THE DETECTIVE AND THE WOMAN TRILOGY

Amy Thomas

First edition published in 2012

Hardcover ISBN 978-1-78705-333-5

Published in the UK by MX Publishing
335 Princess Park Manor, Royal Drive,
London, N11 3GX
www.mxpublishing.com

Cover by Mary Smiecinski

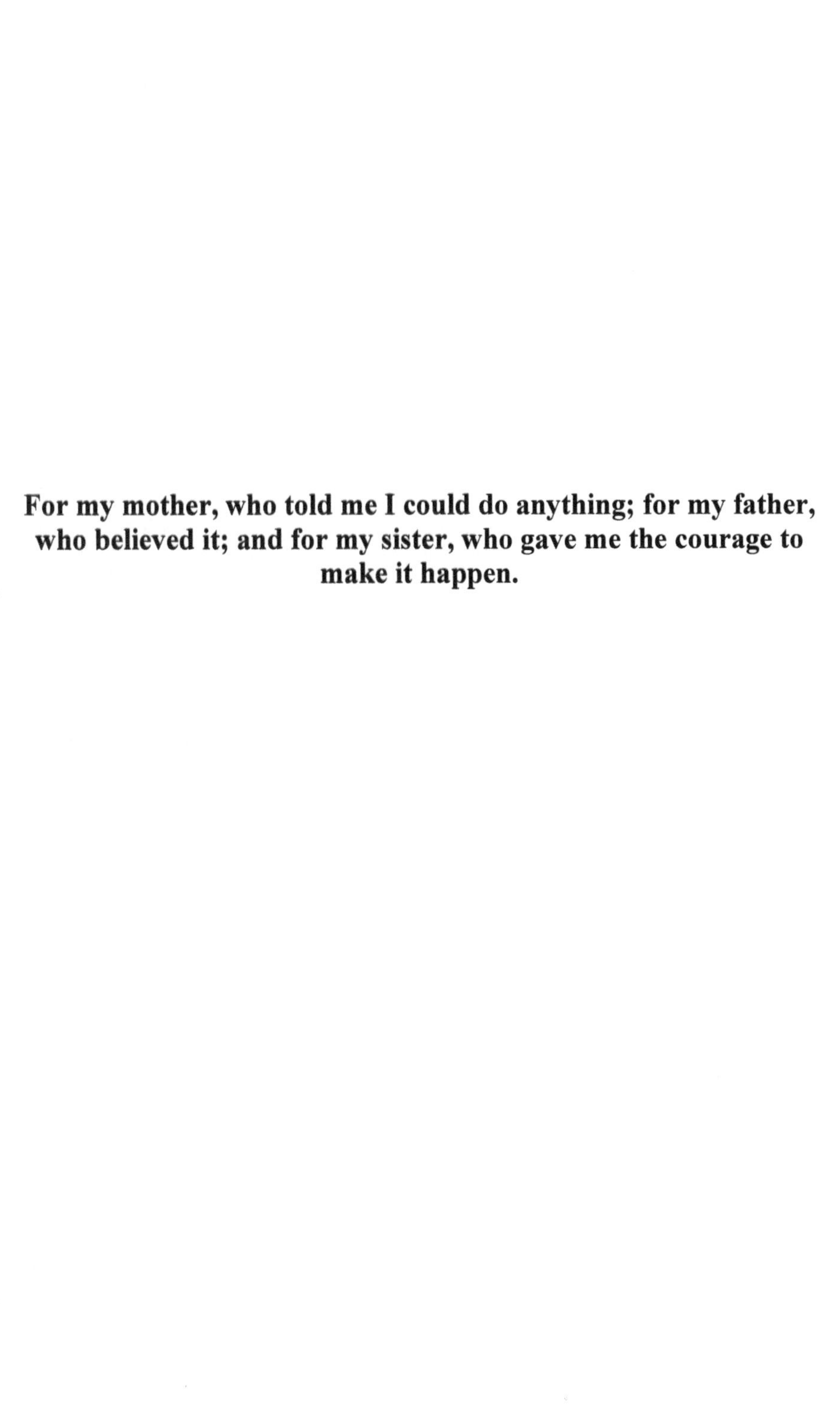

For my mother, who told me I could do anything; for my father, who believed it; and for my sister, who gave me the courage to make it happen.

The Detective and The Woman

Book 1

The Beginning

I stared down at the dead face quizzically, wishing I could feel grief. This wish didn't stem from any guilt on my part, but I thought it would make my next few days easier, days in which I would have to project an appropriate face to the world to keep from raising eyebrows and making my escape less certain. Perhaps the word *escape* is slightly dramatic in retrospect, but at the time, it seemed perfectly reasonable. I digress to assert that I had had nothing to do with putting my husband where his corpse now lay, looking as self-important in repose as it had in life. His death was simply a fortunate tragedy. I've always liked paradoxes. Death by heart attack quite often takes the great and good and elderly, but for once it had claimed a man who was young and brutish. Life is so unfair on a regular basis that it seems to save up fairness like a miser saves coins, only to spend it all on grand moments.

I took one last look at my husband's body and turned toward the door, rearranging my expression to one of subdued sadness. I was glad that in the confusion of the night, I had at least remembered to reach into the recesses of my bureau and take out my one black dress, not a colour I usually favoured. I would put it on now, hoping that the costume would make the role come easier. Emerging from the bedroom, I saw that Dr Park was still hanging about the door, his expression one of assumed sympathy. "I've taken the liberty of arranging everything, Mrs Norton. You have no need to worry about the remains."

"Thank you, Doctor," I said in a low tone, taking care to break on the last word. The portly physician patted my shoulder and strode off, looking pleased at his usefulness. I sighed in relief. One obstacle down, but how many more? I walked quickly to my bedchamber, nodding sombrely to any of the staff I passed, my eyes downcast. My own maid, Millie, met me at my room. It was obvious she had been weeping, and for the first time, I felt genuine emotion pierce me.

"It's quite all right," I said to her, my look appropriately counteracting my words. She helped me off with the rumpled gown that had now encased my frame for over 24 hours and into my mourning dress, an outmoded fashion that enshrouded me and made me feel like a boarding school headmistress. All the better, for the moment. I looked at myself in my glass and saw a face haggard from sleeplessness and worry. No matter that the worry had been caused by the dead man, not the dead man's death—the watching world would see it and pity me.

I dismissed Millie with the command to rest and sat down at my desk. *Dear Barnett*, I wrote, *I need you after all.*

—

Sherlock Holmes refilled his pipe for the third time, staring out the window to take in an alley filled with shops so close they seemed to be built atop one another and dotted here and there with south Florida's ubiquitous palm trees. He found it hard to believe that Fort Myers had been a major military outpost during two American wars. Certainly, the army hadn't left it with any particular evidence of regard, and residents had helped themselves to bits of the fort until nothing was left except a vague impression that something large had once stood in the middle of the city. Of course, he thought, seen in another light, the fort's conspicuous absence was evidence of a more peaceful time when trade and expansion predominated instead of entrenchment and strife. But peace was not without its challenges, he was pleased to note. In fact, crime often flourished during such times.

He opened a leather case by his feet and removed Mycroft's letter, unfolding it slowly. Against his own curiosity, he'd done as he was asked, letting his brother's desires keep the letter sealed until he was safely ensconced in the upper floor of the semi-habitable boardinghouse in which he now found himself. Plenty of nights aboard ship he'd been tempted to digest its contents prematurely, but Mycroft's wishes were never idle, and the detective trusted him as much as he trusted himself. He now read its contents by the piercing light of the early-morning Floridian sun.

Sanchez,

I have reason to believe that our mutual friend will soon again be entrusting her assets to me, assets that have been returned to her by her husband's sudden death. You know as well as I do that she is not to be dealt with carelessly; one false move, and we will find ourselves adrift. Miss A sails on the 19th of September. I will alert you to new developments as soon as they are available.

Barnett

No wonder Mycroft had insisted on his waiting until now. He sat back in his chair and smiled to himself. If it hadn't been for the letter's obvious authenticity, he'd have thought it was his brother's idea of a joke. Unbidden, his mind called up pictures of a boy with unusually bright eyes and hat set at a jaunty angle, a boy who had been a girl.

The three years since the Bohemian case had been taken up with the Irishman Moriarty and other problems, and Holmes had filed The Woman's defeat of him away with his other losses, which were few. He thought about them rarely, only letting himself consider his mistakes on occasion so as to avoid repeating them. No human could ever be perfect, he knew, even one with an intellect as near-flawless as his own. And, indeed, his losses were proofs that the world was not entirely devoid of truly clever people. That thought was a comfort in quiet moments.

Holmes's first inclination, a strong one, was to let Miss Adler handle things herself. Whatever Barnett and Sanchez intended for her, however ominous, he had little doubt she could detect and avert on her own, without the interference of a detective whom she probably considered inferior after their last interaction. But Mycroft had sent him, and that was suggestive of a wider plot. The detective's corpulent brother rarely deigned to entangle himself in anything, and he certainly wouldn't waste his time on a matter of insignificance. No, for Mycroft to take such a direct hand in the matter, it had to be something he considered well worth his notice, which warranted at least a cursory investigation.

The tall detective unfolded himself out of the small wooden chair and shed his dressing gown, throwing it over the rough-hewn wooden desk beside the bed. Watson would have hated that, chided him for being untidy, like a gun-bearing nursemaid—Watson, whose evenings would be spent at home now. Mary Morstan would be pleased.

As he dressed himself, Holmes derived grim amusement from imagining Inspector Lestrade's bumbling investigation at Reichenbach. The dogged detective would have seen what he expected to see, as he always did, and then assisted Watson in declaring the younger Holmes dead. For a moment, Holmes regretted being in rural southern America, where he was unable to procure English newspapers, several of which would undoubtedly have run stories about his demise along with Mycroft's amusing attempt at a grief-filled statement. Lestrade would have waxed positively poetic, he was sure. But Watson—Watson, he thought, would been curiously silent. He refused to let his mind dwell there for long. He adjusted his collar and looked at his reflection in the dirty glass affixed to the wall, finding himself convincingly arrayed as an American businessman of the middle class. Makeup and other more complicated arts of disguise could wait. No one should have cause to know his face here, even if

Watson's stories had somehow reached them. He closed his mind to speculation like a trap and readied it, once again, to belong to The Case.

Chapter 1: Irene

I stared at myself in the mirror. Pink cheeks, full lips, bright blue eyes. I was myself again. "You look beautiful, Miss Adler!" said the voice of Doris the theatre attendant, her painted countenance coming into the reflection behind me. *Miss Adler*. The name hit my ears like cold, bitter water, both refreshing and repulsive. I pushed a curl from my forehead and smoothed my satin gown, standing and turning for her to survey me. "The audience will be dazzled before you start singing!" Doris had a point. The dress was beautiful—flamboyantly violet, trimmed with silver, far from anything the proper Mrs Norton had ever worn. Ten minutes later, I stepped onto the stage and looked out at a theatre full of people gathered to see and hear the spectacle of Irene Adler, Contralto.

It wasn't my first show. That had been in New York City, followed by ten more after the triumph of the first. After that came Boston and then Atlanta, a city still struggling to recover from the devastation of the American Civil War. Those had all been familiar places, places with memories and theatres whose creaky boards I had walked many times in previous years. Now I found myself in Orlando, Florida, a place I had never been before. My American agent, recently acquired through my solicitor, James Barnett, had assured me that the citrus-growers and their secretaries craved entertainment as much as their more established counterparts in the northeast. And so I had agreed to the engagement, looking forward to a change of scenery. I had found it more difficult than expected to put my old life out of my mind, and a singing tour was a welcome distraction.

The crimson curtain opened, and I stepped onto the theatre's dubious wooden platform, hoping the slats wouldn't give way, but I forgot my worries as soon as the music began to play. Singing felt the same way it always had, effortless and at the same time all-consuming, like arms of sound wrapping around me and bearing me away. I willed the audience to fly with me, and as always, I watched them begin to follow, one by one.

Oh Promise me that someday you and I—tears began to gather in the eyes of the blonde in the first row.

Will take our love together to some sky—the man in the upper right private box surreptitiously raised his handkerchief to his face.

Where we can be alone and faith renew—My eyes found those of a man in the fourth row, simply dressed, not nearly as grand as the society crowd. His face was nondescript, but his eyes were mesmerizing, so much so that I looked at no one else for the remainder of the song.

After my last curtain call, I walked backstage to my tiny dressing room, unsurprised to find that the brass lock had been tampered with. The job was professional, likely undetectable by most people, but I was more observant than the average person. I stopped for a moment in the hallway to grasp a solid umbrella as a possible weapon, but I was far from nervous.

I pushed open the door to my dark room, and, sure enough, the nondescript man with the wonderful eyes from the fourth row stood beside my flower-bedecked dressing table. "Hello, Mr Holmes." I affected a breezy, nonchalant tone, since any other seemed as though it would heighten the absurdity of the situation even further.

Mr Holmes smiled a nearly imperceptible smile and bowed slightly. "Miss Adler, it is a privilege to make your acquaintance once again. I'm glad your senses have retained their previous acuity." What a thing to say to a lady—and yet, it felt like a high compliment.

"I'm afraid I can't say the same for you, Mr Holmes, leaving evidence of a break-in like that." I was teasing him, and he knew it. The almost-imperceptible scratches on my door were as intentional as a calling card left on a silver salver. He smiled sardonically and pressed his fingertips together.

Just then, I heard a knock on the door, and Doris popped her head in, her eyes nearly bulging with surprise when she saw Mr Holmes. "Doris, this is my friend, Mr Smith," I said quickly, not sure he'd want his name known.

"I just wondered if you wanted some coffee, Miss Adler," said the girl, while her face said *I'll get out if you say so*.

I smiled. "I'd love some, and please bring a cup for Mr Smith, too. Oh, and make sure no one else comes in." She nodded and scampered off, relieved.

"I must say, you've settled back in nicely," said my companion, looking around the room and then at me. His words held a slight edge, as if the unspoken corollary was that he'd expected something else and been disappointed.

"I did what I'm best at," I answered, my chin slightly aloft. "I escaped."

"Did you?" I didn't like the way he said it, as if he knew all my secrets. In fact, a chill started to spread through my centre and into my throat. Sherlock Holmes didn't do things for no reason.

"Why are you here?"

"It's your—escape, as you express it. I have reason to believe all is not as it seems."

"I can easily believe that something is afoot if Sherlock Holmes is in my dressing room in Florida," I answered tersely, annoyed at my own anxiety. "I didn't suppose you'd come to admire my singing."

"On the contrary," he said, easing onto one end of the garishly pink sofa opposite my dressing table, "your singing was magnificent."

I couldn't help feeling slightly gratified, but I masked it by looking out into the hall for Doris, who came a moment later with a tarnished tray holding two mugs of the theatre's tepid coffee. I noticed no one lurking about outside, so I assumed she'd done a capable job of chasing off any admirers or stray crew. I slipped her a coin as she handed me the tray, and she blushed and grinned. "Thanks, Miss A." She traipsed off like the teenager she was, whatever age her face tried to claim.

I came back into the room to find that Mr Holmes had wiped his face clean of makeup, unmasking the sharp, refined features that were burned into my memory. He had fooled me once, but he would never do so again, I believed. I turned the chair from my vanity table to face him and held out one of the chipped mugs. He took it, his long, tapered fingers closing around the handle. I wondered suddenly if he'd brought his violin to America, the one Dr Watson mentioned so often in his stories.

"Now, Miss Adler, I need to know what brought you here, your story. I hold out hope that it will give meaning to mine." The tall detective sipped the coffee, grimacing slightly at its taste, but continuing without comment. His statement seemed oddly metaphysical, but I knew he meant it literally.

"Why should I trust you?" I asked, knowing that I would, but wanting him to persuade me all the same.

"I'd say the level at which we can trust one another is fairly even," he said drily, leaning back into the sofa and half-closing his eyes. I laughed. It was certainly true. Our last interaction had included mutual deceit, disguise, and blackmail. Strangely, however, it seemed to me that we knew each other very well.

I pushed my feet into the floor and clasped my hands together. I had told my story to no one except Barnett, and even he knew very few details. But Mr Holmes was different; telling him would be like telling a doctor or maybe a phonograph record. Not easy, but not personal, either.

"When I left London, Mr Holmes—"

"Holmes," came a deep, calm voice from somewhere inside his languid form. "Dispense with the Mister."

"I'll be Irene, then," I answered quickly, not wanting to surrender an inch in our long game, whatever it was we were playing.

"Mr—I mean Holmes, after Godfrey and I left London, we went immediately to Belgium for our honeymoon. You will have received my note the day we left, I believe." He nodded his head with his eyes closed, looking for all the world as if he was paying no attention whatsoever. But I knew better.

"Godfrey's character remained steady during the trip. He had never been talkative about his past, but neither had I, so I didn't hold it against him. He had always seemed a kind, openhearted man, and no one had an ill word to say about him, except that he was overly popular, but I saw that for myself and never detected anything amiss in his manner. I was very happy during my honeymoon, happy and still, I admit, proud of my little defeat of the greatest detective in London." I looked up, but Holmes's face did not register any change at this.

"Few, if any, know the truth about Godfrey's family. He was distantly related to an earl, and it had never seemed a significant connection until one month before the wedding, when Godfrey informed me that he had learned that he was the heir to a large estate in Yorkshire. My fortune, gained through my career, was enough to support the manor, which was rich in land but deficient in money. Our friends assumed Godfrey and I meant to move to America, but our intention from that point on was to take possession of the family home. I did not mind the idea of secluded country life. After spending my years from fourteen to twenty-seven touring the world, I felt ready to settle down with a good man—a much better one, I thought, than others I had known."

I stopped to take a drink of my now-cold coffee, and Holmes stood up and turned to the shelf behind the sofa, which was empty except for a tattered grey afghan that was redolent of mothballs. He handed it to me. I hadn't realised I was chilled, but even in Florida, an old theatre can be draughty. "Your hands turned pale," he said, by way of explanation. I thanked him and tucked the afghan around myself, glad for a reprieve before the most difficult part of my recollection, the years I would have liked to forget.

"The trouble started when we reached West Yorkshire. I can't—I still can't explain how quickly it happened. I flattered myself before that I was not a stupid woman, Holmes, but I had been completely taken in. Godfrey was nothing like the man I had known. It immediately became apparent that he had married me for my fortune, the one thing he did not possess to go along with his property and the lifestyle of the landed gentry he sought. He told me very quickly that he had known about his inheritance far longer than he had let on—since before our first meeting, in fact."

"I was shaken, but I planned my escape, determined not to be beaten so easily. He was too vigilant. The man who had been able to deceive me was able to retain power over me by having servants in my way constantly, people who believed he was the kindest of husbands to be so solicitous of his wife's needs. Outwardly, I lived the life of a princess. Inwardly, I felt as if I would die. I could go nowhere alone, do nothing without being watched. My only recourse would have been to injure or kill one of the staff and go alone into the Yorkshire countryside. In London, I would have risked it with a sedative in the teacup of a maid, but in Yorkshire I had access to nothing and no knowledge of the area. I was trapped." As I finished my statement, I saw Holmes's hand clasp into a fist inadvertently, the first sign of acknowledgement he had given in many minutes. I surmised that his quick brain was producing in him the feelings of a trapped mind, my captive feelings.

"I will not explain all the details of my relationship with my husband. It is hardly necessary and excessively painful to recall.

Suffice to say that he did everything to me that a man can do to make a woman's life miserable, both mentally and physically. I had been with unpleasant men before, but his triumph made him crueler than anyone I had ever known. The only hold I had over him was music. During our courtship, I would sing to him almost every night, and he had professed great fondness for my voice. That, at least, was not a lie. When we were married, he would beg me to sing for him, over and over, and I would refuse. It drove him mad, but I never cared what he did then because I knew that I had kept something for myself. It kept me alive, that one thing."

I leaned forward. "One day, Holmes, it happened. We were eating dinner in the evening, and Godfrey complained of stomach discomfort and went to bed. I was relieved because he did not insist that I accompany him. I ate a relatively pleasant dinner under the eyes of the servants and went to my room to allow my maid to undress me for the night. Before she could do so, Godfrey's valet came rushing to the door to alert me that my husband was in unendurable pain and needed the doctor, who was immediately sent for. I went to Godfrey's room and found him sweating profusely and swearing while clutching his chest. I was in a daze. It hardly seemed possible that a figure who held such terrible power in my mind could be lying powerless against some invisible malady. Wild thoughts of murder rushed through my brain, thoughts of the ease of doing away with him in such a weakened condition, but I stood and stared at him as they came and then passed like cooling firebrands. The doctor arrived from the village an hour later and pronounced Godfrey's condition serious. He gave him something for the pain, but that was all he was able to do. My husband died later that night, at about midnight. His death was attributed to heart failure, and the inquest was conducted quickly and seamlessly."

"I was free, Holmes, and the law guaranteed me the return of my money. In the three years we were married, Godfrey had been so concerned about house and grounds that he had been scrupulously careful with my fortune. Had he wished, he could have taken action, I know, to connect the money to the estate more firmly, but he was so convinced of his own ability to manage every detail that he had not yet done so."

"I was tempted to fly immediately, as I think you can imagine, but I maintained an appearance of genteel mourning until all the legal steps were completed. Once my solicitor, James Barnett, assured me that my money was again my own, I arranged to travel to America. Music has been the one friend who never betrayed me, so I took it up again. Singing was my livelihood in the past, but I saw no reason why I could not return to it for different reasons. I planned my life very differently, Holmes, but this is what I have left, a voice and a fortune." I could not help the slightly bitter note that crept into my voice near the end, but I supposed he expected it. He had helped too many unfortunate women to be unaware of the usual results.

"There you have it, Holmes," I finished, sitting back in my uncomfortable chair and looking at him full-on, my eyes challenging him to betray his inner thoughts. He gradually roused from his apparent torpor and sat up straight, his eyes meeting mine without judgement or comment.

"Thank you, Irene," he finally intoned, sounding slightly awkward over my name. "I had surmised the greater part of your circumstances correctly, but your narrative has supplied key details of which I was otherwise unaware." He stared at me for a moment, his eyes curiously bright. "It is not my usual practice to disclose my methods to anyone except Dr Watson during a case, but I am confident that in you I have a listener who will be able to ascertain and comprehend what I say. In short, Irene, I hope that by the end of my tale, we will be allies." His eyes presented a challenge as open as mine had been.

"That is a somewhat extraordinary hope, Holmes," I shot back, "considering our previous interactions."

"Not at all," he returned, with the ghost of a twinkle in his eye. "It is merely a logical assumption." I smiled at him, unable to stop myself, remembering the night I had dared to greet him in the street while dressed like a boy—an unnecessary greeting for an extraordinary man, a man who had been entirely impossible to ignore. Three years had changed me a great deal but seemed to have changed him not at all.

Chapter 2: Holmes

Irene Adler was an unusual woman. That was hardly necessary to consider. Holmes had been aware of it since the moment he'd recognised her as the successful mastermind of his defeat in the Bohemian affair, and now, as he saw her before him, the impression was strong once again. Nevertheless, he knew, the human heart was consistent—consistently susceptible, even in a genius. Men and women, both the stupid and the clever, had been taken in by the opposite sex since the dawn of time, he didn't doubt, and would be taken in until it ended. Like many others, Irene had seen what she desired to see and ignored the rest. She had been foolish—understandably so, perhaps—but she had also been strong. A weaker person would have succumbed to despair long before three years had passed, and he could hardly fault her for being deceived by another when he had been deceived by her. He could not, however, keep himself from wishing that her suspicions had served her better. Weakness was more painful than usual when he saw it in one to whom he had attributed unusual intelligence. But, as he knew too well, no mind was infallible.

The detective leaned forward and rested his arms on his knees, looking into The Woman's delicate face. He wished, as he had throughout the evening, that he had his pipe. The oversight had been deliberate, however, as it had no place in his chosen disguise, and he satiated himself by thinking of it lying snugly in its leather pouch in his hotel.

"The story starts," he began, "with my death." He relished the quick look of surprise that flashed across her features. He always had enjoyed a shocking beginning. "After your departure, my life proceeded largely as it always had, except that I began to detect a hidden pattern that I had never before seen, as if the underworld of London were running according to a shared agenda. There was a regularity to it, a deadly efficiency that nothing so vast can reach without someone or something orchestrating its movements. I will not tax you by explaining all of my processes, but I discovered the unmoved mover, as they say, to be a man named James Moriarty, an Irish professor of unassuming appearance and remarkable mind. He set out to kill me, and it became evident fairly quickly that I would not be safe while the man remained at large, free to use his vast organization as he willed. Watson went with me to Switzerland, and I met Moriarty at Reichenbach Falls, arranging things so that my friend would find evidence of a scene that appeared to be the death-place of both Moriarty and myself. The first assumption was correct; Moriarty met his death by equal parts my hand and the inexorability of the Falls. I escaped, however, and traveled immediately to Florence, Italy, from whence I contacted my brother. My object was to remain absent from England, or, indeed, from the knowledge of the public, until enough of Moriarty's associates had been apprehended that I might return without unreasonable risk to Watson or to the investigation. Such is still my intent."

"Now to the part of the story that concerns you. During my time in Florence, my brother, who works for the British government in a diplomatic role, sent me a letter, a request that I sail to America, and a note insisting that I not open the enclosed missive until I arrived. More than that, he asked that I wait until I had reached a town south of here called Fort Myers, an outpost during the American Seminole and Civil Wars. I didn't know what he meant by the request, but my brother's mind is very like my own, so I did as he asked. Truthfully, without a firm objective, I grow irritable, and I was glad of having a purpose."

Holmes's deliberate omission of the scope of Mycroft's influence was, he considered, entirely necessary. What he had said was technically true and hopefully sufficient to satisfy Irene's immediate curiosity. He trusted her mind enough to believe that she would not betray him in a naive manner, but he did not trust her nearly enough to be willing to share internationally sensitive information in a wanton way. Whatever else was true, Mycroft must be protected. The Holmes brothers did not have a code; they simply shared keen enough intellects to understand the delicacy of one another's positions in the world. Mycroft could certainly take care of himself, but Holmes did not intend to complicate his task by bringing The Woman into more than necessary confidence.

He noted with pleasure that Irene was completely engrossed in his tale, her slim body alert as she followed his every word, her tiny hands pressed against the arms of her chair. "When I reached Fort Myers, I opened this." He handed the paper to her. No need to be irritatingly coy. Her eyes scanned the note once and then again, and her face gradually lost colour and gained it again in a heightened fashion. Holmes watched her expression shift from polite interest to malignant anger in seconds, a remarkable transformation. At once, her demeanor changed to one of focused purpose as her anger was instantly sublimated, a process Holmes recognised and respected.

"Continue," she said very quickly, a slightly breathless note in her voice, but she sat back in her chair, the only evidence of her agitation the vice-like grip with which she still clasped Barnett's letter in her right hand.

"You will have already connected this letter with your recent circumstances, but I had no such references, though I immediately surmised what my brother already understood, that this letter concerned yourself and those who wish to harm you in some way. I believe my brother's insistence that I wait to read it related to the fact that he thought I might be reluctant to help one who had so effectively defeated me in the past." Holmes smiled to himself. "Unlike my brother, however, I do not hold grudges. In fact, since we have been fortunate enough to meet again—(the word *fortunate* came off his tongue with a razor-edge)—I am happy to say that I bear you no ill-will. On the contrary, I find your wit refreshing."

Irene's face remained blank, and Holmes couldn't tell if his admission had had any effect on her. It wasn't a lie, but his inclusion of it at that particular moment wasn't entirely artless, either. He intended to have Irene Adler for an ally before the evening was over, and he was determined to play his cards until the right one hit the table.

"I will help you." Holmes tried in vain to keep his surprise at Irene's words from registering on his face. "You've no need to keep courting me, Holmes." Her eyes burned into him like the coldest ice. "I know that once you've taken a case, you won't rest until it's solved. If I or my property is in danger, I can be in no better hands than yours. That is not a compliment; it is a statement of fact. Do not expect my trust beyond this, but I will help you." She ceased speaking, and Holmes nodded once. She returned the gesture. "Now, tell me what you've learned."

"I knew that Mycroft would not have sent me to south Florida without a definite purpose, and I soon discovered what it was. A man called Alberto Sanchez, a native of Central America, owns a profitable citrus grove ten miles outside of the city of Fort Myers. He is not yet wealthy, but will be once his harvest is concluded. The area is largely peopled by field workers and fruit magnates; he is one of the latter category, of course, a very recent newcomer. In the three weeks I have resided in town, I have received the impression that he is on the edge of polite society—hardly the darling of the most respectable, but with money that makes him more than a pariah. Society I find more interesting than expected, frankly." Holmes put his hands together and pressed his fingertips to one another, relishing what he was about to say.

"The belle of Fort Myers, Irene, is none other than Mrs Mina Edison, the young and lovely wife of the brilliant inventor Thomas

Edison." To Holmes's satisfaction, Irene's smile hid neither her surprise nor her pleasure at learning this.

"But why are they in Florida, Holmes, without all the conveniences of the North?" For the moment, she appeared to have forgotten her own troubles in her sudden interest. Holmes noted that she looked more alive, more like the woman he'd encountered three years earlier, than she had all evening.

"The family divides its time between New Jersey and Florida, spending the cooler months in the South and the warmer in the North, a practice that is not unpopular among Americans with enough disposable income to make it feasible."

"What else have you learned?"

"I will happily tell you, but the story will better accompany our train journey in the morning. If we catch the 7:30, we'll be in Fort Myers by late afternoon."

"You wish me to come with you, then?"

Holmes looked at Irene in dead earnest. "Of course. I came with no other object. Your presence is required to carry the case to a successful conclusion."

"Well, Holmes, when you put the offer in such romantic terms—" Irene looked up from contemplating the faded green carpet and half smiled. "I take it you've figured out a way to explain to the theatre why their prima donna is about to be in absentia for the remainder of her scheduled dates."

"Naturally. On the very morning of the disappearance of Irene Adler, Annie Hart will arrive requesting the theatre for her personal use. The management will be delighted to have the Bowery Girl herself, and the absence of the charming but as-of-yet lesser-known Irene Adler will be a convenience rather than a hardship. Thankfully, Miss Hart owes me a favour. I confess that getting rid of your manager presented a greater challenge, but in the morning, he will find himself in receipt of a telegram supposedly composed by yourself, declaring that your nerves have been frayed by your hectic touring schedule and declaring your intention to rest in seclusion. A hefty sum of money will be wired to him as well, a supposed gift from his appreciative, though delicate, client. He will be instructed to await your communication at a future date."

"You arranged all this beforehand?"

"Of course, I could not afford to lose time after contacting you."

"You were that sure." It wasn't a question. Irene stared at him with what appeared to be a mixture of admiration and something that went deeper than annoyance but stopped short of loathing, something like resistance.

"I hoped," Holmes answered truthfully. He held out a train ticket, and she took it without hesitation. "In the morning, gather your funds and belongings and come to the station. If you see me, do not acknowledge it by look or word, and I will do the same. I am not known here, but I don't want to take chances this close to the scene of events, especially in a place where a stray concertgoer might recognise the divine Miss Adler. Go to the third carriage. I have arranged for it to remain empty."

"Once on the train, your name will be Mrs Lavinia James, wife to Bernard James, a British investor with more money than sense, who is travelling in the new world to enjoy himself and discover whether or not citrus fruit is the key to augmenting his fortune. The emphasis is on the enjoying; Mr James finds it necessary to attend as many social functions as he can and make himself as charming as possible to everyone. He is eager to introduce his American wife, who has been nursing her sick sister but is now joining him."

"Your wife," said Irene drily.

"Well, you could hardly play the role of my valet," said Holmes, smiling to himself, "unless, of course, you still possess that charming outfit you donned during our previous encounter." The Woman did not reply.

—

Irene's hotel was in a much more fashionable part of the city than the detective's. He deposited her at the door and took off down the dark street, musing. He hadn't minded his time alone on the Continent and then in this strange climate where autumn brought nothing more than the slightest addition of a breeze to make the sun less unbearable. He liked the focus that solitude brought, the quiet clarity. And yet, solitude had also been the siren that whispered the craving into his mind and placed the syringe in his hand. Past solitude had made him dependent. Truthfully, he needed the friction of other minds, the whetstone of communication, to keep him from sliding into the grey. When he thought about it, he missed the comfortable ease of Watson, the familiar, practical turns of mind, the errors and the occasional triumphs. He missed the rhythm. He even missed the irritation, the annoyance that reminded him he was more than a machine.

Irene was different. If Watson was a pipe and slippers before a warm fire, she was a Nor'easter, an American storm that blew wherever it chose and sent everything in its path head-over-heels. With surprise, Holmes realised that he felt deep anger, rage against a dead man. No person had the right to lock up something so wild.

Chapter 3: Irene

Two flights of stairs took me to the hallway that contained my room, a generously-sized suite with obscenely opulent wooden furnishings obviously designed to appeal to Florida's new money. The hotels in New York and Boston had installed lifts to save guests from the stairs, but Orlando was a younger sibling playing catch-up in many ways. I didn't mind. I enjoyed the exercise after my mind-whirling evening. Once inside, I lay down for a moment on the hideous yellow coverlet to collect my thoughts.

Hours before, my life had stretched before me in a predictable manner, as predictable as the life of a travelling performer can be. I had not let myself think beyond the singing, the dates that would follow dates for as long as I could continue. I would grow richer, and my memories would grow further away in time, at least, if not in feeling. I would be the world's Irene Adler again, and my mind would be forced to acquiesce, to find its own occupation in between the different places that would all come to seem the same in the end.

Holmes's arrival was like a splash of saltwater to the face, the sting and then the awakening. Perhaps Barnett's dastardly plans for me, whatever they might be, were blessings in disguise, for they had acted as the catalysts to draw salvation near. I laughed at the drama of my own thoughts. What sort of salvation was six feet of arrogance and the promise of endless swordplay? And yet, I experienced relief from a feeling I hadn't known I still had, the desperation of a mind shuttered and set aside. What Holmes offered me was a chance to think freely, and that felt as close to salvation as anything I could imagine.

I allowed myself the luxury of a few moments of contemplation and then roused with purpose. I quickly collected my small belongings from around the room and placed them in my carpet reticule. My clothes went into the sturdy trunk that had served me well through the crossing and all my travels. I felt like a criminal packing my gowns; my manager always arranged for someone to pack them for me at the end of each city's run, and I was far from skilled at doing so myself. I hoped that whatever plans Holmes had for us upon our arrival in the southern city would include enough time for my dresses to recover before being worn. Part of me missed the quick hands of my Yorkshire lady's maid, but I did not miss her constantly watchful eye or loose tongue. My manager, Slade, had begged me to take on a maid or companion of some sort to travel with us and provide company for his secretary, but the haunting memories of my married life had made me desire the freedom to be alone and do as I wished. I usually did very well on my own. In fact, I had begun to think I might never engage another permanent maid. Slade was more than enough, with all of his fussing about my supposed comfort and fawning over my talent. I was grateful for his abilities, which had smoothed my way considerably, but I knew that I would not miss him.

After I had finished packing my possessions, with widely varying degrees of efficiency, I considered the metal safe tucked in the back of the closet. It contained my personal funds and the one piece of fine jewellery I carried with me, a diamond necklace I had inherited from my mother when I was a child in New Jersey. I had a sizeable portion of money in my personal possession at all times, a practice Slade deplored as being unsafe. This, too, was most likely a result of the confines of my marriage, but even before my nuptials, I had been wary. I did not like to be at the mercy of others any more than was absolutely necessary. Slade had no idea how adept I could be at defending myself, should the need arise. I decided to leave the safe opening for the morning, and I decided not to tell Holmes about the money. Wiser to keep something to myself in case of emergencies. He had tried to beat me once and only lost on a knife's-point. I could not afford to trust my wits alone to save me again.

Before I slept, I set the alarm clock for 6:30. The theatre would not expect me until at least 3:00 in the afternoon, and my only other engagement was lunch with Slade and an enthusiastic music lover at 12:30. If all went to plan, I would be far gone and my manager paid off before anyone recognised my absence. Sleep was long in coming, but I didn't mind. Excitement hadn't kept me awake for quite some time.

—

Ding I was fighting a black dress that wouldn't stop wrapping its silky, choking arms around me. *Ding* The corpse on the table kept talking to me, endlessly, about where to place my assets, but it was the corpse of the king of Bohemia with the voice of Sherlock Holmes. *Ding* I fought to the surface, emerging into the smell of stale cigars and the feel of silken bedsheets. I arose quickly, washing my face in the porcelain basin and dressing myself in a plain brown shirtwaist and long tan skirt. I rang for the porter, a near-child, as soon as I was decent and requested a light breakfast, which I ate as quickly as possible. I rang for him once again, and when he arrived I instructed him to take my trunk to the lobby. "Are you going away, Miss Adler?" he asked curiously, fingering his forelock. The hotel staff had been told I was some sort of musical celebrity, and they were aware that I had been engaged for a run at the theatre, a run in these parts usually being construed as anything more than one night. "I need my things at the theatre tonight," I answered with a ready smile. "Someone from there will come by to pick it up." This satisfied the boy, and he took it willingly after being handed a few coins. I was glad that Holmes had entrusted me with a few unmentioned details. At least he trusted my judgement that much.

My last act before leaving the room for the final time was to open the safe. I had an irrational, uncomfortable feeling that the contents might have disappeared during the night, but there they were, as snug as ever. I secreted the roll of American money in a pouch I carried close to my body underneath my clothing. The necklace I put on, taking care to hide it completely under the high collar of my practical shirtwaist. I picked up my reticule and proceeded downstairs, stopping in the lobby to enquire after a cab "for the theatre." The white-haired steward behind the small desk smiled uncomfortably widely and replied in the hushed tones of a doctor addressing an elderly hysteric. News of my "fame" and generous pocketbook must have reached all quarters, I reasoned. He promised me a coach as soon as one could be procured, and I settled in to wait, noting from my watch that I still had half an hour to make the train station, which was only about ten minutes' ride away. I sat down in a faded brocade chair and studied the place, a mixture of American innovation and tasteless nods to old-world finery, emphasizing the worst of each, from the wallpaper (peeling at the very edges) that depicted what looked like palm trees covered with grotesque monkeys, to the fat, unpleasant cherub statues that stood on either side of the oversized staircase.

Thankfully, I was not left to wait in this paradise for long, as a cab arrived within five minutes, driven by an elderly, hunched man, who was too abashed by my presence to make eye contact. The steward simpered proudly at having procured my transportation so quickly, and I thanked him monetarily, taking advantage of the air of good will to enquire after my trunk. "I sent it down for my theatre to collect," I said in my most innocent, whimsical voice, "but I think I'd like to take it with me now." The steward was only too happy to oblige me by yelling for two adolescent porters and having them hoist it onto the coach with the help of the aged driver, who seemed to take it all as a matter of course.

"The theatre, Miss?" he asked before we set off, his voice thin and reedy.

"No, the train station, if you please," I said, sounding unconcerned.

"Very well," he answered, in a tone that seemed to say *none of my business anyway*. I wasn't overly concerned; if he chose to tell the story later, I would be long gone. Nevertheless, I tipped him double the usual amount when we arrived at the platform, and he arranged for my trunk to be stowed. We had arrived with ten minutes to spare, so I purchased a cup of terrible coffee from a slatternly woman who had a vague excuse for a stall in the middle of the warehouse-like wooden building that served as a station. I considered buying two, but I supposed that would arouse the sort of speculation Holmes was trying to avoid. Thankfully, no one appeared to recognise me, and I did not even clap eyes on my travelling companion. I boarded the train considerably more relaxed than I had begun the day, proud of myself for successfully navigating the morning's small pitfalls.

I made immediately for the third car, taking care not to walk too quickly. The train was surprisingly luxurious. I had expected something more provincial, but it had all the accoutrements of the trains that had carried me through New England, the leather and velvet and smartly-uniformed staff with every desire to please. I chided myself for my prejudice. The newness of Florida's prominence did not necessitate a complete lack of taste, hideous hotel vestibules notwithstanding.

I entered the third car eagerly, far more enthusiastic about seeing Holmes than I had expected to be. But there was a problem. The car was occupied, but not by Holmes. Instead, my elderly cabdriver sat placidly hunched over an almanac, sipping coffee from the same stall I had visited. He looked up as I entered, his cloudy eyes barely visible through matted grey locks. My mind raced. Uppermost was annoyance at Holmes. Where on earth was the man, and why hadn't he upheld his promise of an empty car? Furthermore, how could I get rid of the intruder? Just at that moment, the aged driver straightened up, said “Good morning, Mrs James,” and began to take off his face.

Annoyance instantly followed recognition. “Whatever do you mean by this, Holmes?” I hissed, keeping my voice low. I had no idea how far sound would carry on a train (though Holmes probably did, hateful man), but I didn’t want to risk alerting curious listening ears.

“Call me Bernard from now on,” he replied in a low voice of his own, before continuing in a more normal tone. “I couldn’t risk anything going wrong, so I included myself. That is all.”

“Entirely all?” I asked suspiciously, taking my seat on the bench opposite him.

“Well,” he admitted, “after you spotted me so quickly yesterday, I thought I might challenge myself and see if my subtler abilities had lost their sharpness against the recognition of one who knows me. I see they have not.”

I wanted to be angry, but I could see that he meant the statement literally and as no kind of comment on my observational abilities. “It was the eyes,” I said quickly. “Yesterday, they were your own. Today, their cloudiness belonged to someone else.”

“Well spotted,” said Holmes, pulling forth a small pipe. “I did not mind driving a cab with the eyes of another, but only the eyes of the great detective himself could be put to the purpose of meeting Irene Adler again.”

I wondered if he intended to mock me, but he seemed dead serious. He puffed away at his tobacco for a moment and then drilled me with his gaze. “From now on, we are Bernard and Lavinia James. Use those names as often as possible until they are second-nature. We can’t afford to slip.” I nodded, slightly annoyed at his schoomasterish tone. I certainly wasn’t stupid enough to have failed to assimilate the necessity of subterfuge.

"Come, my dear Lavinia, and let me show you the letter I've received from our friends." Holmes motioned to me to join him on his side of the car, and I did so, unable to keep from smiling at the conspiratorial glint in his eyes.

"Very well, Bernard," I answered, sitting myself down primly. Holmes handed me a sheet of paper that contained a handwritten list. I read it with interest.

1) *Barnett is Miss A's solicitor.*
2) *Sanchez is a Central American trying to make his fortune in the citrus-growing industry.*
3) *Both men have some sort of design on Miss A, perhaps on others as well.*
4) *The exact nature of the connection between the two men is unknown.*
5) *Sanchez is a frequent guest of the Edisons, though neither husband nor wife appears to have any particular preferential fondness for him.*
6) *Barnett has extensive ties to both England and North America, though none as-yet-discovered to Central America.*
7) *An ongoing investigation into Miss A's finances, conducted under the supervision of Mycroft Holmes, turns up nothing amiss, though some records cannot be accessed without her personal permission (or that of her solicitor, who is unaware of the investigation and might act in dangerous ways if provoked before he is fully captured). In addition, the finances of her American tour are not fully accounted-for as of yet.*
8) *Barnett represents many wealthy clients, and investigations have begun into the accounts of several of*

the more prominent, though no inconsistencies have been uncovered to date.

9) *Sanchez is almost certain not to know what Miss A looks like; therefore, personal contact will not present unreasonable risk.*
10) *Once Miss A's physical safety is secured, the next phase of the case must include deeper infiltration into Fort Myers society.*

I read the list with interest, noting the mixture of Holmes's terse observations and expanded explanations for my benefit. "I get the impression—I mean, do you suppose the implications of the threat to be wider than a crude plot by a solicitor against a wealthy client?" I asked, looking at my companion curiously.

"I think it likely, as does my brother," he answered, his face in a cloud of grey smoke. "A common criminal would have already betrayed himself in a thousand ways. If Barnett desired to steal, innumerable ways to do so exist before him. But he's been too careful. Why, too, did he include the man Sanchez? The whole thing reads differently from a petty crime."

"I must also ask, Bernard, how my brother-in-law (I nearly laughed aloud) came by the letter from our friend in the first place."

"That, my dear Lavinia, is one of the more interesting facts of the case. A clerk by the name of Michael Morgan caught sight of the letter on his employer's desk right before it was posted. He thought the contents odd and mentioned them that evening when he visited his doctor for treatment of a chest cold. His doctor's name, you might have guessed, is one John Watson, a London physician of considerable reputation who recently lost his dear friend of several years. In the absence of this friend, the good doctor gave the information to the next-best source, his friend's brother, who acquired the letter after it had reached the intended recipient. Even I do not know how that was accomplished, except that Sanchez has recently been enjoying himself in New York, where Mycroft has several associates."

"I begin to see why Dr Watson's company is sought by those who appear to run in such different circles from those frequented by most physicians," I commented, thinking as I did so that the poor man must be enduring a mountain of grief, a monstrously unfair lot for one who had been so loyal.

Holmes grew quiet for a moment before muttering, "At least he had the sense to take it to Mycroft and not try to investigate it himself." I ventured to imagine that perhaps his thoughts echoed my own.

"This evening, you and I are to dine with Thomas and Mina Edison, along with various guests, at Seminole Lodge," said Holmes, and the vision of the tangled dresses in my trunk burst into my mind unwelcome. I would have to try my mother's technique of hanging them in a steamy washroom, a trick I hadn't thought of in years. I didn't complain, however, too interested by the prospect of the dinner to be irritated.

"What character do you wish me to portray?" I asked. The list Holmes had shown me had reminded me that, though I might be a concerned party in the case, I was entering an investigation that had been going on for some time. I was far from overawed by the detective, but I respected his methods.

"One's own character is the easiest to project," he answered. "I must seem eager and naïve, but no such injunctions apply to you. In fact, it may prove more convincing for you to seem like the cleverer wife of a slightly foolish husband. As to specifics, draw out the evening's participants as much as you can. Your appearance should keep the task from being overwhelmingly difficult." At the last line, I laughed out loud. Holmes refrained from comment, but an expression crossed his face that was as near mirth as I had ever seen him.

Chapter 4: Holmes

In many ways, the beginning of the case had proved frustrating for Holmes. The acquisition of the initial letter had been vastly and coincidentally helpful, to the point that he wondered if someone had intended Mycroft to see it. It hardly seemed likely that it had been intended for Sherlock himself, since all of London except, perhaps, a few of Moriarty's associates, thought his corpse was at the bottom of a Swiss waterfall, and anyone remaining in Moriarty's now-defunct organization would have the incentive to keep quiet and low-key for their own sakes. Perhaps a law clerk had simply been especially conscientious and especially ill at the same time. At any rate, the letter was genuine, and that meant the threat was genuine, or at the very least, someone had intended Mycroft to think so.

Since the first information, breakthroughs had been difficult to come by. If only he'd been able to start the investigation in London, where Barnett resided and, more importantly, kept his offices, he would most likely have solved the case in the time he had already spent waiting for letters and telegrams from Mycroft about the progress of his associates and their slow, methodical efforts. Beginning the investigation in Florida, with the recipient of the letter rather than the originator of the scheme, was an entirely backward way to go about things, and Holmes hated illogic even more than he loved logic. Still, even if he could have been in London, with all its resources, he would have had a nearly impossible time enlisting the help of the woman who was seated next to him on the train from Orlando to Fort Myers, dozing in preparation for the work ahead.

She hadn't slept well; he had seen that the moment he'd entered the hotel in the guise of the coachman. Her vibrantly blue eyes had been ringed by dark shadows, her reflexes had been delayed, and her responses to spoken questions had been slightly slower than usual. He reminded himself, too, that her failure to recognise him had not entirely been a compliment to his abilities. He wondered if he had sprung things on her too quickly. He'd known much of the information she had related, but not the depth of unhappiness in her marriage. In the past, his quick perception had made him suspect that The Woman would not be happy in a traditional marriage, the kind he had suspected the ostentatious lawyer sought, but he had not had enough contact with the man to discover the true depths of his designs. Perhaps he'd been too quick to reveal the betrayal of one of her only remaining friends, but he shook his head in denial of the idea. If the intended victim had been himself, he'd have wanted to be told as quickly as possible so that he could assimilate the information and act accordingly. Irene, with her quick wit and systematic mind, wasn't so very different. No, he was sure she'd have wanted to know as soon as possible, even if the knowledge was distressing. Mrs Lavinia James was a formidable force, and he would not have wanted to be the one with designs on her, whatever they might be.

—

"The sun doesn't appear to realise it's autumn, Bernard," Irene observed as the train pulled into the Fort Myers depot, if the dilapidated shack and tiny excuse for a platform could possibly warrant that name. Holmes helped his companion exit the locomotive, taking care to hold her hand gently and smile down at her like a benevolent stork. He was still wearing the driver's costume of the morning, though his bearing made it appear completely different than it had earlier. Still, he left his companion at the door to the grimy women's facilities as quickly as possible and went to the men's, which were unspeakably dirty. He emerged moments later, dressed in a hat and black coat befitting a gentleman of Bernard James's station, which he had retrieved from the depths of his trunk. He was a much neater and more efficient packer than his companion, and his clothing had not suffered much during the journey. He smoothed his collar and proceeded to find a cab to bring him and Irene to Mrs Stillwell's on Monroe Street, the boardinghouse where he had lodged since his arrival. The Woman joined him as he conversed with a quick-looking young man who loaded their two trunks onto his tiny wooden cart straightaway. "Very efficient, Americans," observed Holmes, half as himself and half as Bernard James.

"My dear, I think we must find a new home," said Holmes as their cab bounced roughly down the street. "You will hardly be comfortable in the humble accommodations that have served me these three weeks."

"Not at all, Bernard, I will make do as I always have." Irene took the opportunity to slip her hand into Holmes's with a sickeningly sweet look, which he acknowledged with a benign smile before giving her an amused sideways glance. He had noted with satisfaction that the driver's face as they entered the cab had clearly registered the opinion that Bernard James was vastly and undeservedly fortunate to have married such a beautiful wife, an impression he hoped would be repeated by everyone they met.

In his three weeks of residence, Holmes had become used to the tropical foliage that lined the road—the flowers that bloomed brightly in mid-autumn and the palm trees that shed large coconuts onto the roads. Someone even grew pineapple a few miles outside of town. He had always been affected by atmospheres. The hubbub of London was like a steady hum that called to him and told him secrets about its inner workings. Florida was different, almost silent, save for the growl of the animals that prowled the night-time. He couldn't feel a pulse nearly nonexistent underneath the beating sun, and the lack of bearings unsettled him. But she was here now—The Woman. Perhaps in talking to her, he would see a pattern emerge from the confusion.

—

Mina Edison was the first to greet Holmes that evening as he guided Irene into Seminole Lodge, the home Thomas Edison had commissioned for his family. It was a large white house, not opulent, but beautifully situated on grounds the inventor was already filling with the evidence of one of his many passions—botany. The sound of laughter echoed throughout the premises, and the lady of the house came forward quickly to greet her guests. At twenty-six, Mina Edison was a handsome woman in the height of good health, black-haired and sturdy. She was not a classic beauty, but Holmes thought he understood the middle-aged inventor's fascination with her when he saw the spark of intelligence and wit in her eyes.

"Good evening, Mr James," she said with a friendly smile. "I'm so pleased you've finally brought your wife." Mina took in Irene, dressed in a long, demure blue gown, her chestnut hair piled atop her head, and her eyes widened.

"This is Lavinia," said Holmes, pushing the perfect note of pride into his voice.

"Welcome to Seminole Lodge," said Mina warmly, taking Irene by the hand. "Let me introduce you. We're always happy to have new women down here. It evens the numbers against the male onslaught." Holmes watched Irene smile shyly and laughed to himself. He doubted Irene Adler had ever had a shy moment in her life. "I suppose you can come along, Mr James," said Mina, looking back at him with a mildly teasing smile. Holmes rarely had trouble creating rapport with any woman he chose, and Mina was no exception. It helped that he genuinely liked her.

Mina led them through to a large room with several simple wooden chairs, a white sofa, a grand piano, and a fireplace, something Holmes doubted the Edisons needed frequently, even in the dead of winter. On his first visit to the Lodge, he'd wondered why they had chosen to include it at all, but he had come to learn that Floridians were as enamored of old-world glamour as their northern counterparts, and that those who had come from New England were particularly likely to reproduce their northern comforts in their southern dwellings, whether they needed them or not. And yet, a hint of something different was also present in the light colours and relaxed furnishings, an acknowledgment of the coast and the sea, a curious mixture of familiar and tropical.

Holmes's eyes darted around the room, taking in the evening's participants. To his disappointment, Sanchez was not among the guests. Instead, he saw the inventor engaged in conversation with a short young man he didn't recognise. Another unfamiliar man, tall and broad-shouldered, stood to the side listening to the laugh of a loud, stout, middle-aged woman whom Holmes recognised as Jerusha McGregor, who went by "Tootie." He didn't blame her. Her husband Ambrose, a quiet, prudent businessman who seemed almost extraordinary in his averageness, spoke to Marion Edison, Thomas Edison's eldest child, a strong-willed, attractive eighteen-year-old who seemed to have inherited the bulk of her father's brains. At only eight years older than she, Mina Edison acted as a fond older sister, but was far from maternal. A small party, then, which was fortunate. Easier to draw out individuals with fewer from whom to choose.

Mina brought Irene to her husband, and Holmes followed obediently behind. "Tom, this is Bernard's wife, Lavinia, whom we've heard so much about." Edison's deafness wasn't apparent immediately; he was an excellent lip reader, and his speech was normal. Nevertheless, Holmes noted the way his wife turned toward him when she spoke and took care to enunciate her words clearly. Irene smiled demurely, and Edison greeted her politely. The younger man smiled very shyly and submitted to being introduced as Nelson Burroughs. "I understand, Lavinia, that you are musical," said Mina eagerly after pleasantries had been exchanged. "I hope that after dinner, you will favour us with a song, if your journey hasn't tired you out too much."

"Oh, I hope so too," put in Tootie suddenly, wandering over. "Marion plays, so it will be a huge treat for her." Ambrose calmly followed in his wife's wake, and her conversational partner, the tall stranger, stood at the edge of the group, looking on without comment.

"Oh, Mr Murphy," said Mina, turning toward him after a moment, "I'm sorry I haven't done the honours. Our newcomers are Lavinia and Bernard James. This is Mr John Murphy of Montana, enjoying his first taste of south Floridian life." The large man's voice was predictably booming as he greeted hostess and guests.

"No one's done the honours for us, either," said Tootie once he had subsided, "but we're quite capable of it ourselves. I'm Tootie McGregor, and this is my man himself, Ambrose." Far from embarrassment, Ambrose McGregor seemed massively pleased to be possessed of such an outgoing wife. He smiled at Irene, who said her hellos in a quiet voice. "My goodness, you're lovely," said Tootie, taking a good look at her. "And American. I've no wonder you chose one of those British men to marry. If our boys talked like that, this state would be far more populated." Mina Edison looked vaguely horrified. Her stepdaughter, the only non-speaking participant remaining, appeared vastly amused.

To the relief of the hostess, a young maid came in just then to signal the beginning of dinner. Holmes held his arm out for Irene, who took it and seemed relieved—whether genuinely or not, he was unsure. "I'm afraid I must insist on taking my own wife through, Mrs Edison. Our time apart has been most distressing," he explained, with a benign smile at their hostess. Marion Edison made her own introduction of herself to Irene on the way to the dining room, smiling in a genuinely friendly way before taking the arm of the Montana cattleman. Holmes wondered what age the others ascribed to Irene. She looked younger than her thirty-two years, though she could also look older. Mina seemed to regard her as an equal, which was fortunate under the circumstances.

Holmes's wish for the evening would have been to take on the inventor, to listen to Thomas Edison and exchange ideas with his brilliant mind, but Bernard James did not have such capacities. Instead, his real objective was to draw out Tootie McGregor and her husband, whom he had only met once before in a larger party. They were prominent in south Floridian society and undoubtedly knew the business of everyone in town. The wife hardly seemed like a difficult subject for such a task, though he was less sure about her quiet husband. Burroughs, too, was an unknown quantity, though any connection to a plot between an English solicitor and a Central American entrepreneur seemed farfetched at best. Nevertheless, Holmes kept his eyes on everyone.

Chapter 5: Irene

I was nervous, I'll confess, as I took my seat at the large dining table. Holmes had spent the afternoon briefing me and then quizzing me about the details of the lives of Bernard and Lavinia James, and I had dutifully learned locations and dates and pleasing filial anecdotes. But facts, even emotionally affecting ones, are far from the reality of taking on a character. Holmes had assured me I could behave as myself, but at the same time I was strongly aware of the fact that Lavinia James was far from Irene Adler in her experiences and habits. In addition to this, I would also be required to concentrate on the others in the situation, some of whom Holmes would have met, but all of whom would be strangers to me. Once or twice, I nearly told Holmes to continue the investigation if he liked, but to consider himself divorced from the unfortunate Lavinia, who wished to return instead to her much less complicated life as the celebrated contralto Irene Adler. Each time, one look at Holmes's provoking face steeled my resolve. The *great detective* might be wildly skilled at this sort of thing, taking roles and probing for information as easy to him as breathing air, but it was new to me, and I would not give him the satisfaction of seeing me give up. If he believed I could successfully pull it off, I would do more than that; I would be magnificent.

The beginning of the evening had asked little of me in terms of conversation or activity, so my nerves were on edge when I looked up to find that John Murphy, the mild-mannered cattleman, was to my right. Ambrose McGregor was on my left, but he had already been forcibly engaged in conversation with his wife and the young Burroughs on the way into the dining room. He would have to be left until a lull, which I doubted would ever occur where Tootie was involved, or for after dinner, when Holmes might engage the men separately.

I took a sip of the beverage in front of me and nearly coughed. It was Coca-Cola, an impossibly sweet, fizzy beverage America had produced during my time in England. Mistaking my expression as one of enthusiasm, Marion Edison, who was next to Holmes across the table, eagerly declared, "They say they'll be selling it in bottles any day now, but Papa has it brought in from the drugstore for parties." I couldn't help enjoying her excitement, though I'd have much preferred a glass of wine. Holmes had warned me not to expect the spirits to flow freely, as Mina Edison was a devout Methodist, her husband also held to Methodist teaching, and both were staunchly opposed to the consumption of strong drink of any kind. I smiled politely, and Marion beamed. I appeared to have unintentionally passed some sort of test in her eyes. All the better, I thought. Young people often have open ears and the benefit of not awakening others' suspicions. At eighteen, I had known plenty of things with the potential to embarrass any number of other people. I thought I might find out what sorts of things Marion knew.

The first course included a large green gelatin mould containing all kinds of fruit, and the conversation for a time was taken up with admiring it and with Tootie's insistence that Mina's cook should give her the recipe for her cook, who lacked the proper finesse in preparing such creations. Mina dutifully (and, I thought, with some measure of amusement) offered her cook's services for lessons at any time. In my view, the modern craze for outlandish gelatin was ridiculous. It would have been one thing if the stuff tasted good, but it was horrid. The pile of sticky, indifferent fruit that ended up on my plate reminded me of the one thing I missed about my life in Yorkshire—the plain, unfussy cooking that still predominated in the English countryside. But I soldiered on and managed to fit in a comment about the superiority of American cooks' mastery of the dish.

After a few minutes, the men began to grow restless, and Murphy asked Edison what he was working on. The inventor's eyes lit up at this, and my own interest increased. Everyone else at the table, even the loquacious Tootie, grew silent out of respect for the man. "I will show you all the new Kinetoscope tonight, if the ladies won't mind the laboratory," he said deferentially. Several enthusiastic heads nodded, and Mina looked toward those of us who were newcomers.

"Tom means the new motion-picture device he's been working on. It's terribly clever." She smiled sweetly at her husband and touched his hand lightly, which brought forth an answering smile from the inventor. "The best explanation will be seeing it for yourselves, I think," Mina continued, and I saw that Edison seemed disappointed not to be able to elaborate further.

As the meal progressed, conversation became less formal and more diverse, and I finally found myself able to engage Murphy in conversation over the main course of oyster stew. "I understand that you are from Montana, Mr Murphy," I began, watching as he nearly knocked his delicate china bowl off the table. "I have never been so far West. I was born in New Jersey, and I have spent all my time in the United States on the East Coast. I must ask if the stories of street shootouts and wild Indians are as common as we're told." I wiped my lips daintily on my napkin, priding myself that my inane question was exactly the sort of thing Lavinia James could be expected to wonder.

Murphy smiled broadly and began speaking in a tone of voice that would have worked marvellously if he'd been addressing a ten-year-old child. "Now, Mrs James, you fine ladies with your novels mustn't assume we're all uncivilised. Most of my business is done in banks and offices, and I have employees just like the offices back East do." He leaned closer to me. "Of course, if there's the occasional bit of trouble, we know what to do." His eyes twinkled, but I wondered exactly what sort of *trouble* he might actually have encountered and whether or not it extended to south Florida. He seemed a calm man, but there was a feeling of steel behind his good humour that I wouldn't have wanted to test. I saw that Holmes, while he was engaged in charming Marion, had also been listening, and I wondered what he had gleaned from the interaction that I might have missed.

Dinner was uneventful after that, finishing with brownies, an American dessert that resembled a chocolate cake with the consistency of a plum pudding. I thought it the best part of the meal. Drawing people out over food was more difficult than I'd expected, especially without alcoholic beverages to lower the barriers of the diners. I determined to try harder as the evening progressed. Holmes smiled at me, his face angular in the electric lights against the shadows of falling dusk.

"We should wait for sunset to see the Kinetoscope," said Mina as we took the last sips of our coffee. "It's marvellous in the dark."

"Let's have music until then," Tootie put in loudly, grinning with chocolate-stained teeth. "I can't wait to hear Lavinia. If she's half as good as Bernard claimed last time, we'll all be in tears." I looked over at Holmes, who was staring innocently at the floral wallpaper. He hadn't ever heard me sing before the last time he'd dined with the Edisons and their guests, at least as far as I knew. Impossible man.

Mina seamlessly moved her guests back into the piano room, where the ambiance was pensive in the half light. She gently motioned to the instrument as the others sat down on the sofa and chairs. Nelson Burroughs took the chair closest to the instrument and seemed to be excited at the prospect of the music, the most emotion he'd shown all evening. I wondered if he was a musician himself.

I sat down and began to play, opening with a medium-tempo dance tune. I watched my audience and, as usual, they began to relax as the music soothed them. My second song was a light comic number, a favourite from my time in England before my wedding. Finally, when I had their attention, I went to the popular love song that was the climax of each of my concerts.

I studied them all as I sang. Holmes, in the guise of Bernard, looked enchanted. Mina was surprised and pleased, I believe, having doubted the glowing praise of a husband. Marion seemed slightly bewildered, as if the music pleased her and invaded her at the same time. I felt a pang of sorrow for the inventor until I realised that his hand on the edge of the piano allowed him to experience its vibrations. Burroughs was as into the music as I'd expected, keeping slow time on his knee. The Montanan was quiet and, I thought, the least under the spell. Tootie was wide-eyed and vocal, making unintelligible delighted noises, while her husband smiled kindly and looked as if his mind was far away. I looked back to Holmes at last, wondering if his admiration belonged to Bernard after all, or if any part of it belonged to Sherlock Holmes, Consulting Detective.

After I finished playing, everyone sat quietly for a moment, even Tootie, her face wet with tears as she held her husband's hand. Finally, Mina broke the silence. "Thank you so much, Mrs James. We're fortunate to have heard that." I couldn't help feeling pleased. She turned to her husband. "Now, Tom dear, I think it's time!"

The inventor smiled dramatically and arose, and everyone else followed. He took a lantern from atop a shelf and led us out into the now-black nighttime. The lantern illuminated a well-worn path from the house to a smaller building, a path lined with shrubs and bright flowers I did not recognise, no doubt part of the inventor's collection. Edison opened a creaky door and with the flip of a switch immediately flooded the laboratory with electric light. Our eyes squinted in shock at the contrast between the brightness inside and the darkness of the grounds.

The laboratory was large and rectangular, lined with wooden shelves and with tables covered in all manner of glassware in rows down its centre. I wondered whimsically if the organised pandemonium resembled the inventor's mind.

Edison went immediately to work setting up a large machine made of metal and wood, his wife by his side assisting him at every turn. Clearly, Mina Edison was well-versed in her husband's endeavours. While we waited, Marion amused Tootie by listing for her the names of various chemicals that stood in unmarked bottles on the shelves around the walls. I listened with amazement as the girl explained that her father had all the names stored in his memory, as did his assistants, making labelling unnecessary. Holmes stood at one end of the room, the very picture of affable confusion, engaging Murphy in meaningless conversation about how grand it all was. Ambrose and Burroughs stood apart, watching silently.

Finally, after several moments of congenial work by the Edisons and less successful attempts by their guests to entertain themselves in a room in which they could safely touch nothing, Mina motioned us all to her husband's side, in front of the large brown contraption. "Stay here," she said quietly. "We're going to switch off the lights, and you'll be able to see it one-by-one. Stand in line just here." The men deemed it sporting to let the ladies go first, but the ladies in turn demurred, and so we ended up in a cluster rather than a line, with Burroughs finally nervously volunteering to begin. Mina brought him toward a box she and her husband had assembled at the front of the contraption, and then the room went black.

I realised a moment later that Edison had turned off the electric bulbs, a characteristically dramatic move, leaving us in the darkness of the evening. Someone swore under his breath, Murphy, I thought, and Tootie let out a slight shriek before everyone fell silent.

“That’s cracking good, Edison!” was the next audible noise, spoken, of course, by Burroughs, who had apparently forgotten his host’s deafness. In a moment, I heard the almost imperceptible sound of one hand lightly striking another—Mina Edison translating the words into Morse Code for the benefit of her husband. Holmes had told me that they often communicated in that way.

The lights were again blinding as Burroughs finished and came back to join the group, his face transformed by a wide, unselfconscious grin. He refused to breathe a word of the machine, and the next volunteer was Tootie, who took her place at the box while we all braced ourselves for the lights to disappear. This time, we took it better, a few of us even managing to chuckle; however, I nearly screamed when I felt a hand touch my arm and heard a low voice whisper, “I must have a word with you, Mrs James.” I forced my brain to place the voice as that of Ambrose McGregor.

“Later,” I breathed, glad for Tootie’s frequent exclamations of delight at whatever the contraption did. I felt chilled to the bone, even in the warm weather. Of all the people present, I hadn’t expected Ambrose to be the mystery. There had been something so kind in his quiet appreciation of his wife and his dinner that I hardly knew what to think. Was it possible the man fancied me? I put the thought out of my mind as preposterous (I hoped) and began to conceive of a plan to speak with him alone. When the lights came back on, I stole a look at his face, but he did not even glance in my direction.

My preoccupation consumed me to the point that I hardly cared when Marion finally pushed me forward for my turn at the machine. I bent down according to Mina’s whispered instructions and looked into a hole the size of a silver dollar as the lights went out. Before my eyes was a still picture of a boxer with his fist raised to strike. As I watched, the picture began to move, and the man landed the punch squarely on his opponent’s jaw. For thirty seconds I watched, open-mouthed, as a professional boxing match took place before my eyes. I was still hunched over, marveling, when the laboratory came back to life. I looked gratefully for the face of the inventor and enunciated as best I could, “I’m absolutely stunned, Mr Edison. I’ve never seen anything like it.” His serious face broke into a smile, and I believe he’d have shown us all again if his wife hadn’t stopped him with a small shake of her dark head.

I had been the last of the guests to view the Kinetoscope, so my viewing was followed by Edison and Mina putting the machine away in a cabinet in the corner of the laboratory. This time, everyone lingered nearby, hoping that by watching the Kinetoscope’s dismantling, they might somehow understand its mechanism. I moved slowly toward Holmes, and he sensed my object and moved into a corner of the room, between a table and a large grey cabinet. Without warning, he hooked a long arm around my waist and pulled me close, whispering in my ear. “I heard Ambrose McGregor speak during the blackout, but I could not understand what he said. Was I correct in assuming he addressed you?” I leaned into him like the most enamored of wives.

“He requested a private discussion with me. I intend to lose one of my gloves here and discover the loss once we reach the house. I will require a gentleman to walk me back, but you will be engaged elsewhere.” Holmes nodded once as Tootie’s voice cut into our tête-à-tête.

“My goodness, look at those lovebirds. It’s no wonder, since they’ve been separated.” Her blonde head bobbed in delight.

“Please excuse my enthusiasm, Mrs Edison,” said Holmes with a gallant near-bow. “I fear my wife’s return and your husband’s grand machine have made me quite giddy.” I smiled sheepishly, clinging to his hand.

Mina smiled indulgently. “I’m sure we’re all delighted to have met your charming wife, Mr James.” The guests nodded as one, and I felt a pang of genuine pleasure.

The party's return to the house was almost festive, but dread lay at the bottom of my stomach like a lead weight. Whatever Ambrose McGregor had to say, I highly doubted it was anything I would be overly excited to hear.

When we reached the piano room, Burroughs began to declare his intention of leaving, and Murphy looked ready to follow suit. Before Mina could begin her polite farewells, I made a show of looking down at my hands and finding one gloved and the other bare. At the same moment, Holmes asked Tootie about her favourite topic—her chronically ill son Bradford. He stopped mid-sentence when I lamented, "Oh no, I've been terribly clumsy. I seem to have lost my glove on the way back."

"Don't worry, dear, Tom can go and retrieve it," said Mina kindly, putting a hand on my arm.

"Nonsense," I answered, "your husband has been far too kind already this evening. Perhaps my husband—," but Bernard James looked down at Tootie with the crestfallen expression of a man disappointed at being unable to hear the words ready to fall from her lips. Bless her, she took the bait.

"Ambrose, you can take her," she said brightly. "I was just about to tell Mr James about Bradford's ailment." Her husband nodded wordlessly and proffered his arm to me, using the other to pick up the lantern from the shelf where Edison had placed it.

"Thank you so much!" I said, trying to project artlessly breathless gratitude. Tootie fairly beamed upon me, and I fancied she had decided to take me on as a sort of protégé.

We were halfway between the house and the laboratory before Ambrose spoke. "Mrs James," he said quietly, "I hope you don't think me impertinent. I wish to say at the outset that I mean you no harm."

"I was sure of it, Mr McGregor," I rejoined, supposing it to be the sort of thing Lavinia might say, though it was a blatant lie in the mouth of Irene Adler.

"The truth is—," we reached the door of the laboratory building, and he opened it, shining the lantern inside. I walked quickly toward the side of the room where I had placed my glove. "The truth is, Mrs James, that I believe you may be in grave danger."

"Excuse me?" I said, turning around to face the man, his plain face hardly visible in the shadows the lantern cast against the dark walls.

"This is hard to say," he continued in a slow, stuttering voice, "but I have reason to believe your husband is not who he claims to be." I froze. Of all the possibilities I had considered, this contingency had never crossed even the furthest recess of my mind.

"Whatever do you mean, Sir?" I asked in my most husband-defending tone, moving back outside where the moonlight cast less garish light. Ambrose's expression was filled with pained concern.

"I have reason to believe that the gentleman who claims to be Bernard James is actually an English detective by the name of Sherlock Holmes." I nearly laughed. Only by the immediate application of a pinch to my forearm was I able to keep from making noise. I thought quickly. Holmes and I had not discussed this situation. I was sure that the detective, with his seemingly omniscient mind, must have considered it, but he had most likely dismissed it as a near-impossibility.

Ambrose continued in the midst of my silence. "There is a man who lives in town by the name of Sanchez, and he—well, he is more acquainted with the ways of this person than I am. I first met your husband at this house during a large party a week ago, and Sanchez was also a guest. He took me aside that night and told me he had spotted Holmes, who, I gather, is somehow affiliated with the police. At the time, Sanchez voiced his opinion that the ruse was most likely harmless. After all, the man's reputation is as a champion of good. I could not, however, fail to speak when I realised that you, his wife, seem unaware of his true identity. I am sorry if I have caused you distress, but I could not bear to stand by and watch a lady as fine as yourself be taken in."

I looked up into the kind, concerned face of Ambrose McGregor, and I made a decision. I am generally a good judge of character. Barring the blinders that caused me to marry a monster, I am rarely ever wrong. I wondered briefly what Holmes would wish me to do, but I was in a bind, pinned to the wall like a lab specimen. I had the choice of trying to come up with some wildly elaborate ruse to fool a seemingly reasonable man, or else come out with the truth and trust his judgement and good will. I chose the latter.

"Mr McGregor," I said, standing close to him in the lantern light, "I will be quick, or the others will wonder what is keeping us. The things you say are true, and if you will call on us tomorrow at Mrs Stillwell's boardinghouse, we will explain them to you. I ask you, as a personal favour, to please trust me and keep silent about this until then." The pleading look I gave him was unfeigned.

"You're quite a woman, Mrs James," was all he said as he turned back toward the house.

Chapter 6: Holmes

The moment Irene entered the house on the arm of Ambrose McGregor, Holmes could tell something had seriously rattled her, which he hadn't expected. With sudden horror, he wondered if the older man had bothered her in some personal way. The detective's eyes searched her keenly, but Irene's smile and enthusiastic thanks seemed to convince the others, at least, that all was well. Mercifully, goodbyes were soon said, and within minutes he had his companion settled into a hired runabout. It was hardly elegant, but carriages were hard to come by in Fort Myers. As soon as he had handed Irene up, he retrieved a blanket from the floor behind, tucking it around her knees like a solicitous husband might.

"I'm quite warm enough, Bernard," she said calmly, though none of the others were around to hear. Holmes hopped up beside her and studied her face, trying to ascertain her state of mind, punishing himself mentally for allowing her to go unaccompanied into danger, but she remained quiet, and her face remained impassive until they reached Mrs Stillwell's house.

Holmes willed his hands to be especially gentle as he helped Irene down from the carriage. She was small, he realised. He had never considered it, not properly, not as anything more than a statistical fact. The prints her feet made in the dirt pathway to the back door were tiny, practically a child's prints. Why, oh why, had he been foolish enough to send her off alone with the man? His mind, the fallible organ to which he attached such trust, had painted a picture of The Woman as a force, a tower of strength. He now realised that she was both more and less than that, and he cursed himself inwardly for his lack of concern.

As they mounted the stairs to his room at Mrs Stillwell's, Holmes's hand hovered in the vicinity of Irene's elbow in case she should lose her footing. He did not touch her. She still remained speechless, and he wondered if he would have to employ some unusual method to cause her to explain the encounter. He knew that wronged women were often loathe to speak of their experiences for days or even weeks, and some, he had heard, even refused to speak at all. He could not afford for her to be one of those.

The proprietress of the house was prodigiously proud of having electricity and of living so near the inventor of the lightbulb himself, as she had eagerly told Holmes upon his arrival, and she charged dearly for both. The detective turned on the prized electric light as soon as he and Irene had entered the worn upstairs room, and he watched his companion remove her hat and wash her hands in the basin. Having finished, she turned and looked him full in the face.

"My goodness, Holmes, you look as if you've seen a spectre." The detective sat down in the lone wooden chair and watched her, puzzled. "Since you have not asked me the content of my conversation with Ambrose McGregor, I can only assume you thought it as prudent as I did to wait until we were privately secluded." As she spoke, Irene sat down on the edge of the uncomfortable bed and unpinned her chestnut hair, letting it fall in waves down her back. Holmes supposed that she felt no shame in this, since, after all, the man before her had once seen her dressed as a young man.

"I hope very much that you will not blame me, Holmes." Her eyes pleaded with him, though he saw no evidence of personal injury or offense and began to conclude that his original assessment of her distress had been mistakenly reasoned. "McGregor's aim and purpose was to save me from the unfortunate fate of a deceived woman. In short, Holmes, he went through all that trouble to tell me that my husband was none other than the famed English detective Sherlock Holmes."

At this, Sherlock Holmes of Baker Street, consulting detective to queen and country, threw back his head and laughed, but

The Woman did not join him. "Believe me, Holmes," she continued when he had subsided, "my initial inclination was the same as yours, but the knowledge of Ambrose's source distressed me more than his disclosure amused me. Alberto Sanchez somehow recognised you last week." Holmes nodded, not entirely surprised. Sanchez was the only one with a likely connection. The detective did not yet know exactly what it was or to what it tended, but it would have been almost insupportably coincidental for any person wholly unconnected to the case to have recognised him. Barnett had been more thorough than even Holmes had expected.

"Ambrose said Sanchez called your deception harmless."

"Interesting," said Holmes, pulling a well-worn notebook and pen from his black leather travelling case. "Let us evaluate where this places us. First, I believe we may almost certainly rule out the idea that Ambrose McGregor is lying."

"The thought had occurred to me," murmured Irene, "but I could not think of a reasonable motive, and he gave no appearance of it."

"Well, we may keep the possibility as a remote contingency to fall back on if no other roads lead us to fruitful enquiry, but I doubt it will be needed. Second, we know that Sanchez knows my appearance and is aware that I am alive. This leads to the question: Was Sanchez warned of my continuing existence before and told to be on the lookout for my presence, or was his recognition of me an accident? If the first, then we may suppose a network of people is aware that I am alive; if the second, Sanchez may know of me by some other means, such as a photo of me with someone else whom he has been taught to recognise. I have had few photos taken, but unfortunately some do exist at the cajoling of Watson and Inspector Lestrade of Scotland Yard. Third, where does your solicitor, Barnett, fit into the equation? If he is aware that I am alive, why has he not had me tailed? I can say with certainty that I have not been followed since my arrival in America. As improbable as it may seem, I begin to lean toward the possibility that Sanchez may have recognised me by near-chance. There is one particular photo that appeared in the *London Times* some years ago, after I had helped a certain peer regain a necklace stolen from his wife by a famous jewel thief. My work resulted in the man being caught and imprisoned, not only for the theft in question, but also for several other previously unsolved cases. The picture was notable because it contained the likenesses of several officers of Scotland Yard, Dr Watson, myself, and, most unusually, my brother Mycroft, who had been persuaded to pose for it by the prime minister, who wished the government to receive positive publicity from the incident. The photo's presence in a prominent newspaper means that numerous reproductions of it were produced, and any number of individuals might have procured it easily."

Holmes leaned forward and gazed intently into The Woman's attentive face. "I wonder, Irene, what part Mycroft was intended to play in all of this. As I told you, the letter from Barnett to Sanchez came to him with almost serendipitous chance. I wonder now, more than ever, if my brother was meant to be involved. Perhaps the mastermind, whether Barnett, Sanchez, or someone else, misjudged his character and believed that he would take up where his younger brother had left off—with the same sort of investigation. Perhaps Sanchez was taught to expect to see the face of the elder brother, but instead found himself surprisingly face-to-face with the younger."

"But for what purpose could he possibly need to know your brother's face?"

"That is what we must find out. I am afraid, Irene, that this will be our last taste of fine accommodations for some time. Tonight, Bernard and Lavinia James will receive urgent news that calls them back home to England. Tomorrow, you and I will emerge as merchants to set up shop among the migrant day labourers, our faces different enough to fool even those we met this evening if necessary.

We may safely hope that our roles will not be tested too acutely right away, for I intend us to mix with a segment of local society that families like the Edisons are hardly likely to meet on a regular basis."

Holmes noted that Irene's eyes held excitement rather than fear and trust rather than suspicion. Her beautiful face was alive with the prospect of adventure. "Tell me what you wish me to do, and I will help in any way I can."

"First," he said quietly, "I must thank you for your cool head this evening. Without you, I would be in grave danger with no idea of my own peril. Second, it is obvious that both of us take a great risk by remaining here. I now believe, much more than at any previous point in this case, that the key to the mystery may be found here, but that very fact means harm is not far away. If you wish to extricate yourself, I will not deter you."

Irene put out a small hand and lightly touched the detective's long fingers as they rested on his knee. "I agreed to help you," she said softly, "and I will continue to do so as long as I may be useful. I assure you, I am not afraid." Just then, out of nowhere, she smiled—a rare, wide, bracing smile. Holmes returned it with one of his own. They spent the rest of the night preparing to take on new characters.

The next morning, Gloria Stillwell rose to find on her front hall table a generous sum of money and a note explaining that Mr and Mrs Bernard James had been forced to return to England at their earliest possible convenience to care for a sick friend. Meanwhile, a tall man and a short man dressed in cheap clothing visited the poorest section of Fort Myers and hired an elderly horse and nearly-defunct wagon, which they filled with tattered raiment and low-quality goods. Their afternoon enquiry into the rental of a tiny, empty shop with a dilapidated sign that had once read "Sloane's General Store" proved rewarding, and a few more cartfuls of goods meant that Sherlock Holmes and Irene Adler were in business by evening, proud occupants of a small, square building with sandy floors, empty shelves, and nothing to recommend it except its location and the miniscule flat above it.

The following morning, Holmes dressed himself after a long sleepless night spent in one of the spindly chairs the previous occupants had seen fit to leave in the tattered flat, his pipe forming a pleasant accompaniment to the slight coolness in the evening breeze. Irene had slept soundly, no doubt exhausted from the previous night's sleeplessness and the previous day's transactions. One day was hardly long enough to rent and stock a general store, but that name was generous in this case, and Holmes meant it to be. Forced to be unrecognisable in high society, he intended to work from within another strata of the infrastructure that kept the city moving, that of the migrant day labourers, of whom Alberto Sanchez employed three hundred in his citrus grove on the outskirts of town. If Holmes could not get at the man directly, he would work through his organization. The stakes were higher now. If Sanchez knew his face and knew that he lived, Holmes could not afford to rest.

Once dressed in coarse brown slacks and a slightly ill-fitting grey shirt, Holmes darkened his skin and altered his face, making himself appear weathered and inelegant. He added wrinkles and rounded his sharp features. The cracked mirror on one of the walls revealed him as a middle-aged workman, which was exactly what he desired. He intended that that anyone entering the store should think him a manual labourer whose ambitions had acquired him a dingy store of his own.

After finishing his own toilette, he woke Irene with a gentle shake to the shoulder before leaving the room to give her time to dress. She had been dressed as a male the previous day, but from now on she would portray the lady of the establishment, a woman slightly nearer gentility than her husband, but still coarse and weatherbeaten. Holmes re-entered the room upon hearing a light tap from inside the door. Irene wore a plain yellow cotton dress, worn from its previous owner's use, but she was still stunningly beautiful. Wordlessly, Holmes placed the rickety chair in front of the basin and began to work on his still-sleepy companion, using makeup to create lines of exhaustion and worry where there were none and slight asymmetry in near-perfect features. At last, he took her hair and mussed it slightly, arranging it as sloppily as he could without arriving at a completely inappropriate conclusion. He took care to commit every step to memory so that he would be able to replicate the results as many times as needed.

Irene walked over to the broken mirror and stared at her reflection. "I'm afraid I can't completely eradicate your beauty without more extensive work," murmured Holmes behind her, in a tone laced with irony.

"Don't worry," she said, whirling on him. "Godfrey couldn't manage it either, no matter how hard he tried."

The tall detective stepped back as if he'd been slapped, but regained his composure after a moment. "I've found us a place to eat breakfast before we open." He spoke as if nothing had happened, but Irene wouldn't look at him. Without speaking further, he led the way downstairs and into the morning half-light of the dusty road.

Barcroft's wasn't the sort of place Lavinia and Bernard James would visit, but it was every bit the kind of place Jane and Tom Perkins, junk and supply store owners, would certainly frequent. Holmes and Irene were ushered into the cramped establishment and seated at a round table in a tiny, dubiously-kept corner, away from the few groups of working-class men who had come in for a very early-morning breakfast and, for some, liquid fortification. The other patrons' initial glances at the newcomers gave way to disinterest, so the detective was assured that their disguises were at least marginally effective. Holmes took a sip of the indifferent coffee the waitress brought and declared it vile with a disgusted expression. Irene looked up and met his gaze, then dropped her eyes quickly. "This will not do," he murmured, whether to himself or to her he was unsure. It had been a great deal of time since he'd had such protracted contact with a female of any sort, and he was beginning to recall the pitfalls that invariably complicated such associations. Watson had his days, of course, but a glass of scotch and a good pork pie set him to rights without difficulty. One couldn't ply Irene Adler with a pork pie and expect the same result, more was the pity. The detective's mind extended to the furthest bounds of male existence, but where females were concerned, there had always been certain blanks. The current problem was that communication, which was vital during a case, required the cooperation of two, and one of those two was persisting in her silence.

"I apologise, Holmes." The Woman's voice interrupted his thoughts. "I have no cause to bring my private feelings into the case." Holmes stared at her as if she had suddenly acquired the power of speech after profound muteness.

"Ah," he said.

"Quite," she replied, blushing and staring at the thick white plate on the table before her. Holmes felt fortunate when a plate of irregularly-shaped sausage arrived a moment later, accompanied by white pillows of dough the waitress called biscuits, though they were nothing like the English variety.

"Don't you intend to eat?" Irene asked once she had taken a few bites and noticed his lack of movement.

"Not hungry," Holmes answered. "I rarely require food while I work."

"Well, that's one difference between us," his companion replied between bites, her good humour apparently restored. The biscuits seemed to meet with her approval, as she downed three of them and two large sausages. "I always eat well when I'm on tour," she continued after she had finished her last crumb. "Otherwise, I'm inclined toward irritation." Holmes caught a mischievous glint in her eye.

Watson might be easier to handle, but he was hardly given to mischievous glances.

Chapter 7: Irene

I found, after breakfast, that I looked forward to the day. The sense of impending danger was not entirely absent from my mind, but my unfamiliar clothing and the paint on my face gave me a measure of freedom I had not enjoyed while still in my own guise. I would have to be more vigilant, I realised, not to allow myself to strike at Holmes for being the only available representative of the non-female species. The detective hardly deserved that, and any debt he owed me from our previous skirmish he had more than paid by taking the case.

We returned to the shop shoulder-to-shoulder, and Holmes briefed me on the objectives of the day. For the first time, we were to separate. He intended to visit the site of Sanchez's citrus grove, while I tended the store and learned what I could from anyone I met. Rather than being a cause for apprehension, the idea of being on my own invigorated me.

The idea of it invigorated me, that is. I was less thrilled when no one had come into the store after two hours and I had checked the sign for the third time. I decided to do some reconnaissance on the rest of the street, keeping an eye on the unprepossessing space where Holmes and I plied our temporary wares. My object was the store we had visited the previous day to purchase our ragged clothing, a well-kept secondhand shop with a matriarchal owner who considered herself far above her clientele. On our first visit, I'd been dressed as a boy, and I hadn't spoken. As a result, I hoped and expected that she wouldn't recognise me in my current incarnation.

A doorbell announced my entrance, and I was surprised to find a young man behind the counter instead of an elderly woman. "Good morning, ma'am," he said, his voice thick with the slow drawl of the American Deep South, and I acknowledged his greeting with a nod. I moved quickly through the main room, which held glass cases that cradled expensive items such as silver spoons and brooches of dubious origin, and passed through to a cluttered side room that held clothing racks, piles of dilapidated shoes, and hats stacked high on top of one another. For several minutes, I was the only patron in the store, but my waiting was finally rewarded by the entrance of a woman. I watched her surreptitiously, ostensibly holding up a threadbare coat to test its suitability. She held a baby in one arm, nearly a newborn by the look of it, and her face was worn, though I thought she was no older than I was, if as old.

I listened casually as she began to address the youthful shopkeeper. "Tommy, you better be glad you ain't out today. Bill's gone crazy cause Sanchez is in some kind of hurry to get it all in before the end of the month." At the name Sanchez, I stopped moving and listened intently.

"What for?" asked the boy in a conspiratorial tone.

"Dunno," was the disappointing answer, "but my Jim says Bill's in a temper and screaming at everybody." I took note. Even if this was the only thing I learned all day, at least I had something to tell Holmes. After the woman had left, I bought a pair of shoes with worn-out soles and departed with a word to the young man about the store I'd just opened with my husband. I walked back toward Sloane's General Store, not overly concerned at the prospect that someone might have stolen some of our cheap wares. On my way, I watched the sun's glare in shop windows and discerned nothing important or significant to the case.

Fortunately, the woman from the secondhand store stepped into the store right after me, balancing her tiny baby on her hip and holding a bag of purchases in her other hand. She stared at the cheap cookware, used furnishings, and non-perishable foods that lined the shelves almost haphazardly, picking up a jar of crushed sage. After a while, she brought it to the counter and asked me its price. In order to loosen her tongue, I quoted her an amount much lower than its value.

"You're new in town," she said, with a slight air of distrust. "I saw you in Morgan's just now."

"That's right," I said. "My husband and I just came here from Iowa."

"Well, you're lucky not to be in the groves."

"Why is that?" I asked as nonchalantly as possible.

"Things are getting worse these days. My husband Jim went to work for a new boss because the pay is better, but it looks like he's going to force us all out in the end. It's the deadlines—most of the bosses'll need pickers for at least another four weeks, but he wants it all by the end of the month—only two weeks—and that means the foremen drive the men like slaves."

"I'm terribly sorry," I said sympathetically.

"Well, it's the way of this life," she said, giving me a few coins and leaving.

—

I was vastly relieved when Holmes finally stepped through the door of the shop, looking pleased. "I can see that your day has proved more successful than mine," I said by way of a greeting.

"Indeed," he answered, locking the door and leading the way up the narrow, rickety stairs to the tiny upstairs flat. As we cleaned our faces, he began his story.

"My first object was Sanchez's citrus grove outside of town. I was admitted after a wheedling promise that my shop might be able to stock necessaries like tobacco and liquor at lower-than-market prices. Almost as soon as I stepped onto the premises, I learned a vital piece of information."

"Sanchez is forcing the men to work much more quickly than the other growers' men," I inserted.

"Exactly so," said Holmes, looking gratifyingly surprised.

"I was introduced to an unpleasant character called Bill, who brought me into his office."

"The foreman," I put in, but Holmes ignored me this time.

"I was given to understand that a company office exists somewhere in town, but the field office is in a shed on the edge of the grove itself. I did not expect to be treated well enough to be introduced to the head foreman, and when I was, I began to be concerned that Sanchez himself might be in evidence, a possibility I would like to avoid for the moment. Thankfully, Bill mentioned offhand that his employer would be conducting business in town all day."

"But here's the rub, Irene," he said, stopping dramatically as he finished wiping off the remnants of his altered nose. "*The photograph was on his desk.* There I was, having a normal conversation, if somewhat dishonest in the common way, about cost and supply, with a picture of myself and my brother staring up at me. The man did not appear to recognise me, but I confess I was not entirely comfortable with the situation. The other odd thing is—" and he fixed his eyes on my now-clean face with intensity, "the photo wasn't the one I predicted. I was wrong. It was one from several years ago, a picture of my brother and me on the day of my graduation from Cambridge. I was not aware a copy existed, other than the ones Mycroft and I possess."

"How long has it been since you looked at that photograph, Holmes?" I asked quickly, feeling myself start to blush.

He shook his head. "Not since the day I received it in a letter from my brother three months after the occasion. Since then, it has resided among my personal papers." I stood with my back to him, trying to will my face back to its usual colour."

"Do you remember when Mrs Hudson tried out a new maid, a girl named Sally Hawkins, while you were away?"

"Yes," said Holmes, "but I don't see—" and then the detective fell silent. I winced. He grasped my shoulders and spun me around to face him. "But that was before the King of Bohemia approached me for the first time. What could you possibly have meant by it?"

"I knew that he was planning to come to you, and I decided to strike first in case some sort of bargain was necessary. Mrs Hudson hardly took her eyes off me, but I found five minutes to look through your small collection of photographs. Your disorganization was beneficial to you, or else I'd have come away with much more. As it was, I only had time to conceal one very old photo of you and the man I now know to be your brother, though I did not realise it at the time. I hoped I had been lucky—that if I ever needed the photo as a bargaining tool, it might be worth at least something small to you. I would have tried again, but Mrs Hudson very wisely did not trust me and put me out of the house." Holmes listened to this speech impassively, and I had no idea what sort of thoughts might be going through his mind.

"Listen, Holmes," I finally said, "at the time, I did not know you, and I felt the need to arm myself against the most skilled detective in London."

"And, I've no doubt you would do the same today, if you felt the need," he said drily, looking down at me with a half smile.

"Yes, that's probably true," I replied without flinching, "but I'm sorry it's become a player in whatever it is we're trying to investigate. I kept it with my papers, stored at my bank in London. Barnett must have helped himself to it and probably to everything else as well, whatever your brother's people were unable to access."

"Well, at any rate, we still don't know for sure whose likeness he was after, whether my brother's or my own." He patted my shoulder awkwardly. "I'd have done the same if I were you." From him, the compliment was a high one.

"Well, it appears my news is less than cataclysmic," I said, sitting on the edge of the bed. "We had one customer, a world-weary woman who was eager to share her unhappiness with Sanchez's operation with anyone willing to listen. It seems he lured workers from other growers with the promise of higher pay, but now seems to be driving them like Pharoah and the Hebrew slaves."

"So I gathered," Holmes said, taking his place in the chair opposite me. "I'm glad to hear the comparison, since I did not know if the conditions I witnessed were typical or not. One wonders how long the men will endure the unpleasantness. Certainly, Sanchez could hardly hope for more than two more weeks from them under such conditions."

"I assume they're in something of a bind," I said. "Would the other growers be likely to take them back this late?"

"Doubtful," said Holmes. "Whatever his part in your matter, this Sanchez seems an unpleasant character. Of course, the pertinent question is why he's so eager to get his harvest in before anyone else."

Holmes opened his notebook. "Let us evaluate our position."

"First, we now know that a photo of Mycroft and me has changed hands, leading to recognition. The specific nature of the connection between Barnett and Sanchez remains unknown, but is confirmed, at least, by that. The presence of the photo on the desk confirms that Sanchez considers it important, at any rate."

"Second, we know that Sanchez not only intends to bring in the harvest, but to do so two weeks before his rivals. There is no market value to this; demand is steady. His motive must be completion itself, but why? That is suggestive, I believe, of the fact that whatever part of the plot is to take place on his end will be completed within a fortnight."

"Third, we know that Barnett has tampered with your private papers. We can safely assume that he has been notified by now that his prized songbird has flown the coop, but he should not know where, at least not yet."

"Fourth, we know that Sanchez was not unwilling to mention my presence to someone else, dismissing it as harmless. This suggests that he either does not think I am on his trail, or he is trying to double bluff by appearing not to care. This also assumes Ambrose McGregor is entirely truthful, which seems likely, but is not certain.

"Fifth, there remains no indication that Sanchez is aware of your presence or appearance. That suggests Barnett intended to conduct the Adler side of the affair himself."

"But Holmes, why would Barnett think it necessary for his associate to receive a photograph if he was doing the work on the English side?"

"It could be a precautionary measure, but it's more likely that he expected either Mycroft or me to turn up here." Holmes shook his head. "I begin to think my movements were somehow anticipated."

"Do you think I betrayed you?" I asked the question point-blank, which seemed to me the most logical course of action.

"The thought has crossed my mind," he answered, not unpleasantly.

"Mine too," I said, "I mean, it has crossed my mind that if I were part of the plot, then some of the things we've learned would make much more sense." Holmes let out a dry laugh.

"That would make me the object, rather than yourself," he said.

"That can't possibly—" I stopped. "There's something else I haven't told you."

Chapter 8: Holmes

Holmes watched Irene dig her fingernails into her palms. "Three months after I was married, Barnett contacted me. He came to our house in Yorkshire and requested, as my former solicitor, to see me. My husband was angry, but he didn't want to make a bad impression on a prominent fellow solicitor, so he allowed the meeting. Barnett's reason for coming was to make an offer to help me out of my marriage. He said he could prove Godfrey was an unfit husband and extricate my money if I would only do as he asked. I was suspicious, but I knew that he had connections in the law and on the bench. Obviously, I declined his offer."

"All he asked was for one favour, one job and he would take care of all of it for me." She paused for a moment and smiled at Holmes. "I was told to break into a flat in a dull part of London, the part of London where no one fashionable lives and nothing happens. Once inside, I was to take a particular case and bring it to Barnett's office. This flat and case, he said, belonged to a very bad man, a man who deserved to be thwarted. I asked him the man's name, and he told me: Mycroft Holmes, the brother of the famed detective."

For once, Holmes listened with his eyes wide open and his body alert. Irene continued, "Barnett was aware of the role you played in my marriage and the events surrounding it, but he did not know that our skirmish had convinced me that you were an honourable man or that I considered us fully even and had no desire to continue our little war. You may not believe that I also objected to the idea of petty thievery against someone about whom I knew nothing except his connection to someone I respected. At any rate, Barnett did not seem angry, but he refused to help me if I did not do as he wished. At that point, I owed him nothing, as all my funds were my husband's."

"You will no doubt be wondering now why I appealed to such a man after my husband's death. I am not entirely sure myself, as I can't imagine my doing so under normal circumstances. At the time, however, I was nearly paralysed with fear. I was terrified that the law would somehow contrive a way to keep me bound, to keep my fortune in the estate and leave me penniless. I believed that Barnett could prevent this, and I had never found him dishonest in his dealings with me, but I was surprised when he agreed to look after my property without anything in return except a small fee. I had expected some sort of request like the previous one. I should have known that he had found another way to use me."

Holmes found himself resisting the urge to let his mind travel through the murky hallways of psychological theorising. "You believe he is attempting to use you to get to Mycroft, then," he finally said.

"Yes," she answered decidedly. "I believe it to be the only scenario that fits all the facts. Unfortunately, I have no idea how the man Sanchez fits into it."

"Nor I, yet," answered the detective, "though your disclosures point to the original letter reaching my brother by design."

"You have not asked me the reason for my reticence," said The Woman after a pause. "Does that indicate that you doubt my veracity?"

"Not in the least," answered Holmes, beginning to fill his pipe with inferior tobacco from the shop. "You and I have limited trust in one another. With knowledge of this condition, you chose to withhold information that had the potential to make you appear to be a possible criminal accessory in the current case." He paused to close his eyes and take a drag from his pipe. "More importantly, you're telling the truth now."

Irene folded her arms. "I hoped you'd at least doubt it for a moment," she said, sounding disappointed. The detective opened one eye.

"You have tells, like anyone else, Miss Adler. If you haven't figured them out yourself, I'm certainly not going to enlighten you." Irene let out an unintelligible sound that resembled a *hrff*. "Your solicitor is not a stupid man. He may have misjudged Mycroft's likelihood of involving himself personally, but he did not mistake his willingness to act on information that pointed to criminal activity."

"But what could Barnett have against your brother?" asked Irene curiously. "He's certainly not visible or famous. You said he was some sort of diplomat."

At this, Holmes laughed silently for some time. "That, Irene, is perhaps the easiest thing of all. My brother is entirely unknown and unseen, except by those who have cause to despise him. He is an important man; even I do not understand the full extent of all he knows."

"Is he a bad man, then?" The question was innocent, almost like that of a child, but the tone was ironic.

"Only to those who consider power wielded in the service of order to be an evil."

Irene placed a delicate hand over her mouth and yawned. "What do you intend to do now?"

"Tomorrow, we will deliver supplies to Sanchez's field office, and I very much hope the man himself will be in evidence."

—

For the first time in a good while, Holmes's mind had enough to consider to keep it fully active through the night, mulling over the facts that had come to light through the day and evening. Ever since the concert, he'd suspected Irene of hiding information, and he wished devoutly that she had revealed what she knew earlier;

nevertheless, he didn't blame her for her reticence. She'd been through a great deal, and her still-frayed edges proved that her experiences continued to eat at her psyche. No sense lamenting what couldn't be. The case was beginning to take shape as a simple plot of misdirection, a red herring by the name of Irene Adler, put out to somehow entrap Mycroft Holmes. Mycroft was an audacious target, but Holmes realised that his own presence in Florida was proof that the plot had not been entirely ill-conceived. If he had indeed been dead, would Mycroft have come himself? The detective doubted it, vehemently. Mycroft would have sent an associate to protect Irene, whether she liked it or not, as was his usual practice. Holmes wondered why such otherwise thorough plotters had been so sure his brother would do what his brother had never in his life been likely to do. There must be something, he thought, that he was missing. Now that Sanchez knew he was alive, had the plan changed? Surely, Barnett would be only too eager to use him to get at his brother. Was Sanchez trying to find him? If so, he was doing a fairly incompetent job. And why hadn't he made any effort when he had a chance at the Edisons' party? Holmes had many questions, but they were focused questions. He preferred those to vague certainties.

—

The citrus grove was pleasant in the early morning. A breeze blew the leaves of hundreds of trees, and Holmes enjoyed the pleasantly overpowering aroma of the fruit. The workers were not yet tired from the day, and the serene organization of the harvest gave no hint of the owner's dark purposes.

Holmes led Irene around row on row of trees to the small shack on the far side of the grove. No one accosted them along the way, and he surmised that the foremen knew he was expected. "I wasn't anticipating the smell," said The Woman.

"Indeed," said Holmes. Tom Perkins was a taciturn fellow. His "wife" carried a bag of cigarettes in one hand and held his arm with the other, while he hoisted a box of canned soup on his shoulder. Together, they formed a less-than-savoury picture, he with his sagging eyes and florid face, and his wife with unkempt hair and soiled dress.

Holmes pushed open the door of the office, and Bill, the tall, broad grove supervisor greeted him with a less-than-enthusiastic *eh*. "Good morning," said the detective, his voice ingratiating. "My wife and I have brought the items you requested." Bill ushered them into the tiny building, pointing to a dusty room covered with piles of non-perishable goods.

"We've no mind to leave these until we've agreed on a price," said Irene shrilly, holding tightly to her tobacco and nodding to a dull-acting Holmes not to relinquish his cans.

"I told you yesterday," said Bill, glowering at Holmes and ignoring Irene, "that I can't set a price until I've asked the Boss."

"Well, then, I guess we'll have to take these things back to town," said Irene, staring boldly at the foreman and hugging her sack like a prized turkey.

"Aye," said Holmes after a pause. Bill stared at the couple for a long moment in which he seemed to be contemplating inflicting bodily harm before stomping into a room at the back of the shed and leaving them alone. Holmes winked at Irene.

After a moment, two voices could be heard, one Bill's angry growl, the other quieter and calmer. Bill's irate complaints were easy to understand, but Holmes couldn't make out the contributions of the other man until the door opened and both emerged.

The second man was considerably shorter than the foreman, dark-skinned and dark-haired, with a well-kept moustache and immaculate clothing. He smiled at Holmes and Irene, showing rows of perfect teeth that somehow put the detective in mind of a self-satisfied shark.

"Sir, Madam, what may I do to assist you?" The man's English was perfect, too perfect for a native, too well enunciated. He touched his chin and contemplated the pair placidly.

"Look, Mister, do you want our things or not?" Irene stepped forward defiantly.

"My associate (he indicated Bill with a nod) informs me of your offer. I hope this will be sufficient." He reached into his jacket pocket and pulled out a roll of bills, peeling two off the top and handing them to Irene, who eyed them greedily before surrendering them to Holmes, who glowered at her wordlessly.

"That's…satisfactory," said Irene, attempting to look as if she were excited and trying not to appear so.

"Aye," said Holmes.

"Come back next week with more of the same," said the Central American, smiling and throwing out his arm theatrically. "I'm Sanchez, the owner." Irene nodded sycophantically and took Holmes's arm. The unprepossessing couple left the shack with many thanks from the animated boss and glares from his second-in-command.

The detective led Irene away from the grove, as silently as befitted his character, until they had reached the wagon and he had unceremoniously dumped her into it, like an unprized sack of potatoes. "I thought you might have made a hole in my arm," Holmes finally ventured, once the scrawny rented horse had begun the trek back to town and carried them a safe distance from prying eyes. "You held on so tightly a crowbar couldn't have dislodged you. I'm not entirely sure Jane Perkins is quite so enamored of her lord and master as to make that necessary." He half-smiled drily.

When Irene failed to answer after many moments, Holmes looked over at her and found her pale under her makeup, her eyes fixed straight ahead and hands clasped tightly together. "Holmes," she said, "Alberto Sanchez is James Barnett."

Holmes let the horse drive itself for a moment, blinking rapidly and staring at his companion. For a moment, he wondered if she was foisting some kind of ill-advised joke on him, but her face was far from amused. "You are absolutely sure of this?" He drove again, and his brain began to work.

"Without doubt," answered The Woman, sounding steadier. "When he first came out of his office, I noticed something familiar about him—something about the way he walked, but it was that gesture, when he touched his chin, that let me know for sure. After that, I couldn't stop seeing it—in the shape of his head, his eyes, the way he smiled. I would swear it in court."

"Watson would love this," Holmes muttered.

"Eh?"

"Just like something out of one of his stories, no embellishment needed." The detective felt somehow that a plot twist so outlandishly dramatic was a personal insult, a thumbing of the nose at the rationality he tried to project. Ridiculously irritating.

An unexpected sound interrupted his reverie. Laughter, unfettered. In spite of her fear, Irene's face was filled with amusement. "Well," she said, putting her hand over her mouth, "we will have to tell him all about it one day." Holmes thought so, too, but he didn't answer.

Chapter 9: Irene

I found the sight of our dingy shop oddly comforting after the harrowing events of the morning. Holmes didn't know how close to collapse I'd been, how much it had taken for me to play my part in front of Barnett, wondering if he would recognise me from the same sorts of clues that had unmasked him in my eyes. We had been like a cat and a mouse, but I wasn't sure who was feline and who prey. I felt thankful, for once, for the playacting I'd had to do as Godfrey Norton's wife, the months and years of acting in front of the world as if all was well when I wanted to scream in protest. I had learned to scream on the inside, and that was exactly what I had done when James Barnett's cold eyes had looked into mine. I had screamed in my mind, but I had seen no recognition in his. Holmes's disguises had, seemingly, been effective.

My companion held out his hand and helped me out of the wagon gently enough to make up for Tom Perkins's earlier handling of his wife. Neither of us spoke until we were back inside the shop, seated behind the scarred front counter where we could see anyone who approached. The gun Holmes had kept hidden underneath his bulky clothing during the morning's visit was now lying on a shelf just behind us, where he could grasp it at a moment's notice.

"Sanchez and Barnett are one and the same." Hearing Holmes state the truth somehow made it even more vivid. Only with effort could I even recall the original purpose of the morning's visit, to meet Sanchez and ascertain what sort of purpose he might have for the unholy speed of his operations. Now there was only the realization that one man existed where two were expected and that two plotters were actually one.

"Is it possible, Holmes, that there was a real Sanchez at some point?" I asked after a while, feeling slightly dazed.

"Unlikely," he answered. "Consider the facts. Barnett would have had to take his place before his arrival in Florida. A switch any time after that would have been far too risky. Even the best artists of disguise would have trouble convincingly replacing, overnight, a man who has been seen by many people and has worked closely with at least one. Therefore, he would have had to get to Sanchez some time between Central America and Florida, a risky and complicated operation, not to mention an expensive one. Why not invent some other fake persona and insert himself into Floridian society some other way, if here he must be? No, I believe Sanchez is a wholly fake persona."

I nodded. "How does this affect your view of the ultimate object of the case?"

Holmes shook his head. "I confess that I am somewhat at a loss to understand the man's motivation. He would hardly have created such an elaborate ruse for the sake of making even several thousand dollars from a citrus grove. At the same time, we know that he took the trouble of delivering into my brother's hands a letter indicating a plot against you. He fully intended Mycroft, at least, to believe that he was two different people. Of course, the original purpose for this move had to be to focus attention here rather than on James Barnett, solicitor. He correctly assumed that Mycroft would let Barnett lie for the time being in order to avoid raising suspicion, while he tried to sort out the plot from this end. During that small window of inattention, James Barnett slipped quietly away and took on his alternate character. He probably also preserved the appearance of his presence in London—having his paper brought in, his office lights turned on and off, his radio used, perhaps even going so far as to hire a stand-in. My brother, brilliant but not infallible, almost certainly assumed that Barnett was needed in England to keep his side of the scheme, your supposed side, going, so he did not anticipate such a thing, as I did not. In addition, his operatives would have been instructed to keep a certain amount of distance in order not to alarm Barnett, and that probably also helped to make the ruse successful."

After Holmes had ceased speaking, I took the leather pouch that lay on the shelf beside his gun and opened it. I filled the small pipe carefully, wondering if he would be bothered by my solicitousness, and struck a match, watching its flame whisper a tiny light against the sunshine streaming in from outside. Holmes took the pipe without comment and began to smoke. Neither of us spoke for a long time.

"Your performance today was remarkable," the detective finally murmured, his eyes closed. I stared at him in surprise, having supposed my part in the morning's proceedings to have been taken by him as a matter of course. "I had known you to be resourceful, but your level of bravery I had not realised."

"Not at all," I answered. "It would have been a crime for him to cheat us out of fair pay for our wares." Holmes let out a dry chuckle.

"What do you intend to do after this matter is concluded?"

I watched Holmes smoke and contemplated my future for the first time since I had joined him. "Singing is a life, but I still desire what I wanted when I married—quiet and peace. I have belonged to the world, and I would like to recede in it."

Holmes nodded. "I understand the sentiment, but people like you and me are ill-equipped for ordinary lives, it seems."

"One may be extraordinary in solitude."

"In theory, yes, but not in practice."

"You have certainly lived your belief."

"But you have not lived yours."

"Not yet, Holmes. I'm not in the grave."

"No, certainly not." He smiled, and we lapsed into silence again. I mulled over the details of the case, trying to apply Holmes's own reasoning methods, but I found myself circling back to the same details over and over, unable to think beyond the obvious.

"I admit," I said finally, turning to him, "that I am at a loss."

"Are you?" The question was nonjudgemental in tone. "I wonder if you trust me enough to carry out a few plans that may seem nonsensical, but will, if I am correct, prove invaluable."

"Why not explain yourself, then?"

Holmes set his now-cold pipe down in front of him and turned to me. "I must trust you in this as much as you will have to trust me. We will separate, and you will have as many opportunities to double-cross me as I will have to do the same to you. I am willing to take the chance for the sake of the case. I believe that purposeful ignorance on your part will make your tasks much easier and put you in less danger if anything should go wrong."

"Very gallant of you," I said, in a tone that said the opposite.

"Not noble," he replied seriously, "but necessary." I looked into the detective's face and studied it for a long time. We had been in a position of some trust for several days, but I had not felt particularly vulnerable. I had beaten the man once, and I believed myself capable of doing so again. This was different; this required me to put my concerns aside and believe that he had my interests in mind. It required me to act like a client.

"Fine," I said, none too gracefully.

"It's almost a pity," replied my companion. "You do Jane Perkins terribly well."

"Likewise," I said, arching an eyebrow. "I find Tom Perkins's silence remarkably refreshing."

Holmes motioned me upstairs imperiously. "Disappear Jane Perkins and reappear Lavinia James," but my mind belonged to Irene Adler, and, truth be told, I enjoyed Holmes's dramatic streak immensely.

I found it a strange process to feel Jane's creases and blemishes melt away from my face and Irene reemerge to share her visage once again with the demure Lavinia. With relief, I traded the tattered and stained cotton dress of the morning for one of my own, a conservative brown frock that I usually wore to travel—nothing special, but fully respectable. Finally, I rearranged my hair, laughing to myself at the intentional mess Holmes had made of it. Before I left the room, I couldn't resist dabbing a small amount of the detective's rouge on my pale cheeks. A respectable woman like Lavinia James wouldn't have dreamed of painting her face, but I had no such reservations, and the colour appeared natural. I amused myself imagining how horrified a real Lavinia would be at the amount of paint I normally wore when I performed.

"You'll have to wash your face again," Holmes announced unceremoniously when I again joined him downstairs. "You look painted." I did as he said with the utmost annoyance. He shook his head again when I tried to return to my place behind the store counter. "Lavinia James remains on the other side," he said. "As we currently appear, if we are seen to be familiar, suspicion will be immediately aroused no matter who our observer is.

"Fair enough," I said, taking up a can of beans with mock seriousness. "Are we permitted food, or is that forbidden during this phase of the investigation?"

"Not at all," Holmes answered. "Feel free to eat any of the wares; just take care to do so out of view of the road." I ducked behind a barrel to absorb my meal.

Five minutes later, a customer walked through the doorway of Sloane's General Store. As quickly as I could, I slipped into the furthest recess of the room, a back corner behind tall wooden shelves, trying not to think about what sorts of creatures might have chosen to share such a hiding place.

The customer was a young woman whose white lace dress obviously belonged to someone far too well-heeled for this section of Fort Myers. She turned her face toward Holmes and smiled in response to his abrupt greeting, and I saw who she was: Marion Edison. True to form, Holmes didn't even flinch. "Need anything particular?" asked the American accent of Tom Perkins.

"Nothing," she answered, a little too brightly. "I'll just look around." I didn't move a muscle, hoping she wouldn't venture beyond the shelves near the front of the store. Thankfully, she left within ten minutes, thanking Holmes in a forcedly cheerful voice before she stepped into the street. Once she had gone, Holmes waited a few moments and quietly followed her out. I didn't dare to show myself until he returned several minutes later.

"All clear," he said after he'd shut the door behind him. I emerged and dusted myself off, looking at him curiously.

"I assume you followed her," I said. "Did you discover anything pertinent? Her behaviour was certainly unusual."

"Nothing apparent. She went to the restaurant at the end of the street and was met by a German army officer who was out of uniform. I gather she came here to avoid being seen in the street while waiting for her appointment." I didn't ask how Holmes had divined that the man was a German officer. No doubt, he'd have had a long list of details that yielded the information.

"I wonder if her father knows of the connection."

"Hardly our concern," said Holmes, and I had to agree, though I couldn't help wondering.

"Now," I said, "tell me what you wish me to do in this guise." I walked to the counter and stood in front of him, my arms folded.

"It's simple," he said calmly, "I wish you to reenter society with the story that your husband Bernard has returned to England on business, but that you have remained behind to look after his interests here. You will go to the Keystone Hotel on Park Street and use the money on your person (I had no idea how he knew about that) to procure a room in the name of Lavinia James. You will send notes to the Edisons and McGregors, informing them of your presence and apologizing for your earlier disappearance. You will wait for invitations. If pressed by Ambrose McGregor, you will tell him that you are married to the detective Sherlock Holmes and that a case has called him back to England. The lovely and charming Lavinia James will not be left on her own for long, I'm sure."

"How do you wish me to communicate with you?" I asked the question as soon he was quiet.

"I will communicate with you if necessary. Do not come here or try to contact me."

I stared the detective down as hard as I could. "Holmes, are you trying to get rid of me while you work?"

He looked straight back, equally resolute. "I have already told you this is necessary. Believe me or not as you will."

"Fine," I practically spat. "What information am I to seek?"

"I want you," he leaned toward me slightly, "to make it appear that you have never existed in the world as anyone except Lavinia James and to make her as socially visible as possible. Can you do that?"

"I will do it," I said, "but if it turns out to be without purpose, you won't get away easily."

"Don't worry, Madam," he answered coolly, "I wouldn't dream of putting the great Irene Adler to any extra labour. That would cost extra."

"Holmes," I said suddenly, my tone serious, "Sanchez is part of the Edisons' social circle. How do I keep from being recognised without a disguise?"

"Leave his whereabouts to me," said the detective. "All the while you're working, I'll be just as busy. You will be safe."

"Working," I mumbled, going upstairs to gather my things, "more like being put out of the way."

Chapter 10: Holmes

Holmes was worried. He watched The Woman disappear toward the better-kept part of Fort Myers, and he couldn't help feeling concerned that things wouldn't proceed according to plan. He hated the necessity of separation. If Irene had been Watson, he wouldn't have been so concerned. Watson was used to the procedure and used to the risks. He was also meticulous about following orders and not overly curious about their meanings. But Irene Adler was none of those things. The one thing that comforted him was her frankness. He did not believe she'd have agreed to the plan disingenuously. Far more like her to take a stand and refuse to move than to stab him in the back after agreeing. Still, it was a risk, and he disliked risks when they concerned someone other than himself. The detective forced his mind to stop musing on possibilities and went upstairs to ready himself for his next task.

This time, he dressed as a day labourer but did not change his face. The speed with which he affected the transformation in his clothing made him wish his final objective could be accomplished with the same ease.

Holmes left a badly-written note on the shop door and walked to the grove in the afternoon. It was a walk of several miles, but he wanted to be unencumbered by horse or wagon. He skirted the perimeter of the grounds, moving around the rows of trees to the place where the office stood, approaching it from behind. He hid to the side of the structure, in the middle of a morass of the wooden crates the harvesters used to store picked fruit, crouching down and looking through a gap in the wooden slats. He waited, listening for any suggestion that the office might be occupied. As his ears adjusted, he caught the clicks of a typewriter and low voices. Thankfully, none of the outdoor labourers came near the building or the pile of boxes, but no one emerged from the office, either. Holmes was used to long periods of waiting; he had trained his mind to remain concentrated on the task at hand, but also to go elsewhere and reason through the facts of the case. His body rested, but it was poised to retreat or repel attack at a moment's notice.

The sun signaled late afternoon before he detected any movement. The voices he'd heard intermittently came nearer the door, and a young woman emerged, the source of the typing noises he'd heard earlier. He noted from her clothing and hands that she was a secretary, likely only required on occasion, since she hadn't been in evidence during his previous visits. She walked by Holmes's lair without looking at it. Typical, he thought. People saw things but didn't notice them.

Holmes heard the bang of doors opening and closing and things being moved about before the large figure of Bill the foreman finally left the office. He was more vigilant than his predecessor, as if he was worried that unhappy employees might be lurking in the shadows to accost him. He glanced toward the pile of wooden crates, but didn't appear to see anything amiss and moved on, whistling as he moved further away from the shed.

The building and the area around it were finally silent to Holmes's ears, but he did not move for some time before creeping out of his hiding place and moving slowly around the shack, staying low to the ground and stopping to take cover behind trees and detritus every few feet. He supposed the shed to be empty now, but he had ascertained, from his knowledge of its layout, that he would not be able to hear anything emanating from Sanchez's personal office unless he was on the other side of the building, which presented very little opportunity for cover. Holmes waited until the half light of dusk before skulking well under window height across the back of the structure and to the corner where Barnett's alter-ego conducted his business. The only cover available was a spindly sapling, but Holmes took his chance, knowing that darkness would soon hide him completely. He listened, but no sounds emanated from the dark building, and he began to feel more certain about its emptiness. No one emerged into the growing darkness for another half hour, and when daylight had finally disappeared completely, Holmes waited for his eyes to adjust and then crept to the wall that enclosed the windowless back office. Still no sound.

Confident, the detective quietly made his way to the front door. The flimsy building had no lock on its outside, so he easy pushed it open and slowly made his way inside, his right hand on the gun tucked into his waistband. He moved through the empty building warily, his eyes darting around for any sign of movement, but there was none. Finally, he reached the door of Sanchez's office, which was locked. The *great man* required more security than his associates, then. Holmes took his picklocks from his pocket and made short work of the silly thing.

Sanchez's field office was tiny and bare, containing only two chairs and a large desk with a few papers on its wooden surface. Holmes looked through them carefully, making sure to return them to their exact positions, but he found nothing beyond sales receipts and tally sheets that related to the grove's output. No matter. He hadn't come to find things out. The real information would be at the main office in town. He turned to go, taking a rolled-up handkerchief out of his left pocket and laying it haphazardly on the desk. The blue "IN" on the corner stood out from the white of the cloth like a calling card.

Holmes made his way back to town in the darkness, folding his arms against the rare chill that had infused the Floridian night after the sun's departure. He was relieved that the first phase of his plan was complete, and his mind went to Irene. She was perfectly capable of putting her side of the plan into motion, but it was her willingness that concerned him. He wished he could simply call the Fort Myers police, whatever sort of operation that might be, and have

Alberto Sanchez arrested for criminal activity; however, he had nothing of the man's to prove the connection except the letter, which was addressed to his name but did not indicate his level of involvement. Without more, who would believe the word of two strangers, two foreign strangers, no less, that Alberto Sanchez was actually a dishonest London solicitor? The idea seemed farfetched, even to Holmes, who knew that it was true.

Before the detective reentered the shop, he checked the lock for signs of tampering. He doubted anyone else would want to break into the place, but he had no trouble imagining Irene Adler doing so. Seeing nothing unusual, he went inside and walked around the room, looking for evidence that anyone had been inside. He found none, and upon ascending to the upper apartment and finding it similarly untouched, he became convinced that Irene had honoured her agreement and made no attempt to return, and, furthermore, that no one else had entered the premises. Relieved, Holmes readied himself for sleep. He had slept almost none for the past week, and he could feel himself running down. He hated the necessity of sleep, but he was not stupid enough to try to cheat the inevitable, and so, as he took his place in the chair by the window, he allowed his eyes to close.

When Holmes awoke, he ate absently, downing enough of his repugnant canned wares to keep him moving for the time being, and dressed himself in the expensive clothing of Bernard James. He did not, however, leave his face untouched, but altered his features to resemble a slightly older and less angular man. His walk as he left the shop was that of someone shorter than his six feet. Holmes had long before learned various ways to alter the appearance of what could not be changed. Most witnesses, questioned under oath, would have estimated his height as significantly below the reality when he chose to employ these methods aggressively. He would spend the day uncomfortable, but that was a small price to pay for relative anonymity.

Holmes followed the path Irene had trodden the previous day, moving quickly, like a man with an agenda to keep. He did not greet anyone in the street and gave the impression of someone who considered himself far above the section of town in which he found himself. When he moved into the more fashionable sector, he relaxed slightly and nodded to those he passed, making his way to a tall, imposing red brick structure. This part of town seemed more permanent, somehow, as if even the buildings of the rich were less transient than those frequented by the migrant workers who kept the city's economy moving.

Entering the building, Holmes saw an extremely young, smartly-dressed man at a desk. "I understand this to be the office of Mr Alberto Sanchez," he said, his voice clipped and impatient.

"Yes, Sir," said the secretary, slightly abashed, "but he's out."

"Very well," said the detective, feeling fortunate. "Will he be in today?"

"Yes, Sir," the young man answered, taken aback at Holmes's harsh tone. "He has appointments here all evening." The secretary's eyes were wide. Holmes hadn't expected to be quite so fortunate as to learn his object's plan for the night; the boy's fear had been oddly helpful. The detective studied his face for a moment before determining that he wasn't lying.

"Give him this, please." Holmes handed the young man a card, turned, and left the building before the recipient could realise that the object in his hand read "Irene Norton."

Holmes's next objective was the Keystone Hotel, a small establishment at the end of Park Street. Its small size and white-washed block exterior hardly suggested the grandeur of establishments in larger cities, but it was one of only two hotels offering rentable lodging in town beyond the odd room to let in places like Mrs Stillwell's. Still, as modest as it might appear, it catered to rich speculators and vacationers, the only people wealthy enough to afford its rooms. As a result, it was one of the few places in the city where Lavinia James would be expected to feel comfortable within her own class.

Holmes positioned himself at a table outside a café across the street and ordered coffee from a smiling girl who seemed delighted at the prospect of a tip at a time in the morning when most had finished breakfast and lunch was far away. With impatient bad temper, the detective requested a newspaper and opened it to shield his face. The *Ft. Myers Press* was hardly a goldmine of journalistic scintillation, but he scanned it anyway, looking for inconsistencies and anomalies. Force of habit drew him to the classified advertisements, as the Americans called them. He read down the list: animals for sale, jobs needed, jobs open, and finally, just above the bottom of the paper:

Birds leave their nests and migrate south. M.

The meaning was obvious. How Mycroft had contrived to plant an advertisement in this particular paper, his brother had no idea, but he mentally scolded himself for not thinking of the likelihood before. He understood what the message indicated; Barnett had journeyed to Florida. He gathered that Mycroft did not yet know that Barnett and Sanchez shared a body in addition to a scheme.

Holmes waited through three cups of decent coffee. He watched an elderly couple leave the hotel and a young boy enter and leave again with a parcel, no doubt bound for the town's tiny post office. He scanned the area with his eyes, noting the lack of anyone who seemed to have a particular interest in the hotel beyond the usual. He had hoped he might see Irene leave, but his primary object was to reassure himself that no one was tailing her—or himself.

Satisfied, the detective settled his bill and set down the none-too-generous tip that his character of the day would deem appropriate. He stood to leave, but as he did so, Irene emerged from one of the side doors of the Keystone, dressed in an elaborate green frock, her expression one of wide-eyed innocence. The detective abruptly resumed his seat and watched her over his open newspaper, taking care to keep his face in shadow. He was gratified to note that she scanned the area carefully and obviously noticed the presence of a man at the café, though his newspaper and apparent lack of interest appeared to convince her that he was not a threat, and she continued down the street without alarm.

After a few moments, Holmes left his table and newspaper and set off, following the same path as The Woman. He could see her far ahead, walking with the decorously slow pace of a polite lady. He slowed his walk to match hers, trying to look interested in the insipid shop windows he passed. For the moment, he wished Fort Myers were a bigger town so that two people on the street wouldn't be so conspicuous a sight. He had a close call when Irene turned to look behind her, but he was able to duck into a tiny alley and escape her eye. Holmes approved of her watchfulness. He was glad to know she wouldn't be taken easily.

Irene's path terminated at the edge of the Caloosahatchee River, where the River Cottages Hotel stood, another establishment catering to wealthy visitors. Holmes watched her enter the large vestibule and then exit again, following a young girl who led her around the side of the massive brick building. When the two were safely out of sight, Holmes entered.

"I'm an associate of Ambrose McGregor," he told a stout, middle-aged woman who sat behind a counter reading a novel. "Please point me to his room."

"He's a popular guest," she said. "If you wait for the girl to get back, she'll take you to him, same as she took the lady."

"That's all right," said Holmes, putting impatience in his voice. "If you give me the number, I'll go there myself."

“Fine,” said the woman. “Number sixteen, that way.” She jerked her head to the right, and Holmes nodded curtly and left. Once outside, he went back in the direction from which he’d come. Thus far, Irene was doing exactly as he’d asked, and things were progressing in the direction he’d hoped. Variables were never welcome, but he felt somewhat confident that her side of things would proceed along expected lines—as long as she stuck to plan.

The detective’s next stop was the tiny telegraph office that adjoined the post office, where a sleepy elderly man was hunched over an old machine. He grinned broadly when Holmes appeared, apparently delighted at the prospect of an actual customer with a message to send. The man turned out to be a surprisingly quick and able operator, fortunately for him, since it meant he escaped the ire of the impatient businessman Holmes portrayed. The detective sent a message that he hoped would reach Mycroft in good time.

Our mutual friends are one not two STOP *S* STOP

After sending his telegram, Holmes made the long walk back to Sloane’s General Store and transformed himself back into Tom Perkins. He took his place behind the counter, waiting, watching the road, and thinking.

Chapter 11: Irene

I remained irritated at Holmes for the amount of time it took me to hail a cab, ride to the Keystone Hotel, and engage a room. Once I saw the accommodations, my annoyance evaporated almost miraculously. I hadn't realised, until I saw the comfortable bed with clean white sheets, the immaculate bureau, and modern plumbing, how much the accommodations at Mrs Stillwell's less-than-pristine boardinghouse and the apartment above Sloane's General Store had begun to wear on me. I was willing to endure a great deal to achieve a goal, but I certainly didn't glory in grime and dirt. Holmes didn't like filth any more than I did, but once on a case, his mind was solely taken up with his purpose. I, on the other hand, had plenty of room to think extraneous thoughts about the vermin that might be crawling on my person while I slept. I was glad for the relief of cleanliness.

I waited a few moments in order to give the impression of fragile travel weariness and then rang for stationery. Lavinia James had no calling cards, of course, but I would make do with notepaper supplied by the hotel. I wrote first to Mina Edison and then to Tootie McGregor, stressing my delicate feelings of embarrassment at the brief disappearance of myself and my husband and explaining my current position of loneliness in an unfamiliar city. When I'd finished, I almost believed my own pathos.

The hotel supplied a porter, a fast-moving boy by the name of Simon, who was only too pleased to run an errand for an exorbitant price up front and the promise of the same when he returned an answer. I sent him to Seminole Lodge with both letters, anticipating that Mina would make sure her friend received the one intended for her, wherever Tootie might be. I was willing to perform detective work of my own if this attempt failed, but I saw no reason to take the roundabout way when the direct one would most likely suffice.

As I waited, I rested on an old grey brocade divan by the window and tried to wrap my mind around Holmes's plan. I knew he would take care of Barnett—I trusted him enough to believe that he would not let me be endangered by recogntion, but I couldn't think of a good reason for Lavinia James's reemergence, and my lack of understanding irritated me. Did Holmes also have plans for the inventor and his associates? I wondered, and I mused, and I could not reach an answer.

Thankfully, Simon quickly returned with two notes in tow. The feminine compassion of Tootie and Mina had not failed me. In fact, Tootie invited me to call on her and Ambrose at their suite in the River Cottages Hotel the next day, and Mina offered her home for the following evening. Holmes would be pleased, I thought, if he knew.

The rest of the afternoon and evening, I did something I had not done for some time—I read a novel, taken from the recesses of my trunk. It was about a lost soldier, a young detective, a flat, a German word scraped on a wall, and the colour red. I thought of Holmes, and I thought of Dr Watson and what I knew of them, and I smiled to myself. Most people thought the Holmes of reality was somehow less than the one they read about—less sharp, less brilliant, less exacting. The few who knew him well realised that he was actually more.

I slept well, and the morning found me ready to continue my half of the investigation, not that I understood what it was I was actually meant to be accomplishing. With a clear, rested mind, I could almost imagine that Holmes had good reasons for what he'd asked me to do, reasons beyond ridding himself of my presence.

I dressed in dainty green ruffles, all the better to appear as a timid and bereft wife for my visit, and ordered a vast breakfast. I derived a small amount of satisfaction from the notion that wherever Holmes might be, he certainly wouldn't be as comfortable or eating as well as I was. Sacrificing one's self for a case is well and good, but there's nothing wrong with a little enjoyment, one fact of which Holmes seemed sadly ignorant. I considered, though, as I speared an egg yolk and watched the decadent liquid spread, that enjoyment is a most subjective thing.

I waited until midmorning before asking the porter the way to the River Cottages and setting out on my way. I considered a cab, but the weather was too fine, and I fancied a walk to the river. For the first time since I had agreed to help Holmes, I took the gun from my trunk and tucked it into my handbag, imagining Lavinia's horror at such a thing. Nevertheless, it made Irene Adler feel secure.

The sun was bright as I made my way outside and swept the area with my eyes. I noticed a businessman engrossed in a newspaper at a café across the street, but otherwise, the street was clear. As I walked, I checked for followers a few times, but found no one. Still, I kept my hand on my bag, ready to retrieve my weapon if needed. I couldn't entirely shake the nagging fear that Sanchez—Barnett—had recognised me as his client during our previous interaction.

I reached the River Cottages in good time and was shown to the McGregors' vast suite, which overlooked the Caloosahatchee River. Tootie admitted me herself with a smothering embrace, though I noticed that she had a maid with her, a tall, middle-aged woman who looked as if she might be near-equal in determination to her employer. Ambrose stood up from a chair as I entered and greeted me gravely and politely. His eyes were curious and insistent, and I knew that I was not likely to escape an explanation. I considered trying to attach myself to his wife to avoid a private encounter, but considering how long Ambrose had lived with her, I didn't doubt he would have plenty of ways to get around her insistence. I decided to let things unfold as they would.

"My dear, you look positively famished," said Tootie, as soon as I was seated on a plush chair. "Look at her, Ambrose. She's wasted away since we saw her." I managed not to smile at the thought that it had been a mere few days since the Edisons' dinner. I was gratified at the thought that I looked slightly unwell. I had chosen the particular shade of green I was wearing because it made my fair complexion look even paler than usual. All the better for Lavinia to appear frail. Tootie called for a meal, which turned out to be a somewhat appalling array of baked beets, fried artichokes, greasy beef, and canned pineapple. My long walk had made me slightly hungry, but I was relieved that the decorous Mrs James would never have been expected to eat very much at a time. I could pick at the fare without appearing impolite.

"Now," said my hostess, spearing an overcooked beet with great force, "tell us what happened to your Mr James. I sent a note to your boardinghouse and was told that the two of you had simply vanished. It was quite shocking, my dear! Quite shocking!"

"I apologise," I said weakly, covering my face with my hand as if I were somewhere near tears. Tootie found a large yellow handkerchief somewhere on her person and handed it to me.

"I don't blame you, dear, but I'm terribly curious," she continued. I thought quickly. I had considered a few different explanations I might use, but had ultimately decided to let the inspiration of the moment guide me.

"It was very surprising," I began, which was true, since whatever I was about to say would certainly be a surprise to myself. "The morning after we left the Edisons, we received a telegram that my husband's London partner had fallen ill, a man named Smith, who has been in business with him for many years. As a result, Bernard was needed right away so that the directorship of the English branch of the company would not be left vacant." I said some of this as if I were slightly confused, the way a business-ignorant Lavinia might be.

"What sort of business is your husband in? I'm afraid I didn't catch it the other night," Ambrose put in quietly. I resisted the impulse to react, wondering what he was trying to accomplish.

"Canning," I said. "He was hoping citrus might be a *helpful avenue of expansion*, as he likes to say. That's why I'm still here." I turned to Tootie, smiling. "He was so upset about his partner that he was ready for us both to go home, but he decided after thinking about it that I should remain here for the time being, in the hope that he will be able to return."

"All by yourself!" Tootie shook her head, "without even a companion! Well, don't worry. Mina and I will take good care of you. Even Marion seemed to like you, and she's usually difficult to impress." I smiled thankfully.

"I'm ever so grateful, Mrs McGregor."

"Don't worry, dear. That man is so delighted with you that he won't be able to stay away. And who could blame him?" Holmes's face came into my mind, and I had to exert great effort to keep from laughing. The detective hadn't warned me of the odd moments during a case when something so strange or humourous happens that staying in character is an almost superhuman skill. Maybe he didn't find it so.

I spent another hour with the McGregors, admiring their river view and listening to Tootie's plans for them to purchase property and build a home of their own in town. Finally, she declared that I looked weary (after purposeful yawning and dullness on my part) and that I must rest until the evening's dinner engagement. She said that she would hire a cab, but I said that I would prefer the fresh air. I had not anticipated that Ambrose McGregor would insist on accompanying me, though I wasn't surprised. His wife beamed and sent me off with a kiss.

Once we had cleared the hotel grounds, Ambrose spoke. "You're a very good liar, Mrs James—Holmes, I mean." I fought the automatic urge to say *thank you*, as any polite American child is raised to reply when praised, but he hardly meant it as a compliment.

"First, Mr McGregor, I didn't intend to lie to you at dinner. I planned to meet with you and explain, but unforeseen complications beyond my control arose that required my husband and me to disappear briefly."

"Yes," he said drily.

"As you said, my husband is not Bernard James, but Sherlock Holmes, the consulting detective. We came here to investigate a case that concerns interests both here and in England, but he was called back by developments there. I will remain here until he returns, learning whatever I can."

"Are you investigating my family or anyone else who was present at the Edisons' that night?" The direct question was in keeping with the man's direct nature, and it did not shock me. I was relieved to be able to answer honestly.

"No, we are not. Our investigation concerns others. I wish I could tell you who they are, but I must keep my husband's confidence." The last bit was half true. I wished I could trust him with the details of the case. At the same time, his very impression of solid respectability made me doubt him. Had he truly been the chance receiver of a comment by Sanchez about Holmes's identity, or did he play a larger part? I wished Holmes were with me, hearing and seeing what I encountered so that he could give his opinion. I disliked coincidences as much as he.

Ambrose nodded calmly. "I suppose I have to accept that." I felt sorry for the man I hoped he was. As we approached the entrance to the Keystone Hotel, he turned to me. "I have not—Mrs Holmes, I consider myself a gentleman, and it has never been my habit to importune respectable ladies. If you and your husband are on the side of right, then please accept my apologies."

The only repayment I could give his kindness was my widest smile, but, without being ridiculous, I must admit that men usually seemed to find it a plentiful enough reward. He went on his way, and I returned to my room to make sense of things using the hotel's cheap stationery and my fountain pen to write down my thoughts.

Chapter 12: Holmes

Number 14 Charles Avenue. Holmes studied the rudimentary map of the city that the cheerful clerk of the town's one real general store had sold him just before closing. While he thought, he smoked a cheap cigarette in a repugnant alley where many others had obviously done the same, given the amount of refuse that littered the ground and the stale smell than lingered in the air. The map showed that he was in the right part of the city for the address he sought, and he didn't want to make his taxed feet walk all the way back to Sloane's to wait for dark. In the guise of Tom Perkins, he was below most people's notice, and he was able to move closer and closer to his object without attracting attention.

Finally, when the Florida night was covered in thick, humid darkness, he took the last steps to Charles Avenue, a street lined with opulent mansions, some of them even grander than the Edisons' home. He crept through a few well-kept lawns and skirted two that showed signs of having dogs somewhere on the premises. Number 14 wasn't vastly different from the others. It had the same appearance of new money, whitewash, and pride built into its wide porch and numerous windows. Holmes walked around it silently, ascertaining that the first floor was dark and silent while the second showed signs of occupants who were awake and active. All the better for his purposes. He stepped silently toward the front porch, hunching over to make himself as short as possible. When he reached it, he took a box of ladies' face powder out of his pocket and dropped it willy-nilly on the porch floor. Not waiting to see if the sound had roused anyone, he ran back to the road and didn't slacken his pace until he was far away.

Holmes again forced his weary feet to carry him to the Keystone Hotel. No one was around its outside, so he went to the door from which Irene had emerged during the day, a door into one of the large ground-floor suites. He listened, but he could hear nothing. It was too late for her to be at dinner, but he hadn't expected her to be asleep, either. He wanted to be unsuspicious, to trust that Barnett had conducted meetings in the guise of Sanchez all evening and taken no time for a society dinner party, but he couldn't silence the worry in his mind.

Concerned, Holmes went into the front entrance. A young porter, not more than fifteen at the oldest, sat behind the desk, playing cards. "What do you want?" he asked, taking in the unpleasant visage and attire of Tom Perkins.

"Has Mrs James come in?" Holmes asked in an ingratiating tone.

"Why would I tell you that?" asked the lad, staring belligerently.

"Because of this," Holmes spoke in his normal tone and produced a group of coins whose combined value was more than a porter would be likely to make in a week. The boy's eyes bulged.

"No harm, I guess," he said, holding out his hand. "She ain't come in anyhow."

Holmes wished the boy were lying, but the detective could tell he was sincere. He handed him the coins. "Now," he said, still in his own voice, "if you tell anyone else where the lady is, I'll know about it, and you won't get off so easily." The boy looked nervous, but Holmes turned tail and left. Once outside, he ran.

The detective didn't know the last time he'd done so much legwork in one day, but he didn't care. He had one place in mind, and if that failed, his case would be about more than identity and theft; it would be about finding a missing woman. *Just until tomorrow* he thought angrily. Today was the day—the only day—the only time he'd had to leave things to move as they would. He hadn't believed the man would act so quickly. Mistakes—he'd made them before, but not often. Had he been incorrect now in thinking he had time?

Holmes's weary body finally carried him to Sloane's General Store. With sinking heart, he looked at the lock and found it intact. Cursing his own faith, he took out his key to open the door and give himself one last chance not to be entirely wrong. He nearly called out when the door opened of its own accord. The Woman stood on the other side, dressed in a purple gown. "Good evening, Mr Holmes," she said, opening it wide to admit him. His fear threatened to turn into wrath for a moment, but logic subsumed it. He had expected this, had known that no matter what he said, she was likely to return. Relief, too, had its place—larger, perhaps, than he had anticipated.

"I'm sorry," were the next characteristically blunt words out of her mouth. "I needed to talk to you, and I didn't know what else to do." As she had done once before, she went behind the counter and retrieved the detective's pipe, filling and lighting it before handing it to him.

"I'm entirely unsurprised," said Holmes after a few drags of his pipe, forcing himself not to betray his previous worry. "What is it you wish to tell me?" Irene sat on the edge of the counter, not seeming to care what impression her presence might give to outsiders, her dress strangely out of place among the grimy wares.

"I think Ambrose McGregor might be in league with Sanchez," she said. "I'm not sure his knowledge is as coincidental as we thought."

"What did he say?" asked the detective calmly. Irene gave a detailed account of her meeting with the man, ending with a restatement of her questions about his possible motives.

"Let us consider," said Holmes quietly. "If he is part of the plot, why would he make a point of speaking to you? Furthermore, why would he emphasise that he knows me?"

"To try to discover your whereabouts for his accomplice?" Irene asked. Holmes opened his eyes and looked at The Woman.

"A fair question," he said. "I'll grant you that it's not entirely possible to rule him out. Still, if he had designs on you, he had a perfect opportunity to act on them."

"That I grant you," said Irene quickly, "but if your brother—or even you yourself is the object, then his actions make more sense."

Holmes did not tell her what he suspected. He still believed, even after the evening's worry, that she must not know, for fear that she would unwittingly do something to make the entire plan come crashing down.

"I take it," he said after a while, "that your dinner with the Edisons was uneventful, since you haven't mentioned it."

"Very," she said simply. "It was only a family party with me and the McGregors as additions. Ambrose didn't say a word to me the whole evening."

"I see," said Holmes quietly. "You may be interested to know that the case is progressing exactly as it should. Until this unexpected change of plan, you had played your part admirably."

Irene looked over at him as if she'd like very much to hit him. "How dare you?" she said, getting up and standing in front of the counter to face him. "I know what your clients feel like now, how manipulated, like chess pieces. I don't know how they stand it."

"My clients do as I wish because they trust the outcome," Holmes said drily.

"Well, pity I know you're not infallible then," she threw back, her eyes on fire. "You give me no way to contact you, force me into a character that leaves me vulnerable to recognition, and now—you have the gall to complain that I've *deviated from plan*."

Holmes wondered how he'd arrived here, to a point at which he had a partner who was intrinsic to the case but impossible at the same time. Watson trusted him, almost too much sometimes; he was brave, but his bravery was rarely creative. He served the plan, whatever it was. The clients, too, almost always followed whatever parts of the plan he gave them, out of desperation and trust. Even the police grudgingly came around to his way after a while. Lestrade had been proven wrong too many times.

The Woman was different. She had beaten him, and it made something different between them. She had seen his cracks, and she could not see him uncritically. Against the odds, she seemed to have mustered some sort of trust in him over the previous days, but that appeared to have evaporated in the midst of her worry over Ambrose McGregor.

Irene turned her back to the detective, her arms folded. "Tell me why I can't know, Holmes," she said from between clenched teeth. "Make me believe you."

"I can't," he said simply. "I have a plan, and I believe it will succeed. I can guarantee you my best efforts and my protection, but as you know too well, I cannot guarantee perfection. There was a time when I was very young that I thought myself invincible, but that was a long time ago. You must make your choice based on what you know of the man I am—based on logic."

After a very long time, Irene turned slowly and faced him. "I wish I didn't trust you," she said, then turned and walked out of the store.

She didn't know that moments after she left, the bone-weary detective followed her. She didn't see him mirror her steps all the way to the Keystone Hotel, and she was ignorant of the vigil he kept while she slept.

This phase of the plan was new. The Woman had no idea that the day of separation was over, and now Sherlock Holmes was determined not to let Irene Adler out of his sight. He sat in an empty lot beside the hotel, his arms propped on his knees, his body finally at rest. No one was out so late at night in the fashionable part of town, and he had only insects for company. He welcomed the physical rest, but he had no desire for sleep. He was beyond that now and at the point in the case that made his blood rush and his body cease to desire food or sleep. All he craved was the end, the solution. Other things receded, even his conversation with Irene. He recognised the near-disaster her refusal to help him further would have caused, but he did not dwell on it. She had made the right decision, and now it was for the man, the villain of the piece, to make his move.

Holmes thought, for a moment, of Watson, of how much the doctor would have enjoyed the waiting and the hunt. John had always been a soldier, and he always would be. They'd have sat together under the stars, not speaking, both alert, and he'd have felt the confidence of having a brother-in-arms.

But The Woman was inside. Walls separated them, but not purpose. She had agreed, and Holmes had seen the resolve twisted inside her anger. She would play her part, and she would play it well. She was no brother, but she was enough.

Chapter 13: Irene

I hated everything about my room. I hated the heavy tan drapes, the ugly floral wallpaper, the insipid lace coverlet. Everything seemed different now. I lay down on the bed in my purple gown and closed my eyes, but my thoughts were far too tumultuous for sleep. The most infuriating thing was that I had made the right decision, and I knew it. For savage amusement, I tried to imagine stolid Dr Watson railing angrily at Holmes for the part he'd been told to play in a particular case, but I couldn't manage it. Watson trusted him too much.

And so did I, irritatingly. I trusted him the way I had once trusted Godfrey. That was different, though. I had trusted Godfrey without really knowing him, staking my claim on a personality and a reputation, but not on my own knowledge and experience with the man. My trust in Holmes was just the opposite sort. What name and reputation had failed to do, my experiences with him had accomplished. Now that I knew him, I could not fail to trust him. Once again, I had entrusted a part of myself to a man, and that was something I had promised myself never to do again. But it was the right decision, the inescapable right decision. I finally fell asleep with my mind going around and around in circles, berating me on one hand and soothing me on the other.

The next morning, I awoke at peace, as if I had crossed some sort of barrier. I was committed, but I wasn't stupid. I took my handgun from under my pillow and put it back into my bag. It would accompany me wherever I went.

A few minutes after I finished breakfast, Marion Edison came to call. I received her in the hotel's main sitting room, wondering, when I saw her pale face, what secrets she might have, particularly about the German she had met. I doubted they concerned Holmes and me, but I was unwilling to ignore any anomaly.

"Good morning, Mrs James," Marion said a little shyly as she joined me.

"Please call me Lavinia," I answered, smiling and holding out my hand. She took it, and I noticed that she was strong.

"Would you walk with me?" she asked after a moment.

"Of course," I answered. "I'm new in town. Perhaps you can show me what I should see." I couldn't remember the last time I'd taken a walk with another young woman, and I found it ironic that the case was what caused me to do so now.

For a long time, we talked about nothing in particular. She asked about London fashions and I about American ones, we laughed at a duck crossing the street, and finally we retraced our steps back to the café across from my hotel, thirsty and ready for a rest.

"I hope my husband is well," I said as we sipped our tea.

"You must miss him," said Marion quietly.

"I do," I answered, "very much." I felt sorry for deceiving the girl so blatantly, but I hoped to draw her out by revealing personal feelings. Another part of my brain tried to remind me that if I had been a different kind of wife with a different kind of husband, I also might have felt those same feelings when I thought of Godfrey Norton, but I pushed it away.

"I—have someone to miss, too," said Marion, hesitating.

"Oh?" I said noncommittally, thinking I might know something of what she was about to say.

"Last year, I took a trip to Europe with my aunt. The trip was difficult. I got smallpox, and the doctor thought I might even die." She looked at me with the wide-eyed stare of a child who could not yet fathom the finality of her own death. "But," she continued, leaning forward with intense excitement, "I met *him*." I felt a surge of empathy. Some things are universal.

"His name is Karl Oeser, and he's a lieutenant in the German army." I nodded and tried to look surprised. Marion lowered her voice, “He’s—come here, and I don’t know how to tell my father and Mina. My aunt never knew how much we cared for each other.”

I tried to think of what Lavinia James would say to this, finally settling on, “I’m afraid you’ll have to tell them some time,” about which Lavinia and Irene could safely agree.

“I know,” said Marion, back to her usual directness. “That’s why I’ve told you first, to practise.” I smiled encouragingly, and she continued. “I think he’s going to ask me to marry him.”

“I hope you’ll be very happy,” I said, and meant it.

I finished my tea, feeling a sense of satisfaction at having one mystery cleared up. As Holmes and I had both suspected, Marion’s secret was a private one. It was a strange thing, I thought, to unravel someone’s personal story in the midst of the danger and uncertainty of a case. There was something wrong about it, almost, as if people’s personal lives should be spared the magnifying glass of detection, but it didn’t work that way. As I knew from experience, private lives were often exactly where mysteries lay, and truth usually only emerged after invasive scrutiny.

Marion’s enthusiastic thanks and impulsive kiss on my cheek as she left me at the entrance to the hotel reminded me that not everyone minded being found out. She was radiant in the knowledge that I knew her secret, and I couldn’t help but hope that she would not regret her choice.

When I entered the Keystone once again, I was met by a porter with a note from Tootie McGregor, asking me to accompany her and her husband to the theatre that night. I was not excited at the prospect of meeting Ambrose again, but I could think of no way to refuse. I sent back my acceptance, glad that a theatre would, at least, provide little room for private encounters.

With the prospect of nothing to do until evening staring me down and no desire to put myself in needless danger by wandering around outside, I ran a bath in the gold-footed tub in my suite’s opulent washroom and hung one of my finest dresses to be unwrinkled by the steam. I sat on the white tile floor while the tub filled, watching fog cover the mirror and wondering what Holmes was doing. My mind turned to Barnett, and I shuddered at the thought of the moment I'd realised he was standing in front of me as Alberto Sanchez. I hadn't known I could be brave enough to stay silent when I had so much fear. How often did Holmes feel afraid, I wondered, during the long nights and dangerous days? I realised then that I'd never thought of him as brave because he never showed his fear.

I luxuriated in the bathwater for ages. I had no idea how long I'd be Lavinia James, so I was determined to enjoy her luxury as long as I could. It was refreshing to be alone, with no maids and no husband, free from being Irene Adler, even. The case tugged at the back of my mind, but at the same time I felt curiously light, as if the bonds that had tied me down were finally loosening. My own decisions had gotten me where I was—no one forcing or pushing me, not even Holmes. As much as he his reticence had angered me, he had left my choices in my hands. There might be concealment between us—I could not forget that I had failed to tell him everything at first—but there was no underestimation or manipulation. We were equals in The Game.

As I stepped out of the water, I was determined. I put on my black silk gown and felt it glide over me like confidence. I would be Lavinia James tonight, demure and sweet, but underneath, Irene Adler would watch and wait, never knowing when the part I didn't understand would turn to something more, when the thin form and bright eyes of the detective would ask, and I would be swept away to become someone new. As I picked up my bag, the pistol in its depths felt natural, an important part of my ensemble.

The McGregors came for me in their carriage at half past six, and Ambrose helped me inside, his face blank. In contrast, his wife was an explosion of life in a red gown that accented the red in her cheeks and complemented her excitement. She eagerly seized my hand and declared her joy at the prospect of seeing *Hedda Gabler*, a reportedly shocking play by Henrick Ibsen, a Norwegian with extremely liberal views.

"My goodness," she said, lowering her voice conspiratorially, "I've heard the poor heroine shoots herself, right on stage! Mrs Warren does the part beautifully, they say." I didn't tell her that I had seen many of Ibsen's plays and knew of this one, since I couldn't imagine that Lavinia James would care about such things. Ambrose sat across from us, staring at the floor. His wife seemed used to his taciturn ways and didn't mind filling up the space with her own words, for which I was grateful.

The theatre was one of the grander buildings in Fort Myers, a neoclassical edifice with columns, which served as town hall, meeting place for Freemasons and other civic clubs, and, as it would this night, a theatre for travelling companies. Society considered acting a less-than-respectable profession, but in Fort Myers, as everywhere, very few seemed to mind enjoying its product, and we were joined by many others as we entered the vaulted vestibule.

Tootie knew everyone and was quick to greet young and old and to introduce me as her friend. I gave out many a simplistic smile, all the while watching for Barnett, anyone else who looked as though they might recognise me as Irene Adler, and Ambrose McGregor, of whom I did not want to lose sight. Strangely, my different purposes made me calm rather than agitated, as if they formed the steps to my own mental dance of which I was leader. A step here, and I clasped the hand of a woman Tootie introduced as Mrs Johnson. A step there, and I ruled out a man with Sanchez's hair but someone else's face. A twist to the right, and I caught Ambrose McGregor in the corner of my eye, engaged in conversation with a man I didn't recognise.

Was this what Holmes felt, I wondered? The intense focus, the knowledge of one's purpose and task, the surge of adrenaline that came with danger, and the answering calm of total awareness—I knew them all, and I began to believe things might end well.

We finally took our seats in the fourth row, and I stared at the red plush curtain, thinking of the many times I had been on the other side, waiting to be revealed to audiences in countless theatres. I didn't know what I would do after the case was over and Holmes and I had parted, but I saw now with absolute clarity that I would never again sing to please a theatre crowd. Once, I had left singing to start a new life, but the tragedy of my marriage had caused me to seek solace in what I knew. After the case, I would need it no longer.

I leaned back in my seat and flicked my fan up and down in front of my face, welcoming the mental escape the play would bring. As the lights dimmed, anticipation washed over the audience like the tide coming in, and I could hear Tootie take a sharp breath beside me. Lavinia James watched the stage, to all appearances as excited as everyone else, but Irene Adler kept her hand on her bag, ready to produce her pistol at a moment's notice.

Chapter 14: Holmes

A tall, well-dressed man slipped into the theatre just before *Hedda Gabler* began. He allowed an usher to hurry him to a seat in the back row, but as soon as the man had gone, he got up quietly and slipped into a back corner. Sherlock Holmes stood in the darkness, his black suit blending into the shadows. This night, he firmly believed, was when the man would make his move.

For several moments, Holmes kept his eyes on The Woman's dark head. Her body was relaxed, but he could tell by the position of her arm that her hand was clutching something. Knowing Irene, he thought, it was most likely a weapon. He applauded her vigilance, but not the presence of a complication. With aversion, he realised he would have to rob her himself, provided Barnett gave him time. He was repulsed at the idea of betraying a partner, but the idea of a plan gone wrong was even more unthinkable.

Holmes enjoyed the first act. He appreciated Ibsen; the man was like a detective who had solved a case and then rewritten it with all the hidden motivations and human frailties on the surface instead of buried the way they usually were. Detection would be far easier, thought Holmes, if people behaved so transparently in real life. He ducked into a seat as the audience clapped for Act I and the lights rose.

A local tenor by the name of Steven Bartholomew shuffled to the stage to entertain in the interim, looking nervous. Holmes felt a surge of something surreal as the man's accompaniment began and he tentatively bleated out his first notes. The love song sounded nothing like it had in the mouth of Irene Adler, but Holmes's mind cast him back to the night when he had first seen her again, divine in violet, staring him down with every perfect note.

He made his mind return to the present, forcing himself to focus against distraction. A supposed plot against Miss A had brought him here, and he would not let himself lose concentration until the case was complete. Besides, Steven Bartholomew was one of the worst singers Holmes had ever heard.

Polite applause for the man's unfortunate effort heralded the dimming of the lights for Act II. Once again, the detective quietly slipped from his seat and took his place in the back corner of the auditorium, his eyes looking up and down each row to discern any changes. There were none. The same audience of well-to-do Floridians stared straight ahead, waiting to witness Hedda Gabler's ever-crumbling life played out in front of them.

As the second act drew to a close, Holmes waited for the intermission, his nerves taut. He sat again, waiting through a short speech by a member of the Fort Myers Salvation Army, then sprang to life as soon as the audience was dismissed.

Holmes's eyes found Irene in a few seconds, in the middle of a group of people pressing toward the door. He stayed well to the edge of the crowd, waiting for most of the theatregoers to move into the hall before he followed, but he did not allow Irene to pass out of his line of sight. Once in the vestibule, Holmes kept to the edges of the room and watched as Tootie purchased refreshments for herself, her husband, and her guest. He smiled to himself as Irene was plied with a drink that he could see she didn't want. Finally, Tootie shepherded her charge back toward the theatre, and Holmes prepared to make his move. The detective had made himself up to look slightly dissipated and beyond his own age, but he didn't want to risk Irene's notice through a direct confrontation. He would have to be quick.

Using the press of people to hide him, he made his way to a drink seller and purchased a glass of wine. Slowly, he moved closer and closer behind Irene, until only a few people separated him from The Woman and her companions. In a frantic split second, Holmes dropped the entirety of his wine on a large man in front of him, then ducked down in the midst of the confusion and extracted the pistol from Irene's handbag while she tried to calm Tootie, who was in danger of panicking. He couldn't tell if Irene had noticed the theft, but he knew she hadn't seen him. Even if she desired to report the loss, how would she explain her reasons for carrying a pistol? It wasn't the most elegant operation Holmes had ever carried out, but it had accomplished its purpose. He followed the crowd back inside the theatre and sat down, thankful for the dimming of the lights a moment later.

Holmes once again took his place in the shadows, but this time, he found the difference for which he had been watching. He counted the number of people in each row and found one extra in the last seat of the sixth, a man with dark hair—hair the colour of Alberto Sanchez's dyed locks. Holmes's pulse quickened as he studied the man in the darkness, trying to be sure. If he didn't plan to move that night, Holmes thought, then he was a greater fool than the detective supposed. The end of Act III brought back the unfortunate tenor, and Holmes sat again, wishing the play would end. He couldn't imagine Barnett risking a panic in the theatre, so he doubted anything would happen before the final curtain. The last act was torture for the detective, his mind pushing forward to whatever might be coming. He watched Irene, surprised at the calmness in her demeanor in spite of the anxiety she must be feeling after the discovery of her loss. He had done what he knew to be necessary, but he despised the thought that he had caused her to be afraid. For a split second, he questioned himself and wondered if he should have disclosed the entirety of his intentions to her, but just as quickly he reminded himself that the plan depended on her not knowing. The fact that she might not agree once the operation was over had occurred to him, but it had no effect on his resolve.

Finally, the curtain closed after the suicide of the protagonist, and the stunned audience waited a few seconds before breaking into enthusiastic applause. As the lights rose and the cast members took their bows, the detective made his way to the entrance and waited unobtrusively until the attendees began to drift out, watching for horses and carriages to take them home.

Alberto Sanchez exited before the McGregors, and Holmes let him pass out of his line of vision and waited instead for Ambrose, Tootie and Irene, who were near the back of the departing crowd. Once again, he stayed at the edge of the press of people, watching and waiting, keeping pace with The Woman though physically separated from her. He had to be careful; Irene's watchful eyes were everywhere, and he could clearly see how ill-at-ease she was. To anyone else, she simply seemed agitated by the crowd, but he knew her thoughts were much darker.

Holmes was poised in the limbo of the moment, knowing that something was about to occur to change everything, but unsure exactly where or exactly how it would take place. He would have given a great deal to stop it before it began, but that would have broken the deal he'd made with himself. He wouldn't jeopardise the case because he was afraid for the lady, and he couldn't afford to put her in more danger later by eliminating the current peril. He felt as if his hands were tied, and she looked as if she anticipated the worst. He hated the increasingly desperate confusion he could see on her face. Irene Adler was meant to be strong. Irene Adler was meant to be brave. Irene Adler wasn't meant to look like a lost little girl.

Finally, the detective followed the thinning crowd outside. He stepped behind a white pillar and watched as Irene and her hosts stood on the steps of the hall and waited for their carriage. Irene stayed close to Tootie, as if she thought the older woman's presence might offer some protection.

The McGregors' carriage was one of the last to arrive, and Holmes watched as Ambrose helped his wife and The Woman inside before getting in himself. Was it possible, then, that he had misjudged Barnett's intentions? Suddenly, as the carriage left, he caught a glimpse of the driver's thick leather gloves. Bill the foreman had been wearing those gloves the night Holmes had seen him leave work.

The detective sprang into action, no longer caring if the remaining theatregoers saw him. He raced across the street where a horse and cart waited for him, threw himself onto it, and began to drive. He followed the McGregors' carriage, and so did several others carrying oblivious members of the crowd back to their homes. Bill could not afford to gallop, and neither could Holmes. After a maddeningly sedate few minutes, the other carriages began to pull off into side streets, and Holmes became concerned that he might have to change course quickly to avoid having his purpose detected.

Holmes's concern turned to relief when it became apparent that the last two carriages between him and the McGregors had longer journeys than the others. He hung back, and as the four vehicles traveled further and further, he realised Barnett was doing exactly as he'd expected. One of the other two carriages finally turned onto a dirt road, and Holmes quietly followed its driver into the night.

In a few short minutes, the detective had doubled back and taken a totally different route out of town, into the long dark where the roads were hardly marked. As soon as he found himself alone, he urged the horse forward, as fast as it would go. He rode through the night, passing trees and hearing hooves beat the sandy ground, with no thought but his destination, cursing the necessity of taking the roundabout way. Thankfully, the horse was strong, and it kept up the fierce gallop that matched the pounding of the detective's heart.

He wondered if Irene realised what was happening to her. Of course she must, but she would be calm. The Woman wouldn't let her fear destroy her judgement. She would fight back, but Holmes didn't believe she would succeed, and as perverse as that thought felt as it came to him, he knew that she must not, or the plan would be incomplete. Three to two might be decent odds, but Holmes had seen the foreman's musculature and knew that he was strong, and while

Barnett's physical strength was unknown, he would undoubtedly be carrying a gun to help him force obedience from his unwilling captives. Unless Tootie or Ambrose McGregor possessed unexpected skill, Holmes had little doubt the three would remain subdued by Barnett and Bill.

It felt all wrong somehow, to be on a different road than the one carrying the object of his concern and to be wishing that she and her companions would be held hostage instead of finding their way out of an impossible situation. He hoped that Barnett had planned well. He needed the man's plan to succeed partially before his could be fully effective.

After a long time, Holmes turned his horse onto a dirt road and followed it beyond a group of trees. He stopped and looked around, carefully seeking any sign of the presence of another human being, but no one else was present and no sounds could be heard except the calls of crickets and tree frogs. The detective alighted from his cart and went toward an unlocked door, ready for the next phase of the plan to commence. He took his place and waited, hoping devoutly that nothing had gone wrong along the way.

Holmes crouched, his every sense at the highest possible level of alertness, his mind filled with the calm that always came when a case was about to reach its climax. Watson never understood that calm, but it was the calm of a man waiting for events to unfold the way he'd pictured them and thinking through every possible contingency in order to avert it. After what felt like ages, he heard voices.

Chapter 15: Irene

Someone stole my gun during the theatre interval. I don't know how it happened, but one moment I was trying to keep Tootie from succumbing to claustrophobia, and the next I found my bag empty of its only important item. I forced myself to silence my self-flagellating brain and instead reason through the theft and whether it was more likely that my weapon was now in the hands of someone significant or a random pickpocket who had chosen to target theatregoers that night.

I wondered how Holmes would rate the likelihood of a coincidence. The idea that a woman who was involved in a criminal case would also be involved in a petty theft, randomly chosen out of a group of hundreds, hardly seemed creditable. I didn't appear noticeably richer or more opulently dressed than others in the crowd. Why choose me?

The other alternative was much more horrifying, but I forced myself to consider it. I ruled out Ambrose McGregor immediately because I had seen his whereabouts the whole time, and then I began to scan the crowd systematically, looking for anyone familiar. I found no one unexpected and finally had to take my seat again for the third act.

I remained outwardly calm throughout the rest of the play, but I felt as if a weight were pressing on my chest, making it hard to breathe. In some grotesque sense, Hedda Gabler's elaborately staged desperation seemed to mirror the growing desperation I felt. I now realised that it had been a mistake to come to the theatre. In public, I felt like a clay pigeon on display in a shooting gallery.

When the curtain finally closed, I wanted to escape the auditorium as soon as possible, but the crowd and Tootie's friendliness caused us to be one of the last groups to leave. Ambrose sent for our carriage, and I waited nervously, trying to answer Tootie's banal chatter but feeling as if I would like to run away.

Finally, the carriage arrived, and Ambrose glanced at the driver and commented that "Bryce has sent someone else." The McGregors rented a carriage for their use in Florida, and they hired drivers when they needed them. I thought nothing of the comment. Nothing, that is, until Ambrose had helped me inside and I saw Tootie's pale face, her words silenced by the cocked pistol at her temple. I looked over into the cold eyes of my solicitor. "If you so much as call out, I'll pull the trigger," he said matter-of-factly as Ambrose took his place beside me. I believed him.

At that moment, I understood why my handgun was gone and why the theft had been so expertly carried out. Excellent foresight on Barnett's part. The terror on Ambrose McGregor's face struck me as vastly ironic, a combination of genuine fear for his wife and horror at a friend's betrayal. His innocence was apparent, and in the midst of my fear, I felt the letdown of having been wrong, of having fallen for a classic red herring. Oh, how Dr Watson would enjoy the story if he ever had a chance to hear it, I thought wryly.

We rode in silence for some time until Barnett finally rested his hand on his knee with his gun pointed firmly at Ambrose. "Why are you doing this?" the poor man finally asked, a question that even I had no real answer to as of yet, in spite of my part in the investigation.

Barnett, as Sanchez, smiled and addressed me instead. "Do you know me, Miss Adler the Divine?"

I nodded, projecting as much calm as I could manage. "I knew you from the moment the wife of the tobacco supplier laid eyes on you."

He looked surprised for a moment, then smiled. "I didn't envy her husband that day. Now I see that I was mistaken. But no matter. It's all worked out in the end."

He finally turned to Ambrose, shaking his head. "You're a good man, Mr McGregor. You and your wife have no reason to be afraid if you do as you're told. This operation (he looked at me) is about Miss Adler, myself, and Mr Holmes. Both Mr Holmes, if you like, but I only ever had the younger in mind as part of this particular plan."

"I wouldn't do that, Miss Adler." The gun was trained on me in a split second, and Barnett shook his head. "It's no use inching your hand toward the door latch; at this speed, you'd fall out and injure your skull, not to mention that we're currently in the middle of nowhere."

I wondered what Holmes would have done in this situation—in a closed carriage with a gunman and two innocent people. He'd have had a solution, I was sure, but I was at a loss, and it infuriated me.

"You might like to know," Barnett continued, "that my office in London received Irene Norton's new will today, leaving the bulk of her property to her faithful solicitor, who will transfer it to his good friend Alberto Sanchez as soon as Mrs Norton is dead."

"But don't worry. I won't kill you if you sign over everything instead. The detective is the only one who has to die, and that's not my job."

Tootie hadn't uttered a word since the beginning of the ordeal, and she still sat with her hands clenched, pale and terrified. I had never seen her silent for so long, and there was something grotesquely humourous about it. I hated myself for thinking so.

"Holmes isn't here," I said. I considered saying something about his death, but I could see no use in doing so since Barnett knew very well that he was alive.

"No," said Barnett, "but he will be. You're excellent bait."

At the word *bait*, something connected in my mind, and I understood. That was my role in the case. Holmes had been using me to attract Barnett the way the solicitor was now trying to use me to attract the detective. That was the reason for the lack of caution and insistence that I play a role so near my own character. Unwitting bait, that's what I'd been. And now that the bait had been taken, Holmes was nowhere to be found.

I wasn't angry with Holmes, but I was disappointed. For a short space of time, I had believed in him fully, trusting that he would complete his plan, whatever it might be. I had also trusted his promise of safety. *Bait is never safe* I thought bitterly. Whatever Holmes had expected to happen, the current situation was obviously far from it, I knew, or I wouldn't have found myself stranded in a carriage with a criminal and no recourse. The man I had fooled once had made another mistake, and this time it was to my extreme detriment.

"I have no idea," Barnett continued after a few moments, "if you and Holmes are working together, and I don't care. Either way, he'll follow you."

"How do you know he's in Florida?" I asked, thinking quickly. If Barnett didn't know for sure that I'd been working with Holmes, then I had the upper hand of information, at least.

"I saw him two weeks ago," he said. "He's tracked you, I'm sure, whether you know it or not. Also, thank you for the calling cards, my dear. It would have taken me much longer to realise you were here and might be in society tonight without them. I don't have the slightest idea what you hoped to accomplish, but I'm glad I circumvented it." He smiled nastily.

I also had no idea what I'd hoped to accomplish or, indeed, what he was talking about, so I kept my thoughts to myself and tried to look upset at being thwarted, which wasn't difficult, since I was frightened and angry.

Finally, our miserable journey ended with an abrupt stop, and Barnett herded the three of us outside into the dark night. I realised immediately where we were when I smelt the sharp aroma of citrus in the air and turned and saw the shack in front of us, the ramshackle building that contained Alberto Sanchez's field office.

The driver hopped down and took off his hat, revealing himself to be Bill, the surly foreman Holmes and I had met during our previous visit. He took out a handgun and pointed it in our direction, helping his boss force us inside.

The shed was dark, but Sanchez lit a lantern and pushed us into his office. Ambrose gave the two chairs to Tootie and I, and he stood, his face dark. Bill stood watch in the front of the building, and Sanchez sat behind his desk, staring at his captives with gun in hand.

"What do you intend to do?" I asked, hoping to hear something I might be able to use.

"I intend to wait until Sherlock Holmes arrives, release our friends, get a signed statement from you giving me your assets, and take the detective to the lighthouse," he said, with a chilling lack of hesitation.

"Why do you want Holmes?"

"I don't want him, but Sebastian Moran does. He's meant to be dead—Holmes, I mean. I have no idea why he isn't, but Moran knew right away. It's a good deal for me, Miss A. You've always been a good client, and I don't want to hurt you. That's why I'm going to leave you enough money to go wherever you like."

"What's the benefit to you? I know very well you don't do anything without getting something back."

He laughed. "You know me well, Miss Adler. The convenient part of this plan is that the bait is also the prize. In return for Holmes, I get to keep your fortune."

"You have a loose tongue," Ambrose suddenly put in quietly, his face stormy.

I turned to the McGregors. "You deserve to know that this man is no more Alberto Sanchez than I am. He's a crooked London solicitor named James Barnett." Tootie's eyes widened.

"How do you know him?" Ambrose's meaning was clear; he thought I was in league with Barnett.

"I was stupid enough to let him handle my affairs," I said honestly.

"Far too few affairs," said Barnett, with an ugly insinuation in his voice, "but plenty of money."

"Holmes won't come," I said. "He has no idea I'm here, and if he did, he wouldn't care."

"You're wrong there, Miss A." Barnett sat back and folded his hands over his stomach, looking self-satisfied. "I've no doubt he's on his way right now."

"If that's true," I said, "how do you know he won't bring the police?" I stared him down.

"Doesn't matter if he does. They'll let me go to save you three. I didn't take the McGregors for no reason. Bill and I will be happy to fill any of them with lead, though, if they try anything." He turned to Ambrose. "You, at least, should know that Sherlock Holmes is on the way."

Ambrose shook his head. "It appears I haven't been very smart about all this. Whatever happens, please accept my apologies, Miss Adler."

"That's all right," I said, trying to smile. "I did lie about my identity."

"I knew there was something more to you than a simple socialite," Tootie's voice suddenly cut in. "I don't know who you are, but I'm not surprised."

"I'm sorry," I said without explanation, seeing no reason to give Barnett more information than he already had.

"It's all right," she said unexpectedly. "We're all more than we seem."

"That's certainly true," said Barnett, pulling a handkerchief out of his pocket. "I should give this back to you, Miss A." I looked at the piece of cloth, a white background with blue letters. Mine. I took it without comment.

I was disappointed in myself. I'd always imagined that if I were in mortal danger, I'd be resourceful and fearless, able to think my way out of anything. But I was just Irene Adler, frozen in the face of danger the way I'd been powerless to stop my husband.

"I suppose I should have you sign the papers before Holmes gets here," said Barnett after a while. "Things might get ugly, and I want to have everything in place." His calmness infuriated me.

The solicitor produced a stack of legal forms, the paper that represented my not-insignificant worldly property. "Sign these, or I'll put a bullet in your head," he said calmly. I stared down at them, my eyes swimming.

Just then, Alberto Sanchez's desk took on a life of its own and flew forward, crashing to the floor as I jumped backward to avoid its path.

Chapter 16: Holmes

Sherlock Holmes rushed to his feet and tackled James Barnett, his long-constricted muscles screaming from the sudden exercise. The altercation was over in seconds, the shocked Barnett clumsy and slow in his surprise. Holmes pushed his gun against the man's head as Bill rushed into the office, astonished by the crash.

"Nice to see you, Mr Holmes." He touched his forelock in respect to the detective.

Holmes laughed noiselessly. "Thank you for your assistance, Mr Waverly. I'll put in a good word with my brother." The detective noticed Irene's pale, unreadable face watching him attentively.

"Miss Adler, I have something that belongs to you." He took The Woman's gun from his waistband and handed it to her, smiling. She took it with a blank expression.

"Allow me to introduce myself, Sir and Madam. I am Sherlock Holmes, consulting detective," said Holmes, turning to the McGregors, who looked dazed. "I believe, Sir, that there has been a misunderstanding, for which I apologise." His eyes took in Ambrose, who bowed his head slightly.

"Not at all, Mr Holmes. I now comprehend that my wife and I have been mixed up in something far larger than we realised."

"I'm grateful to have two such reliable witnesses to this man's intentions," the detective replied, indicating the furious Barnett, whose face under his makeup was a violent shade of red.

"Will we have to testify in court?" asked Tootie, suddenly finding her voice again.

"Indeed, Madam, I would expect so," Holmes answered with a smile. "I hope it won't be overly distressing."

"Not at all," said the lady, looking almost pleased, her equilibrium apparently returning. She moved to her husband's side, and he put an arm about her.

Holmes looked at The Woman, wondering about her thoughts. He had never seen her so pale, but otherwise, she looked perfectly composed. "Miss Adler," he said after a moment, "I believe our friends have arrived. Please be so kind as to usher them inside." His keen ears had detected the sound of more than wind approaching, and soon voices and boots could be heard. Irene went outside, and no one spoke until the door of the shed was forcefully pushed open and a stocky policeman entered, followed by Thomas Edison, who looked characteristically calm, and little Nelson Burroughs, who was attempting to look fierce. Irene followed last, still looking somewhat dazed.

"Welcome, Gentlemen," said Holmes, standing up straight and nodding to the newcomers.

"I'm Sheriff Samuel Morris," said the solid, middle-aged officer of the law. "I assume you're Mr Sherlock Holmes, detective of London."

"I am indeed," said Holmes quietly.

"And this is Miss Irene Adler, legally Mrs Norton, subject of a plot put forth by the gentleman here, Mr James Barnett, known locally as Alberto Sanchez."

"That is correct, Sir," answered the detective. "I'm afraid we haven't time for conversation. This man's associates, under the orders of a criminal named Sebastian Moran, are even now awaiting the delivery of my person. We have a chance of apprehending them if we move in haste."

Thankfully, Holmes realised, the policeman wasn't as slow as some of his counterparts across the Atlantic. He immediately produced handcuffs, which Holmes assisted him in placing on the surly suspect, then led the entire group outside. His quickly-uttered "What do you propose to do, Mr Holmes?" endeared him eternally to the detective.

“Mr and Mrs McGregor, Mr Thomas Edison will take you home in your carriage. You’ve been through plenty of surprises this evening,” the detective began. “Miss Adler, you will accompany me and our friend Barnett in my cart, with Sheriff Morris and Mr Burroughs following behind. We’ve no time to lose.”

Holmes was relieved when everyone did exactly as they were told, moving rapidly, propelled by the force of his personality. He used his gun to push Barnett forward, and Irene followed to where his cart was hidden in the darkness, his horse tethered to a tree. Irene trained her gun on the solicitor while Holmes freed the horse and prepared to drive. As he had anticipated, Bill was nowhere to be found, as if he’d melted into the night. No doubt, Holmes knew, he’d resurface wherever he was assigned.

The detective watched The Woman force Barnett into the cart. Holmes wondered what the man was about. He was too quiescent, and Holmes had every belief that he was plotting something, but The Woman could handle him, at least until they reached the beach. The detective drove quickly, and his horse, rested from its long wait, was delighted to run. Holmes was optimistic, pleased with Irene’s perfect handling of her difficult role and with the outcome. Barnett had been entirely fooled, both by Bill, Mycroft’s agent, and by Miss A, who had been magnificent both intentionally and unintentionally. The night was far from over, but he knew now that he was in control.

The oppressive darkness, punctuated by moonlight, was almost like a living thing as the detective drove the cart to the coast, with the clop of the police horse behind, reminding him that the law and the young Burroughs were with him, ready to provide backup. Holmes didn’t know exactly what they would find at the drop-off point. He hardly hoped to nab Moran; unlikely the man would have made the journey himself. Instead, they would most likely capture a few of the mid-level operatives from Moriarty’s vast but splintering organization. At any rate, capturing any of them would be a positive outcome, especially if it could be accomplished without bloodshed. He was well aware that the situation was likely to be complicated.

"If you move again, I'll put a bullet in your leg." Holmes heard Irene's voice, calm and deadly, break into his thoughts.

"You've never shot anyone," rejoined the solicitor derisively.

"No, but I'm the sort of person who could."

After that, silence reigned, but Holmes glanced behind him to ascertain that all was well. The Woman looked oddly peaceful, her gun resting on her lap, pointed squarely at Barnett, who sat still with his hands cuffed. Holmes smiled to himself. Irene was all right. She wouldn't be taken by surprise.

—

The coastline was eerily beautiful in the moonlight. Holmes had heard a local rumour that pirates had once patrolled these waters, quartering captives on an island nearby. He could well believe it. What was idyllic in daylight had a savage edge in the nighttime.

Holmes drove until he saw a lighthouse in the distance, giving off a faint glow. He stopped his horse at the edge of the sand and jumped down as the policeman halted his own cart. Catching glimpses of Irene's face, Holmes saw that she was relieved that the long ride spent staring at the solicitor was complete. He trained his gun on the man as Morris and Burroughs joined them.

"You see the lighthouse," the detective said quickly. "No doubt they have a boat waiting to carry them out to sea as soon as the drop has been made. I gather that's how Mr Barnett was to get out of the country as well." He looked at the solicitor, "If you'd like to confirm that, it wouldn't go amiss." Angry eyes stared back at him.

"Here is what must happen now. One of you will impersonate Mr Sanchez and follow me to the lighthouse, after which the others will wait until we start for the boat and converge with us there, in order to capture not only those on land, but also those who may be waiting on the water."

"Needless to say," he continued, "this is a risk, but not as much as it would be if our solicitor friend were involved. Sheriff Morris, I must ask you to remove the man's jacket." Morris stared at Holmes briefly before taking off the solicitor's handcuffs. For a moment, Barnett looked as if he might make some sort of attempt to fight, but the joint effect of Irene's and Holmes's guns on him, as well as the beefy arms of the policeman, kept him subdued. Burroughs's eyes were enormous with confusion.

"Irene," said Holmes, once he held the jacket in his hand, "I believe you're the only one who will suffice. Mr Burroughs is too short and Sheriff Morris too robust." The Woman looked surprised, but she comprehended his meaning and took Barnett's evening jacket from the policeman, putting it on and using it to cover her figure. "Now, Mr Burroughs, your hat." Burroughs was frozen for a moment, as if he hadn't heard, then removed his highly fashionable hat and handed it to Holmes, who placed it on Irene's head, hiding her hair. The Woman looked up at him with a roguish smile that passed in a second. "The darkness will hide your dress long enough for my purposes," the detective added, noting that Irene looked relieved. She appeared to have wondered if he intended her to exchange clothes completely with the solicitor.

Holmes handed his gun to Burroughs, who stared at it as if it were some kind of ferocious animal in his hand. "Sheriff Morris and Mr Burroughs," the detective continued, "I trust you will take care of our friend while Miss Adler and I begin the operation. A gag might be in order to keep him from making noise. Once we're ready to rendezvous, Mr Burroughs can keep his gun on the prisoner while Sheriff Morris helps us subdue the others." He helped the policeman re-cuff the solicitor, who spit in his face. Holmes merely wiped his cheek and didn't deign to reply.

"Now, Irene," he said, turning his back to her, "please be so good as to jam the barrel of your pistol into the small of my back, and we will proceed." Irene did as he asked, none too gently, and he began the walk across the sand to the blur in the distance that was the lighthouse. Behind him, he heard muffled curses and the calm voice of the policeman, noises indicating that he had taken Holmes's advice and decided to gag the prisoner to prevent him somehow giving them away by shouting. *Not entirely stupid*, thought Holmes, gratified.

"Are you all right?" the detective finally asked in a low voice as he and Irene made their way across the wide expanse of sand.

"Tolerably," she answered.

"You won't have to speak. I'll make sure of that."

"Very well."

"Remain in the shadows and stay behind me, and I'll keep you from being detected until the men emerge and we make for the boat. Morris will join us then."

Holmes continued, "Just keep your head down and don't be afraid to use your weapon if things don't go to plan. We're taking a risk, but I don't wish to lose any of the perpetrators."

"No more do I," Irene answered. "At least Morris doesn't seem a complete fool. He'll come to our aid if he sees or hears anything amiss. Have you any idea how many are in the lighthouse?"

"A few at the most. More would have attracted local attention, and Moran has to allocate his resources carefully these days. The Yard have been on him heavily since Moriarty's death. His outsized faith in Barnett results from the man's previous service to the organization, I gather."

"What previous service?"

"That I do not know. Even Mycroft's people hadn't uncovered it at the time of his last letter."

It was odd, Holmes thought, to be conversing with The Woman in an almost enjoyable way under the present circumstances.

Watson was nearly silent at these times. With his back to Irene, the detective couldn't see her face, but their words flowed back and forth as usual, and she sounded strangely normal. He wondered how the evening's events were affecting her, how long it would be before her adrenaline gave way to weariness. He hoped she would be able to stay with him, to keep her senses keen, until after it was all over. He needed her mind to be clear.

Both fell silent for several moments. As they drew closer to their destination, Holmes heard Irene's breathing quicken. "Steady on," he whispered.

The structure itself had the usual appearance of a coastal lighthouse, tall and sturdy with a large door in its side. He hoped the men had a reliable lookout and were not waiting for some prearranged signal from Sanchez. That would, he thought, be inconvenient. The detective raised his arms and gesticulated as they came close, giving the appearance of a man under great duress.

Holmes's wish was granted a few feet from the lighthouse, when he heard a male voice shout and saw a man appear at the door, brandishing a rifle. "There's no need to be dramatic," the detective said loudly but icily, "Mr Sanchez's gun in my spine speaks loudly enough." Two men came out the door and faced Holmes, who kept his thin body squarely in front of Irene in order to shield her from view as much as possible in the moonlight.

"A gentleman might think it unsporting to capture a man by dressing as a lady," said Holmes in an indignant tone, hoping to buy a few more moments by selling Irene's unexpected attire.

One of the men, who was tall and young, let out a hearty laugh. "Didn't expect such creativity from you, Mr Barnett. Moran told us you were a by-the-book man."

Excellent, thought Holmes, they hadn't met Barnett. Irene stayed silent, as he'd instructed. "Oh, he's plenty creative," he said, sounding angry.

"Be quiet," said the other man, who was of middle age and seemed jumpy. "Let's get to the boat before Sammy falls asleep."

Holmes saw movement out of the corner of his eye, and suddenly Barnett came rushing toward them, yelling against his gag. The detective was forced to move, revealing Irene. The young man from the lighthouse immediately grabbed her gun. At the same time, Holmes pinned the hysterical Barnett on the ground while the older man trained his gun on the detective's temple.

At that moment, Morris and Burroughs burst toward the group, and confusion reigned. Morris tackled the older man, and Burroughs stood at the edge, looking bewildered. Finally, the voice of the younger lookout cut through the madness. "This is all well and good, Mr Holmes, but if you don't come with us, I'll shoot the head off the la—" A deafening, close-range shot rang out, and he lurched forward, blood beginning to spurt from his mouth; he was dead almost instantly. Immediately, Irene jerked the gun from his hand and pointed it at Barnett, while Morris dragged the older accomplice to his feet. Burroughs stood behind Irene, his face deathly white, with a painfully hot gun in his shaking hand.

His pistol firmly trained on his prisoner, Morris looked gratefully at the bewildered Burroughs. "Well done, Sir," he said. "I hope you still intend to make this town your home one day." The small man didn't answer, but his colour slowly returned.

Holmes hauled up Barnett, who was practically foaming at the mouth in rage. "As I said a few moments ago," the detective intoned calmly, "there's no need to be dramatic."

Morris put a hand on the detective's shoulder. "I'm afraid we've lost the boat, Mr Holmes." Sure enough, in the beginning half-light, Holmes saw the outline of a small craft moving further away from the Florida coast each moment. It was a pity, but not a contingency he'd seen as particularly unlikely.

"It's all right. I'll alert the proper authorities." He meant Mycroft, but saw no need for a lengthy explanation. Sammy, whoever he was, would be long gone before the American authorities could track him. Morris nodded, and Holmes was surprised once again at the man's sense. Lestrade could afford to learn from him, the detective thought.

"I'll send the boys out for the body," said the policeman after a moment. The corpse looked vulnerable in the dawning light, nothing like the surly young man who'd threatened to kill Irene Adler.

Holmes led the way, and Irene, Burroughs, and Morris herded Barnett and the other man toward the wagons and impatient horses. Without a second pair of handcuffs, the policeman was forced to tie the older man's hands with twine found in the bottom of one of the wagons, a task he seemed to enjoy. He took charge of both prisoners, with Burroughs, less shaky than before, consenting to drive the police wagon. To Holmes's surprise, Irene waited at the front of the other cart until he helped her up next to the driver's seat, which he filled himself. He took the reins, relief beginning to settle over him. Both he and The Woman were safe.

Chapter 17: Irene

I was comfortable beside the detective. For the moment, that was enough. It was too soon for the anxieties of the previous days to leave me or for my mind to make sense of all the twisted threads that had entwined to create the events of the evening. I just was. I smelt the smell of the water and sand in the early morning, felt the breeze and the brush of trees as we made our way back to the road, and enjoyed the presence of another human being.

I am Irene Adler, I thought. Not Irene Norton or some combination of the two. Just Irene Adler. It was a deconstructed feeling, but I didn't mind. I felt lighter, almost as if Barnett had succeeded in taking everything from me and I didn't care. He had shown me my life with nothing, and the vision hadn't destroyed me. Now that I once again possessed all that was mine, my grasp felt stronger and lighter at the same time. Even if everything in the whole world was taken from me, I would not break, and I would not die.

After a long silence in the warm autumn morning, Holmes turned to me. "My shoulder is not the most congenial of pillows, but I have no objection to its use," he said quietly. I realised that I was exhausted, bone-tired from danger and exertion and too little sleep. I wondered how Holmes managed to keep his eyes open, but I drifted to sleep leaning against him before I could finish the thought.

I awoke as Holmes stopped the horse in front of the police station and jail, a tiny building in the middle of town, situated next to the home of the volunteer fire brigade, judging by the accoutrements lying about. I watched sleepily as Morris and Burroughs pushed the unhappy Barnett and the older man inside, then waited for Holmes to help me down. I was too disorientated from sleep to climb, so he proffered his arms instead, and I put my hands on his shoulders. His long fingers around my waist were warm and strong as he effortlessly swung me down and placed me on solid ground, smiling down at me.

I saw that his eyes were closing with weariness and that his face, always almost painful in its thinness, was gaunt.

Inside his own kingdom, Morris was all business. He imprisoned the two men quickly, doing the necessary paperwork to start the state's process, then sent a boy who was loitering in the street to collect his part-time deputies, brothers who worked as carpenters in their father's shop. In the meantime, he produced adequate coffee, which he gave to all, including Barnett and the other man, who claimed to be named Joshua Mason. Now that the guilty were contained, I noted that Morris had the quality of many a good policeman, human objectivity that boggles the mind, that can put aside terrible acts of even moments before and treat the guilty simply as human beings—human beings in limbo, but human beings nonetheless. Holmes also possessed this quality, but I did not.

I could not yet look at Barnett or Mason with any objectivity. My eyes were clouded by the sight of the dead man and the horror in Nelson Burroughs's eyes at having killed him, the terror that silenced the gregarious tongue of Tootie McGregor, and for myself, the feeling of claustrophobic danger that had all-too-poignantly recalled my life with my husband. Perhaps some day, not far off, I would be thankful for what I had learned about myself, but I could not feel grateful yet, and the sight of the criminals turned my stomach.

My faculties had once again become reasonably alert from movement and coffee once the Bartholomew brothers arrived, strapping young men who each had at least half a foot over their boss. "Good morning, Sir," they said deferentially, almost in unison, and I realised they were twins. Morris told them where to find the body, and they went off eagerly, apparently glad for some actual police business to attend to. Fort Myers didn't seem to be a hotbed of illegal activity, especially not the sort that concerned more than one country.

Deputies dispatched, Morris set about taking statements, choosing out of his own kindness to begin with Burroughs. With a gently businesslike manner, he ushered the still-shaken young man into a tiny back room, while Holmes and I drank second and third cups of coffee in the front of the station. I was glad we were removed from Barnett and Mason, even if only by a thin wall. I had no desire to see the solicitor's face again.

"My brother will take care of getting your assets into the proper order if you wish," said Holmes after a while. "Otherwise, I fear you may face undue delays in recovering them."

"Thank you, Holmes," I answered, wanting to say more but unsure how to begin.

"Our solicitor is very discreet," he added. I nodded in acquiescence.

At once it struck me how odd it was to be drinking coffee with the detective again, but to feel so differently. Only a few days had passed since our memorable meeting in my dressing room, a meeting of seemingly disparate minds united by a single piece of paper and two names that had turned out to be one. But we had never really been dissimilar, Holmes and I. The case had shown me that the hints of things I'd discovered about the detective during our last interaction—trustworthy, kind things—were far stronger parts of him than people realised. Neither of us was soft; we were both honed edges that could cut in an instant, but if we were sharp, we were also straight.

After half an hour had passed, Morris and Burroughs emerged, and the policeman clapped Burroughs on the shoulder. "You're a true hero, Mr Burroughs, and I hope you won't let this unfortunate incident cloud your view of our city."

Burroughs looked at us all with relief on his face. "Just glad I could help, Sir, Mr Holmes, Mrs, I mean—"

"Miss Adler," I supplied with a smile, and he smiled back.

"You'll be called to testify, Mr Burroughs, and I wouldn't be surprised if the mayor sees fit to give you a commendation," said the policeman with finality. The young man nodded and left the station, but I didn't think any mayor's commendation would be sufficient to compensate him for what he'd been through.

Once Burroughs was gone, Morris turned to me, and I noticed that in spite of all the events of the nighttime, his brown hair was still perfectly coiffed. "I'd like to get your statement now, if you don't mind, Miss Adler." I didn't mind, but Holmes put a hand on my arm as I started to get up.

"Sheriff Morris, I'd be grateful if you'd let Miss Adler and I give statements together. I realise it's slightly irregular, but given enough time, I could produce permission from as high as you'd like."

The policeman sat back down and seemed to be contemplating how much he trusted Sherlock Holmes. "Very well," he finally said, "I know there's more to this than meets the eye. There was that fellow Bill, the one who alerted me, for one thing. He had identification from a government organization I won't mention."

"Very wise," Holmes put in.

"Here's the thing," said Morris, looking at both of us. "I have a dead body to account for. What I want are statements that explain it. I'm not fool enough to think the entire case, whatever it entails, is under my jurisdiction."

"What we need, Sir," I put in, "is for Holmes to be nonexistent in this case." The policeman raised one eyebrow, a signal that he was about to become obstinate.

"Give me twenty-four hours, and I will have all the reasons you need to keep me out of it," said Holmes.

The policeman nodded abruptly. "I trust you, Mr Holmes, but for this, I need solid proof. I'll give you the day you request."

"Understandable," I murmured, and I noticed that the detective didn't seem perturbed either. I wondered if he meant to flee.

I couldn't help feeling a little bit of regret at leaving Morris without a satisfactory explanation, but as soon as Holmes and I emerged into the sunshine, my spirits lifted. It was fully daytime now, and people were about in the streets, shopping and working. I looked around, and the city of Fort Myers looked different, friendlier, without the spectre of an enemy hanging over my head.

Holmes re-hitched the wagon. "I was thinking, Mrs James," he said playfully, "that perhaps it might behove us to use the hotel instead of the flat above Sloane's General Store, now that we have our choice."

I laughed, and we made our way back to the Keystone. My opulent room seemed far removed from all the things that had happened to me since I had been in it, but there it was when I returned, just as I had left it. Holmes appealed to the office for his own room and was given one adjacent to mine.

My companion did not bother to close the door between our rooms before sprawling across his bed and falling into a much-needed sleep. In a reversal of our former positions, I sat by the window and watched him, and I wondered if he had also watched me in a similar way. In sleep, all of his strength and control were gone, and he was simply a man. I realised in that moment that I had become his friend.

Holmes slept for three hours, and I spent them in contemplation, examining my feelings one by one and trying to put to rest as many as I could. I had never been so near death before, and I found that I was different afterward—calmer, less afraid that the world would pass me by, and happier just to be in it. Time would tell how far that difference went.

Holmes finally awoke in the late morning and came into my room, instantly alert. "You look better," I commented. "Better still with food."

"Agreed," he said simply, so I had some brought up, soup that tasted canned, a beef dish with noodles that the hotel called "stroganoff," and a bakewell pudding at the end. Both of us ate with abandon and determination. I had read Dr Watson's descriptions of the succulent dinners he and Holmes sometimes enjoyed, but I'd never actually seen Holmes eat heartily before. With amusement, I realised the accounts weren't lies after all. The detective was quite capable of taking in energy when he needed it.

Once finished, Holmes perched on the ancient divan in my room and gazed at me with an uncertain expression. "I feel I owe you some explanation of the events of the past few days." I met his eyes, and he looked away, almost as if he were avoiding the intimacy.

"After you recognised the solicitor, I began to suspect where matters stood. If harming or capturing me had been the man's sole object, it would have made little sense for him not to have devised a way to entrap me the night we first met. He had a decided advantage since he knew my face, but I did not know his. He would, at least, have had a good chance. As it was, I knew he must be waiting for something else. The presence of the letter pointed two ways, to you by its content and to Mycroft by the ease with which it was procured and the presence of the photograph in Sanchez's office. I couldn't dismiss the notion that if the man knew my brother well enough to target him, he would also know what an impossible target my brother would be. The Florida connection would have been senseless in that situation. As a result, I began to be convinced that you were as much a target as I, if not more."

"That's why I insisted that we separate. I realised that the man knew of my presence but did not appear to know of yours. I surmised that he'd known you were coming to Florida for your singing tour and assumed that I would follow Sanchez here, but he didn't seem to know that we were together and both in Fort Myers. I decided to force him to make a move."

"That's why you used me as bait," I put in.

"Yes, I—" For once, the detective looked as if he were at a loss. "I understand that it caused you a vast amount of—

unpleasantness—" he trailed off. It was the least fluent speech I'd ever heard him give.

I rose from my chair and went to him. "Get up, Holmes," I said forcefully, hoping to startle him into obedience. He did as I asked, his tall frame dwarfing mine once he was standing.

"Thank you," I said, and I stood on my toes and wrapped my arms around his neck, holding him tightly for a few seconds. When I pulled back, he looked more shocked than I'd ever seen him. I returned to my chair, but he seemed entirely unable to speak for quite a while, sitting on the edge of the divan with a bewildered face.

"I'm afraid the logic of this situation escapes me, Irene," he finally managed, which caused me to laugh uproariously for some time, while he stared at me as if I'd gone mad.

"Please continue your tale, Holmes," I finally sputtered. I breathed deeply for a moment and gathered my wits again. "I simply wished to express my thanks for your rescue and my lack of anger all at once. That seemed the simplest way." I gave him what can only be described as a coy look, which he received with a raised eyebrow.

"Very well," he said, looking at his hands. "While you were living the somewhat frustrating life of Lavinia James, abandoned by her business-bound husband, I was busy. I visited Sanchez's grove office, his town office, and his home." I looked up in surprise. This I had certainly not expected.

"I left the man three items: a handkerchief embroidered with IN, a lady's powder box, and a calling card. These things, of course, were meant to make him believe that Irene Adler was indeed in Fort Myers and was on to him. My additional hope was that if he thought you responsible for these tokens, he would not realise the two of us were working in unison, as he apparently did not."

"Well, that explains one of the mysteries," I said, remembering Barnett's comments about my helpful calling cards. "Nicely done, Holmes. I'd not have thought to taunt him in that way."

"It was expedient," Holmes answered quickly, "an irresistible temptation to act, but it allowed him time to contact his associates and arrange the dropoff. He was most likely aware that Bernard James had disappeared, but he is not a stupid man, and his familiarity with me no doubt kept him from assuming I'd actually gone."

"Now we reach movements of mine that you do not know. The day you visited Tootie and Ambrose McGregor, I followed you. I will readily admit that I wanted to make sure you were following the plan, but," he looked at me steadily, "I was also concerned for your safety. Satisfied that you were with the McGregors, whom I did not believe to be part of the plot in spite of all of Ambrose's quiet discomfort, I continued my errands. I believe you may have seen me, hidden behind a copy of the *Ft. Myers Press*."

I shook my head in annoyance at myself. Sure enough, I had seen the man, but since he'd made no effort to follow me, or so I thought, I'd dismissed him. "Expertly carried out," I said with a wry laugh.

"That afternoon," Holmes continued, "I returned to the store to wait for the evening, at which time I planned to pay Barnett's home a visit, which I later did. Before that, however, I received a visitor."

"Bill," I put in. I wanted to remind Holmes that I wasn't a complete fool, whatever my lack of observation of him might have suggested. He smiled appreciatively.

"Exactly so. It had taken him my two visits and a critical look at the photograph his boss possessed to understand who I was. Our disguises fooled Barnett, but Bill, or whatever his real name is, figured us out after we had made our exit. I was not entirely surprised to see him, or, rather, to see an emissary of my brother. Mycroft had sent him here as soon as he'd first received Barnett's letter to Sanchez—strange to contemplate now—and Bill had insinuated himself into Sanchez's organization. He had been told to expect me, but since he didn't move in the polite circles of his boss, he was not able to find me as quickly as the solicitor was fortunate enough to do. Barnett never mentioned that he'd met me at the Edisons' party, so Bill was left on his own. Fortunately, he put the pieces together and finally approached me that day, meeting me at the store on the pretext of doing an errand for his boss in town. He showed me identification that proved his claims, and I explained the situation to him. We agreed that Barnett was unlikely to wait long to act once he realised you were taunting him. Bill promised to help me, but we could not make firm plans without knowing how the solicitor would act."

"That night, you came to see me." I looked away from him then. The memory was painful. Thinking back, I couldn't fault myself for my anger, but I also couldn't praise myself. I had acted according to my understanding at the time; that was all. "Don't trouble yourself," he continued, correctly interpreting my expression. "Your distress made me strongly consider the downside of the plan, but I still considered it essential that you be as innocent as possible. When one is aware of such an operation, it is nearly impossible to act completely normally. Forgive me for the observation, but your relative lack of experience in these matters also made me wary of giving you more information that would require you to be deceptive. You had shown yourself to be an admirable actress, but I didn't want to tax your powers any more than necessary. I needed Barnett to think he had taken you completely by surprise, and the best way to accomplish it was for you to feel the part you had to play." The detective spoke quickly and avoided my eyes again, as if he was afraid of the response he might receive.

"I agree with you," I said quickly, to put his discomfort to an end. "I was afraid, as afraid as Godfrey ever made me, but I see now the value of that fear. It was like a lullaby to soothe Barnett into thinking everything had gone as he expected. Had I known you were already in place, I doubt I'd have been able to act so convincingly." I nodded to Holmes, and he nodded back, relieved.

"At the theatre that night—"

"—You stole my pistol," I interrupted, smiling. "You can imagine what a turn that gave me."

"Indeed," Holmes replied. "I knew it would severely risk our ability to thwart the whole operation if you succeeded in getting yourself and the McGregors away from Barnett prematurely. I didn't yet know if he planned to act that night, but I expected it. I apologise for the theft. It felt ungentlemanly at the time and still seems so now, though I consider it to have been necessary."

"Not at all," I answered, "though I did curse the thief roundly to myself."

"If curses had power, one would think I'd be dead from all the lurid ones that have been directed at me by various persons," Holmes said absently.

"Let me tell you something for a moment, Holmes," I said, suddenly remembering that I, too, knew the solution to a small mystery. "You were right about Marion Edison."

"Oh?"

"She met the German lieutenant during an apparently heinous trip to Europe, but the attachment endured. He's here visiting, and now the young lady is trying to figure out how to break the news that they'd like to marry." After a moment I added, "She came to see me yesterday morning."

"I know," said Holmes quietly.

"Indeed?" I was intrigued.

"I am aware of all of your movements of that day," he said, which was enough of an explanation for me to understand what he meant.

"Thank you," I said simply.

"Not at all." He coughed quietly, as if to change the subject, and continued. "I considered the theatre a likely place for Barnett to act for a number of reasons, but I saw nothing amiss until after the interval. You noticed, I believe, that he was not in the audience before that."

"Yes."

"After I had relieved you of your weapon, I realised Barnett had joined us at the beginning of the second half, though I believe that fact eluded you. My subsequent movements made me nearly unable to keep myself from being seen by you. You have a very vigilant eye, Irene. Barnett would not have escaped it if you had been unencumbered by your hostess." I grinned inadvertently as he went on. "I thought I had been mistaken when it appeared that you and the McGregors would be safely conducted home in your carriage, but just before you left, I recognised that Bill was the driver, as he intended me to do. He gave me a nod, and I knew that his boss's plan was fully in motion. That nod also signaled that he had summoned the police, as he had promised he would do during our previous meeting. I had put a large store of trust in the man, but my brother's operatives are as trustworthy as he is."

Even though I knew the order of events after that, I found myself eager to hear them. In my mind, I could see myself and the McGregors entering the carriage and losing hope, but now I could also see Holmes, watching over us. It seemed silly now to remember how sure I'd been that he'd failed.

"I followed your carriage in my cart for as long as I could without attracting attention, until I was sure Bill was making for the citrus grove. Then I made my way there as fast as I could, staying off the main roads. I arrived several moments before you did and took my place under Sanchez's desk, grateful for the sense of grandiosity that had prompted him to purchase such a large one. I still considered that you and the McGregors might have managed to overpower Barnett, but Bill was sworn to his role and had promised to help his boss if you began to succeed in taking him down. I needed his plan to remain intact in order to hear enough information to convict the man and lead us to his associates."

"You played your part brilliantly, as did the McGregors, and I waited, hoping to hear enough to bring Barnett down without waiting long enough to endanger you or your companions. Bill stood by to assist if anything began to go wrong. A very useful man, I must say. I also hoped the police would not arrive too early. Bill had instructed Sheriff Morris to take his time, and he had agreed, though not without some concern. Thankfully, by the time Barnett decided to force you to sign his very unfortunate papers, I had heard plenty. That, of course, was when I emerged."

Chapter 18: Holmes

The detective couldn't help his enjoyment of the delight on Irene's face when he said the word *emerged.* He knew she was remembering the moment and probably experiencing once again the relief of knowing she hadn't been abandoned to a nasty fate. She had surprised him many times during their long conversation. He'd expected to have to explain himself, to have to apologise, but instead, she understood. She didn't even act as if she'd forgiven him; she acted as if she found nothing to forgive. He found it comforting to know that The Woman was so eminently reasonable, even when she'd been through so much.

He stopped speaking, his part of the tale concluded, and the two associates sat looking at each other in silence, enjoying one another's company and understanding. "For the most part, a very successful case, Irene," he said at last.

"Yes," she answered, "though it's a pity about Burroughs and the dead man and Sammy, whoever he is."

"True," he replied.

"You couldn't have done it without me." Irene's expression was teasing and playful.

"That, Miss Adler," he answered, leaning toward her, "is most certainly true."

—

The middle part of the day was spent in sending a telegram to Mycroft, using the shorthand code the brothers had worked out years before, and taking tea while waiting for a response, which came promptly. It contained a set of words and names Holmes didn't recognise but assumed Sheriff Morris would, since its function was to convince him to expunge all mention of Sherlock Holmes from his record of the case.

"You intend to cooperate with Morris, then?" Irene asked, as the two left the telegraph office with the message in hand.

"Of course," said Holmes.

"I thought perhaps you meant to leave without a trace, or something equally dramatic," said The Woman mischievously.

"Certainly not," said Holmes, "the weather's far too nice not to enjoy it to the fullest." He was glad to hear her laugh, such a contrast from the anxiety of the previous day.

Upon returning to the Keystone Hotel, the two were met with a note from Mina Edison, asking them to dinner once again and explaining that the McGregors would be guests as well. Irene shook her head. "I can't believe the poor woman even wants us after all this. I'd have thought we were pariahs by now."

Holmes smiled. "No reason not to make our thanks in person, especially to Ambrose McGregor, who, it seems to me, has been particularly unfortunate throughout the case."

"Yes," said The Woman, "though I admit I'm not looking forward to seeing everyone I've deceived, good reason or not."

"Not a compunction that seems to affect you in connection with deceiving me, however," said the detective drily. Irene gave him a quick look and burst out laughing again, not stopping until they parted at the door to her room.

Holmes dressed elegantly, in the clothing he would have worn for an evening out in London. He was relieved to be himself again, not that he minded playing a part. The end of a case was always pleasant, before the monotony seized him, and he planned to enjoy himself. Irene, too, seemed pleased as she emerged to join him, dressed in a turquoise gown that set off her brown hair and made her look far more like Irene Adler than Lavinia James. He proffered his arm, and the companions went down to catch their cab.

Seminole Lodge was beautiful in the moonlight as they arrived, the grounds lit by paper lanterns that Mina Edison had purchased for the occasion. Holmes led Irene to the door of the white mansion, and she seemed nervous, even more so than she had when she was in the guise of Lavinia James. He lightly squeezed the small hand that held his arm. "Steady," he whispered. She was capable of more timidity than he'd expected.

"Good evening, Mr Holmes and Miss Adler," said Mina Edison without hesitation. She was smiling and radiant.

"Good evening," said Holmes, smiling down at her kindly.

Irene blushed and nodded as the other woman motioned her inside. "Marion's wild to see you." Holmes watched The Woman walk away with the hostess, her confidence obviously rising.

As he entered the piano room, Holmes saw that the dinner party was the same as that of the previous occasion, except that the Montanan cattle rancher had been replaced by the German officer with whom he had seen Marion Edison. The inventor was speaking to the lieutenant, and timid Burroughs was engaged in conversation with Tootie McGregor, whose spirits appeared to be completely restored. As usual, her husband hung back slightly, listening.

Holmes approached Burroughs and held out his hand. "I must thank you, Sir, for your assistance."

"I'm grateful I could help," said the young man. "The deputies were away from town until morning, so Mr Edison and I figured we could do our part, Mr Holmes." He stumbled slightly over the name.

Holmes smiled warmly and looked around the group. "My name is Sherlock Holmes, and my companion is Miss Irene Adler." He didn't elaborate further, but since he seemed to expect everyone to accept the names, everyone did, out of respect for the detective and his companion. He watched Irene in the corner of the room, engaged in conversation with Marion, and she seemed herself once again.

Dinner was a subdued meal, and no one seemed inclined to mention the case, except for Edison, who asked Irene, seated next to him, whether or not the criminals were in custody. Holmes had noticed that Marion seemed especially nervous and looked often at the German, whose name was Karl Oeser. Finally, she spoke. "Mr Oeser and I have an announcement." When all eyes turned toward her, she blushed bright red and took Oeser's hand. "Mr Oeser—Karl—has asked me to marry him, and I've accepted."

Holmes looked quickly at Edison and Mina, but neither seemed surprised by the news and both appeared genuinely pleased. Irene beamed across the table. "I'll sing for you after dinner," she said to Marion, who couldn't stop smiling. The Woman's equilibrium had returned.

The good feelings remained through dessert, which was a new French recipe called Crepes Suzette that Mina had ordered to accompany her stepdaughter's announcement. After many compliments, the party finally made its way to the living room, and Irene sat down at the piano. Holmes wondered what sort of song she would choose, if she would again sing the bittersweet anthem that had captivated her audience before. But her fingers began a different tune:

At Clapham Town end lived an Old Yorkshire tyke
Who i dealing i horseflesh had ne'er met his like.
'Twas his pride that i aw the hard bargains he'd hit
He'd bit a good mony but but nivver been bit.
Chorus: Wi' me dum a dum dary,
Dum a dum dary,
Dum a dum dary,
Dum a dum day.

By the beginning of the second verse, everyone in the room was laughing, and Marion had grabbed Oeser's hand and started to dance. Holmes watched them all is if he were seeing one of Edison's moving pictures, but his eyes were drawn back to The Woman in her element, singing as if nothing else in the world existed. She looked up and smiled at him, and her eyes were warm.

The evening continued with other songs and impromptu dances, and the members of the party tried to laugh away the darkness as the detective looked on, finally forced to participate by the persistent Tootie, who seized him in her arms and forced him to dance a waltz with her. Marion, alive with joy, played the piano and laughed with the abandon of the young and engaged. Weariness eventually forced the guests to consider leaving, and Irene came to Holmes's side. In spite of the fact that they were no longer portraying a married couple, the proximity seemed normal to both of them, and he gave her his arm once more.

"Thank you for everything!" said Marion, taking Irene's hand. "I'll miss you." Her voice was sweet, but she had eyes only for her fiancé, who was quiet and polite and appeared to dote on the girl. He led her away to her father, and the McGregors took her place.

Holmes felt Irene's hand on his arm tense, and he saw that her nervousness had returned when she was confronted with the large woman and the quiet man. He cleared his throat, "Please accept my apologies for everything that has occurred over these past few days, Mr and Mrs McGregor." Tootie smiled instantly and gave Holmes a loud kiss on the cheek, which took him aback considerably.

"Don't worry, dear," she said, "we're ever so grateful for all you've done. We'd love to read it in a story some time, if Dr Watson has a notion to write it up, of course." Holmes could feel Irene laughing noiselessly at this, but she gathered herself quickly and turned to Ambrose.

"Mr McGregor," she said quickly, "I'm sorry— for everything." Holmes nodded, adding his own quiet assent. Ambrose smiled one of his rare smiles, an expression that completely changed his face from serious and dour to kind and welcoming in an instant, allowing the detective to finally see what had attracted the gregarious, generous woman to him.

"Miss Adler," Ambrose said, "you are an extraordinary woman, and I can only say that Mr Holmes is very fortunate to have your assistance." The Woman blushed crimson at this, to Holmes's great amusement.

The final goodbye was to the Edisons, who offered their home and company if either Holmes or Irene should ever be in town again. Holmes regretted the necessity of leaving the inventor. He'd have liked to spend a year or more observing the man's work, but it was not to be.

Just before the party broke, Holmes commanded everyone's attention. "I have a favour to ask of each of you," he said, making and holding eye contact with every person in the room. "You now know what kind of people wish me harm. In order to protect me, yourselves, and others from such people, I ask one thing. Do not mention my name or tell anyone that I am alive. You are all bearers of a secret that must not be told." Wide-eyed stares greeted his request, and one-by-one, each of them nodded in agreement, even Oeser, who seemed to be in awe of the tall Englishman. Holmes didn't suppose they would all keep the promise, but he hoped they would at least manage to do so until he was so far away that even the remaining members of Moriarty's gang could not find him.

Out in the night, the detective could tell by the ease in Irene's movements and breathing that she was relieved. Once they were ensconced in a cab and on the way back to the Keystone, she spoke. "Now I feel like it's really over, Holmes."

"As do I," he replied. "I don't like facing the consequences of necessary deception any more than you do." She nodded.

"I understand, Holmes. I don't know how you always manage it."

"One builds up walls of objectivity."

"I don't think I could," she said, a slightly brittle note in her voice. The night had been difficult for her.

"Your singing was marvellous."

"Thank you, Holmes."

"You're welcome." He smiled, and she returned his with one of her own.

"I took the liberty of consulting a train schedule," he said after a while. "I'll speak to Morris in the morning, and we should be free to leave by ten o'clock, if you wish it."

"I do," Irene answered.

Chapter 19: Irene

That night, I tried to sleep, but I couldn't stop thinking about the future. Holmes had promised that Mycroft would make sure I was taken care of until my assets were sorted, so I didn't worry about money, but I felt adrift. Singing had been one purpose and the case another, but now I no longer had a desire to sing or a case to concern me. I supposed I would go to London, where I had been before all my trouble started. I had no family to return to in America, and the great British metropolis seemed like my most sensible option, a place I had lived and with which I was intimately familiar. I didn't look forward to the press of people and the call of society, but I had nowhere else to go, and I knew that Holmes must move on as well. Somehow, as unexpected as it was to realise, I knew that I would miss him.

The next morning was appropriately gloomy, with a light rain and grey clouds overhead as we made for the train station. Holmes had visited the policeman while I dressed, and he assured me that Morris had understood Mycroft's telegram and agreed that not only Holmes, but I as well, should be kept out of further record or investigation. I was vastly thankful to Mycroft, though I never expected to meet him and express the sentiment. Holmes assured me that, like his own, his brother's work was its own reward.

As the train carried us away from Fort Myers, I felt as if I had spent far longer there than the days actually indicated. The journey to New York was to take us through the night and the following day, and after that, Holmes and I would part. It seemed strange to leave one another as suddenly as we had come back into each other's lives.

I sat back in my seat and studied my companion. His long fingers flipped the pages of his newspaper with rapid dexterity, and his eyes flitted from column to column like a fly hopping from one thing to another, taking in all the things he deemed important and leaving the rest. His body was relaxed, and he looked slightly less gaunt than he had at the height of the case, though he would never be anything other than spare.

After a long while, Holmes looked up and met my eyes. "I have an offer to make to you, Irene," he said slowly. "You told me that you desired nothing more than a quiet life."

"That's true," I answered.

"I own a cottage on the Sussex Downs," he continued. "It's small—nothing grand or luxurious, but situated in a picturesque part of the country. No one lives there at present, but a lady named Mrs Turner takes care of it for me. I had intended to keep it for my eventual retirement."

"I offer this home to you, for your use." He looked down, as if slightly embarrassed. "I offer it as a friend."

"As you know, I'm supposed to be dead, and I do not know if I will ever return to England to live. Watson and Mycroft are the only others who know of the property's existence. Without me, Watson has no reason to ever think of the place again, and Mycroft will never trouble you. You'd have no companions unless you sought them for yourself. The place would be yours entirely, for as long as you cared to remain there."

"I'll think about it," I replied quietly.

I thought about it. My mind turned to nothing else as we barreled toward separation. Holmes's offer had nothing to do with money. We were both wealthy, the man who couldn't return home and the woman with no home to return to. I longed for quiet, for contemplation, for a place where my weary mind could rest. Sussex was exactly what I desired, a place where I could be inconspicuous and do as I wished, where the world would not trouble me, nor I it. I accepted Holmes's offer an hour before we reached New York.

"Where will you go?" I asked my companion.

"Tibet," he answered. I saw a gleam in his eye, and I knew that he looked forward to his journey. Because of his kindness, I also looked forward to mine. I felt at peace as we pulled into the station.

Holmes and I parted outside the Central New York Railway. "I trust you have enough money to take you to Sussex. Mycroft will send more within the month," he said, concern on his face. I nodded.

"I do."

"Be careful. We don't know where Moran may have eyes and ears."

"And you, Holmes." The tall detective leaned forward and touched my face for a moment, tracing my cheekbone with his finger, and then he was gone. He disappeared in a crowd of people down the street, blending in the way he was always so capable of doing. I watched the spot where he'd been a moment before, as if he might somehow magically reappear. Then, I squared my shoulders, turned around, and went to book a passage to England.

—

On the Sussex Downs, time had an odd way of passing. The days seemed long and luxurious, unburdened by the speed of the world and the concerns of others in it, but the years, in contrast, passed quickly, as if they'd come and gone without my notice. I learned to garden and cook and clean, all things Mrs Turner was more than willing to do for me, but that I desired to do for myself after a lifetime of being waited on by others. I began to feel self-sufficient, like a stronger version of the weary Irene Adler who had dragged herself into the cottage after a grueling ocean passage.

I liked living alone more than I ever would have before James Barnett's gun had made me confront my own fears. I liked waking up to the sound of my own thoughts and then choosing who would share them, if anyone. I became friends with women in the village who simply knew me as the widow Irene who lived on the hill. They did not intrude on my life any more than I desired, since their families clamored for their work and attention, and I even became friendly with their husbands and children. I was somewhat of a mystery, I knew, but I appreciated the locals' willingness to let me have my secrets. I believe they enjoyed having such an eccentric resident among them.

After a year, I bought a piano. At first, I only sang for myself, but after one of the village farm wives walked up the hill and heard me practicing, I became something of a desired commodity. I played for funerals and sang at weddings, and I enjoyed being a part of the life of the community as much as I had ever liked singing under theatrical lights.

My other passion was my bees. I discovered them as a result of my habit of subscribing to all sorts of magazines and journals. I was happy to lead an uneventful village life, but I still enjoyed reading about the exploits of others and learning what I could about many things, so I collected many periodicals, one of which was published by naturalists. One day, I came across an article about beekeeping, a perfectly normal sort of animal husbandry analysis of which the publication was inordinately fond, but I was intrigued in a way I had not been before. I pored over the drawings of hives and the advice about how to make the environment harmonious enough for good honey to be produced. The information about bee existence fascinated me—their logical, methodical lives that all contributed to the good of their society. The perfect collectivists, bees.

Soon, I ordered one book about beekeeping and then another. I thought the passion was to be a purely academic one, a quest to learn all I could about the bee kingdom and amuse myself by applying what I knew in my imagination, but the itch became too strong. I determined that I must have bees.

I spent months methodically acquiring all the necessary equipment, crowing with delight over the bee paradise I intended to create. Finally, the creatures themselves arrived, buzzing with life, and I became a beekeeper. I didn't love the pastime at first, and I made many mistakes, some of which angered the bees and resulted in painful stings. But I kept at it. After several months, my hives were in good order, and I was devoted to beekeeping in earnest.

—

One windy morning in April, I went to my hives to check on the bees and see how they were getting on. I'd been in Fulworth nearly three years then, though I rarely thought about the passage of time. I was due to sing for a wedding the following Saturday, and I hummed a love song to myself, hoping the weather would be nice for the couple.

Unbidden, my mind turned to the disturbing tale I'd read in the newspaper that morning. Reportedly, a London man named Ronald Adair had been shot in a seemingly impossible way—by soft-nosed revolver bullet in a locked room that had no signs of being breached. The story was strange enough to reach even the country papers, and I tried to reason it out for myself, though Scotland Yard was reportedly baffled by the scene.

I thought of Holmes then, of course. I wondered what he'd have said about the case, whether it was one he'd have solved simply from reading the account, or if he'd have wanted to inspect the scene. Those thoughts brought others forward, and a pang inside me told me that I still missed my friend. Very few days went by that I failed to think of him, because my gratefulness for the life he'd offered me was often in my mind. I wondered if he was still in Tibet, or if he was even still alive. The world, at least the small part I inhabited and the larger part I read about, seemed to bear no imprint of the detective's life whatsoever.

Later that day, I went into the village to purchase dry goods at the shop on Lamb Street, and I was met by a disturbance. Lionel

Warren, who operated the village's seldom-used telegraph, was standing on the street surrounded by Mr Sykes, who owned the shop, and Mrs Carlyle and Miss Rose of Wilmont Farm, all of them speaking over each other in excited voices.

"There's a telegram for you!" said Miss Rose excitedly as I approached. Lionel nodded, his eyes bulging.

"First telegram I've had in weeks!"

I was surprised that I'd received a telegram at all, but its contents shocked me far more:

Coming to visit 12th on 9:40 if convenient STOP and *Watson* STOP *Please advise* STOP *SH*

I gave my affirmative reply to Lionel in a shaky voice that he interpreted to be the result of my amazement at the immense honour of receiving a telegram, and then walked home, my heart beating rapidly. Holmes, alive in England! And then the doubts began. What if someone was impersonating Holmes to get to me? I began sleeping with my pistol near my pillow and listening for any odd noises in the night. Florida had been far away for some time, both in place and memory, but the case returned to my mind with absolute clarity. I dreamed about the face of James Barnett, long in jail, and the dead young man who'd threatened to put a bullet in my head. In my waking hours, I hoped for Holmes.

April 12th was a beautiful day, sunny and pleasant, and I went to the train station early in the morning to wait for my visitors. I took a seat on a bench, keeping my hand on the gun inside my bag. I hadn't carried it even once since my arrival in Sussex, but I didn't want to take a chance that one of Holmes's enemies would be getting off the train.

I had hardly let myself think about what I would say to the detective or how I would feel when I saw him. The strength of my anticipation had surprised me, and I was glad, too, to think that Dr Watson was no longer grieving as the result of a deception. But I had no idea how I would respond when the spare form stepped off the train. I had supposed for so long that he would never come that my mind had trouble accepting the notion that he would soon appear.

I was still lost in thought when the train arrived. Startled by the noise, I came out to watch the passengers disembark, but only two emerged: a short man in a bowler hat and a tall man with piercing eyes.

Chapter 20: Holmes

Irene was the only person on the platform. Holmes watched her as the train pulled into the station, noting with approval that her hand was inside her handbag, no doubt clutching her firearm in case she should need it. She looked well, better than she had been in Florida, with colour in her cheeks and bright, clear eyes. Fulworth had agreed with her, as he'd known it would.

Watson got off the train first, complimenting the country air, and Holmes followed. Three long years he'd been away from England, and even now he'd only been in London for a few weeks. He'd missed the English countryside. He'd also missed the company of The Woman, which he hadn't expected. She stood calmly, waiting and watching. He wondered if she was pleased to see him.

"Good afternoon, Miss Adler," said Watson in his gallant way, stopping in front of Irene.

"Dr Watson, I'm glad to see you." Her smile showed relief.

"Not at all," said the small man, smiling broadly, "it's Holmes we're all pleased to see." He meant it, Holmes knew. John Watson hadn't given more than a moment's thought to his years of thinking his best friend was dead. He'd simply accepted things as they were and his friend back into his life.

"Indeed we are," said The Woman, smiling first at the doctor and then up at the detective.

"I'm glad to see you well," he said.

"Likewise," she answered. It felt natural to be with her again, as if mere days had passed since the Floridian case.

—

That night, Mrs Turner insisted on cooking the two men their favourite foods, almost as excited to see the younger Holmes as Irene seemed to be. That was the thing that gave the detective the most satisfaction. For all The Woman's calm coolness, he could tell that she was genuinely delighted to see him, and he was glad.

Watson went to bed early in the evening, tired from the journey and eager to read his beloved medical journals, but Holmes and Irene stayed up late into the night, talking and drinking tea. They spoke about Florida, and then he told her in detail about the case of Ronald Adair and how it had intertwined with the apprehension of Sebastian Moran. He could see the worry leave her as he finished his tale, as if some part of her that had remained tense ever since the Floridian case had now relaxed.

"Thank you for telling me, Holmes," she said quietly. "Now, will you tell me about your time away?"

The question was so artless that it took Holmes by surprise. He hadn't intended to tell Irene about the dark nights and hungry days or the near-misses and tense moments, but he found himself doing so, more fully than he had told anyone else. His words painted the simple life of the Dalai Lama, the fjords of Norway, and the worshippers of Mecca. She even wrinkled her nose as he described the tar pits of France.

"I nearly returned to Tibet at the last," he said, as he neared the end of his tale. "It is curious how many similarities exist between the life of the logician and the life of the mystic."

"But you came back to England."

"Yes, I came back."

"Why?"

"It was The Game, Irene. I am hardly suited to a life of contemplation." She laughed then, and he enjoyed hearing it as much as he had three years before.

"And what of you?" he asked after a moment.

She smiled mischievously. "I am a beekeeper."

He stared at her a moment, wondering if she was joking, but her eyes were serious.

“Logical creatures, bees,” he said. *Like we two*, he thought to himself, but he didn’t say it aloud.

The next morning, she showed him her hives. He watched as she carefully, almost reverently, opened each door and pointed to queen and subjects, explaining the functions of each part of the society. It was odd, Holmes thought, how much it suited her. She was at home in this activity that seemed simple on the surface but was vastly intricate and complex just below it. Her perceptive mind took pleasure in the tiny details that made her hives the pinnacle of perfection, and she cared not one whit if any other human being ever knew or cared. The detective admired her precision, but he knew that he could not have borne such serenity. He needed friction to keep his engine running, but she was like a tree that simply needed the earth and the air.

She was different here, freer. Her world was smaller, but she was less constrained within it, less wary and afraid. He no longer heard the brittle bitterness that her voice had contained before. She was once again the Irene Adler who had fooled the greatest detective in the world. No, he thought, she was more. She was older and more complete, and happiness sat well on her.

The three friends walked to the station five days later, amid Dr Watson’s effusive compliments to Miss Adler’s home, which she received with a smile. She truly liked the little doctor, and that fact gratified Holmes. Watson bid The Woman fond farewell at the train, but Holmes was silent, and his eyes were upon her as the locomotive pulled away.

Once again, she was alone on the platform. She was dressed in a brown skirt and blue shirtwaist, a plain outfit, but her face was anything but plain. The eyes that watched him depart were deep and quiet, and the mouth was ironic, as if The Woman would be ready to make a joke at any moment. But her hair—her chestnut hair was bundled loosely on her head, far wilder than she’d ever worn it in her life before the cottage. The day was windy, and pieces of it had escaped and framed her face. She lifted a hand and waved goodbye to the detective, and he waved in return.

Holmes didn't know when, but he knew he would come again.

—

It was two years before the detective again made his way up the hill to the little house. This time he was alone, since Watson had chosen to attend a medical conference in Zurich. As before, he found The Woman in good health and spirits, and pleased, as ever, by her bees. She had purchased more hives, and now the honey they produced had begun to bring her a small income, which amused her greatly.

For three days, they roamed the countryside together, and Holmes told Irene about plants both poisonous and curative. She seemed far from alarmed when he explained the connections of various herbs to cases he'd solved, and the accounts of even the most grisly of murders appeared to interest rather than sicken her. He acted out for her the circumstances one of his more mysterious cases in which a body had been found with no tracks leading to its resting place, using the Sussex grass as his stage, and she clapped delightedly and solved the case herself before he'd told her the solution.

The third night, he found himself discussing his current case, a slow, delicate affair involving a foreign head of state, which had required him to be absent from London for a short time. Irene listened intently before offering her own thoughts, to which Holmes listened objectively. That night he did not sleep, but he considered what The Woman had said and realised that it might help him reach a solution. When he left for London two days later, he asked if he might write to her in future and ask for her opinion of perplexing cases.

So began a correspondence that was sometimes frequent and copious and other times filled with long silences. If Irene helped Holmes and Dr Watson with several cases after that, no one ever knew, and if her opinion occasionally kept them from erring, Watson promised to keep her secret and never write a word of it in his stories.

The detective visited the white cottage twice the next year, both times after the end of a case when dreaded boredom gnawed at his mind. Each time, he found the woman unchanged, except, if possible, that her company was even more restful and her wit more engaging. Each time, too, she succeeded in drawing him out and keeping his mind occupied until a new problem presented itself.

After that, he came to Sussex whenever he was between cases, sometimes with Watson and other times alone. No doubt the villagers wondered about the relationship between the tall man and the lady beekeeper, but they kept their thoughts to themselves because they liked her, and after a long time, they began to like the man as well, in spite of his strange ways.

—

Holmes had noticed Irene's piano during his first visit, and he'd been glad to see that she had not abandoned her music. In subsequent visits, he often brought his violin to Fulworth and spent many evenings playing whatever she or Watson requested. At those times, he wished The Woman would follow suit, but he did not press her, and she did not offer.

Christmas Eve of 1902 was different. Holmes came to the cottage alone, as Watson had chosen to spend the holiday with his family. The doctor had been unwell, and the detective believed he might soon retire from medical practice. He, too, no longer felt young, but when he saw The Woman waiting for him on the platform, those thoughts vanished.

How was it possible, he wondered, that she had stayed the same? The world had changed—Mycroft had told him that international war would not be long in coming, and even London, his friend of so many years, was beginning to fill with motorcars instead of hansom cabs. But Irene Adler looked the same as the girl who had so cheerfully beaten him more than a decade before.

"Good morning, Holmes," she said, taking his arm. He could tell that she was cold in the December chill, so he took off his wool scarf and wrapped it around her neck. She smiled up at him, and they continued up the hill in companionable silence.

They spent the day visiting the bees and talking about cases they had solved, until evening came and Holmes opened the bottle of champagne he had brought to mark the holiday. "To your health, Miss Adler," he said, raising his glass to her.

"And to yours, Holmes." Her spirits were unusually high, and the detective tried for several moments to deduce the cause, but he could not.

Finally, when she had drunk her fill of the golden liquid, Irene went to the piano on the far side of the room and sat down at it, smiling at Holmes. "I would like to sing tonight," she said quietly, her eyes shining.

She lifted the lid of the instrument, and he could see in her face that the act was significant beyond the present. When she began to play, he understood why. The song was becoming old-fashioned then, reminiscent of a vanishing time, but it was the song between The Woman and the detective.

Oh, promise me that someday you and I
Will take our love together to some sky

Where we can be alone and faith renew,
And find the hollows where those flowers grew

He looked into her eyes, and for the first time, she was singing to him.

Epilogue

Baker Street
December 10, 1903

Dear Irene,

These separations between visits grow irksome, and as Watson declares his intention of soon limiting his practice to near-retirement, I shall come down on the 20th by the 8:00, with no intention of ever returning to Baker Street. I think—I hope, at least, that this will be as congenial a prospect to you as it is to me and, of course, to your bees.

Yours,
S.H.

Fulworth
December 15th, 1903

My Dear Holmes,

The bees find your message quite congenial, as do I. I will meet your train, and you will find me prepared to become Mrs Holmes.

Yours,
Irene

Afterword

Several of the individuals mentioned in this story walked the streets of Fort Myers, Florida, at the turn of the 20th century, though they might be surprised to return and find themselves part of a case involving the great detective Sherlock Holmes. Thomas Edison and his second wife Mina spent many happy winters at Seminole Lodge. Marion Edison married Lieutenant Karl Oeser and lived with him in Germany until 1921. John Murphy built a beautiful home that was later bought by Nelson Burroughs and his wife, who became prominent citizens of Fort Myers. Tootie and Ambrose McGregor also made Fort Myers their permanent home, and Tootie was a respected humanitarian and citizen, whose contributions to her city are still enjoyed. Both the Edison and Burroughs homes are historic sites today.

The Detective The Woman and The Winking Tree

Book 2

The Beginning

The wedding of Edward Cox Rayburn and Julia Ellworth Stevenson was, without a doubt, the biggest event in the village of Fulworth since Mr Percival's sheep overran the parish graveyard. I preferred the latter event—I didn't have to perform, and I was allowed to laugh. Nevertheless, I couldn't refuse when Julia's overexcited mother begged me to try to wrest something resembling music from the ancient piano in the front room of the Stevenson abode for the benefit of wedding party and guests.

I watched the crowd as I played and sang after the ceremony. Father Murphy, the vicar, stood next to the banister, eating cake and listening to Mrs Dunaway, who, from her level of animation, appeared to be extolling the virtues of her "little darling Annabel," a child of thirteen who was neither little nor darling in my estimation. The Rayburns, family of the groom, looked slightly uncomfortable in the Stevenson home. They were well aware that their son's legacy as a country farmer was not looked at with boundless favour by Charles Stevenson, a barrister who had only been moved to give his consent by several weeks of his daughter's tears. I knew this as everyone did. Villages have few secrets.

Julia herself clung to the arm of her groom and smiled radiantly, nearly as tall as her new husband. I thought her the much stronger-willed of the two, though Edward's affable grin gave a hint of the kind heart he possessed. He wasn't handsome. His face was a rough-hewn, homemade thing rather than a piece of high art, but I thought I understood his appeal.

My eyes had drifted toward the other side of the room, where, unmarried and on the prowl, Maria Ramsden was talking determinedly at the oblivious butcher, when something occurred that eclipsed even the wedding in the local consciousness. Mrs Phillimore of Oakhill Farm burst through the front door, nearly collapsing with breathlessness, her seven-year-old daughter Eliza by her side. "James is gone," she panted, as soon as she was able.

I had wondered why the Phillimores were not in attendance at the wedding. Edith Phillimore was the sort of person who never missed a chance to socialise. In contrast, her husband was taciturn and *given to moods*, as it was described locally, but seemed entirely devoted to his wife and followed her everywhere. Their absence had struck me as strange, but the events of the day had left me little time to ponder it.

The vicar was the first to react to the dramatic entrance, moving quickly toward the distraught woman and placing a large hand on her shoulder. "Gone, Mrs Phillimore? Gone where?"

"I haven't the slightest idea!" she said, looking as if she might burst into tears. "He only went inside to get his umbrella, and then—he wasn't there any more."

—

"Thanks from Colonel Digby for the return of his dog. An invitation to Lord Lewisham's party. A request to help Simon Bainbridge find out who's been stealing from him. I'll send that to Lestrade. Even he can't be fool enough to miss the secretary's obvious motive." One by one, Sherlock Holmes took up sealed envelopes, deduced their contents, and discarded them without deigning to open them.

Finally, his flatmate handed him the parcel he'd saved for last, a neat, square box covered in brown paper. "The Woman," said Holmes quickly. "High-quality dark rosin, an early birthday gift."

"Not honey this time?" asked Watson.

"Certainly not. The shape is entirely wrong, and there's a stain on the outside of the paper where the rosin dripped." Holmes took the parcel from his friend and carefully untied the strings, revealing a box containing a tin of rosin, just as he'd expected, and, to his annoyance, a jar of honey as well. He looked up and met Watson's eye. The doctor was smiling broadly.

The detective pulled a note from the recesses of the package and, as he had not done with the rest of his post, he opened it and read the contents aloud:

Dear Mr Holmes and Dr Watson,

I hope this parcel finds you well. You will undoubtedly already have discerned that the tin of rosin is meant for Holmes, while the honey belongs to Dr Watson, who, I recall, enjoyed it immensely during your last visit.

Now for my primary purpose, which is to recount a puzzling situation. A week ago, the parish saw the wedding of a farmer's son and barrister's daughter, an occurrence overshadowed by the disappearance of a moderately prosperous farmer, who vanished without a trace as his family was preparing to leave for the ceremony. The local constabulary combed the village and surrounding country, and official reinforcements were sent from London, but none of them uncovered anything that pointed to the man's whereabouts. Knowing me as you do, you will realise that I have not been idle. I enclose a list of my observations and ask for your suggestion as to which line of enquiry I should pursue.

Yours truly,
Irene Adler

Holmes handed the second sheet of paper to his companion, who peered at it in the lamplight. "Read it to me, please," said the detective, leaning back into his chair and putting his fingertips together in front of him. Watson's steady voice filled his brain with images:

1) *The missing man, James Phillimore, is 38 years old, husband to Edith and father to Eliza.*
2) *He has been in possession of his family's farm since his father's death five years ago.*
3) *He is financially solvent but not wealthy.*
4) *Edith claims he did not seem agitated on the day of the wedding.*
5) *His disappearance occurred when he re-entered the family abode, ostensibly to fetch his umbrella, and was not seen again.*

6) *No physical evidence can be found that he left the farmhouse by the back entrance.*
7) *According to the police, the house itself shows no evidence of foul play.*
8) *No motive can be found for Edith herself to have done violence to her husband.*
9) *The umbrella is still in the house.*

"Infuriating woman," muttered Holmes, which caused his flatmate to stare with a certain amount of astonishment. "She means to lure me to Fulworth with these half-truths."

"Half-truths?"

"A great deal of surface fact, but no specifics about her observations of individuals and relationships," explained the detective. "Those she saves for my visit."

"And will you go?"

"Of course I'll go. I have nothing else on at present." Holmes glared at the frankly amused expression on his friend's face. "You will accompany me?"

"I'm afraid not." The doctor looked mildly apologetic. "I have a dinner engagement at the home of Miss Willow in three days' time." The detective did not answer, but his exit from the room was decidedly icy.

Oh, she has turned all the men's heads down in that part.

—A Scandal in Bohemia

Chapter 1: Irene

"You are a most charming woman, Miss Adler, most charming indeed," droned the nasal voice, as thick fingers wrote slowly in a yellowed notebook. "I've no doubt Inspector Graves will be delighted to hear your—observations on the case."

I had no doubt of two things. The first was that Sergeant Chipping would have been instantly less enamored of my charms if he could have heard my thoughts, and the second was that Inspector Graves, if he ever did hear my observations, would receive some version of them that would make me sound like a busybody and a fool. At such moments, I could have cursed my pretty face. Oh, how I missed Holmes, to whom facts were facts, regardless of who delivered them.

Finally, the burly policeman closed his notebook and smiled down at me, and I had the terrible premonition he intended to say something personal. I put on my iciest and most discouraging expression and was apparently successful, because he dropped his gaze and left the front room of my cottage, rather like a chastened puppy. I smiled to myself. I didn't dislike the man particularly, just his utter lack of original thought.

Ten minutes after his exit, I heard an unceremoniously loud knock at my front door. I opened it to find a tall, thin man holding a black bag and a violin case.

"Hello, Holmes," I said, failing to keep my mouth from curving up into a half-smirk.

"Good afternoon, Irene," said his low voice. "I hope you're prepared for a lodger. It's the least you can offer after your transparent effort to lure me here."

"An effort I doubted would be anywhere near so successful," I said, peering behind him. "Is Dr Watson not here?"

"Dr Watson," huffed Holmes, "is courting a Miss Willow."

"Ah," I said, thinking I understood the reason for his short temper. "Come in. Mrs Turner is shopping in the village, but I can put the kettle on."

Holmes came into the house and deposited his things in the larger of the two guest rooms, a ponderously-decorated space with dark curtains and heavy wood furnishings. It suited him quite well, I thought, and he had naturally claimed it for his own during his visits. Dr Watson always took the smaller of the guest rooms, which was lighter and more cheerful.

I made tea and took out a plate of Mrs Turner's excellent biscuits, then joined Holmes in the sitting room, where he was seated comfortably in the one gothic-looking piece of furniture I owned, a plush black wing chair.

"You look very well," he observed, with a scowl that belied his words in a comical fashion.

"As do you," I said, speaking relatively. Holmes always looked uncommonly thin, but his eyes were bright and clear, and he seemed vigorous.

"Of course I'm well," he groused, putting long fingers through his dark hair.

"Well and cross," I murmured, smiling. "But I will speak to you of the case, and perhaps that will cheer you." Holmes looked daggers at me in response to my school marm-ish tone, but I could tell that he was eager to hear the full story of the disappearance of James Phillimore. I leaned back on the flowered sofa and prepared to speak.

"Holmes, do you wish me to begin with the sequence of events, or with my assessment of what is important?" To look at my companion, it seemed as if I was speaking to a person deep in meditation or sleep, but I knew that the detective's closed eyes and relaxed body concealed a mind that was acutely aware of all it heard.

"Your discoveries, if you please," he said. "The order of events I divined from your letter and from the perusal of a local paper, which I purchased upon my arrival."

"Very well," I said, unsurprised. I knew that Holmes was not overly fond of personal conjecture, but I had rightly judged that he knew my mind's capabilities and respected its processes enough to admit space for my observations.

"As I informed you, Phillimore was last seen when his family was preparing to attend a wedding, the nuptials of Julia Stevenson and Edward Rayburn, which is where I'll begin. I had known for some time that the Stevensons did not consider Edward a suitable son-in-law, since Charles Stevenson is a barrister and had more elevated hopes for his daughter. For their part, the Rayburns were equally proud of their agricultural heritage, but they liked Julia, who did not share her family's disdain. If Charles had gotten his way, the wedding would never have taken place, but I understand from village gossip that Julia wore him down with ceaseless tears and entreaties."

I leaned forward, resting my elbows on my knees, and stared intently at Holmes, though he did not acknowledge my increased intensity in any outward way. "My acquaintance with Julia," I continued, "is not a close one, but from what I have observed of her character, I believe her desperation was played as a calculated move to extract her father's blessing, rather than out of any genuine despair."

"You believe she did not love her fiancé?"

"Not so," I answered, "but I do not believe her to be the kind of woman to ever succumb to that extent of hysteria."

"Love has done stranger things to the human mind," Holmes's deep voice rejoined, "but let us move away from the uncharted territory of psychological supposition."

"Very well," I said. "I simply wished to begin by briefly sketching the characters who feature prominently in the drama."

"Continue," said Holmes, stretching out his long legs in front of him.

"The groom, Edward Rayburn, I have had occasion to meet a few times, since I often accompany Mrs Turner to purchase milk and eggs from his family's produce. He is well situated on a vast farm a few miles outside the village. I understand him to be more than able to support a wife and family. The Stevenson objection is generally known to concern his lack of elegance and social prominence, as opposed to a financial deficiency." I was silent for a moment as I bit into a chocolate biscuit and allowed the combination of sweetness and bitterness to delight my tongue.

"Almost as soon as I learned of Phillimore's disappearance, I began looking for connections between him and the families involved in the wedding, in case his absence should have to do with the particular event for which his family was bound. The associations are certainly ample, but they do not strike me as unusual. The Rayburns bought a horse from the Phillimores two months ago, and Charles Stevenson has given the Phillimore family legal advice once or twice over the past several years. Fulworth is not large, as you know, and the majority of its residents and those from the surrounding farms are connected in similar ways to one another."

"Another of my primary objectives, once it became clear that no man or corpse would be recovered easily, was to gain understanding of the missing farmer's family. Edith, his wife, is well liked in the village for her gregariousness, but her husband is known to be her opposite in temperament. I have seen him at many social events, standing near a door or side of a room, looking completely discontented until his eyes light on his wife, whom he appears to adore. Their only child, Elizabeth, is seven years old and seems uncommonly intelligent, from what I have observed."

Just then, the door opened, admitting Mrs Turner, tall and imposing in her black dress and black hat. "Good afternoon, Mr Holmes," she said, looking him up and down with a sharp eye. "You've not had anything decent to eat in weeks, I'll wager." Her disdain for Mrs Hudson's cooking was legendary, though I could not ascertain that she had ever encountered it personally. "I see you've produced tea, Miss Adler," she continued. *Produced* was the word she invariably used instead of *made* in these cases, since she believed me incapable of concocting a truly legitimate tea.

"Yes," I said, smiling. Her severity had the perverse effect of amusing me and making me adore her, a fact that I had been concerned might dismay her at the beginning of my time at the cottage. I had quickly realised, however, that for all her crossness, she enjoyed my affection.

"I hope you've brought the ingredients for one of your excellent pork pies," said Holmes, earning the ghost of a smile at the corners of the housekeeper's mouth. I laughed to myself. He knew very well that she always cooked pork pies on Monday evening. Dr Watson was particularly fond of them, and I found myself hoping that Miss Willow, whoever she might be, would accommodate him in that and other ways. I hated to think of such a kind man having any advantage taken of him.

Mrs Turner disappeared into the kitchen, a domain I was not allowed to enter when she chose to occupy it. I had tried to alter this inexorable rule a few times to offer help, but the frigid stare that greeted me had caused my resolve to evaporate. I didn't mind the arrangement. Truth be told, I had never been fond of domestic work. Some of the farm wives undoubtedly thought my retention of a housekeeper absurdly frivolous, since many households in the Fulworth area could afford little household help, even those with establishments much larger than mine.

I relaxed into the sofa cushions and heard the words "go on" issue forth from the environs of Holmes's chair, as if nothing had interrupted my story.

"I, of course, looked to the others in Phillimore's household as well. He has the managing of a moderately-sized farm that has been in his family for several generations. He inherited it upon his father's death and is assisted by a man named Peter Warren, with whom he has a complicated association."

Holmes opened his eyes briefly. "Explain."

"I have been told that until his death ten years ago, Warren's father had more or less the same position with Phillimore's father that the son currently occupies. As a result, James and Peter grew up together, attended school together in the village, and had the run of the farm. They were friends."

"David and Jonathan," murmured Holmes.

"More like Jacob and Esau," I retorted. "According to village gossip, the break in the friendship happened five years ago, when Phillimore's father died. The claim is that Warren had felt himself a part of the family for so long, especially since his own father's passing, that he had expected to be treated differently than a hired man, more as a sort of partner. Phillimore apparently did not agree and took the full birthright for himself, while offering a continued position to his friend."

"I have not spoken to Warren about his decision to stay at the farm, but the general consensus is that he couldn't bear to leave a place with so many ties and old memories. Everyone in the village knows about the disagreement, and sentiment is extremely divided.

The two men rarely speak about anything other than the management of the property, though they are constantly in close proximity."

"Would Warren have anything to gain by Phillimore's death?"

"That I do not know. It seems unlikely, but I haven't yet been able to extract information about a will from anyone, since no body is in evidence."

"It's enough to begin with," said Holmes.

—

That evening, we dined on Mrs Turner's succulent pork pies, and I surmised from Holmes's healthy appetite that his mind was not yet entirely consumed by the case. Indeed not, for he talked of Paganini, and I happily joined in, enjoying the rare treat of musical discourse. After the conclusion of the meal, Holmes freed his violin from its encasing prison, caressing the smooth contours in the wood like an enchanted lover before playing a piece I had never heard before that he called *Meditation*, from a new opera by Massenet. It was exquisite.

I enjoyed watching Holmes play, as the music kidnapped the mind of the detective and made it her own. It wasn't as if he became someone else—to say so would be ridiculously limiting. No, it was as if all of the dreamy abstraction and mystery that lived behind his eyes became suddenly and starkly and beautifully evident on his face and through his fingers. Mrs Turner cried. I did not, but I understood. Once the piece was complete, Holmes played a cheerful quartet of popular beer hall dance melodies, humorously endowing them with all the gravity of a funeral dirge. Mrs Turner and I both laughed without concern for dignity, and I thought Holmes was pleased, though he did not break his comically serious character.

The housekeeper went to bed as soon as Holmes had finished, but I sat up with him and watched as his eyes drifted toward my piano in the corner. I thought perhaps he wished me to play, but I did not volunteer to do so. We sat silently for a very long time, neither of us seeking sleep or wishing to disturb the tranquil atmosphere.

“Holmes,” I said after a while, “You have a performer’s flair for the dramatic when you choose the juxtaposition of your violin performances. You had us crying and laughing at will.”

“Yes,” he said, sounding less cross than he had since his arrival, “Watson has often commented that I might have been an actor.”

“There’s more to it than that,” I answered, looking him full in the face. “An actor parrots the lines of the playwright. When you perform, Holmes, you choose your own lines. Given your success, I’m very glad you’re not a confidence man by trade.”

Holmes laughed, suddenly and drily. “You are hardly less skilled in the art of manipulation. You have already succeeded in luring me here and elevating my mood. Good night, Miss Adler.”

I watched the tall form leave the room and smiled to myself. Any boredom my village routine might have engendered was no longer a concern. Sherlock Holmes’s presence was anything but monotonous, especially when he had a case.

Safely tucked into my own bed, underneath a quilt that had been given to me by Miss Rose from the village after I had helped her end an unfortunate liaison with a carpenter, I realised that I was more glad than sorry that Holmes had chosen to view my letter as a summons. I had not expected him, knowing that if he had an engrossing case in London, he would not be likely to put it aside for a village concern; however, I was not entirely surprised, either. No one can command Holmes when he is set against something, but he’s equally resolute when he’s interested in a problem. I had chosen my written words carefully, revealing enough to tantalise but also concealing much. I had attempted to manipulate him, purely and simply. He had seen through me, of course, but that had not stopped him from taking the bait. I had offered him a pretty problem, and he had thanked me by consenting to play my game, at least for the moment. I fell asleep contented.

—

The morning dawned bright, as mornings tend to do in Sussex and elsewhere. I stared at the white ceiling of my bedroom for a moment before remembering my guest in the spare room. I was glad

Holmes had come, both for the sake of the investigation and for my own sake. I was happy in Fulworth, ridiculously so, but occasionally I craved repartee with someone whose experience extended beyond the Downs, and the village afforded few such individuals. I had long since resigned myself to the fact that a certain sort of local man invariably underestimated me because of my gender, and plenty of women did as well. This could, at times, be a decided advantage if I found myself needing to extract information or achieve particular outcomes, but I preferred meeting people on an equal footing, without subterfuge if it could be avoided. Living near the coast was glorious, but sometimes I required more than invigorating scenery.

Holmes's presence was welcome, for he treated me as his experiences with me warranted. Sometimes a pretty face—not, I admit, usually a cause for complaint—could be troublesomely distracting to others. Holmes didn't even seem to see it. No, that's not quite right. He observed my face and catalogued it as part of me, the way he assimilated Dr Watson's moustache or Mrs Hudson's jet black hair. He observed, but what he observed did not prejudice him. These thoughts accompanied me as I readied myself for the day, feeling a certain air of excitement as I completed my toilette and joined Holmes at the breakfast table.

"Good morning," he said, taking a sip of coffee but not touching the vast spread Mrs Turner had provided. The long fingers of his right hand held the village's attempt at a newspaper. It was a poorly-written thing, to be sure, but certainly revelatory of local viewpoints. I often laughed at its amateurish writing style, but as a mirror reflecting popular opinion, it was without local equal.

I created what I considered stunningly beautiful artwork on my plate, consisting of liberal quantities of toast, bacon, sausage, and eggs before deigning to reply to my companion with more than a nod.

"The paper's still full of the 'Phillimore Tragedy,' as they're calling it," I observed. "It's been nearly two weeks, and without evidence of the man, people are naturally thinking of foul play."

"No one supposes him to have fled?" Holmes raised one eyebrow slightly.

"It's a hard theory to find any motive for," I admitted, "even for me. Of course, he might have been in some sort of trouble no one knew about. That seems to be the most likely cause, though I'd have thought the police might have come up with something by now if it was at all plausible. He was an enigmatic man, but one who displayed thorough devotion to his family and his duty."

Holmes nodded. "I don't share your hopeful view of the official police's capabilities, but I don't discredit your observations or conclusions. Still, such outward correctness does not always tend where it seems."

"True," I agreed. "At first, the police were enthusiastic about the idea of an escape plot, but no way was discovered for how it might have been done, and no evidence was found that he used a train or any other transportation. Edith, too, insists that he could not have fled in front of her eyes."

"And if she's lying?"

"Then she's exceptionally skilled."

"I would like to meet her," said Holmes, swirling the last dregs of coffee in the bottom of his cup as Mrs Turner glided up behind him to refill it.

"If you intend to view the scene of the disappearance, you will hardly be able to escape her," I replied, looking down and giving my full attention to my breakfast.

As he spoke the door opened and a young lady entered the room.

—The Adventure of the Copper Beeches

Chapter 2: Holmes

The detective finished his coffee in silence as his brain wove together the disparate threads of the Phillimore case into some semblance of a coherent whole. It was by no means a complete whole as of yet, but he sought something that would suggest lines of enquiry.

He was unconvinced that Phillimore was deceased. In fact, he would have been highly unsurprised to learn that the man was in London, glad to have left duty and family behind. Plenty of other men had done the same. He intended, if he was unable to ascertain the man's location himself, to enlist his brother's help. The city was a vast beehive, filled with places to hide and disappear, but Mycroft Holmes had ways of finding out people's whereabouts.

At the same time, he could not fail to acknowledge the puzzle of the case—the seemingly impossible way it had all been done. Years of dissecting crimes and criminals had taught him that crime of any sort was a nearly impossible thing to conceal in a village as small as Fulworth. Someone was sure to know something, and the police, however incompetent, invariably came up with some sort of theory. The fact that no one whatsoever had come forward and that the police had come up with nothing certainly suggested a case that had features of interest beyond the ordinary. Someone wasn't talking, someone who knew facts that were relevant to the case.

Holmes's last sip was interrupted by a nearly-imperceptible tapping on the cottage door. Neither of the two ladies heard it, for Mrs Turner was loudly washing dishes, and Irene had gone to her beehives. The detective waited a long moment and went to the door himself, a highly unusual practise, but he wanted to see the person who had chosen to announce his or her arrival in such a timid sort of way.

He opened to door to nothing—until his eyes traveled down to take in the small body of a little girl. She was of average height for a seven-year-old, with pin-straight brown hair and large grey eyes, which widened upon seeing such a large and imposing stranger. Any moment, she would bolt.

"Hello, Love, where's Mummy?" said a voice behind the child, and The Woman materialised from the direction of the hives, her chestnut hair askew and a smile on her face. She took the child's hand.

"Cottonwood's," answered the voice of the tiny person, naming a shop in the village.

"This is Mr Holmes, Eliza. He's come to visit." Irene indicated the detective with a tilt of her head.

"Hello, Mr Holmes," said the little girl seriously, taking in the stranger's dark clothing and sharp features. Holmes smiled a smile he usually reserved for the youngest members of the Baker Street Irregulars, the children he employed to prowl the London streets in search of helpful information. He was aware of his propensity to appear forbidding, a quality for which he had often been grateful, but it was one which was not universally advantageous.

"Hello, Eliza," he answered, bowing politely and extending his hand, as he would have done in the presence of royalty. He caught Irene's smile in his peripheral vision.

"You're very pointy," said the child.

"A solid observation," answered Holmes, nodding respectfully. "You have the makings of a detective."

"And you have the makings of someone far sillier than I had supposed," said Irene, grinning as she ushered the girl inside and passed her to Mrs Turner, who smiled indulgently. He followed the women inside, wondering what information he might be able to gain from the missing man's daughter.

"I've already questioned her," said Irene in a low voice at his elbow, as if she had read his mind. "She's clever, but she didn't see anything."

"Perhaps," answered the detective, "but I would still like to speak with her."

"I'm afraid you'll have to anyway. She was intrigued by you—and your angles." The Woman smirked saucily.

"I have angles enough," Holmes mused, taking his usual seat in the wing chair.

Eliza emerged from the kitchen within ten minutes, wearing traces of berry pie on her face. She stopped in the doorway when she saw Holmes and stared at him intently. The detective stared back with no less frankness. "Are you Miss Adler's friend?" asked the little girl after a long while.

"Yes," said Holmes with a wry smile. "Miss Adler and I have known each other for a long time."

"Do you live in London?"

"Yes, on a street called Baker."

"Is it very noisy?"

Holmes leaned forward slightly with his elbows on his knees and peered at Eliza from under his dark brows. "In the daytime, the air is filled with the noise of hansom cabs passing by and people selling flowers and fruit and sweets of all kinds. In the night, the darkness is broken by the sounds of horses' hooves and people yelling from too far away to understand what they say." By the time he had reached the end of this dramatically-delivered speech, he had lowered his voice to a near-whisper, and the little girl's eyes were wide open with amazement. He sat back in his chair, satisfied that he had effectively silenced her for the time being.

"Is my Papa there?" The sound of Eliza's voice disrupted the detective's complacency, and at the conclusion of her question, he looked at her with no small amount of astonishment.

"Go let Mrs Turner wash your face, and then we'll talk about it," Irene put in, and Holmes nodded to her gratefully as the little girl left the room. Once Eliza was gone, The Woman left her seat on the sofa and perched on the arm of Holmes's chair. She spoke quickly in a near-whisper. "Right after the disappearance, her mother told her that her father had gone to London and would return. Unfortunately, one of the stupider policemen assigned to the case assumed she was too young to understand and said something that made her think he was never coming back. Her mother told her it was a lie, but she's been asking about it incessantly ever since."

Holmes answered in a rapid whisper, "Normally I would advocate telling the unvarnished truth, but since the object of the obfuscation is a seven-year-old child, I can't fault the mother's reasoning. She may yet have something useful to add, though. She's certainly clever enough to have observed something significant."

"Just don't frighten her," Irene hissed into his ear before bolting back to the sofa as the child reappeared.

Holmes held out a hand to the little girl, and she came and stood in front of his chair. He took her tiny right hand in both of his and addressed her honestly. "I haven't seen your Papa, but I will work very hard to find him."

"Mr Holmes is good at finding things," said Irene.

Suddenly, the little girl became exceedingly animated. "Can you find Charles?"

"If I am to find him, you must tell me who he is," Holmes answered, as seriously as before. He stole a glance at The Woman, who simply nodded and remained silent.

"Charles," said Eliza, "is a rabbit." She looked as if anyone who was unaware of this obvious fact must be an imbecile of the highest order.

"Stuffed rabbit," Irene contributed.

Holmes allowed himself a moment to let the full absurdity of the situation pass through his consciousness, but he did not mind the humorous turn of events. The child's trust might end up proving useful, and he knew that direct interrogation was far from desirable where young children were concerned. He would allow things to unfold naturally.

Taking his small, black notebook from his pocket, Holmes began. "When did you last see Charles?"

"Last week, in Wonderland," Eliza promptly answered, exactly, Holmes thought, as if she had said "Brompton."

"How did he arrive in Wonderland?" Holmes asked, infusing all the patience he could muster into his tone. He glanced over at Irene, who appeared surprised and gratified. If The Woman thought he was unequal to managing the little girl, he would certainly prove her wrong. Small children were nothing to Scotland Yard, and sometimes, there wasn't a great deal of difference between Inspector Lestrade and a seven-year-old child.

"From the Winking Tree," said the child. "We sat down and closed our eyes and went to Wonderland, just like Papa said."

"Then what happened?" asked Holmes.

"No more Charles," said the child, with an expression of utmost dramatic woe.

Without further comment, Holmes closed his notebook and rose, taking the child's hand in his once again. "Take me to the Winking Tree."

The little girl started toward the door in an instant, pulling Holmes as if he were a dog on a leash. Irene followed, and the detective felt her amusement as if it were a living thing.

—

The Winking Tree, Holmes discovered, was in the very middle of the village, on a green in front of the local parish church. Irene did not follow him and his tiny captor all the way, instead taking a lane toward Cottonwood's to inform Edith Phillimore of her determined daughter's whereabouts. As a result, the detective found himself in the dubious position of being alone with an unfamiliar female. Age, he thought, was largely immaterial when it came to the fairer sex. A woman was a woman, as his association with Irene constantly reminded him.

As the two stepped onto the grass in front of the large beech tree, Holmes stopped the little girl with a hand on her shoulder. "Point to where you were when you went to Wonderland," he said. The child's tiny finger indicated a spot under the tree, where the grass was flattened, obviously from her seated form.

"Charles was sitting there." She pointed to a low-hanging branch.

Holmes took out his magnifying glass and scanned the ground. He knew from a conversation he had overheard on the train that the weather had been uncharacteristically dry for several days, and very little moisture had muddied the green or destroyed the imprints of shoes in the soft earth. He made out the child's prints and another set that were the size and shape of a woman's slipper. The mother's, most likely. He saw other footprints, but none of them approached the trunk of the tree. The child did not speak at all while he completed this examination, a fact that did not occur to him until he straightened back up to his full height and remembered her presence. She followed him to the base of the tree and continued to watch silently as he shifted branches and looked for any sign of the missing toy.

After a few moments of careful observation, a flash of white caught Holmes's eye. Taking a set of tiny metal forceps from his pocket, he captured the strands of white from a twisted branch. The little girl's face lit up. "That's from Charles." The inference was a logical one, but not one the detective would have expected a child to make so readily.

Holmes dropped the threads into a bag and looked for more, though he did not find any. He studied the tree and the ground for a few moments more before taking Eliza's hand and turning back the way they had come. They found Irene at the edge of the green, joined by a short, plain woman in grey. Eliza broke free of the detective's grasp and ran to her mother, whose smile transformed her face into something nearly pretty.

A quick study of Edith Phillimore revealed to Holmes that she was genuinely worried about her missing husband, a fact he had desired to ascertain for certain before he made further judgements. Her eyes were rimmed with darkness in her pale face, and her dress showed signs of a lack of care that belied the good quality of the fabric, a lack of care she had not displayed when clothing her child. Even as she embraced Eliza, her gaze scanned the village, as if she thought she might yet see some clue she had missed. After a moment's observation, the detective was willing to concede that Edith's concern over James was natural and unaffected. He caught Irene's eye, and her small look of triumph seemed to indicate that she understood his thoughts.

The Woman introduced her friends to one another, and Edith smiled tensely. "Mr Holmes, thank you for your kindness to my daughter."

"It was no trouble," answered the detective. He leaned down to the little girl. "Miss Eliza, I'm sorry I cannot produce Charles immediately, but I hope to be able to do so very soon." Eliza nodded and stared at him with her large eyes.

"May we come to your house?" Irene asked, ending the awkward silence that followed. "Mr Holmes would like to see it."

Edith nodded. "I doubt that you will find anything the police missed." Her voice was terse, almost bitter.

"Perhaps," said Holmes, "but I have been known to do so in the past." He thought he heard the slightest hint of a snort come from The Woman, but he said nothing else as he followed the women and child away from the green.

—

Holmes's first glimpse of Oakhill Farmhouse was unsurprising. The house was a square, two-storey structure with a chimney and two rows of front windows. It was clearly the home of a moderately prosperous family, neither mean nor opulent.

He alighted from the Phillimores' wagon and offered his assistance to Eliza, who giggled as he swung her to the ground. In the meantime, Irene and Edith alighted with the help of a large, grey-bearded man and joined the detective and the little girl in front of the house while the man led the horse away toward the nearby barn.

"That's Styles," said Edith. "He's been here forever."

"Mrs Phillimore," the detective began, "would you mind taking me through the particulars of the day your husband disappeared?"

"Yes, of course," she answered. "Eliza, show Miss Adler how big the chickens are getting." Irene understood this to be her cue and submitted to being dragged away by the little girl, a fate Holmes knew she relished, judging by the sanguine expression on her beautiful face.

"It's probably silly of me, Mr Holmes," Edith continued, "but I don't like to speak of it before her. Not until—not until we know something for certain." Holmes didn't answer, but he considered how typical it was of parents to underestimate the understanding of children. He would have bet money on the fact that Eliza knew far more than her mother realised.

"Miss Adler has probably told you that the whole village was invited to the Stevenson wedding. I dressed Eliza in the morning while my husband did chores with the men, and he finally readied himself with only moments to spare. Styles brought the carriage around for us, but James said it looked like it might rain and that we'd better have an umbrella with us, so he went back inside. That was all, and then he wasn't there."

"Was there no one in the house at the time that your husband returned to it?"

"No, I had given the maid the day off. She was a friend of the bridal household and wanted to help with preparations. The cook left for the wedding just before we did."

"Where exactly was the carriage brought?"

"The same place where we left the wagon just now."

"How long was it before you became alarmed?"

"Well, my husband keeps his umbrella in a large carved vase by the door, so I expected him to emerge within a few seconds. When he didn't, I thought it was strange, but I waited until nearly ten minutes had elapsed. At that point, I was more irritated than worried. I couldn't imagine what was keeping him. I told Eliza to stay in the carriage, and I walked back into the house, but James wasn't there."

"I'd like you to retrace your steps, please, as nearly as you can remember them."

"I remember them well," she said. "I've had to repeat them to the police many times."

"I am reasonably convinced that this time will produce better results."

She half smiled, but her voice was brittle. "It was very kind of you to come here, Mr Holmes. I'm sure you have far more important things to do than look for one missing farmer."

"Not in the least," answered the detective. "I came because the case interested me, and I will not leave it unsolved." Edith looked unconvinced as she led him into the house.

The first thing that caught Holmes's eye was a large wooden receptacle with two umbrellas sticking out of it. "His umbrella was never touched," said Edith.

"Interesting," said Holmes. He did not utter them aloud, but his brain immediately catalogued the available options: either Phillimore had never intended to fetch the umbrella at all, or whatever had happened to him had occurred before he had a chance to pick it up. The third option, that Phillimore or someone else had picked it up and then replaced it, he considered possible but unlikely.

Edith led him through to a parlour with a piano, a sofa, and a few hard-looking chairs. There were no signs of a struggle, but Holmes wished devoutly that he had been on hand more quickly, before the police had obliterated most of the potential evidence. Still, even the regular force was usually competent enough to see the signs of a fight, and the woman of the house seemed too intelligent to have missed them herself.

"May I see the upstairs, please?" he asked, after an extensive perusal of the room. "You may leave me to my own devices." Holmes uttered the phrase in a tone that left no doubt of his desire to be left alone to complete his observations. Edith nodded once and left the room. The two weeks since her husband's disappearance had apparently acclimated her to the invasion of her home by unfamiliar and unwanted guests, though the set of her shoulders indicated that she still felt slight displeasure at the intrusion.

Holmes made his way up the modest staircase, noting the presence of obligatory portraits of stern-looking relatives, and found himself in a long hallway with rooms on either side. He began at one end, entering a room that obviously belonged to a servant. Its furnishings were neat but meagre, and no personal objects were in sight other than a small, cheap mirror with a cracked silver handle. He quickly searched the small, rough-hewn wardrobe before leaving the room and proceeding down the hall.

Two other similar rooms completed the accommodations of the live-in staff, and Holmes determined that, depending on the conclusions of his findings in the house, he might also contrive ways to enter the homes of the farm hands and their wives to see if their occupants might be inclined to tell tales of what they knew.

The detective set his steps toward the family rooms, ready to uncover any detail the police had missed. Nearly two weeks was a long time—for a wife to hide whatever she did not wish to be seen, for the careless tread of policemen to obscure delicate clues, or for a resourceful criminal to destroy evidence. But Holmes knew himself, and he was equal to the task.

Detection is, or ought to be, an exact science and should be treated in the same cold and unemotional manner.

—The Sign of Four

Chapter 3: Irene

The chickens looked exactly as they had every time I had submitted to having them shown to me. More than anything, my acquaintance with Eliza Phillimore had reminded me of the astonishing, stubborn love of repetition that exists in childhood, until adulthood robs us of the wonder of sameness.

I knelt down obediently beside the little girl and watched as the largest chicken, which was named Mrs Merriwether after the family's rotund cook, pecked mercilessly at the tiny rooster, who was known as Rogers. I watched the child, too, wondering how much she knew or could possibly suspect about her father's disappearance. Her mother never spoke of it to her, but I wondered if that was the best course of action, given that he might never return.

Presently, Eliza's seven-year-old mind tired of chickens, and she dragged me toward the large, weather-beaten barn, which was as grey as her eyes. "Miss Adler," she said, pulling my hand as if it were a toy, "is Mr Holmes nice?"

A host of amusing thoughts crowded into my mind, but I answered honestly, "Mr Holmes is interesting, and that's even better." I bent down to adjust my shoe and hide the laugh that I couldn't keep from coming. Eliza stopped, too, and fingered a blade of green grass as if it were the most exquisite lace.

I had only been inside the barn once, a year before, when Eliza had insisted on showing me a newly-born foal, but it had not changed since I had seen it. The same smell of manure assaulted my nose, and the same men, busily at work, stopped just long enough to nod in my direction. I felt the crunch of hay under my feet and heard the sounds of horses in the yard beyond. My eyes were fascinated by a building that was immense, but at the same time filled with all manner of nooks and crannies and tiny spaces. I wondered how many of them had been the recipients of Eliza's tiny body and what she might have seen and heard while resident in them.

I noticed with interest that Peter Warren, known locally for his bitter conflict with Phillimore, was in one corner of the barn—off to himself, polishing a leather instrument that I did not recognise. Holmes would want to speak to him; of that I was sure. For myself, I couldn't help thinking that the man's severe, spare appearance did not indicate a charitable temperament, though that did not necessarily indicate murderous intent.

Eliza didn't utter a word until she had brought me through the barn and into the smaller carriage house, which was connected by a side door and opened onto the yard. It was dark and quiet, and once we had passed into it, we found ourselves alone. "This is Eliza's place," said my companion, pointing to a tiny, claustrophobic corner behind the family's one ancient carriage. It held a small, tattered blanket spread out over straw, a tin of biscuits, a yellowed lace shawl, and a picture book. Eliza sat down, and I crouched beside her, wondering why she had chosen to let me into her tiny world. She arranged a straw throne for me, and I stretched out my legs and leaned against the structure's ancient back wall, wondering what discoveries Holmes might be making inside the house.

"Charles!"

In the dark, serene atmosphere of the carriage house, the child's shocked screech nearly made me let out an answering scream, but I recovered myself and looked over to find her clutching a grimy, stuffed white rabbit to her chest.

"Where did you find him?" I asked, slightly perplexed. I knew Holmes would have found it unforgiveable, but I had allowed myself to drift off and miss the moment of discovery.

"He was under here," she said, lifting up the edge of her tiny blanket.

"Ah, you must have forgotten and left him here," I said, in the exact knowing way that had irritated me when adults had used it during my own childhood.

"No!" she said, shaking her head vehemently. "I looked." I stared at her a moment, trying to evaluate the truth of what she was saying. If she were right, then things had certainly taken a peculiar turn. I resolved to let Holmes decide.

"Let's go back to the house and show Mummy," I said brightly, hoping to lure the child without a fight. In her usual fashion, she took my hand wordlessly and began to pull me back toward the house, clasping the rabbit in her other hand. I considered that if the toy were actual evidence, then Holmes would probably fault the fact that I had not seized it, but I didn't relish trying to pry the prodigal rabbit from Eliza's eager clutches.

The quick trot to the house gave me enough time to consider the implications of a disappearing stuffed rabbit. I tried to think like Holmes. How small did a coincidence have to be before it was allowable? Was a child's mysteriously-appearing toy insignificant enough to be unrelated to the disappearance of her father? I did not have Holmes's knack for weaving together the seemingly unrelated strains of a problem. I could understand events as they occurred, but I could not always perceive their interconnectedness.

Eliza and I found her mother in the farmhouse kitchen, joining the cook in the preparation of lunch. She looked up in surprise as we entered, though her face was not unpleasant. I would not have inserted myself unceremoniously into the kitchen of every home in Fulworth, but the Phillimores had never kept a formal household.

"Mummy, I've found Charles!" burst immediately from Eliza's throat, sparing me from having to explain the situation. In excited tones, she explained the circumstances of the rabbit's sudden reappearance, all the while cuddling it in irrepressible joy. I watched Edith carefully, thinking Holmes would want me to catalogue her reaction as closely as I could.

She seemed genuinely surprised, and after a moment, she looked up and met my gaze solidly. "I can attest that she looked there before. We searched it together right after she lost him." I nodded, wondering what Holmes would make of it.

I didn't have long to ponder the question, because the detective soon appeared with a wide-eyed young housemaid in tow. "The tone of voices I heard across the house indicates that something of import has occurred," he said mildly, smiling benignly but in a way that suggested to me his annoyance at having missed something.

"Charles has reappeared," I intoned softly. Holmes's eyes flashed triumph for a split second before he resumed his air of harmless pleasantry.

"May I see Charles, please?" he asked, bending down to Eliza's level. I thought the child might be reluctant to give up her recently-regained treasure, but her nascent fondness for my angular friend won out, and she handed the rabbit to him readily. Her mother was just behind her, and I almost thought I saw her flinch, but the impression made no sense to me at the time, so I pushed it aside.

—

Holmes and I returned to my cottage in silence. I knew him well enough to tell that he was deep in thought, and I had no desire to awaken his irritation by disturbing him, though I dearly desired to know what he had made of the recent events.

As we approached the front door, he seemed to remember my existence and looked down at me with a smile—his genuine one, not the falsely benign one of the morning. "I didn't think things would move so quickly," he mused contentedly, as if he were commenting on the weather. I resisted the urge to pinch him.

"What things do you mean?"

"I didn't suppose the rabbit would be returned so quickly," he said. "Certainly not when we were present. Mrs Phillimore nearly turned green when I touched the thing. I assume you observed her reaction."

"I did," I said coolly, trying not to sound as if I had almost discarded the observation as irrelevant. "I didn't understand it, though," I added unashamedly.

"No," said Holmes, "and I believe she thought me equally befuddled, but I was far from it."

"Of course," I rejoined archly. "The great Sherlock Holmes is never befuddled by anything."

"Very few things," he answered in dead earnest, though I caught a faint twinkle in his bright eyes.

"I see that you're brimful of curiosity," he continued. "I'm no less curious about your experiences with the child, but I assume you'll require some sort of edible nourishment before you'll be able to manage complicated conversation."

"Indeed," I answered, laughing to myself. I wanted to think of some withering reply, but in truth, I was starving, and my brain didn't wish to cooperate. Thankfully, as we entered the house, it was immediately apparent that Mrs Turner had seen us coming up the hill, for she was setting out a meal of boiled eggs and cold meat.

Holmes did not join me at the table, electing instead to make his way to his chair in the sitting room. Mrs Turner's annoyance at this amused me, since she was certainly well acquainted with my companion's tendencies, but I said nothing. I was too busy eating eggs and regaining a sense of mastery over the world.

Once I'd had my fill of luncheon, I joined Holmes, who was reading over pages in his small notebook. "You look better," he said without looking up.

"You look attentive," I answered.

"And therein lies one of the chief differences between you and Watson," Holmes intoned, his gaze still on the page before him. "When he points out the obvious, he simply means to draw attention to it. When you point it out, you mean something else entirely."

"Exactly," I answered, "and what I mean to say now is that I'm going to burst if you continue to be cryptic and uncommunicative."

"Very well," said the detective, shutting his book and sitting back in the wing chair like a king on his throne, with his fingertips pressed together in their usual position. "I expect you observed that the ground floor of the home bears no evidence of a physical struggle. I can add that the upstairs is similarly without such signs. Of course, Edith Phillimore would have had ample time to try to obscure them if she'd wished, but doing so with absolute completeness is nearly impossible for accomplished criminals, let alone amateurs." (I sniggered at the way he said "amateurs," as if crime were analogous to sport.)

"No," he continued, "I became convinced fairly quickly that Phillimore's disappearance had been, if not willing, at least effected through means that did not incite a struggle."

"A chemical anesthetic would have had to be administered and then Phillimore's inert body would have had to be dragged out of the house, I suppose," I said, thinking aloud.

"Just so," said Holmes, "and there was no evidence of that either, on top of the fact that the process would have required the kidnapper coming up to the farmhouse, which would have alerted Mrs Phillimore and anyone else who was around the property at the time."

"It looks bad for Edith, then," I mumbled.

"Yes," said Holmes, "though consideration of her potential involvement presents its own set of problems. If she killed Phillimore in the house, for instance, then she certainly did it in the least messy and most efficient way possible and without leaving any evidence whatsoever, a practically impossible feat, on top of which is the question of what she did with the body."

"Could she have lured him outside and done it?"

"Possibly, but the property was far from deserted when she departed for the wedding. I intend to question the man Styles to corroborate her timeline of events, but if she was honest about how quickly everything took place, then the realm of possibility narrows."

"He will corroborate it," I said, glad that I had something to add. "One of the reasons Edith wasn't badgered even more by the police was because of his statement. He said that he brought the carriage, saw husband and then wife re-enter the house, and then finally saw Edith drive away very quickly. He wondered where Phillimore was, but said he didn't think too much of it because Edith often drove herself and the child, and everyone in the village knows that James Phillimore has his moods."

"It's an attractive problem," said Holmes, sounding far from displeased. "Usually, people disappear from public places or open spaces. A house leaves such little room for error, either on the part of the perpetrator of the disappearance or the investigator."

"Aren't you going to ask how I learned the man's story?" I asked.

"Not at all," said Holmes. "I already know. The two possibilities are that you asked him yourself, or you found out from the police. If the former, you couldn't be sure that he had told you exactly what he told them. The latter, then. You asked Sergeant Chipping, and he, being enchanted by your face in the usual way, told you everything you wanted to know."

"How did you deduce that?" I asked, slightly impressed, though not overmuch shocked, knowing Holmes as I did.

"The day I arrived, I saw a sheet of paper in the bin in your cottage. It was the size and shape of the usual contents of a police notebook. It had your name at the top and the beginning of a line of text, and then the writer's pen obviously ran out, at which time he scratched over the paper to try to force ink to flow but was unsuccessful, leading to the discarding of the page. From that I deduced that a policeman had been in your house and taken some kind of statement from you. I could hardly believe you had given information without taking plenty in return, even if the man was unaware of it."

"And Chipping? How did you know it was him?"

"The newspaper mentioned an Inspector Graves and a Sergeant Chipping as being connected to the investigation. The inspector would be unlikely to take time to conduct the interview himself, no matter how much your observations might have actually warranted his attention. He would have considered it beneath his notice and sent one of his subordinates instead. It was simply a matter of probability."

I was reminded of the many times that Dr Watson, after hearing his flatmate's chain of reasoning, had declared it to be simple after all. It was, and yet it wasn't. Anyone could see the links; few could chain them together into something that held up. Holmes could.

"True," I said simply. "But what about the stuffed rabbit?"

"What about the stuffed rabbit?" Holmes echoed. "My perusal of the tree revealed that Eliza and her mother were the only ones who had approached the place where the child fell asleep. In that case, the rabbit had to have been removed by Eliza, her mother, or by someone else, but using a tool that would allow him or her to grasp it without approaching the tree. Such an action would have been pointless; unless the person expected an immediate and detailed investigation, there would be no reason to avoid approaching the tree. The fibres I found in the branches indicated, too, that someone had carefully grasped the rabbit rather than wrenching it with an apparatus, which would almost certainly have left far more residue. I concluded, then, that Edith had removed Charles while her daughter slept."

I stared at my friend. "Why in the world would she have done such a thing?"

"In time, Miss Adler," said Holmes, unable to suppress a slight smile. "I will elaborate in an orderly fashion." The detective leaned back slowly, and I secretly wished I could simply read Dr Watson's version of the tale and skip to the significant parts—Holmes, of course, found all details significant in some way.

I pursed my lips as Holmes continued. "My conclusions about the probability of the rabbit's disappearance indicated to me that Mrs Phillimore knew more than she had revealed to anyone. She showed the appropriate signs of genuine worry for her missing spouse, but from then on, my communications with her were tests of sorts. You asked if we might visit the house, and she consented. From that, I inferred that she expected either to be able to keep me from discovering evidence in her home or else that she believed there was none to be found. I also noted that despite the local description of her as exceptionally gregarious, she did not appear so at all when she spoke to me. Could a missing husband account for this discrepancy? Perhaps, but it has been my experience of many years that even the most extreme calamity doesn't change a person's demeanor completely, especially after several days have passed."

"Most people give many allowances of temper to one who is perceived to be in distress or grief, as you and the villagers have done with Edith Phillimore, but her manner was too studiedly depressed for one of normally sanguine disposition, even in a time of difficulty. In other words, I began to believe that a portion of her behaviour was affected. And yet—" Holmes's eyes gleamed, and I could see that he was enjoying himself—"she didn't seem completely disingenuous. Her look and movement betrayed real concern, though she took care to emphasise it purposefully."

"You were not present for my next test of our hostess, which was to request to examine the upstairs of the home on my own. If she had been concerned with a need to direct my investigations, she would have balked at this, but she was willing, if somewhat short of congenial. Nevertheless, I conducted my examinations in the usual way. Just because someone believes that no evidence is present does not mean that it is actually the case. The police's inability to turn anything up was equally insignificant in my mind, given the official force's common inability to discover anything that is out of plain sight."

"Did you find anything?" I asked, trying to trick the least susceptible man in the world into hurrying his narrative.

"I began in the servants' rooms," said Holmes, exactly as if I hadn't spoken. "I saw nothing out of the ordinary. The family rooms, too, seemed to corroborate the wife's claim that her husband had taken nothing with him, though it was a difficult assertion to either prove or disprove without an intimate knowledge of the man's possessions. It was not until I was nearing the conclusion of my investigation of the man's own room that I found one significant absence: tobacco."

"How did you know he used it regularly?" I asked, finding it unnecessary at that moment to affirm that I had seen the missing man smoking a pipe on more than one occasion.

"Telltale signs," he said. "Dusting of the stuff around the room, the lingering odor. Most significantly, the surface of the side table beside Phillimore's bed revealed a trace of ash next to the faint outline of a commonly-sized tobacco pouch, as if it had been laid there regularly for several years. If nothing whatsoever had been moved in the room, then where was the pouch? Edith's claim to police and local newspaper was, as you know, unequivocal—Her husband, she said, carried nothing with him when he returned to the house except the clothes he wore."

I was so interested in Holmes's tale that the insistent knock at my cottage door seemed unreal at first. I didn't move until it sounded a second time, the rapping of a fist that obviously had no lack of physical force behind it. I was already at the door when Mrs Turner emerged from the kitchen, and I opened it to find a blue-eyed officer of the law.

"Good afternoon, Sergeant Chipping," I said automatically, my brain whirring through any possible reasons he might have for coming back to my house in spite of the force's obvious disdain for my feminine observations. I hoped fervently that his mind was not amorously inclined, as I had previously feared.

"Good afternoon, Miss Adler," he said, his gaze moving past me to take in Holmes, who had joined me in his noiselessly graceful way.

"This is my friend, Mr Sherlock Holmes," I said by way of an awkward introduction.

"The detective?" Chipping seemed bewildered for a moment, but he shook his large head and went on. "I've come about Mrs Phillimore. They've found her husband's body, and she asked us to notify you, Miss Adler. She's very shaken up, you may imagine."

"What?" I uttered.

A minute examination of the circumstances served only to make the case more complex.

—The Adventure of the Empty House

Chapter 4: Holmes

The Woman was obviously shocked. Holmes stepped forward and smiled at the young policeman. "Where is the body?" he asked evenly.

"They found him at his farm," he answered, "in the carriage house."

"Didn't the police look there before?"

"Yes, Sir," said Chipping. "I looked through the place myself. He wasn't there a week ago, right after he went missing." Holmes was glad the young man wasn't tight-lipped.

"Quite right, I'm sure," he answered. "Miss Adler will follow you to Mrs Phillimore."

"Inspector Graves sent a wagon for her," said Chipping, looking over at Irene's white face quizzically, "if she cares to come along."

"As long as Mr Holmes accompanies us," said The Woman suddenly. Holmes almost laughed aloud. She might be momentarily stunned, but Irene Adler never really lost her wits.

"Of course, if you wish," said Chipping uncertainly, obviously weighing his options and finding the prospect of refusing a distraught lady beyond his sensibilities.

"Thank you," murmured Irene faintly, and Holmes could tell that she was making the most of her influence over the sergeant.

The detective held Irene's arm as they followed Chipping outside, trying to assist her in continuing her appearance of frail femininity in case either of them should need its advantage as the afternoon progressed. If the policeman wondered what a famed London detective was doing in Irene Adler's house, he didn't betray his curiosity, instead retaining his businesslike manner as the three situated themselves for the short journey to the farm.

—

As Holmes surveyed the Phillimore farmhouse for the second time in one day, he took in an atmosphere that was radically different from the one of the morning. There were people everywhere—workmen, police, and women from the village loitering around the edges, trying to grasp whatever morsels of information they could. It was always the same in villages. Nothing could be concealed, and nearly everyone could be on hand in moments, it seemed. The detective took in every face and the manner of every observer, storing them in his memory in case he should need to recollect them.

Holmes followed Sergeant Chipping through the gawking crowd, noting recognition in the eyes of a few who had seen him on previous visits to Fulworth, though he had never made an effort to enter village life. Irene was more communicative, speaking subdued greetings to those she knew, as befit the circumstances.

Only a small group had been allowed inside the house, and the body had been laid out in the front parlour, Around it stood an elderly man who was obviously a doctor, a policeman Holmes knew to be Inspector Graves, a well-dressed gentleman he did not recognise, a hired man, and the widow, who looked as shocked as anyone Holmes had ever seen. His first task as he stepped into the room was to scrutinise her face, but he could no longer detect any sign that she was exaggerating her feelings. Whatever she might or might not know about her husband's disappearance, his death had caught her off guard.

"Holmes?" The police inspector looked up and met the detective's eyes, his face a mask of irritated surprise.

"Good afternoon, Inspector," said Holmes evenly, concealing his repugnance.

"Sergeant Chipping," said Graves, ignoring the detective, "I told you to bring Miss Adler," *and no one else* was implied by his chilly tone of voice.

The unfortunate younger policeman cleared his throat and answered deferentially. "The lady took a turn when she heard the news, Sir. She asked for her friend to come along."

Inspector Graves looked as if he might devour his subordinate on the spot. "Very well," he sputtered. "Mr Holmes can help Miss Adler keep Mrs Phillimore company."

Edith Phillimore looked up as if she had just noticed their entrance and walked over to Irene in a daze. The Woman took her hand. "Let's go to the kitchen," she said gently.

"You'll have to go, too, Mr Holmes," said Graves in his high-pitched voice. "Only those with official business can stay."

"Very well," said Holmes, in no mood to argue. At the present time, he had more interest in seeing the place where the dead man had been found than in seeing the corpse itself. Graves's preoccupation with the body meant the detective's chances of examining the carriage house were far higher than if the inspector had been roaming the grounds himself.

Holmes followed Irene, who led Edith to a chair in the kitchen. He smiled at the family's lone housemaid, whose acquaintance he had made earlier in the day. She seemed to be hiding in the recesses of the small room, trying to fade into the corner. The cook was not in evidence.

Edith stared at her hands for a few seconds before speaking. "Peter Warren found him," she said softly. "He had gone to fetch one of the wagons, and there James was, seated on top of the carriage with a blanket around him and a bullet through his forehead." She laughed a short, stabbing laugh, and then she cried. Irene knelt down and put an arm around her. Holmes slipped out quietly, making his way from the house.

When the detective arrived at the carriage house, he found Chipping inside, supervising two policemen who looked young enough to be schoolboys. He nodded to the three officers of the law, but the sergeant looked uncertain. "No one's supposed to be in here," he began, clearing his throat.

"I won't disrupt your work," said Holmes, cutting him off genially and thinking to himself that the work being performed, which included much stamping about and stroking of surfaces, had more to do with destroying evidence than collecting it. Chipping relaxed a little, and a smile crossed his thickly amiable face.

"I suppose it won't hurt anything."

"Very wise," Holmes intoned, careful to stand out of the way of the concentrating boy policemen, who had ceased moving and were staring hard at the ground as if it might open its mouth and utter something profound. "Is that where he was found?" The detective's eyes traveled to the top of a large hulk of a carriage, the sort that had, by its obvious age, been passed down through the family over several years.

"Right there!" came the overly enthusiastic voice of one of the investigating infants, a short lad with sandy hair, who dropped his gaze as soon as he had spoken, as if he was abashed by the sound of his own voice.

Chipping nodded gravely. "Sitting up there like he was going to drive away any second. Gave the man who found him quite a turn."

"Who found him?" Holmes asked, enquiring about a fact he already knew as a further test of the sergeant's good humour.

"Hired help by the name of Peter Warren," came the reply. After a moment, the policeman dropped his voice and added, "No love lost between him and the dead man, they say." Holmes realised that the large young man had begun to consider him an ally.

The detective's mind started to tease out strands of the web. A murderer might try to avert suspicion by finding the corpse himself, but Warren's part in the drama certainly changed the look of things.

After a short time, Chipping and his subordinates left, consenting to give Holmes a few minutes alone. The detective shook his head in exasperation at the police footprints that covered the floor and the evidence of interference on nearly every surface. Still, he was determined to discover what he could.

Systematically, he walked a perimeter around the carriage, then climbed onto it. The one place the policemen hadn't touched was where the corpse itself had rested, and he saw where the dust had been displaced. With irritation, he realised that he couldn't ascertain how the body had been placed there because it was impossible to distinguish evidence of the murderer's movements from the police's. From atop the carriage, though, he was able to visualise the possible entrances and how the corpse might have been conveyed.

After a few moments, Holmes jumped down and walked outside by way of the entrance that faced the house. He saw with relief that the police had managed to get rid of the village crowd and that no one else was in sight. He scanned the area, and, when he was satisfied, returned to the farmhouse and entered it by the staff entrance.

Just inside, he found a man waiting for him. "Peter Warren," barked the newcomer gruffly, inclining his head toward a small room near the kitchen, a dirty place where the household staff kept their shoes and coats. Holmes followed him inside, bracing himself for anything; an attempted punch wouldn't have surprised him, nor would a flood of tears. What he did not expect was for the man's face to break into a friendly smile. "I'm glad it's you, Mr Holmes," was next, followed by a proffered hand. It took the detective a moment to accept the enthusiastic handshake, though years of practise allowed him to disguise his surprise.

"I'm equally pleased, Mr Warren," he said smoothly, "given your unique vantage point on the day's events." The man smiled again, an action that seemed somewhat foreign to his face, and motioned to Holmes to sit down on a rickety wooden bench, while he occupied a chair opposite.

"The thing is, Mr Holmes, I don't know how they done it," he began.

"In that, you are not materially different from the majority of the rest of the world," said Holmes drily, beginning to feel irritated.

"It's just, how did it get there without no one seeing it?" said the hired man.

"Perhaps you might begin at the beginning," said Holmes, carefully keeping his tone level.

"I was on the other side of the barn from the carriage house—it was just me and Simmons—and I told him to go off for something to eat. He went back to the house; the men who live further away eat there. My Em and I live closer, so I usually go home. I decided to walk through the carriage house, and there he was. I didn't know he was dead at first."

"What did you do then?"

"I called to him and then climbed up and saw the bullet in his forehead. I think—I might have figured it out sooner if I hadn't been shaken up. I didn't know what I was seeing at first."

"Continue," Holmes murmured, finally engrossed in the man's tale.

"That's about all. I went back to the house and raised the alarm—"

"To whom, exactly?" put in the detective's deep voice.

"I saw the cook, Mrs Merriwether, and she told the rest of the house."

"I see," said Holmes, opening his eyes for the first time in several moments to find the hired man nodding intently.

"That were—exactly like you do it in the stories, Mr Holmes, as if you're asleep, but I'll wager you heard every word." Not for the first time in his existence, a certain number of uncharitable thoughts toward his loquacious flatmate entered Holmes's mind, but he dismissed them as irrelevant to the present problem and returned his focus to the matter at hand.

"You must know, Mr Warren, that you are a prime suspect," he said sharply, watching the man's face to ascertain his response.

Warren went slightly pale, but he answered after a moment. "That'd be a strange way for a murderer to act, wouldn't it, finding the corpse for the police?"

"Killers have done odder things," Holmes rejoined, "but you're not a murderer. Still, it's going to take some doing to make the police as firmly convinced of that as I am. They're unlikely to take my word for it." He met Warren's eyes for a moment.

"You played your cards well by speaking to me. Keep playing them well, and you may avoid the noose." The detective left the room.

No; he is not a man that it is easy to draw out, though he can be communicative enough when the fancy seizes him.

—A Study in Scarlet

Chapter 5: Irene

I am not the sort of person who goes around comforting people in their every distress. Fulworth, like all other villages in the world, I'll wager, has its share of people who leap at the chance to feed off tragedy, but I find that a quiet word or a smile a few weeks after something has occurred is usually more welcome. I am not, however, without feeling.

As I held Edith Phillimore, I understood the spectacular aloneness that can sometimes crowd around a popular person. Edith was known everywhere in town and by everyone, but she was close to no one. She had called for me because I was the closest thing she had to a friend, the other woman in town whom everyone knew but no one knew well. The difference was that I had chosen my aloneness intentionally, while she seemed to fight against hers with every fake laugh she uttered.

After a few minutes, I thought of Eliza, and I felt a pang of guilt that she hadn't crossed my mind sooner. I looked up over Edith's bowed head and mouthed a question to the maid, who mouthed back *outside with cook*. I wondered where the woman was keeping her, and the question bothered me enough that I started to contrive a way to settle the mother so that I could find the daughter.

Edith obeyed me with the compliance of a dazed child when I shepherded her upstairs, and the timid maid helped me get her into bed. I left the girl, who did not seem unintelligent, with instructions to stay by Edith's bedside until the doctor appeared.

I made my way downstairs with a determined step, knowing that I was about to re-enter a decidedly male domain. I saw no reason to create conflict without purpose, but I never had any trouble asserting myself when the situation demanded, or should I say suggested it, as Holmes was well aware from our previous encounters.

Indeed, as I stepped into the parlour, I could practically feel the ice in the stares that greeted me. Having been banished to my proper female sphere, I was neither expected nor welcome to return to this one. Thankfully, I have been plenty of places in my life where I was not welcome, and the impression has had no lasting effect on me except a lingering sense of amusement. I smiled at the police inspector and then addressed Dr Clarke, who was still studying the body. "I've put Mrs Phillimore to bed. I believe she might benefit from a sleep aid of some kind." He stared at me for a moment, and then nodded wordlessly and left the room, clearly irritated at my interference, but even more so by the fact that my suggestion was undeniably reasonable.

"Very good, Miss Adler," came a voice from the recesses of the room, and I looked over to find Julia Stevenson's father coming toward me, using every inch of his considerable height to intimidate me as much as possible. Charles Stevenson always seemed to be looking down at one from a physical and moral height of some sort, as if he saw a flaw in every character but his own—and his daughter's, for he doted on her. I realised he had been in the room when Holmes and I had first entered the house. An unpleasant man, but I supposed he might be useful under the circumstances, since he had a great deal of legal knowledge.

I excused myself quickly, much to the relief of Inspector Graves, who looked as though he would have liked to arrest me for something but couldn't think of any legitimate reason. I determined to ask Holmes about the man's obvious dislike of him at the earliest possible opportunity. Graves wasn't the most delightful of men at any time, but seeing Holmes had brought something out in him that I had not previously observed.

Holmes's whereabouts didn't concern me. Knowing him as I did, I expected that he would be at the scene of the discovery, taking in the details that would have eluded me. My mind, instead, turned to concern for Eliza. The maid had offered no suggestions, but I had an idea of my own: the chicken house.

Sure enough, I wasn't forced to employ my skills of deduction any further. The portly cook and the little girl were right where I had expected, in the midst of the hens, Eliza looking as if nothing in the world had ever been so enjoyable, and the cook looking as if she'd like very much to be elsewhere.

The bright face the child turned toward me suggested that she knew nothing of what had transpired, and I didn't know whether to be glad or sorry. Mrs Merriwether was certainly a poor choice to be the bearer of terrible news, but the truth couldn't wait forever.

"Eliza," I said suddenly, "how would you like to stay at my house on the hill tonight?" Her face turned serious, and she nodded in wonder, as if the idea was beyond her comprehension. I smiled as brightly as I could and took her hand. "Come inside, and we'll get your things ready."

The cook was obviously relieved. She seemed to have expected Eliza to be her personal charge for the foreseeable future, and my willingness to take on that dread duty earned the one and only smile I ever received from her during our acquaintance.

I, of course, did not normally find Eliza an onerous duty. Her inquisitive mind and willingness to explore any subject made her, I thought, a far better companion than many of the village's adults. This time, however, I didn't look forward to her company. My thoughts swirled with the desire to keep the truth from her and the ever-growing assurance that I could not.

The sun was low in the sky as Eliza and I walked across the yard hand in hand. She was quiet, as usual, but I could feel her excited anticipation of a night at the cottage. As soon as we entered the house, we found Holmes looking at scuff marks under the stairs, and I recalled that I hadn't considered his feelings on the matter of having the child stay with us.

"I see you're to come back to the village with us," he said promptly, addressing Eliza, who immediately let go of my hand and took his, staring at it and touching his long fingers one at a time. I didn't blame her; he had magnificent hands.

"Yes," I answered. "I decided that would be best."

"Indeed," said Holmes, but I couldn't tell from his face what he thought about it.

—

The police wagon was crowded on the way back to the village, but we were nearly silent. Chipping seemed afraid to say anything with the child present, for fear of upsetting her, and Holmes was in a world of his own. I held Eliza in my lap and let down a few strands of my hair for her to play with, and she seemed content.

Chipping left us at the cottage with a subdued goodbye, and Holmes swung Eliza down from the wagon, making her giggle and cling to his neck, which didn't seem to bother him. The case filled his mind, I could see, to the exclusion of almost everything else.

The child's delight was matched only by Mrs Turner's, and upon arrival at the house, the little girl was immediately taken from Holmes's arms along with her tiny suitcase to be settled into the second guest room and then plied with tea and as many pink frosted cakes as she could eat.

My friend and I took our familiar places on wing chair and sofa. "Holmes," I said. "I need your advice."

"You want to know how to tell the child that her father is dead, since her mother is in no condition to tell her, and she will no doubt hear from someone in the village if she is not told very quickly," he rejoined, and I realised that, as usual, he had not been as oblivious as he'd appeared.

"Exactly," I answered, looking down at my hands.

"I will do it," said Holmes, and my head jerked up.

"Are you sure?" I asked.

"Completely," he answered.

Part of me wanted to argue, but I had learned to trust Holmes, especially when he was as certain as he was about this. Besides, I truly had no idea how to break the news to her myself.

Dinner was a cheerful affair, with Eliza jabbering excitedly and Holmes proving that he could talk nonsense as well as anyone. I tried to join in, but a lump kept forming in my throat whenever I looked at the little girl. Finally, after we had all eaten our fill, Eliza began to realise that things were not as they usually were.

"Is mummy coming?" she asked, peering out the window into the darkness.

"No, love," I answered. "You're going to stay the night. Remember?" She pressed her face into my skirt then, and I looked over at Holmes for assistance, which he provided with his violin, playing a series of happy tunes that finally forced a grin out of the little girl. In the end, he was the one who ended the evening by asking Mrs Turner to get Eliza ready for bed. The child looked stormy for a moment, as if she might balk, but Holmes lifted her chin with a single finger and promised to come and tell her a story, which filled her with curiosity.

"You don't intend to tell her right before she goes to sleep, do you?" I hissed as soon as she had tripped off with the housekeeper to be put into her nightdress.

"Certainly not," said Holmes with annoyance. "I shall tell her the story of Ali Baba and drag it out so long her body will be forced to give in to sleep."

I confess to sneaking into a shadowy recess across the hall to watch Holmes as he seated his spare frame on the end of Eliza's bed and went so far as to put out a long finger and tickle one of her small, pink feet, eliciting giggles.

"Hush, Madam," he said in a deep voice. "Keep still for the tale of *Ali Baba and the Forty Thieves*." Eliza's eyes widened, and she sat up against the pillow with rapt attention, clutching the much-loved Charles to her chest.

I don't know why it should have surprised me that Holmes was an excellent storyteller. He certainly had a large enough streak of the dramatic in him. His voice was by turns as quiet as a whisper and as loud as a thunderclap, and his fingers formed fleeing thieves and camels in the shadows on the wall. Eliza listened patiently, but I could see her eyelids beginning to droop after a while. My friend also noticed, and he made his voice quieter and his details more intricate, until the child's head rested on her pillow and he could make his exit without disturbing her.

"Come along," whispered Holmes, putting a light hand on my shoulder and propelling me into the sitting room. Of course he'd seen me watching, as I'd known he would.

"Marvellous performance," I said, once we were seated again.

"I hardly doubt you'd have done the same."

"Perhaps, but why did you do it? I don't suppose you're in the habit of telling bedtime stories to Dr Watson."

"Only if there's a case to be mulled over," said Holmes drily, leaning back in his chair and stretching his long legs. "I know, Irene, what it is like to lose one's parent."

"Oh," I said, unsure how to respond. I waited several long moments in the flickering light, but he did not continue.

"So do I," I ventured, though the silence had been so heavy that it seemed as if the previous comment had been uttered days before. "Both of my parents died during my first singing tour. I left a normal home, but there was nothing to return to when I came back." I didn't say this as bleakly as it sounds. Holmes and I had never spoken to each other about our distant pasts, and I found that I didn't mind revealing some of mine to him, though the intervening years and, hopefully, a measure of maturity, had lessened the sting of grief. Holmes nodded, but he did not reply.

After another long silence, I went to the kitchen to make tea and forestall the sleepiness that I could feel attempting to overtake me. Mrs Turner always went to bed early, and late-night tea was my one rebellion against her insistence on preparing all the food and drinks in the house herself. I did not know if Holmes wished to discuss the case, but I had no intention of going to bed without receiving an explanation of his thoughts.

When I returned with the tea tray, I found my friend looking through his notebook. "I hope your curiosity has not failed you to the point that you intend to go to bed without filling me full of questions like a Christmas goose," he teased, obviously aware of my intentions.

"I hope you're prepared," I rejoined, handing him a flowered teacup. I had purposefully selected the most hideously embellished one I owned in hopes of annoying him. It was, unaccountably, Mrs Turner's favourite.

"I believe," said Holmes after a few sips of the fragrant Darjeeling, "that we were finishing the discussion of the missing tobacco pouch."

"Yes," I said, casting my mind back.

"You will have realised, Irene, that the intentional removal of the man's tobacco pouch would have been a very strange move for a murderer to make. If the killer had wished to make it look like Phillimore had left of his own volition, then taking more than a tobacco pouch would have been the logical action. Edith, too, struck me as far too intelligent to have failed to notice the object's absence if she wasn't expecting it. That, coupled with the odd incident of the rabbit, began to suggest a chain of events to me."

"I don't suppose you intend to reveal it yet," I said, resigned to the wait.

"One must not guess, Miss Adler," he said, "and I was at the time unsure."

"Very well," I groused, not really irritated.

"The timing of the rabbit's sudden appearance, as I said before, surprised me, though I had expected it to be returned at some juncture. The material point is how much Edith Phillimore did not want me to look at it. I had already observed a certain amount of resistance in her to my taking the case at all. She purported to be pleased, but her demeanor told a different tale. Strange behaviour from a woman who was supposedly longing for her husband's return and had no particular reason to dislike me."

"At the house, too, she did not seem overly pleased with the idea of me poking about upstairs without her to guide me, though she took pains to act as if she didn't mind. Again, a peculiar way of behaving considering that the police have been over the place many times without uncovering anything. I could only attribute it to the fact that she had more faith in my powers of discovery than in the police's."

I rolled my eyes. "Very flattering. Do you think she killed him, then?"

"Certainly not," said Holmes. "All of this points to her not being the murderer."

"I don't quite follow," I admitted.

"Consider," said Holmes. "We have evidence that a missing man took his tobacco pouch with him when he disappeared, the one thing he could not be without because of his habit. His wife says nothing of this to the police, who are too focused on the presence of the man's clothing and umbrella to notice where something as small as a tobacco pouch ought to be. At the same time, a little girl's white rabbit goes missing and reappears without an explanation. No doubt, had we not been present, the mother would have passed it off as a child's forgetfulness. Finally, we have Edith Phillimore's obvious shock at her husband's death."

"Yes," I murmured. "She was even more surprised than I would have expected. The duration of the time that James has been missing would have suggested a very real possibility of foul play to most people."

"Just so," said Holmes with satisfaction. "Therein is the key. As strange as it is to contemplate, the evidence points to Edith knowing where her husband was all along, or at least being aware that he intended to leave. His death, though, was apparently not part of the plan, whatever it might have been."

"Isn't that unbearably coincidental?" I asked.

"I don't care about coincidence if it's the only possibility," said Holmes. "The reason for the disappearance will very likely provide at least a beginning for the investigation of the murder, and will probably do much more than that."

"Do you intend to tell the police?" I asked.

"Tell them what?" asked Holmes, smiling. "That I suspect that the child's white rabbit was some sort of signal between husband and wife? That a little tobacco dust indicates that Edith Phillimore has been successfully deceiving them the entire time? I would hardly be believed, and anyway, I have no desire to involve Inspector Graves more than necessary."

"What is your prior acquaintance with him?" I asked, unable to restrain my curiosity.

"Unfortunately, he was a protégé of Inspector Lestrade. He took that venerable gentleman's side in a disagreement during a case several years ago, and his dislike was hardened by the fact that I turned out to be correct."

"Naturally," I rejoined archly.

"I had no idea he'd ended up in the country, but I see that his abilities haven't eclipsed his teacher's."

"At least Chipping is agreeable," I put in.

"Very," said Holmes, and I suspected that he was teasing me.

"What do you plan to do now?" I asked, thinking I could predict his answer.

"I'll tell Eliza in the morning, and then I think we must question her mother. It may be the only hope for finding the murderer, and the longer the trail has to go cold, the more difficult our task will be."

"I agree," I answered. "And Holmes—" I added as I rose to leave the room, "are you sure you want to tell Eliza yourself?"

"I am," answered my friend, showing no sign of going to bed.

"Why?"

Holmes stared at nothing. "Perhaps because she reminds me of Mycroft."

"What?" I stopped halfway down the hall and turned back to face him.

"Oh yes," he answered, "Mycroft was a very fanciful child." My last look at him before I went to bed found him smiling to himself.

She was fond of him, too, for he had a remarkable gentleness and courtesy in his dealings with women.

—The Adventure of the Dying Detective

Chapter 6: Holmes

Holmes didn't sleep, a usual occurrence when he was mulling over a case. This night, however, his mind was partially occupied by the little girl sleeping in the guest room next to his, the child with a mind so much like his older brother's. That was what unsettled him. Mycroft, even at Eliza's age, would have seen something. The question was how to tease information out of the mind of a seven-year-old to whom flower petals were as important as human beings.

At present, though, his task was to tell her that her father wasn't coming back. The detective didn't think about his childhood often, but now he let himself remember the day of his mother's death. He had been barely old enough to speak in full sentences, and Mycroft hadn't been much older than Eliza was. Strangely, he could hardly remember his own response, but he could recall with absolute clarity the horror on his brother's face when the second housemaid had told them. He had spent years trying to wish that moment away, not to bring his mother back, but to erase the look of helpless pain on Mycroft's face. Eliza was not his brother, but she had a similar mind, and he would do his best.

—

Eliza awoke early in the morning, and Mrs Turner dressed her for a walk outside, as Holmes had requested. He felt very old when he saw her emerge from the guest room with Charles tucked under her arm. She wasn't smiling. "Good morning, Miss Eliza," he said. She simply nodded.

The detective took the child's hand and led her out of the cottage and down the hill toward the village. The morning wind was chilly, and he bent down to make sure her coat was secured around her. She stared at him before touching his nose with her finger, ostensibly to see if it felt as pointy as it looked. "Where are we going?" she asked.

"To the Winking Tree," said Holmes, and he felt his hand suddenly tugged forward by the excited little girl. Hardly anyone was about and none of the shops were open at the early hour, for which Holmes was grateful. He listened to the crunch of leaves under his feet and felt the brisk air sting his cheek, all the while hoping he was not a fool for endeavoring to tell the child himself.

When they reached the large beech tree, Eliza sat down underneath it immediately, and Holmes joined her. She looked surprised, but he took his magnifying glass out of his coat pocket and gave it to her. She spent a happy ten minutes looking at everything in sight under the glass. Finally, Holmes held out his hand and took it back. "Eliza," he said, "do you know where your father is?"

"At home," she said promptly. With effort, Holmes did not show his surprise.

"When did you last see him?"

"I went to put Charles in bed for a nap, and Papa was on the carriage. He was sleeping, too. He didn't wake up."

"What did you do then?" asked Holmes evenly.

"I went and told Mummy, and she sent me away with Mrs Merriwether." Holmes leaned against the tree trunk, thinking.

"Eliza, your father wasn't asleep." The little girl turned toward the detective and looked at him with wide eyes.

"Was he dead?" Holmes nodded wordlessly. "My cat Tiger died," she continued, "so Papa bought Charles for me because he said Charles couldn't die."

"That's right," said Holmes, trying to ascertain where her mind was headed.

"When will Papa come back?"

"He's not coming back," said Holmes, feeling something thick in his chest and beginning to wish he hadn't undertaken his current task.

"Oh," said Eliza. "Is he still in Wonderland?"

Holmes thought about this for a moment before replying. "You can always keep him in Wonderland in your mind."

Eliza seemed satisfied with this, and she fell silent. The detective didn't try to rush her. After a while, she crept close and buried her face in his coat. He did not move to touch her, and she did not cry.

A long time later, the little girl stood up. "I'm hungry."

"Me too," said Holmes, and he realised that he was.

Breakfast was an odd affair, with Eliza showing no signs of her newfound knowledge except an unusually subdued demeanor and The Woman giving Holmes meaningful glances every few moments that betrayed her insatiable curiosity about what had transpired. Mercifully, Mrs Turner took Eliza away to help her fold laundry as soon as breakfast was over, which gave ample opportunity for the detective to join Irene in the sitting room and submit to her questioning.

"Well?" she hissed, keeping her voice low so as not to carry to the back of the cottage where Mrs Turner and Eliza were working.

"The task is complete," said Holmes simply, knowing he wouldn't get off so easily.

"How did she take it?"

"A seven-year-old child, however intelligent, can hardly be expected to fully understand the finality of death, but the material point is that she took it even better than I expected on account of already having a subconscious inkling that it was true."

"What in the world do you mean?" asked Irene, staring at the detective as if he'd turned purple.

"She found the body," he replied succinctly, watching his companion's face drain of colour as the sense of what he'd said reached her mind. "Her brain appears to have interpreted her father's lack of response as sleep, but I believe she knew something more serious had happened."

"Didn't she tell anyone?"

"Unless she's lying, which I can't quite credit, she told her mother, who bundled her off with the cook."

"And then what?"

"I'm not clairvoyant, Miss Adler, but it appears that Edith waited for someone to find the body accidentally. The other possibility is that she told Warren what had happened and arranged for him to find it, but after speaking to him, I don't believe so."

"You spoke to him?"

"He encountered me at the house yesterday and told me the story of finding the body purely by chance, which I believe is true. There is simply no indication that any of his actions would have benefitted him if he was the actual killer."

"I see. Are you confident that we may eliminate him as a potential suspect?"

"Nearly so. If things continue in the same way they're going now, I believe we'll find ourselves looking in another direction entirely."

"I suppose we'll have to question Edith now, though I confess I'm not looking forward to it."

"I, however, am," said Holmes, in the midst of lighting his pipe. "Her feelings notwithstanding, I'm ready to hear the truth about what she knows and am not inhibited by bonds of friendship. Perhaps you might prefer to miss the interview. I'd be happy to conduct it alone."

Irene was silent for a moment, as if she was considering the offer. "Very well," she finally said, "but I'll expect a full rendition of events." Holmes was slightly surprised at her easy acceptance, but he said nothing.

Mrs Turner brought Eliza back into the room then, and Holmes held out his hand. "Miss Eliza, would you like to go home?"

The little girl looked from the housekeeper to The Woman as if she was afraid of answering incorrectly. "I want to see Mummy," she said finally.

"And you shall," answered the detective, letting a smile reach the corners of his bright eyes.

—

Eliza was nearly silent on the ride to the farm, her tiny hands twisted into her green frock. Holmes didn't disturb her. He had been a quiet child himself, and he saw no reason to interrupt the little girl's process of thought. Children, he believed, were capable of far more logic and understanding than adults usually admitted.

Finally, when the farmhouse was nearly in sight, he heard the child's quiet voice. "If papa is dead, I won't see him any more." The assertion was decidedly a statement rather than a question. "Will they put him in the ground?"

"Yes," answered Holmes.

Eliza didn't speak again until they reached the house and Holmes swung her down from the wagon. "You are a nice, pointy man," she said seriously. "I like you."

"The impression is—mutual," said Holmes, caught off his guard. No matter how well he thought he understood the fairer sex, its members still had an almost infinite ability to surprise him.

He followed the child into the servants' entrance, where he found the cook in conversation with the housemaid. Mrs Merriwether gave him a frosty look. "Mrs Phillimore was about sick with worry when she woke up and didn't see the child."

The detective almost snorted, his private opinion being that her desperation probably had as much to do with worrying about what the child might say as it did with worry for her whereabouts. "I assume you informed her that Miss Adler was taking perfectly adequate care."

"I knew nothing of the sort," retorted the old lady. "Miss Adler is widely known to be almost *bohemian* in her habits." She spoke the word as if it was akin to insanity of some kind, and the watching housemaid's blue eyes seemed in danger of falling out of her head if she opened them any wider.

"Shocking," murmured the detective, sounding as if he meant the opposite. "I wonder, then, that you let her go so easily yesterday. As you see, the child returns in good health. Where is her mother? I would like to deliver her back personally."

"That's not possible," snapped the cook. "She still hasn't left her room."

"Nevertheless," said Holmes coolly, "I believe she will see me. Please inform her of my presence."

Mrs Merriwether stared at him a moment as if trying to ascertain her likelihood of winning a battle of wills, but she finally nodded curtly to the diminutive maid. "Lewis, go and ask if Mrs Phillimore wishes to see this man."

The girl looked confused for a moment. "The name is Sherlock Holmes," the detective reminded her, trying to put her at her ease. It was obvious the cook wouldn't be won over to his side, so he determined to cultivate a positive relationship with the younger girl in case the association might prove useful later.

Eliza followed the housemaid upstairs, leaving Holmes alone with Mrs Merriwether, who showed her disdain by returning to her task of preparing vegetables as if the detective were not present, which suited him very well. Watson, he thought, would have been of great use in the present circumstance. He had a way with females in households everywhere that was unequalled by anyone else the detective had ever known.

After a few moments, the housemaid returned, standing in front of Holmes with a look of official purpose about her. "Mrs Phillimore says that if you please to wait downstairs, she will see you." The look the cook gave him was filled with malevolence.

The detective followed the girl into the parlour and took his seat on one of the uncomfortable chairs. He was not surprised that Edith desired to see him in a formal setting. She was obviously an intelligent woman, intelligent enough to have realised that he was likely to have some idea of her subterfuge. The cold formality of the parlour would afford her, he thought, a stronger feeling of confidence than would a more intimate setting.

The woman who joined him ten minutes later was pale and self-contained, though there was a desperation in her eyes that the detective hadn't seen there before. He rose and smiled at her. "Good day, Mrs Phillimore. I'm sorry to importune you at a difficult time."

"I doubt it," she answered weakly. "I assume you have questions for me." She sat down opposite Holmes with resignation written in her every movement.

If I had been less cautious I might have been more wise, but I was half crazy with fear that you should learn the truth.

—The Adventure of the Yellow Face

Chapter 7: Irene

As soon as Holmes and the child had left for the farm, I made ready for my intended tasks. Perhaps it was petty of me, but I relished knowing that I had been able to conceal from Holmes my wish to make an investigation of my own. I dressed in one of my finer frocks and prepared to visit the home of Charles Stevenson, barrister, and his wife, Jane.

The Stevenson home was on the coastal edge of the village, one of those houses that looks as if it would be bad tempered if it could speak. It was large and white and ugly and undoubtedly worth a great deal. I didn't look forward to entering it for the second time in my life, but I was determined to find out why Charles Stevenson had been in the Phillimore farmhouse on the day of the murder and if his presence had been a result of the discovery of the body or something prior to it. I couldn't get him out of my mind; the idea of a man like him coming to discuss business with a woman seemed hard to credit. Perhaps it was an insignificant detail, but I didn't like to leave anything unexplained.

I put on my most simpering smile and tucked a wisp of hair behind my ear—small ears are not always an advantage when one wishes to keep one's hair under control—and made my way up the tree-lined path to the door. I could see a maid's face pressed against the window, and I expected to see her starched self in the doorway.

Instead, the tall, ornate door was opened by a large-boned, dark-haired girl with a determined chin. "Julia," I said, surprised, "I didn't expect to see you."

She smiled with a look of defiance in her eyes that I couldn't place; we had never been enemies. "Come in, Miss Adler, I'll tell Mother you've come."

"No need," I said suddenly, improvising. "I'm just as happy to visit with you." I did my best to look as though nothing was amiss in the world.

Julia nodded, though she did not smile, and told the maid to order tea. I followed her into a small breakfast room, thinking all the while about how I might ask her what she knew about her father's involvement with the Phillimore tragedy.

We sat down at a small table that was arrayed in a lace tablecloth of ridiculous intricacy and stared at one another. Julia's taciturnity was uncharacteristic, but I knew her to be direct, and I made a decision to be the same. With her mother, I would have been far more subtle, but I knew the daughter to be boldly honest.

"I came to find out why your father was at the Phillimore house yesterday," I said. "You have heard, I am sure, that Sherlock Holmes of London is currently my guest, and his intent in being here is to unravel the James Phillimore case. I simply wish to know when your father arrived at the house."

Julia turned as white as the lace tablecloth, and the hand that held her teacup shook. For a moment, I was afraid she might faint. Her discomfiture shocked me and sent my thoughts into a whirlwind. Of all possible scenarios, this was certainly not one I had anticipated. For a moment, I wondered stupidly if she might have misheard my question, but I had spoken clearly.

"I—I don't know," she finally stuttered out. "My father isn't here, and my mother wouldn't know either. I'm afraid I can't help you."

It's not to my credit to admit that I accepted her answer, but my amazement at her response had disturbed me to the point that I let her usher me out before the tea had even been brought. I walked home without realising where my feet were taking me, lost in an attempt to figure out what had just happened.

Once I was alone, I thought through events. Julia's presence at her parents' home wasn't unusual in itself; a new bride living near her parents has every right to visit them. At the same time, her relationship with her father was widely known to be strained, ever since he'd tried to prevent her marriage with Edward Rayburn. The fact that he had eventually relented had not, apparently, healed the breach. Of course, I reasoned, no one knew of any bad blood between Julia and her mother, which could account for her visit.

Her reaction to my question was another matter entirely. I'd fully expected her to say she knew nothing of the matter at all. Barring that, I'd anticipated a mundanely businesslike answer relating to her father's professional capacity. What I had certainly not expected was an emotional reaction, particularly one as extreme as she had expressed. Clearly, it pointed to something, and I determined to puzzle it out while drinking a pot of tea.

I found Mrs Turner darning socks, a pastime she enjoyed to an extent I could not fathom. She looked up with a certain kind of disapproval when I entered, a look that I had learned meant she was pleased to see me. I smiled. "I've just finished a most unaccountable social call," I said, "and I need tea to help me think it over." This appeal was successful in its blatant attempt to move the heart of my housekeeper, and she rose majestically and went into the kitchen. I knew, to my delight, that a pot of tea also meant an array of biscuits and cakes.

I sat down at the table with a few sheets of notepaper. At the top of the first sheet, I wrote, "Julia Rayburn Problem," but before I got any further, I heard someone at the door. After the excitement of the previous two days, I felt I was prepared for anyone to be standing in my doorway. I was wrong.

The form that greeted me was that of none other than Edward Rayburn. He took his hat off and stared at me uncertainly, as though I might bite.

"Please come in, Mr Rayburn," I said, taking pains to conceal my considerable surprise. "It's a pleasure to see you."

The young man followed me like a large puppy and sat on the edge of the sofa as if he was afraid of soiling it. My unflappable housekeeper immediately materialised with two teacups instead of one and a variety of edibles which would have satisfied eight people as well as two.

Edward held his teacup gingerly, as if it might come alive in his hand, then cleared his throat and blurted out, "Miss Adler, my mum was a midwife."

"Yes—I know," I answered, slightly shocked. I didn't mind the discussion of such things, but they were usually far from the lips of the villagers, especially men.

"It is—I mean, when I was a little boy, she used to take me on her rounds with her. I wouldn't be in the room, you understand, but I knew what went on."

"Very proper, I'm sure," I said, trying to encourage his halting narrative.

"The thing is, I think Julia—is—" He couldn't continue. I waited for a moment, but it was obvious that uttering the word in my presence was more than he could manage.

"You mean that Julia is going to have a baby?" I asked matter-of-factly, hoping that my tone would help to put him at his ease. He nodded, blushing red to the tips of his large ears.

"I didn't know who else to talk to, Miss Adler. It's—you know, it's too soon for that with us, at least for—for any of the signs. I didn't want to believe it, but it's getting more and more obvious."

"You came to me because you know my past reputation," I said.

"It wasn't just that," he answered, raising his head and looking at me with clear green eyes. "Julia likes you. She doesn't like many people around here, but she likes you."

"I see. You understand what this means if it's true," I continued.

"I do," he answered.

"What will you do? You'd have reason to leave her."

Edward fixed me with a steady gaze. "You're quite mistaken, Miss Adler, if you think I'd ever do that."

"What?" I'm afraid I looked at him as if he had lost his mind.

"My feelings have not changed," he said simply.

"I don't like the idea of you as a martyr," I returned with equal directness.

He laughed, and his face transformed into a boy's. "I'm much too happy to be a martyr. Julia is the best company I've ever had. I can't do without her."

"You don't mind?" I asked, still unable to comprehend his position.

"Yes," he said, "but all the minding I've done has only reminded me of how much I care for her. I know that she did not always care for me, but I believe she does now."

"I cannot argue with you," I said, "though I urge you to consider your position."

He smiled again. "I used to wonder what I could possibly do for her, how a farmer could ever give anything to a woman like her. Now I have something to give, and it's mine alone."

"What would you like me to do?" I asked.

"I want to know if I'm right," he said, "from her own mouth. I can't ask her, but I believe she would tell you. I don't want to hear it from someone else. I just—want her to tell me herself. I would forgive her if she would just tell me."

I paused before answering. "Very well. I will do what I can." He left then, and I sat alone in my house for a long time. I had little doubt that Rayburn's suspicion was correct. He wasn't a stupid man, and he adored Julia. That, coupled with her strange behaviour, made me think that he was not likely to be mistaken.

I did not claim a position of moral superiority, but my sensibilities revolted from the idea that Julia had married the farmer simply for his name or the status of marriage. Had she thought he was stupid enough to accept a child as his own without question, even if the timing was wrong? Of course, most men did not have Rayburn's knowledge of the first signs of pregnancy. That was the curse of irony, it seemed. Julia had married the one man in Fulworth most likely to figure out her situation.

Mrs Turner brought lunch to me after a while, but I didn't eat. For once, knowing what I needed to do chased away my appetite completely. I didn't want to speak to Julia, didn't want to be part of a something between a man and his wife. But there was something in Edward's manner that wouldn't let go of me. He was, I thought, a good man. I had known very few of those in my life. I had known plenty of women in trouble similar to Julia's, victims of men with hearts as small as Edward Rayburn's was vast. As much as I sympathised with whatever might have led to Julia's circumstances, though, I could not condone the use of a good man by a woman who simply needed his name. And yet—I had seen the look of love in Julia's eyes when she watched her husband. I had observed the way she spoke to him and watched her smile when he took her hand, small moments when she thought no one else was paying attention. Given what I had seen, I would never have doubted her affection, and I still found it difficult to do so. I didn't know what to think. Truthfully, I wished for Holmes, to be able to explain the situation to him and hear his assessment. Unfortunately, he was at the farm, and in any case, his presence was not conducive to the task I had agreed to undertake for Edward

I was beginning to feel as if I were in some strange, enchanted state in which everywhere I visited must be visited again and again—first the Phillimore farm and now the Stevenson house, where I expected Julia to have remained. I didn't let myself speculate about what I would find when I arrived. A great many of Holmes's opinions were not shared by me, but I found his revulsion to guessing extremely reasonable. I could not manage to be as religious as he was about eradicating the practise altogether, but in the present circumstance, I forced my mind to focus on other topics. If Julia was pregnant, the ramifications would be ample, but since I could not yet know, I filled my walk to the house with thoughts about the Phillimore case and the things I knew of it, though they did not seem a great many when I'd added them all up in my mind. I hoped Holmes might have something of value to add when he returned.

But the deception could not be kept up forever.

—A Case of Identity

Chapter 8: Holmes

Holmes looked at the pale woman opposite him, and he saw neither a cold-blooded killer nor a greedy swindler. "Perhaps it will be easier for you if I begin with what I know," he said.

"Very well," she answered listlessly.

"Some time before the wedding of Julia Stevenson and Edward Rayburn, your husband got into some sort of trouble, serious enough for him to consider fleeing Fulworth. You decided to stage his disappearance as a mystery, so that whomever he felt threatened by would think that there was no hope of finding out his whereabouts from you. Not wishing, I suspect, to disrupt a wedding, you waited until after the ceremony had concluded to deliver your shocking news. The police were called, but you had been careful, and they did not find any clue to your husband's whereabouts." While the detective spoke, Edith's face remained impassive.

"The importance of Eliza's rabbit took me a little while to puzzle out, but I determined that he was a signal between you and your husband. Once you had played your part and alerted the village to James's disappearance, you posted it to him, mailing it to a predetermined location. In return, your husband posted it back to you to confirm that he had reached his destination without issue. I assume a servant was used to post and retrieve it so that it could be placed in a way that made it seem as if Eliza had simply misplaced her toy."

"I began to suspect all of this when I perceived your distaste for my presence and your strong reaction to my interest in Eliza's rabbit. You had fooled the police, but you did not fool me, as I think you realised."

"When do you intend to tell the police?" asked Edith, defeat in her voice.

Holmes drilled her with his eyes. "As you have probably ascertained, if I told them this, they would immediately believe they had found the murderer—a wife with knowledge of her husband's whereabouts that no one else had, who stood to do quite well if he died. This is why I do not intend to tell them anything until I have discovered the murderer."

"You don't believe I'm guilty?"

"Of deceit, yes. Of murder, no. If you wish the real murderer to be found, however, you must tell me the entire truth about your husband's flight."

"Very well." Edith looked away from Holmes then, clenching her hands as if she were a nervous child. "Six weeks ago, my husband started acting strangely. You will have heard that he is—was—not a sociable man, but he became even less so than usual. He hardly spoke, and he seemed absent, as if he were with me in body but not in spirit."

"After a week, I asked him what was wrong. He—had never acted to me the way he acted to everyone else. I had always been his confidante, so I could not understand his newfound reticence. He wouldn't answer at first, but finally he told me the truth: He was being blackmailed."

"By whom?"

"You may have seen the doctor who was here yesterday—Dr Clarke from the village. He blackmailed my husband in several letters."

"May I see them?"

"I'm afraid not. James took them with him. They haven't been found. I never saw them. James was too ashamed to show them to me." Holmes let out a nearly imperceptible huff of frustration.

"What was the matter of the blackmail?"

"I suppose it doesn't matter now. Dr Clarke has been the family physician since before my husband was born. He threatened to reveal that James's real mother was the family's housemaid, who died several years ago."

"A fact that had been known to your husband?"

"No, he'd never known until he received the first letter."

"And what was the doctor hoping to gain?"

"Money. James never told me how much, but he paid him regularly for a while. There was no proof of what he said, of course, but my husband couldn't bear the thought of having the whole village wonder about his father and drag the family's name through the mud. He hated being singled out."

"But why now?"

"James said it was because Dr Clarke had speculated and was trying to glean money from whatever possible quarters he could."

"I see," said the detective. "What led to the disappearance?"

"After I had finally convinced James to tell me what was troubling him, he also told me that things could not continue as they were, or we would be unable to pay. I tried to convince him to go to the police, but he, I'm afraid, had given up. Dr Clarke is a powerful and respected man."

"James began to insist that he couldn't stay in Fulworth. I begged him to reconsider, but he believed that his position was untenable here. What he hoped was to leave and bring Eliza and me to join him later, taking care of selling the farm from afar and anonymously. You may—you may, Mr Holmes, think that my husband's actions were extreme, but you didn't know him. He valued his pride very, very highly, and he'd always felt that as a farmer, he could never match the power of men like the doctor."

"Please continue with the specifics of the plan," said Holmes, beginning to tire of the subjective aspects of the narrative.

"It was as you said. We determined that James would leave on the day of the wedding so that I could reveal his disappearance in a place where the whole village could hear of it, including the doctor. He went back inside for his umbrella and hid in the cellar until the property was clear of people so that it would seem as if he'd simply vanished. Once the police investigation was concluded, I was to depart the village with my little girl and meet him, leaving the farm in the hands of Warren and the other farmhands until it could be quietly sold. I didn't know precisely where he intended to settle, but he was to write and tell me in a few weeks. The return of Eliza's rabbit was assurance that all was proceeding smoothly—until yesterday." Edith's voice faltered, and she ceased speaking for a moment. "I—didn't expect to never see him again, you know. It's like he really disappeared, Mr Holmes. My husband went back into the house, and all that's left is his shell." She dabbed hard at her eyes for a moment.

"Who posted the rabbit?" asked Holmes.

“The cook, Mrs Merriwether,” Edith replied. “I think she would kill for me.” After she realised what she’d said, she shook her head sharply. “I didn’t mean that.”

“I didn’t expect so,” said Holmes. “I had already observed her loyalty to you.”

“Do you know the vicinity of your husband’s destination?”

“That’s the problem,” said Edith. “I don’t know. The rabbit was sent to a specific address in London, where my husband’s cousin resides, but James didn’t plan to stay there. I thought—I thought he was somewhere else in London, but I have no idea where.”

“I believe you,” said the detective. “Now, Mrs Phillimore, have you any idea who might have killed your husband? Did anyone other than the cook know of the plan?”

“No,” said Edith, “and even she didn’t know the particulars. She refused to let me tell them to her. I thought of the doctor, but I don’t know what he would have gained by killing a man who had been paying him regularly.”

“No,” said Holmes. The detective rose. “Thank you for your help, Mrs Phillimore. I will do my best to put an end to this mystery.”

The widow half smiled. “It’s ironic, Mr Holmes, but now I’m actually thankful to have you on the case.”

“Understandable,” he said, turning to leave, but Edith stopped him with a hand on his arm.

“I should thank you for being kind to Eliza. When I awoke, I was scared to death she’d found out about James by more difficult means. I’m so very glad she learned the truth from friends.”

“I’m glad you consider me a friend in this matter, Mrs Phillimore,” was all Holmes answered.

Holmes found the small maid beating rugs outside the farmhouse. “Miss Lewis,” he said, which turned her face red from the politeness of it, “do you know where I might find Dr Clarke from the village?”

“You know the Winking Tree on the green?”

“Yes.”

“Go beyond it to the big, ugly houses down the lane. His is the plainest one. Be careful he don’t dose you with something.”

"Thank you," said Holmes, smiling to himself as he took his leave.

—

The housemaid, the detective soon realised, was not incorrect in her observation. The wealthiest members of Fulworth society had a row of houses that skirted the village, as if they were too rich to quite allow themselves to be a part of daily life, but too fond of recognition to be entirely out of it, either. One house, however, was noticeably plainer than the others, as if its size was for function rather than form. To this home the detective went, and he was met at the door by a solidly-built, middle-aged woman—Mrs Parkfield, the doctor's assistant.

"Dr Clarke isn't seeing patients today," she said stiffly.

"I am not a patient," said Holmes. "I wish to see him about the Phillimore murder."

Without another word, the woman turned and disappeared into the house, her black skirt swooshing around her as if it was trying hard to keep up with its wearer. Holmes looked around him, and he understood the impression of functionality that seemed to pervade even the exterior of the house, for its front, at least, was furnished as a doctor's surgery more than a home.

The woman in black returned after a few moments, and she motioned to Holmes. "Dr Clarke will see you in his study," she said, already starting down a wide hallway. The detective followed, lengthening his strides to keep up with her brisk pace.

She led him to a large, book-lined room. "Here he is," she said tersely, leaving Holmes just inside the door, facing a huge wooden desk at which was seated the elderly form of Dr Isaac Clarke.

"Good day, young Holmes," he said.

"Doctor," said the detective, taking his seat in a chair in front of the old man.

"I count that it has been above thirty years since I last laid eyes on you."

"Quite right," said Holmes. "When we last met, you were simply Clarke, a young man trying his hand as a doctor's assistant."

"I'm still simply Clarke," said the doctor with a sardonic smile, "though hardly young any more. I knew you at Oakhill Farm, but I thought you might prefer not to be recognised while you were acting in your professional capacity."

"I appreciate your discretion, though even now, I am acting in my professional capacity. I have heard a story today, and I wish to hear your explanation of it."

"Indeed?" said the doctor, leaning back in his large chair.

"In short," said Holmes, "Edith Phillimore claims that you blackmailed her husband into disappearing."

"What?" The doctor sat forward in his chair and pushed his palms down on his desk forcefully. "What sort of motivation could have driven me to do such a thing?"

"Money," said Holmes simply. "I would not suggest such a thing if I could avoid doing so."

"Believe me," said the old man with heightened colour, "it is only fondness for the boy you once were that is keeping you in this house at this moment."

"Very well," said the detective, unperturbed. "The widow claims that you extorted money from her husband by threatening to expose that he was the child of his father's indiscretion with a household servant."

The doctor's face suddenly changed, and he threw back his head and laughed. "I don't mean to be irreverent about a man's death, Holmes, but Edith Phillimore is having you on or has been deceived herself. Robert Phillimore was as pure as the driven snow. I wasn't the doctor who attended the birth. I confirmed Mrs Phillimore's pregnancy, but she gave birth elsewhere, at her sister's home in London. The family had three servants, all of whom were at home at the time. I am hardly the only person still living who was alive and would recall that no one in the household was with child except Louise Phillimore."

"Thank you," said Holmes. "I suspected this, but I am glad to hear your confirmation. The story the widow told me was deeply flawed, but I did not wish to dismiss the possibility until I had spoken to you."

"Since you're not likely to get much out of Graves, I should tell you that Phillimore had been dead for some time when he was found, several hours at least. His corpse showed signs of being dragged before it was placed in the carriage house. Here are my notes, if you care to see them." The elderly doctor handed Holmes a stack of pages written in his spidery hand.

"Thank you," said the detective. "Edith Phillimore knew that her husband planned to disappear. The question now is what happened to cleave soul and body in the mean time, causing him to never be seen alive again. I will take my leave to ponder the question."

"Humour an old man and stay for tea—or perhaps something stronger," said Clarke, smiling. "Since my dear wife's death, I welcome rational company. I experience it so rarely."

"Not today," said Holmes, "but I promise to return before I leave the village."

"Don't forget that I used to let you read my books."

"Certainly not," said the detective, smiling.

There is nothing new under the sun. It has all been done before.

—A Study in Scarlet

Chapter 9: Irene

"Hello, Julia," I said when she again opened the door of her parents' home. I had been afraid she might try to keep me out, but she ushered me in with a quizzical expression.

"If you wish to speak to my mother," she said softly, "I might be able to fetch her for you."

"On the contrary," I said, "I am here to speak to you."

"Whatever for?" she asked, making no effort to seat me, but continuing to stand over me awkwardly in the opulent front hallway of the house.

"Your husband came to see me," I said bluntly, hoping to shock her into a response.

"I see," she answered, her face betraying nothing whatsoever. "Shall we walk outside?" I nodded, and she led the way out to the lane and away from the village. I respected her silence for several minutes and let myself enjoy the pleasure of being outdoors, but the sky began to turn grey, and I knew that rain was not far away.

"Come to my house," I said, and Julia followed absently, as if her mind was entirely elsewhere. Had I not recognised the coming rain myself, I believe she would have stayed out in it and hardly noticed.

As it was, we reached my cottage just as the first fat drops began to make their acquaintance with the ground. I installed Julia on the sofa with one of Mrs Turner's afghans and took my seat in Holmes's wing chair, which seemed oddly appropriate under the circumstances.

"Julia," I finally ventured, "I can't think of an easier way to go about this. Your husband came to see me because he had a question that he didn't want to ask you himself, but I have one that I'd like to ask first: Do you love him?"

The girl didn't look up. Instead, she twisted one finger through a lock of her black hair and fidgeted with her other hand, staring hard at the lace pattern in the afghan on her lap. "I do love him," she finally said, and the sudden intensity in her voice surprised me. "I wish I didn't, but I do."

"You know," I said gently, "that his mother was a midwife."

“Yes,” she answered, and the colour drained from her face. “You don’t mean he—”

“He’s not a stupid man,” I said evenly, watching her. “He knows the signs, without even trying.”

What little doubt I’d had of the truth of Edward’s claim was immediately dispelled by the sob that burst from his wife’s throat. Julia put her hands in front of her face and leaned forward, weeping into her lap. I moved to sit beside her and put an arm around her shoulders the way Mrs Turner had used to do for me when dark memories clouded my first months in Fulworth.

As the distraught girl began to calm, my mind made a leap of intuition of which Holmes would not have approved. Or, perhaps, he would have said that my subconscious mind had somehow assimilated evidence that pointed where my conscious mind finally led me.

“Julia,” I said, “James Phillimore was the father of your child, wasn’t he?” In that moment, I knew what Holmes must feel when he revealed a deduction that held monumental power over someone’s very life.

Julia’s voice faltered, “Yes, that’s true.”

“I believe I know what happened,” I said. “Will it be easier for you if I suggest events? You may correct me if I’m wrong in particulars.”

She nodded. “Please.”

“Last year, you returned home from school. You had left Fulworth as a child, but you returned as a woman, in appearance if not in wisdom and experience. Somehow—perhaps at church or a village fete, you met a farmer.”

“The Harvest Festival,” she murmured. “He was showing flowers.”

“I won’t claim to know exactly what happened,” I said, “but believe me, I understand more than you could possibly realise. He asked for things, and you gave them. I think that you were not forced, but your naïveté was exploited.” She looked as if she might disagree, but she said nothing.

“He had a wife, but he said he didn’t love her, and you believed him.”

"No," she said suddenly. "He told me that he loved her very much, but that he loved me even more. That is why I gave him what he asked for."

"The two of you were discreet," I continued, "and nothing disturbed you for a few months."

"Except conscience," Julia muttered, almost to herself.

"Then the worst thing of all—you were pregnant."

I stopped speaking, and Julia continued instead. "I didn't want to believe it, but I finally knew that it must be so. I didn't go to the midwife; I knew my shame would be all over the village."

"I expect you're wondering where poor Edward comes into it. He's always been in love with me. Before we were ten years old, we used to plan our life together. He was heartbroken when my parents sent me away to school, and when I came back, he asked to court me. I declined several times. James Phillimore was a mystery and a prize. Edward had always been available whether I wanted him or not."

"After I knew the baby was coming, I wrestled with myself. Edward, I knew, would come the moment I called him. His name and standing were a way out of my difficulty. Other women in the village have given birth before their times, and I knew that Edward would propose very quickly if I would let him. I could, I thought, make it seem that the child was his, and if any tongues wagged in the village, they would think that any indiscretion had occurred between a couple who were now married. With luck, however, I planned to pass it off as a premature birth."

"You may not believe me, but I could hardly bear to do it. I had a sister's affection for Edward that was left over from childhood, but it became even worse than that. As we began to court, I finally understood what kind of man he was. I saw him with new eyes. Phillimore could be cold and even cruel, but Edward was kind and gentle. He respected me as James never did. The regret, you may imagine, was excruciating, as I realised what I had given up for a few occasional moments with a man who had never truly loved me."

"Phillimore took monstrous advantage of you. Where was he when all of this was occurring?"

"He never saw me again after I knew about the baby. He said it would be better for me not to be seen with him. The only promise he made was that he would leave the village."

"Better for you, my eye," I snorted.

"I know that now," she said, "but it was like he'd cast a spell on me. I can see why Edith married him. He could be very, very charming in a mysterious way, as if you might just come to know him if you stayed around a moment longer, but the right moment never came, and he never gave anything of himself."

"I understand," I said, meaning it.

"I'll have to leave Edward, of course," she faltered. "He's far too lovely a man to be chained to a woman like me."

"He is a good man," I agreed, "but there's no need for you to be a martyr. He's willing to forgive."

"I don't care," said Julia. "I'd no right to try to trap him this way. Even if he hadn't figured it out, I don't think I could have managed to go through with it. At least, Miss Adler, you can think that much good of me."

"Believe me," I answered, "I'm not claiming any sort of superiority. I know that my past is a rumour in the village, and believe it or not, the truth is more sensational than the whispers."

"Really?" Julia looked slightly incredulous. "I'd always assumed it was just because you're a bit—unusual and unmarried and American."

"I am all those things," I said, "and I'm a widow, but I've also been a thief and other less mentionable things. You should ask Mr Holmes about it some time."

"What about your Mr Holmes?" she asked, half smiling for the first time since she'd entered my house.

"Holmes," I said, "is as the Bible says: The same yesterday, today, and forever."

"There's a great deal to be said in favour of that," Julia mused, unconsciously touching her belly. "Ed thinks I'm spending the night at my mother's," she continued. "Tomorrow I'll figure out where I'm to go."

"Must you be so hasty?" I asked. "Can't you give your husband a chance to prove his love?"

"He's already borne far too much," she said resignedly.

"Phillimore is at least as responsible as you are, and in my eyes, much more," I said, trying again.

"I don't dispute that," she said, "but I'm the one who duped Edward into giving me his name."

"True," I said, "but now that he knows, he gives it willingly." I hesitated for a moment. "Julia, I am more than ten years older than you are, and I know how rare men like Edward Rayburn are in this world."

"Do you also know what it's like to contemplate incurring a debt to someone that can never possibly be repaid?" she asked bitterly.

"Yes," I answered, looking around at the home Holmes had given me, "I do."

Julia rose then, and she left the cottage without another word, walking home to her mother through the afternoon rain.

—

I did not notice when Holmes entered the house, so deep was I in thought. He took his place opposite me on the sofa. "I see that Rayburn paid you a visit. His boots left traces of a peculiarly-coloured clay that is only found in the part of the county where his farm is situated."

"Yes," I said, "both he and his wife came to see me, but separately."

"I see," said my friend. "Had these visits anything to do with the case?"

"I don't know yet," I answered. "Edward came to tell me that he suspected his wife was pregnant with the child of another man, and Julia corroborated his suspicion."

"Indeed," said Holmes. "Was Rayburn asking for help to extricate himself?"

"No, he doesn't want help," I said quietly, looking out the window into the falling dusk.

"As I would have expected, from what you said of his character before," said my companion, lighting his pipe with long, steady fingers.

"I did not," I replied.

"Perhaps you credit the fairer sex with a better-developed ability to forgive."

"Or perhaps I think us undeserving of such profligate kindness," I retorted, a trifle bitterly.

"Kindness is far from profligate when it is bestowed on the object of one's regard," said Holmes quietly. I stopped myself before I asked him how he knew.

I have not lived for years with Sherlock Holmes for nothing.

—The Hound of the Baskervilles

Chapter 10: Holmes

The detective watched his companion carefully. He had learned that like Watson's, but unlike his own, her moods were subject to change based on the fluctuations of a case and the information she uncovered. He sometimes wondered what it would be like to inhabit such a mercurial existence, to be at the mercy of whatever one happened to discover. He did not relish the idea.

"I take it, by your obvious eagerness to tell me more, that these encounters of your afternoon somehow potentially relate to the Phillimore case, as opposed to simply being a tangle of human affections in the common way," he finally said.

"Yes," The Woman answered, twining her fingers together. "I've something to tell you that may change things considerably. When you left today, my intention was to ascertain why Julia's father, Charles Stevenson, was present at the examination of Phillimore's body. I found Julia at her parents' home, and her reaction to my question was so strong as to be bizarre. I have since learned from her visit and her husband's the reason for her behaviour, but it relates to our investigation much more than I'd realised."

Irene took a deep breath, as if for dramatic emphasis. "James Phillimore was the father of Julia's child."

"Indeed," said Holmes, not begrudging The Woman her moment of triumph. "That puts certain discoveries of mine in their proper places."

"Yes?" she said, leaning forward.

"Edith Phillimore was as forthright as I expected once she knew she had been found out. She readily corroborated the fact that Charles the rabbit was a messenger between her and her husband. She also told me the reason for her husband's flight, the fact that he had been blackmailed by Dr Clarke."

"I can't believe that," said Irene immediately.

"Your skepticism is to your credit in this case," said the detective. "Fortunately, I have known Dr Clarke for many years, and I found the idea of him extorting money based on a rumour about someone's illegitimate origins beyond credibility. I went to see him, and he put the idea to rest."

"So Edith was lying once again?" said Irene, incredulous.

"No, I think not," said Holmes. "I believe she herself was deceived by her husband."

"That certainly harmonises with the picture of his character that Julia provided," Irene added.

"After hearing your additions to the story," the detective continued, "I believe that Phillimore was desperate after finding out about Julia's pregnancy and concocted a story to convince his wife to help him disappear. We have no way of knowing if he ever actually intended for his wife and child to join him."

"Disgusting," said The Woman, repugnance written all over her beautiful face.

"Quite," said Holmes, "though he does seem to have had real affection for Eliza."

"What does this mean for the case?" asked Irene after a moment of silence.

Instead of answering, the detective went to the door of the cottage. "I hear footsteps approaching," he said.

"Mrs Turner should be returning from the shops now," said Irene.

"No," said the detective, "the footfall is heavier."

"Why not open the door and see which of us is correct?" said The Woman, slightly exasperated. Holmes did so, and a burst of wet wind entered the house, along with a ruddy man wearing a luxurious moustache.

"Hello, Holmes and Miss Adler," said Watson, and he looked past his friend to nod to Irene, who had risen and was surveying both men with surprise.

"Welcome, Dr Watson. I'm sorry we didn't anticipate your arrival," she answered.

"It's no matter," said the doctor, "I suppose my telegram didn't make it to you."

"I'm afraid not," she answered. "The office in the village is not always reliable."

"Then please accept my apology for my importunate arrival," answered Watson gallantly. "Miss Willow," he added, looking up at his tall flatmate, "has eloped with a curate. I certainly hope it was fully her own doing and not assisted by the machinations of anyone else."

"Your implication does me dishonour," Holmes answered, but he could hear The Woman inelegantly smothering a laugh in the background.

"Please do settle in, and I'll make a pot of tea," she said, gliding into the kitchen and leaving the two men alone. Watson took his small suitcase and black doctor's bag into the guest room next to his friend's, then rejoined Holmes in the sitting room.

"I'm glad you've come, Watson," said the detective, relaxing on his winged throne. "I've grown so accustomed to your ever-faithful presence that I find your absence more inconvenient than ever."

Watson smiled. "And I, I'll admit, find London dreadfully dull without a case to keep me occupied. I'm afraid you've acclimated me to your ways, old friend. How is the Phillimore disappearance progressing?"

"As often happens," Holmes answered, "the disappearance has become a murder. The interesting feature of this particular case, however, is that a certain amount of proof exists that the disappearance happened significantly before the murder. In other words, the man did not disappear because he was murdered; rather, the murder took place at an as-yet-undetermined time afterward."

"I do," Holmes continued, "find myself in need of your particular speciality."

"What sort of speciality?" Watson asked curiously. "I have my revolver."

"Not that," the detective rejoined. "One of your more delicate specialities. I need you to worm your way into the heart, as it were, of the Phillimores' sour-tempered cook."

Watson huffed resignedly. "If you're certain. What sort of information are you seeking?" Holmes spent the next ten minutes giving his friend an overview of the case, a process that felt nearly as natural as breathing, so often had he done it.

Irene finally returned with a tray and sat down next to Watson on the sofa. "I confess, Holmes," she said, "that I am in the dark as to our next logical step."

"In general," the detective answered, "we must find the missing link between the murder and the association between James Phillimore and Julia Rayburn. There can hardly fail to be one. In particular, I wish to know what Mrs Merriwether knows, which friend Watson will find out for us."

"Do you want me to tell Edith that her husband was a philandering liar?" asked The Woman, spitting the words out with distaste.

"Soon," Holmes replied. "First things first; I wish to examine the notes made by Dr Clarke, who viewed the body right after it was found."

"You didn't view it yourself?" asked Watson incredulously.

"Unfortunately," said Holmes, "I was obstructed by the presence of an Inspector Graves, whom you may remember as an assistant to our friend Lestrade."

"Unpleasant," said Watson, wrinkling his nose.

"Nevertheless," said Holmes, "I have the doctor's notes, which are nearly as thorough as my own would have been."

"Goodness," said Irene, looking up from her teacup, "high praise indeed."

The detective looked at her coolly. "When I was a child, my parents sent me to Fulworth one summer to stay with a distant cousin. Dr Clarke, merely a medical assistant at the time, solved a highly sensational murder in Fulworth simply by viewing the corpse. I have rarely seen the equal of the performance. I read all his books that summer, hoping to absorb the ability."

"The osmosis appears to have been successful," answered The Woman, smiling.

"We share a certain similarity of mind," Holmes replied, momentarily transported back to his youth, but forcing himself to return to the present immediately.

For the next half hour, The Woman and the doctor conversed quietly while Holmes read the sheaf of papers given to him by Dr Clarke. He was well aware that if Clarke had been somehow involved in the murder, then his information would have been compromised. After seeing the old man, however, he was convinced that it was not so. Furthermore, in the few moments he'd had in the room with the corpse, while his attention appeared to be focused on the distasteful Inspector Graves, he'd actually had time to make a few deductions of his own, which the doctor's notes corroborated. That fact, coupled with the fact that he'd found Edith Phillimore's story of the doctor's involvement entirely preposterous, assured the detective that he could trust his old friend.

Sometime during Holmes's perusal, Mrs Turner arrived at the cottage laden with packages, which she nearly dropped upon beholding Watson. "Doctor," she stammered, "what a surprise. Miss Adler didn't inform me of your intention to visit, or I would have had something ready for you." She looked severely upon Irene, who grinned back with, Holmes thought, perverse amusement.

"Please don't trouble yourself," said Watson, rising and taking the housekeeper's hand. "Miss Adler didn't know herself. I'd intended to stay in town to fulfil certain obligations, but they have since disappeared, and here I am." Mrs Turner blushed and whisked away the tea tray Irene had produced, glaring down upon it as if she approved of neither its contents nor its arrangement.

"Sometimes," said Irene, "she reminds me a great deal of a girls' school headmistress."

"Or headmaster," said Watson. "I'll wager she could do battle with either of the ones I experienced."

"I love her for it," said Irene quietly, and Holmes saw a soft look come over her. He was glad. Uniting The Woman and the housekeeper had been his own doing, based on his knowledge of each. He had done well, he thought with satisfaction. Not all of his cases were large ones. Sometimes he used his abilities in quieter ways, but he was no less satisfied when he succeeded.

That night, Watson and Mrs Turner went to bed before the detective and his hostess, as was the usual practise when the flatmates visited. Holmes was quiet, pondering the developments of the day and putting them into their proper places in his understanding of the case. From the evidence of his own trained eyes and Clarke's notes, he was fully convinced that Phillimore had been killed somewhere other than the Oakhill premises and then dragged there by a particularly vindictive murderer or, perhaps, a vindictive accomplice. The placement of the corpse atop the ancestral carriage seemed particularly brazen, the work of someone who was fully convinced that he or she could not be caught or else didn't care, instead wishing to make the strongest statement possible. It suggested a combination of hatred and an impression of power that intrigued Holmes and also perplexed him. As of yet, no one he'd considered had impressed him as having the proper temperament.

"Holmes, are you sure Edith is innocent?" asked Irene, breaking the silence after a very long time.

"Yes, I am," said Holmes, "though I have considered at length how she might still be a viable suspect. However, I find the idea even more difficult to entertain than that of Peter Warren as the killer. For one, her whereabouts can be accounted for at significant moments. For another, we know that Phillimore was not killed until after he'd run away; for Edith to have subsequently killed him and then displayed his body for all to see would have been madness, and she is not insane. The one thing I find incredible is her willingness to believe her husband's story of being blackmailed by Dr Clarke without seeing the letters he'd supposedly sent or any other proof whatsoever."

"That part I comprehend," said The Woman, staring into her long-cold tea. "When my husband first began to turn on me, to show me who he truly was, I couldn't believe it. For months, I made excuses for his behaviour and deceived myself into thinking he would change and once again become the man I thought I'd married. I don't know if it was my own pride, not wishing to admit that my judgement had been flawed, or a more altruistic inability to believe something so dreadful of someone I loved. Perhaps it was a combination of the two."

"I wonder," she continued, "if Edith suspected that something was wrong, but convinced herself that leaving the village would solve the problem. Or maybe she truly forced herself to believe, out of an inability to even bear to consider alternatives."

"The human mind can be a ghastly thing," Holmes observed. The Woman nodded in agreement.

"Good night, pointy detective," she said then, rising and going to her room. Holmes didn't go to bed that night. He'd never understood how other people could simply turn off their brains in the midst of deep thought, suspending their reasoning processes for hours while their bodies slept. Ever since he could remember, his way had been to think until his brain could think no more, to let the engine run itself out.

He was glad of Watson's presence, but he realised with some measure of surprise that his moments with The Woman were not now as unlike his moments with the doctor as they once had been. Like his flatmate, she had become a friend and then an ally, a trusted listening ear and occasionally, a very useful associate. Her ways were different, but that did not make them unhelpful. He had missed Watson, but he had not been alone, and the realisation made him feel strangely comforted.

A little later a rakish young workman, with a goatee beard and a swagger, lit his clay pipe at the lamp before descending into the street.

—The Adventure of Charles Augustus Milverton

Chapter 11: Irene

When I awoke the following morning, I was filled with what I can only describe as a devilish sense of amusement. I loved having both Holmes and Watson in my house, endlessly amused by their affectionately barbed exchanges. Adding in Mrs Turner and her ways made for a ceaseless buffet of delights for me to savour.

I rose early to see to my bees, who also seemed to be in a buoyant state, though I suppose the impression was in my mind alone. Returning to the house, I found Holmes alone at the table, drinking coffee and going over his notebook. "I've told Watson that he must attempt to infiltrate the Oakhill Farm household today," he said without looking up.

"How will he manage it?" I asked.

"I will be with him," said Holmes, "but in a guise other than my own."

"I see," I answered. "What do you wish me to do?"

"Tell Edith the truth about her husband. Involve Dr Clarke if you must. We may need her help to catch the murderer, and I want to ensure her full cooperation before that happens."

"I think, perhaps, the easiest way would be to produce Julia Rayburn," I said. I wished I hadn't, even though it was true.

"I agree," said Holmes, "but I did not think you would be open to the idea of attempting it."

"I believe it to be the only way of doing what you ask successfully," I answered, feeling my joyful frame of mind evaporate as my thoughts grew darker.

Watson emerged then, looking as fresh as a gentleman on a country holiday. "I hope this is appropriate attire for the day, Holmes," he said, standing at attention in the middle of the floor, as if he were undergoing a military inspection.

"Haven't you brought anything shabbier?" Holmes asked critically.

"No," said the doctor. "I didn't come down with the object of insinuating myself into a farmhouse."

"Very well," groused Holmes.

"I—might have something that would be useful," said the voice of my housekeeper from her vantage point in the kitchen doorway. "I'm afraid it's below Dr Watson's dignity, but I have some clothing that's meant to be donated to the church."

"Excellent," said Holmes. "Bring the possibilities here, please."

A surreal scene followed, in which Mrs Turner surrounded my friend with piles of dingy garments, as if he were a bird in a nest, while Watson and I looked on in amused amazement.

Holmes picked out an outfit worthy of a gardener or farm labourer, a grey shirt and brown trousers that looked as if they had seen much better days. "Here, Watson," he said, "this is far more like it."

The doctor took the clothing gingerly. "Well," he mumbled, "I suppose it's not the worst thing you've ever asked me to do." Mrs Turner looked conflicted, pleased to have been helpful on the one hand, horrified at the impeachment of the doctor's dignity on the other.

"Thank you, Mrs Turner," I said quickly. "You've saved us."

"Yes, indeed," said Dr Watson, blushing. "We'd have been hopeless without you." He turned tail and disappeared to dress himself in the guise Holmes had dictated. The detective vanished as well, to turn himself into whomever he planned to be for the day. I stole a look at my housekeeper, who was still standing motionless in the kitchen doorway with a slight smile on her face.

I waited on the sofa, amused that for once, I was free to remain in my own character while the two men changed theirs. I knew Holmes's love of the drama of disguise, and I was glad that he had a reason to employ it. He would never have admitted it, but it seemed to provide an outlet for the part of him that might have enjoyed treading the boards of the London stage.

Dr Watson emerged quickly, looking more ordinary than I had ever seen him. Normally, there is a pervasive neatness about the doctor, an air that marks him out as a former military man, but Holmes had chosen his clothing well, and he looked like a farmer or one of the working men of the village.

Holmes took longer, but when he came into the sitting room, he looked as ordinary as his friend, an accomplishment that was far more difficult to achieve. I had seen his powers of transformation during the Florida case, but years had elapsed, and I saw with fresh eyes. He smiled at my obvious astonishment.

"I hadn't expected to create such an impression in one accustomed to my methods," he said, clearly pleased with himself.

"You both look your parts very well," I said, not willing to allow him a victory. "I wish you the greatest of luck."

"No need for luck," said Holmes. "Watson and I are old hands at this sort of thing."

"Though I am not usually in disguise," said Watson, not sounding overly pleased at his lot.

"I would hardly call it a disguise, Watson," said his flatmate. "It's merely a way to gain you an entrance. You've no need to speak or act differently than you normally do."

"Well, that's merciful," said the doctor, and I thought I detected a note of sarcasm in his voice.

"Your task, I fear, may be more difficult than ours," said Holmes quietly, looking at me with a steady gaze.

"Difficult but not impossible," I answered. "It will be better, I believe, for Edith to know the truth as quickly as possible."

"Better, perhaps, but no less painful," said my friend, and I was reminded that he understood human emotion far more completely than his reputation indicated.

—

We parted after breakfast, the two men beginning the journey to the farm on foot, which befit the station they planned to imitate. I began my much briefer walk back to the Stevenson house, a journey that felt shorter than I wished it to be, so much did I loathe making it. Ever since Holmes had connected the threads of Julia's shame and Edith's sad deception, I had known that a moment like this must come. If Edith believed in her husband's innocence against the evidence of his own odd behaviour, then it was unlikely, I knew, that she would take the word of someone else without the proof of her own eyes. Whether she would believe that Julia's baby was actually her husband's, I didn't know. I hoped, however, that all of the circumstances would align in such a way that she would be forced to accept the truth, even if she could not do so at first.

My own experience with my late husband's duplicity had taught me the value of the brutal truth. Lies may feel safer and more comfortable, but they are poison. Better to know the ugly reality than a beautiful fiction.

I found Julia pruning flowers in front of her family's home. She smiled when she saw me approach, but her pale face and dark-rimmed eyes showed that she had slept little, if at all. "Good morning, Miss Adler," she said softly, rising and taking my hand.

"Good morning, Julia," I said. "May I have a cup of tea?" I couldn't face broaching the day's subject in the front garden of the Stevenson home. The girl led me to the kitchen, which was part of the servants' domain. I was surprised, but the maids and footmen we passed only nodded, and a few greeted "Miss Julia" as if they were used to her ways.

"Mrs Teague," said Julia, once we reached the environs of the kitchen, "I would like to make Miss Adler a cup of tea." The cook nodded, and I watched as Julia made tea, an act that would have been quite normal for most of the people of the village, but which was, for the daughter of Charles Stevenson, almost an act of rebellion.

Once the tea was made, Julia and I took our places at the servants' table. "Please forgive my eccentricity," said the girl, taking a sip of tea from her china cup. "I've always liked this part of the house best. When I was a little girl, I would come down here and learn all sorts of things from Teague and the others. I can polish a pair of my father's shoes better than either of the current footmen. My parents thought I would grow out of my below-stairs enthrallment, but I never did. My visits became more discreet, but I was still a frequent guest up to the day of my wedding." She flinched after she spoke the last word.

"Don't they mind the fact that you don't keep your place?" I asked, more out of a desire to understand Julia than because I actually wondered. My experience with household servants made me well assured that they were likely to mind a great deal, though they would take pains to appear as if they did not.

"My parents don't know, and the others are used to me. They have to warn any new arrivals, but everyone adjusts in time. I've often thought the staff was more like my family than my parents are," Julia finished. I couldn't help doubting that the hardworking maids and footmen I saw could possibly feel the same way about the privileged daughter of the house.

After a few moments of drinking my tea and bolstering my courage, I began. "Julia, I need you to do something that will be very difficult."

"Anything," she said. "It doesn't matter now." I looked around to confirm that we were fully alone.

"I fear you will feel differently in a moment," I said, speaking quietly. "The truth is, James Phillimore deceived his wife as much as he did you. Rather than disappearing, he left the village on purpose to escape what he claimed was blackmail by Dr Clarke over something that concerned his parents. Edith chose to believe him. We need her help now, but I don't believe we'll be able to get it without you to corroborate your story. It may—it probably will be very difficult, but I see no other way to make Edith comprehend the depth of her husband's deceitfulness."

"Penance is never easy," said Julia.

"It's obvious that Phillimore actually fled to escape his wife finding out about the child and his relationship with you. I assume he convinced you to keep quiet to preserve your own reputation."

"Yes," she answered. "He made it seem like my idea, but he assured me that if I breathed a word of what he'd done, we would go down together. He was afraid, though. I could see it in his eyes the last time we spoke."

"I'm sure, then, that part of his desperation was fear that you would tell his secret."

"He said he had always admired my discretion, and he made it seem like I would be a disappointment to him and to myself if I gave in and told anyone."

"Miss Adler—" she met my eyes with fire in her own. "I'm glad Ed knows. Please, when I'm gone, tell him that I helped you. He might not think so ill of me if he knew."

"Tell him yourself," I said, feeling a flash of something that was either inspiration or madness. "Speak to him before you go. You must agree that you at least owe him that."

"You're sure he'll see me?" she asked.

"I'm sure," I said.

"Very well," she answered, her eyes fixed on her pale hand as it rested on the table. "If you believe he wishes it, I will do so."

"I'm convinced he wishes it more than you can bear to believe," I answered.

—

Julia and I drove to the farm in silence. I had nothing more to tell her, since her part in the day's events would depend on Edith as much as on either of us. I simply hoped I could avoid causing a scene that would bring unbearable pain to either of the two women. I like to pride myself on a certain measure of emotional objectivity, but I could not manage to detach myself from my dread of what I was about to undertake.

We gained admittance to the house easily, and we were shown into the parlour, where Edith soon joined us. She looked surprised when she saw Julia, but I saw something flash across her face as she came into the room that suggested she might not be as shocked at what we were there to reveal as I'd feared.

"Now, Watson, the fair sex is your department," said Holmes, with a smile, when the dwindling frou-frou of skirts had ended in the slam of the front door.

—The Adventure of the Second Stain

Chapter 12: Holmes

The detective and the doctor reached the Phillimore farm by midmorning, but instead of going to the house, they made their way across the fields to the gathering of homes where the workers lived with their wives. "I thought we were to infiltrate the household," said Watson, who looked confused, but followed his flatmate in the usual way.

"So we are, in a manner of speaking," said Holmes, "but I happen to know that the cook is married to one of the men, and today is her day off. We will find her in her lair."

Watson sighed wearily, and Holmes stopped and looked at him for a moment. "I'm sorry, old friend. I didn't mean to sap your strength."

"No matter," said Watson. "It's only my old injury. Perhaps if you tell me more about what I'm to do, it will help distract my mind from the discomfort."

"Very well," said Holmes. "We know that Mrs Merriwether acted as an emissary of sorts between Phillimore and his wife, meaning that she was aware of Phillimore's whereabouts. According to Eliza, the murdered man's young daughter, Mrs Merriwether was also the first person called by Edith Phillimore when the child found the body."

"The child found the body? How dreadful for her," Watson interjected with a pained expression on his amiable face.

"She seemed to handle it decently enough," said Holmes. "She thought her father was asleep."

"Seeming is different from being," said the doctor. "I have attended at the homes of many children who were the unfortunate discoverers of a parent's death, and not one of them was without a scar of some sort."

"Set your mind at ease," said Holmes. "I spoke to her afterward and explained the truth."

"Very well," said Watson. "Having witnessed your uncanny way with the children of London, I can hardly fail to believe in your capability when it comes to a child of Fulworth."

"Your concern does you credit," said Holmes.

"Our story," the detective continued, "is that we are looking for work and heard that Mr Merriwether might be hiring extra hands. He's in charge of the labourers and takes responsibility for many of those things. Of course, Oakhill Farm isn't looking to take anyone on, and we won't find Merriwether at home. Once we gain admittance, however, you can begin to work your usual magic on the cook."

"Why not go alone?" Watson asked. "You know the case much better than I do, and you're familiar with the lady in question."

"Unfortunately," said Holmes, "familiarity is not a blessing in the present circumstance. She deplores me in my normal guise. I believe I will succeed in not being recognised if I act like your nearly-mute friend. If I went alone, however, the risk of discovery would be much greater. Besides, Watson, you are far too modest. I have nowhere near your ability to put ladies of all ages and societal stations at their ease, nor do I wish to cultivate it."

"Your confidence in me is touching," answered Watson drily. "If I am unable to succeed in gaining the information you require, what will you do then?"

"I have every assurance that your conversation will be beneficial, but I will explore other avenues to the same conclusion if I must," said Holmes.

"I left my revolver at the cottage," said Watson.

"No matter," his friend replied mildly. "I picked it up myself. Normally I would not take it upon myself to carry your weapon, but in the present situation, I will take your place as the silent witness with his hand on the trigger."

"You mock me, Holmes," said the doctor. "It's not sporting."

"Certainly not," rejoined the detective. "Your silent vigilance has saved us from a tight spot many a time, and I'm not likely to forget it."

Finally, the two men reached a row of modest homes. Outside of the first, they found a girl putting clothes on a line. Her dress was torn, and she looked tired, but she smiled in a friendly way. "Where might we find the home of Mr Merriwether?" Watson asked, returning her smile.

"It's just there," she said, pointing to a house three down from her own. It was a drab grey colour, much weathered by wind and rain, but respectably kept and slightly larger than the others around it. Holmes noticed that the girl did not look entirely pleased at the question, and as they turned to move on, she called after them, "You won't get any help there."

"I fear she's correct," said Watson, once the two were out of earshot and nearly to the Merriwether home.

"You are determined to sell yourself short," said Holmes. "Besides, I'll be here to rescue you if anything goes wildly amiss." His flatmate shook his head resignedly and followed the detective up to the door.

As Holmes had predicted, it was opened by the cook. Instead of her usual white apron over a practical grey frock, she was dressed in a garish yellow colour that reminded Holmes of the time he'd seen a child get ill on a train from London to Birmingham.

"What do you want?" she asked suspiciously.

"Please excuse our intrusion," Watson answered smoothly. "My friend and I are looking for work and thought your husband might have some to offer."

Mrs Merriwether looked the doctor up and down. "Well," she said, "you don't talk like most of the men around here, and I rarely have visitors. Come inside and have a cup of tea."

"Thank you," said Watson. "That would be very welcome." The two men followed the cook into a small parlour that was as drab as the outside of the house, but neat. Holmes scrunched himself into the corner of a threadbare chair, folding into himself so that he would look like the more insignificant of the two companions, while Watson took his place on the doily-covered sofa. The lady of the house went to fetch something edible, and Holmes tried to look as if he didn't notice the irritated look Watson bestowed upon him.

When Mrs Merriwether returned, she bore a plate of iced biscuits that instantly repulsed the detective. He took one, however, along with a cup of tea that appeared more promising. "Now," said the lady when both men had been served, "what sort of work were you looking for?" She fixed Watson with a sharply appraising stare. "You don't seem much like a field worker, not with those hands."

Well done, thought Holmes, willing to acknowledge merit wherever he happened to find it. The doctor looked momentarily discomfited, but he rallied quickly. “My name is John Morstan. I’m a veterinary surgeon, and this is my friend Smith who assists me with the larger stock. I thought some of the animals might need looking after. I understand your husband has oversight of them.”

“No,” she said, “for that you’d need Peter Warren, but Williams was just by not a week ago, and he looked them all over. Won’t be needing any more of your kind.”

“That is unfortunate,” said the doctor. “I haven’t had biscuits as good as these since my wife passed away. It’s a pity we’ll have to move on without tasting more.” The cook blushed with pleasure at the compliment.

Watson had a gift. Holmes couldn’t deny it. He might not be brilliant, but he was certainly skilled. The combination of compliment and pitiable revelation had obviously begun to win the woman over.

“Stay and have a few more, then,” she said. “It’s not often I get to entertain in my own home. They’re always running me ragged at the big house.”

“That must be difficult,” said Watson, “especially given the excitement of the past few days.”

“Heard about that, have you?” she asked. “I suppose it’s all over the county now.”

“I’m sure it must have been terrible for you,” said the doctor, “losing a member of the family with whom you have such a close association.”

The cook sniffed meaningfully. “I don’t mean,” she said. “Never could bear the man. I only stayed around because of his wife, Edith Pope, as was. For her sake, I never said it when he was alive, but it doesn’t seem to matter now.”

“Oh,” said Watson, “I understood him to have been a very pleasant man.” Holmes had told him nothing of the sort.

“People always say the most ridiculous things about the dead,” said the woman. “He was a bad-tempered man until the day he disappeared. His only redeeming quality was his love for Edith, but even that failed at the end.”

"I see," said the doctor. "How did it fail?" He had gone too far. Holmes could feel the woman's reticence return in an instant.

"Nothing worth speaking about," she said. "I ought to get back to my mending. I'm sorry I couldn't be of more help." She ushered the two men out the door as if she was afraid to keep them in her house.

Once outside, Watson shook his head dejectedly. "I told you it would come to nothing," he said. "I'm not cut out for this sort of thing."

"Not at all," said Holmes pleasantly. "You did brilliantly."

"What do you mean?" asked his flatmate. "She barely spoke before I ruined the whole thing."

"My dear Watson," said Holmes, "you must learn to view these things with a more careful eye. It is true that Mrs Merriwether did not reveal the entire plan of Phillimore's flight and her involvement in it, but I hardly expected her to do so, and I know some of her part anyway. What she did reveal is that she was aware, at least to some extent, of James Phillimore's marital indiscretions. Her inclusion of the phrase 'at the end' suggests strongly that she was speaking of his relationship with Julia Rayburn."

Watson stared at his friend, and Holmes let out a dry laugh. "Well," said the doctor, "if I've been of help, then I'm pleased."

"Always, my friend," said Holmes, leading him back across the fields.

—

The two men returned to the cottage, and Holmes transformed himself back into his usual guise. He could feel his brain working to make cohesive sense of the fractured pieces of information he now possessed, so he took his black notebook in hand and went to Irene's bees.

The detective spent the next half hour simply observing. First, he watched every tiny movement as if it were its own single event. Only after he had done that did he allow himself to watch them all together, to see the elaborate dance that made up the life of the hive. Such was the case, he thought. Such was every case, every collection of seemingly disparate events that nonetheless affected each other and connected intrinsically with one another.

A man was dead. That was the beginning point, no matter where it fell in the narrative. The man had left home to escape the consequences of an illicit affair, ostensibly to never return. Instead, he had been killed and his body dumped in a prominent location at his own farm. Supposedly, only two people had known of the affair, the two who had engaged in it. But there was a third. The cook had known something, and that meant that others might know as well. The important question was who and what they had chosen to do with the information. That, Holmes realised, was almost certainly the key to unravelling the whole mystery of Phillimore's death.

In an experience of women which extends over many nations and three separate continents, I have never looked upon a face which gave a clearer promise of a refined and sensitive nature.

—The Sign of Four

Chapter 13: Irene

"Inspector Graves just left," said Edith as she took a seat across from Julia and me. "They've been combing the grounds again, looking for new evidence, but they can't find anything."

"I'm sorry," I said. "That must be very difficult for you."

"I would put up with a lot more if it would help them find my husband's murderer," she said, and I took my opportunity, fearing that if I did not do so right away, I wouldn't manage it at all.

"That's why we've come," I said. "We want to tell you something that may have power to alter your view of events. I'm afraid—" I looked over at Julia, who was deathly pale, "that it may also prove distressing for you, and for that I apologise in advance."

Edith laughed. "I hardly see what could be more distressing than what I've already experienced."

Suddenly, I wanted to laugh, in that horrible, untimely way that hits one at funerals or at the most sombre moments in church. The irony was piercing. I stifled the laugh, but as a result, there was a moment of quiet.

"Miss Adler, I'll do it myself," said Julia very softly, finally breaking the heavy silence.

I looked at her in surprise. "Would you like to be alone?"

"Yes," she answered, with her old resolve back in her voice. Edith's expression was guarded, and I had no idea what she might be thinking or anticipating, but I trusted Julia, so I took my leave and went outside. Truthfully, I was delighted to be relieved of an unpleasant task, and it seemed like a certain kind of poetic justice for Julia to be the bearer of the news.

The midmorning was slightly cool, and I took the path away from the house, not really intending to do anything in particular but hoping I might observe something useful. I had spent so much time at the farm over the previous few days that it seemed impossible that I would miss anything that hadn't been there before.

As I approached the barn, I saw two men standing outside the door, and I heard one of them say, "I don't understand why we're even working. Phillimore's dead, and his wife don't care one way or the other."

"We will work as long as there's work to be done," answered another voice, and Peter Warren appeared at the door to the barn. He saw me and removed his cap, which caused the other two to turn and do the same.

"Forgive me," I said. "I had no intention of disturbing your work."

"Seems to me, Miss Adler," said the tall foreman, "that you're very good at disturbing people's work." I was prepared to be affronted, but he smiled then, and his smile changed his face so completely that I was amazed. No longer was he the severe man I'd imagined him to be; instead, he was the husband and father I'd never quite been able to picture him being.

He came toward me and spoke quietly. "The little girl's in the carriage house. She might need some company."

"Thank you," I answered. I didn't wish to walk through the barn and endure more stares, so I went back around to the outside entrance, thinking as I did so that James Phillimore would never again drive out of it, except if he were to do so in his ghostly form. It was an extremely fanciful image, but I could almost visualise the spectre of the dead man riding restlessly through the grounds of his farm.

I dismissed the picture from my mind as I crept back to the dark corner where Eliza had brought me before. The sound that greeted me was one I hadn't heard before; she was crying.

As quickly as I could, I sat down on the dirty floor and gathered her close, rocking her in my arms. She clung to me and buried her wet face in my shoulder, holding Charles tightly. "They took all my things away," she sobbed, her voice muffled by the cloth of my green shirtwaist.

"I'm so sorry, darling," I said. "It was dreadful of them. We must bring new things."

"No!" she said, shaking her head emphatically against me. I just held her then, not knowing what to say to ease her sadness. I am no psychologist, but I wondered how many of her tears were due to the death of her father and how many to the maelstrom around her.

After a long time, she sat up and wiped her eyes with the back of her hand. "Is Mr Holmes here?"

"Not now," I said, smiling.

"Charles wanted to see him," she said.

"Then he shall," I answered. "You and he and Mummy must come to my house very soon." This seemed to content her. She leaned against me once again, and very soon, she fell asleep.

I carried Eliza, who was heavier than she looked, back to the servants' entrance of the house and handed her to Lewis the maid, who smiled at the sight of her sleeping form. I didn't relish the thought of returning to the cold parlour where the two women were, but didn't think I could forestall it any longer. With head held high, I made my way back to the front of the house, determined to make the best of whatever sight was to greet me.

I don't know what I expected, but I certainly did not anticipate finding Edith Phillimore holding Julia Rayburn's hand gently and smiling at her with a look of genuine peace that I hadn't seen on her face for some time.

Both women looked up when I entered. "Sorry to intrude," I said, feeling like I'd been apologising a great deal that day, something that is not my usual practise.

"It's all right," said Julia, and I saw traces of tears on her face, though she smiled at me.

"I understand," said Edith, "and I will help any way I can, though Julia and I both ask, if possible, that my husband's—associations be kept private, if they may be."

"I will do the very best I can," I said, "and Mr Holmes has no intention of publicising them."

"I know that it may not be possible," said Julia, "but for my husband's sake, I hope that it is." I wondered to myself what Edith might have said to her on that topic, but I didn't pry, and our ride back to the village was as silent as our ride to the farm had been until we were nearly to the Stevenson house.

"Thank you for that," said Julia suddenly.

"You have yourself to thank," I said. "I was just the messenger."

She laughed. "That's what you really think, isn't it? No wonder you and Mr Holmes get on so well."

I left her at her parents' home, but extracted a promise from her that she wouldn't leave Fulworth until the conclusion of the case, which she was only willing to give on the assurance that she might be needed by Edith, depending on developments.

I made my way back up the hill, glad that I did not know what had passed between the two women. Edith had surprised me slightly, though I thought I understood her reaction. There's a kind of stubbornness that clings to a flawed way of thinking but is actually relieved to be proven wrong, to have legitimate doubts confirmed. I had known that stubbornness and the relief that comes from being delivered of it.

—

When I reached home, I went to check on my bees and found that they had a strange companion, a detective with long fingers and luminous eyes. "Hello, Irene," he said without turning around as I came up behind him.

"Hullo, Holmes."

"The bees seem well contented," he mused.

"They are," I answered. "I am happy to say that their care is rather less complicated than solving criminal cases."

"I don't know," said my friend. "Both are a matter of small parts that fit into a unified whole."

"When it comes to the murder of James Phillimore, I fear that I understand a great deal of the parts and very little of the whole," I admitted.

"Well, Watson and I were not entirely unsuccessful," said Holmes. "Come inside, and we shall tell you our discovery."

"Poor Watson," I said.

"Not so," said Holmes. "He performed his task with success."

—

When my friend and I reached the cottage, we found Dr Watson and Mrs Turner conversing congenially over cold meat pies. The sight of food reminded my stomach that it was starving, and I sat down to relieve my hunger pangs. Holmes didn't seem to notice the spread, making his way to the wing chair instead. My curiosity warred with my hunger, but physical cravings won out over mental ones, and I began to eat.

"I hope your errand was successful," said the doctor kindly.

"Very," I answered between mouthfuls. "Edith Phillimore is fully on our side and apprised of the situation."

"I can't help feeling our task was less elegantly done," said Watson, "but Holmes seems to have gleaned something useful out of it."

I noticed that Mrs Turner smiled a great deal whenever the shorter man spoke, though she did not comment. It was her usual habit to eat her meals with me, but I had been surprised at her readiness to do so with my guests, not from any reticence on my part but an expected hesitation on hers. I was beginning, I thought, to understand.

I ate quickly, wanting to combine my thoughts with Holmes's as quickly as I could, wondering if he had come any closer to apprehending what was still impenetrable to me. When I'd had my fill, I rose from the table. "Excuse me," I said to doctor and housekeeper, "please don't feel the need to hurry. I wish to discuss the morning with Holmes."

Dr Watson nodded. "Yes, before you came, Mrs Turner was telling me about some of the local legends. I would like to hear more if she isn't bored with the subject." The lady in question blushed like a schoolgirl and showed no sign of leaving the table.

I joined my friend in the other room, surprised to realise how comfortable I felt as I settled onto the sofa and looked at his face with its languid expression that denoted acute mental activity. "Now, Holmes," I said, "relieve my misery and tell me the result of your attempt at Mrs Merriwether."

"Watson's attempt," he corrected. "I'm happy to say that our mutual friend more than outdid himself, albeit somewhat accidentally."

"I'm well aware of Dr Watson's talents," I said sharply, not meaning the comment ironically, though given what was occurring at my table at that moment, I suppose it was.

"Very well," said Holmes, with infuriating mildness. "We went to the woman's house, were treated as strangers, and Watson engaged her on the subject of the Phillimore murder after a well-placed comment on the excellence of her iced biscuits."

I laughed. "I take it she said something significant."

"She spoke few words, but she insinuated that she knew Phillimore had not been faithful to his wife. More specific she would not be, but she certainly knew something."

"If she knew, why would she not have told Edith?"

"It's a fascinating question to ponder," said Holmes. "Given her vital role in the man's flight, I expect that she intended to tell Edith at a later date and convince her to never rejoin her husband once he had left. She seems uncommonly attached to her."

"That I can corroborate," I said, "but mightn't she be the murderer?"

"A sour disposition does not necessarily single one out as a killer," said Holmes, smiling. "A murderer would have been far more careful with his words than she was, though I believe our appearing to be strangers loosened her lips to an unusual extent. At any rate, I don't believe she killed the man."

"I suppose it's helpful to rule her out as a suspect," I said.

"Very," said Holmes, "but the question now is, would she have told someone, and if so, who?"

"I fear we have a great many possibilities," I said.

"Fewer, perhaps, than it seems at first blush," said my friend, his voice taking on a schoolmasterly tone. "In every case, there is a limited number of concerned individuals with probable involvement. If none of them prove to be the culprit, then the gaze must widen, but the first task must be to rule each of them out."

"We know that neither Edith nor Julia was aware that she knew. We can also rule out Phillimore himself because he must have known she was to be in charge of the posting of the rabbit, and he would have been very unlikely to trust her or quietly allow his wife to do so if he'd known. Warren, one of the police's favourites, is clearly unaware, or he would have used the information to throw suspicion off himself. Dr Clarke, who by rights shouldn't even be involved, would certainly have told me if he'd suspected anything. We know Julia didn't consult him or the midwife, so that's another pathway taken to its conclusion."

"Julia's father," I said. "We don't know why Charles Stevenson was there." Suddenly, a host of possibilities crowded into my mind that hadn't been there before I'd learned Julia's secret. Her revelation and the subsequent events had banished her father's presence from my mind, but the memory of my encounter with him in the Phillimore parlour rushed back forcefully.

"Precisely," said Holmes, and I could see with infuriating clarity that he had known where the conversation was headed all along and was simply waiting for me to catch up to his reasoning.

"Clearly, you're ahead of me," I said, a trifle testily. "What do you have in mind?"

"I plan to visit him this afternoon. Do you care to join me?"

"I hadn't anticipated such a direct approach," I answered.

"Give me a small amount of credit," said Holmes. "I don't plan to greet the man with an accusation of guilt. I have my methods of encouraging revelation."

"Very well," I answered, "but don't expect an easy time of it. He's unpleasant at the best of times."

"Watson," called Holmes to his flatmate, who was still at the table conversing animatedly with my housekeeper, "three will be too many for this task, I fear. If you are favourably disposed, Miss Adler and I will leave you to your own devices."

"Certainly," said the doctor, looking excessively pleased.

—

"Holmes, you are positively a romantic," I said as we strolled down the lane that would take us to the office of Charles Stevenson.

"Nothing of the sort," he retorted.

"You can't claim," I replied, "that you are ignorant of the attachment currently developing within the walls of my house."

"Watson," said the detective, "has many talents, one of which is the ability to form absurdly rash attachments."

"But is it rash?" I asked. "He has known Mrs Turner for some time, and she has always admired him."

I looked up at my friend with a mischievous glint in my eye. "Holmes, I believe you would consider attachment of any kind to be unforgivably rash, except that of yourself to your chemistry set."

"Nonsense, Irene," he answered. "I'm at least as attached to my tobacco." My laugh rang out in the clear, open air.

Presently, I spoke again. "If there is a perfectly logical explanation for Stevenson's presence at the farm, what do you intend to do?"

"If that happens," he said, "we will follow the clues and see where else they lead us. I do not believe, however, that we will have to concern ourselves with that."

"You believe Stevenson is the murderer?"

My friend spoke soberly. "I deal in certainties rather than probabilities, but I saw something interesting as Watson and I made our way back to the village. Another person was making his way toward the farm workers' cottages. He was far away, but I could tell by his gait and shape that it was the man I had seen standing over Phillimore's body."

"Stevenson was going to speak to Mrs Merriwether?"

"I am not certain," he answered, "but it's highly suggestive. None of the families who live in those houses could ever hope to afford his services, so it's unlikely he would have been calling in his professional capacity. It's also hard to imagine a man with his love of outdoing his neighbours idly visiting one of the poorest places in the area unless he had a pressing reason."

"Upon my word, Holmes," I said, "will you never stop concealing vital clues from me?"

"I meant no such thing," he answered calmly. "I merely meant to give your mind ample time to process our earlier conversation before I added this development." I folded my arms, irritated.

“That hurts my pride, Watson,” he said at last. “It is a petty feeling, no doubt, but it hurts my pride.”

—The Five Orange Pips

Chapter 14: Holmes

The detective continued, undaunted by his companion's annoyance. "I also wished to share the information right before we see the man. I thought it might inflame you to your present state of aggravation, which I hope will prove helpful in our exchange."

In a moment, The Woman had stepped in front of Holmes and turned around, effectively barring him from continuing down the lane. He looked down at her with a mixture of amusement and perplexity.

"I am glad I'm able to provide you with the day's entertainment," she said, "but before we continue to the man's house, I insist on a full explanation of what you intend to do. I have been content with limited information when my own safety was in question, but I see no reason such reticence should be necessary now."

"No matter," said Holmes. "It's just that I had anticipated the value of having someone with me who is less knowledgeable and therefore likely to perform naturally."

Irene sniffed. "Holmes, your powers of manipulation grow ever larger with each passing day. Dr Watson credits you with a straightforwardness that you begin to lack. Perhaps I should tell the poor man to watch out for your machinations." She spit out the words with great pique, but as she did so, she moved out of the way and allowed the detective to continue walking.

"I take it you agree to leave me to my methods," said the detective mildly.

"I wish I didn't trust you as much as I do," said The Woman. "I will consent to be the ignorant partner. Do you have anything you wish me to say or do?" As much as she tried to seem resigned, she was, he thought, also filled with a conspiratorial sense of excitement.

"Simply play along and act as you normally would," said Holmes.

"Very well," she answered, as they approached the low brick building that housed the office of Charles Stevenson.

A ring of the bell produced a short young man who looked as if he was so clean he was likely to sweat soapsuds if warmed. "What is your business?" he asked curtly. "You have no appointment."

Holmes cleared his throat. "Please inform Mr Stevenson that Sherlock Holmes and Irene Adler wish to speak with him."

The young man looked up at the detective, seeming to evaluate whether or not it was within his ability to get rid of the visitors himself. Holmes stared down at him sharply until he dropped his gaze and ushered the companions inside, disappearing behind a closed door.

The barrister's vestibule was furnished simply, but the wood of the young clerk's desk was of the highest quality, as was the bench on which Holmes and Irene took their seats without being asked. The companions waited five minutes and then ten. "Do you think he means to bore us into losing interest?" asked The Woman.

"No," said the detective, "but he does mean to make us uncomfortable, something he does very well in the courtroom, I'd imagine."

"Have you never seen him perform his role as legal advocate?" Irene enquired. "I understood him to be very active in London."

"I have heard of him, but our paths have not crossed," said Holmes. "I would expect him to have heard of me."

The door opened again, and out stepped Charles Stevenson, barrister, wearing a suit that Holmes priced at roughly the yearly income of one of the men who worked on the Phillimore farm. "Please come in," said his smooth voice, and the detective and his companion passed into a large, dark office. The clerk went back to his desk, giving Holmes a cold glance as he did so.

"You'll have to forgive my young man," said Stevenson, motioning to the two to sit down. "His father is a peer, and it seems to have affected his disposition." He laughed drily. "A peer with no money to speak of, but still, a peer." Holmes thought that it must have been one of the man's great regrets that he himself had not been born to rank.

Stevenson sat down behind his desk and folded his long, pale fingers. "Well, Mr Holmes," he said, "I can't fathom that the great detective of Baker Street has come to me for legal advocacy."

"I would like your help," said Holmes deferentially. "I've been retained by Edith Phillimore to investigate the circumstances of her husband's unfortunate death, but I find the details very difficult to unravel," he lied smoothly. "If you have any information that might help, I'd be indebted to you. As you know, villages are very difficult places to glean anything of value. A great deal of talk goes on, without clarity or intelligence."

The barrister smiled. "I hardly think that you, Mr Holmes, would be foiled by the unreliability of village gossip. I thank you for your flattery, but it is unnecessary. I will help you in any way I can."

Holmes smiled. "Excellent. As you were on hand the day the body was discovered, I hoped you might shed a little light on the circumstances. I've spoken to Dr Clarke, but he was so focused on the corpse that I fear he may have missed some of the surrounding details that a man of your expertise would have noticed."

Stevenson leaned forward, and his fine white hair fell over his forehead. The detective noted that he appeared to relish the opportunity to give his account. "I only learned of the unfortunate event because I was supping at the home of the good doctor that night. We went to the house together and found them laying out the poor man's body. It was obvious he'd been killed long before, but still an arresting sight. The widow was distraught."

"If you don't mind a question, who fetched the doctor?"

"Mrs Merriwether, the cook at Oakhill Farm."

"Were the police present when you arrived?"

"Only just. Graves has been resident in the village for the duration of the investigation of the disappearance, and he roused Chipping and those ridiculous boys. It's a good thing they didn't find any evidence. With their methods, I doubt it would hold up in court."

"You favour the London police, then?" asked Holmes.

"On the contrary," said Stevenson. "They're equally inept, but with fancier pedigrees." Holmes didn't particularly like the man, but he had to agree. "I remained at the house until Dr Clarke left. Miss Adler saw me just prior to our departure."

"True," said Irene.

"Had you any theories about Phillimore's disappearance before that time?" Holmes asked.

"None whatsoever," said Stevenson.

"Thank you," said Holmes, "you've been very helpful," though he was thinking the opposite. "Miss Adler, I believe we may take our leave."

"Won't you stay for a cup of tea?" asked the barrister, looking as if he didn't mean it.

"I think not," said Holmes. "We have other pressing engagements." The young man showed the detective and The Woman out in the manner of a housewife throwing rubbish into the dustbin.

Once outside, Irene looked up at Holmes in perplexity. "If you've managed to glean something important from that conversation, then you've outstripped me by miles."

"Few miles," Holmes answered. "The man is less susceptible to appeals to his vanity than I'd anticipated. We do know now that Mrs Merriwether sounded the initial alarm, though this was a frustratingly elaborate way to arrive at that detail."

"I don't believe my ignorance was of much assistance after all," said Irene, "though I did appreciate your subservient act."

"I confess," said Holmes, "that I hoped the man would betray that he knew something of his daughter's predicament."

"An excellent motive," The Woman murmured.

"Still a possible one," said Holmes, "but if it is true, we will have to discover it by different means."

"I almost think I prefer cases in which my own life is in danger," said Irene. "The excitement is much enhanced."

"Stay the course," said Holmes. "We will find the murderer."

"Do you not worry that he or she will have fled?"

"No," said Holmes. "A person who places a corpse or arranges for a corpse to be placed in as prominent a location as Phillimore's murderer did is almost certain to remain and survey the effects of his handiwork."

"Insanity?"

"Not necessarily, but a desire for recognition, certainly."

"Then why not confess, as some do, and receive all the credit?"

"I believe our murderer feels stronger than that, invincible and not susceptible to detection. Of course, in truth, all murderers are susceptible to detection because they invariably make mistakes."

Holmes would have continued to speak, but as he and Irene turned to start up the hill to the cottage, a yell behind them stopped them in their tracks. The detective turned to see the frantic form of Edith Phillimore, flushed and wild-eyed as she approached.

"Whatever is the matter?" asked Irene.

"It's Eliza," panted the breathless woman. "I can't find her anywhere."

I confess that I have been as blind as a mole, but it is better to learn wisdom late than never to learn it at all.

—The Man with the Twisted Lip

Chapter 15: Irene

"What happened?" I asked, putting out a hand and lightly touching Edith's shoulder. "She was at home earlier. I saw her in the carriage house, and then Lewis put her to bed."

"I know," she answered. "She got up and went to the chicken house, and she never came back. I sent the men scouring all over the property for her, but she was gone. There's no chance she had enough time to get away under her own power."

"Have you told the police?" Holmes asked.

She nodded. "They're forming a search party, but I came straight to you from them." I had observed that while Holmes did not admire the police's methods when it came to more refined tasks, he had the sense to see when they were needed.

"Of course, we will do all we can," said Holmes.

I could see that Edith was near tears, but she used powerful self-control to hold herself together for the moment. "Inspector Graves told me to go home and wait for developments," she said. "I'm going to ask Julia to come with me."

"Very wise," said Holmes, and she walked away toward the Stevenson house, her shoulders bowed with dejection and fear.

"What do we do?" I asked my friend.

"We go home," said Holmes.

"Whatever for?"

"To figure out what I've missed."

—

The inside of the cottage was empty, and it didn't take Holmes to deduce for me that Dr Watson and Mrs Turner had gone out together. My friend immediately made for the wing chair, and I sat opposite him so that he could talk through the details in his mind if he wished. He was beyond me then. I saw facts, and my brain refused to stop making surmises, but I had no idea which direction to proceed or what might be in my companion's mind. After a long silence, I got up to make tea, but when I came back and pushed a cup into Holmes's hand, he did not acknowledge my presence.

"Tobacco," he said after what seemed like an age. I was almost asleep by this point, drowsy amidst the quiet of his thoughts, but the insistent tone of his voice woke me, even though he spoke quietly.

"What?" I asked.

Holmes leapt to his feet, colour rising in his cheeks. "We must leave at once. There is no time to lose." I knew better than to argue, following him outside as quickly as I could.

"The tobacco, Irene. He tried to fool me, but the tobacco gave him away."

"Who, Phillimore? Stevenson?" I breathed hard, trying to keep pace with Holmes's long, quick strides.

"No," he said, "Dr Clarke."

"What?" I said again, walking along and staring at my friend with disbelief. "I thought we ruled out the possibility of Edith's story."

"We did," said Holmes, "but nevertheless, it's him. I saw traces of Phillimore's tobacco in his study."

"How do you know it was Phillimore's and not someone else's who uses the same sort?"

"Clarke doesn't smoke, and he never allowed tobacco anywhere near him from notions of it being harmful to the health. The traces I saw were ground into the floor of his study, as if dropped by accident and not heeded. He would never have allowed the stuff if he could have helped it. The pattern of droppings suggests that the tobacco fell out of Phillimore's pocket, perhaps during an altercation." Holmes related these facts in a monotone that suggested he was agitated on the inside. I wondered why these signs had not been evident to him before, but I didn't comment. There would be plenty of time for that.

I quickly ascertained that Holmes was leading me to Dr Clarke's house at the edge of the village. A shouted greeting by Miss Rose as we passed the butcher's shop was not returned, and I hoped in passing that I had not mortally offended her.

"We won't find Clarke here," said Holmes. "I only hope to find clues to where he might have taken the child."

"Should I find the police?"

“No,” said Holmes. “They will be half way to the farm by now. There isn’t time.”

Clarke’s house was dark and quiet, with no sign of anyone to let us in. Holmes dexterously picked the lock on the front door and led me through the suite of rooms that the doctor used as a surgery. The light from the afternoon sun cast strange shadows, and I felt a strong sense of foreboding as I looked around at the coldly formal arrangements. Holmes quickly passed through, entering an unusually broad hallway.

“What are we seeking?” I asked.

“Any sign of the child and where he might have taken her,” said Holmes briefly. “Barring that, any sort of disturbance.”

My friend undoubtedly knew what he meant by this, but I was less sure. I found myself peeking into obviously-unused rooms and then coming out again into the passage, feeling as if I were Alice in Wonderland trying to make sense of a strange world. Holmes, meanwhile, went straight for a large room at the end. After a few minutes, I joined him, less than satisfied with my own efforts. He was searching Clarke’s dustbin.

I knew better than to say anything and proceeded to walk around the perimeter of the room with as little luck as I’d had previously. I was about to give up and search through the jumbled papers on Clarke’s vast desk, a task Holmes had already performed, when something caught my eye. There was a flash of white tucked between the cushion and the back of Clarke’s chair. It was the smallest of fibres, but it looked out of place.

“Holmes,” I said, “look.”

To his credit, the detective trusted me enough to stand to his feet and look at the wisps in my hand. “Charles the rabbit,” he said shortly. “Eliza was here.” As gratifying as the realisation was, it also chilled my blood. Until we had found evidence, the reality of Eliza’s kidnapping had seemed further off, almost as if it might not really be happening. Now, there was no mistaking the truth.

I stood back as Holmes made his way around the room again, looking at each surface. Finally, he glanced over to where I was, standing next to a small table on which the doctor had placed a decanter and a glass. The detective ran toward me and grabbed the glass, putting it to his lips and turning it slowly. His eyes grew alarmingly bright.

"They're here!" he said

"What?" I asked dumbly, unable to process what he was saying.

"The lip of the glass is warmer than it should be," he whispered. "Speak softly."

"There's no need for that," said a voice in the doorway, and a woman with a ramrod-straight spine, a black dress, and a large gun met my gaze.

"Mrs Parkfield," I said pointlessly.

"I've no idea what you hope to accomplish," Holmes said coolly. "You can't possibly keep us here."

"I have no intention of keeping you after Dr Clarke gets what he wants." She trained her gun on me. "This is quite simple, Mr Holmes," she said, and the detective and I sat down in the chairs that stood before Clarke's desk. I looked over at Holmes, trying to ascertain what work his brain might be doing, but his face was totally impassive. Mrs Parkfield sat in Clarke's chair, not taking her eyes off either of us. I had never liked her when I'd met her in the village, and my ill feeling was finally justified.

My mind went back to the day I had been held prisoner in a tiny field office in south Florida. I had felt hopeless then, but the circumstances were hardly the same. Holmes had been with me then as well, but I had been unaware of his presence, ignorant of the fact that he was about to rescue me. Now, he was seated next to me, and his presence was comforting, though the irony was that he, too, was a prisoner.

After a few short moments that seemed much longer than they really were, I heard a noise in the hallway, and Clarke passed the doorway with the sleeping Eliza Phillimore in his arms. He stepped into his study, and I saw that the child was more than asleep; she had obviously been drugged.

"What is the meaning of this, Clarke?" asked Holmes, not as if he was addressing a criminal as much as an old and disappointing friend.

"It's your fault, you know," said Clarke. "I was getting away with it before you came. When you arrived and started nosing your way around the village, I knew it was only a matter of time before you figured out the truth one way or the other. After all, you learned some of your methods from me, though you've far eclipsed my modest achievements."

"What do you want from me?" asked Holmes.

"You're going to write to the police, assuring them of the guilt of Charles Stevenson for the death of James Phillimore, a murder motivated by the fact that the man had meddled with Stevenson's daughter Julia. Miss Adler will deliver this letter, along with proof in the form of letters in the man's own hand—or the hand of someone near enough for the ineptitude of Inspector Graves. Mrs Parkfield, my trusted assistant, will make sure this occurs. After that, I will personally escort both of you to the train station. You will leave Fulworth, never to return. After that, and only after that, I will return Eliza to her unfortunate mother. You must see, Holmes, that for all your cleverness, you have no option. I don't want to hurt you."

"Very well," said Holmes, sounding defeated. Mrs Parkfield smiled unpleasantly and handed him a piece of stationery and a pen, her gun still pointed firmly in my direction. The detective went to the side table and placed the paper upon it, beginning to write, his non-dominant hand fidgeting nervously in his pocket. Clarke watched him carefully. "It's dull," he said after a moment of wrestling with the pen.

"Mrs Parkfield, get him another," said Clarke, his old shoulders slumping from the little girl's weight.

At that moment, Holmes's lazily fidgeting hand sprang to life, and I saw a blur of light that suddenly blazed up with heat and shooting sparks. At the same time, the decanter rolled toward me across the floor, and in a split second, Holmes had snatched Eliza from the dazed Clarke, and we ran for the door.

"Fire! Fire!" screamed my companion as we hurled ourselves outside, and one of the inevitabilities of village life began to work immediately in our favour. People came running from everywhere. Mothers streamed out of Cottonwood's with babies in their arms. The butcher came running out of his shop with a leg of mutton in his hand,

and Miss Rose, who didn't appear offended after all, gamely took Eliza in her arms. The news spread from around us and seemed to bring out every able-bodied person in the village. Meanwhile, I was relieved to find that Holmes was now the one with the gun, and as my eyes scanned the mayhem, I saw the hapless Clarke and his assistant skulking away at the back of the crowd.

"Stop the doctor and Mrs Parkfield!" I screamed as loudly as I could, no longer caring how insane I might or might not seem. "They killed Phillimore!" As could be expected, this assertion produced a flurry of aimless noise and activity, but thankfully, a young man with strong arms and an equally strong mind laid hold of the man, and his action prompted the vicar, who was next to him, to take hold of Mrs Parkfield's wrists. Edward Rayburn looked nothing like a knight in shining armor, but as he paraded Dr Clarke over to Holmes, he looked as heroic as any subject of a romantic painting that I had ever seen. Father Murphy seemed less comfortable with the task of dragging a substantial, angry woman in our direction, but he did so. At that moment, someone in the crowd screamed, "There's a real fire!" and I realised that I had actually managed to forget the flames that Holmes had set on their merry way.

"The fire brigade must form immediately," said Holmes, "and Miss Adler, Edward Rayburn, and the vicar will help me restrain these two until the police arrive." The sound of my friend's commanding voice worked wonders among the crowd, who almost magically broke apart to follow his instructions.

The detective led the group of captives and captors to the village green, where the Winking Tree greeted us with its usual green solemnity. "This will be best," said Holmes. "Impossible to escape in plain sight with the whole village outside." He sounded, I thought, quite pleased. "Now, we will send to the farm for the inspector and sergeant," he continued.

"I could drive Miss Adler," said an eager voice, and I looked behind me to find that Jimmy Simms, a young man possessed of dimples and oversized hands, had run over and was eagerly awaiting instructions like an energetic puppy.

"Very well," said Holmes, "but first, fetch us some rope." The boy was quick, and in a few minutes, the resolute Edward and tired vicar were relieved of the task of subduing Clarke and Mrs Parkfield.

—

"How did Mr Holmes get them?" asked Simms eagerly once we were on our way.

"He surprised them," I answered, "by starting the fire."

The boy's eyes grew large with amazement. "He might have gotten burned himself."

"That's true," I answered. I hadn't thought of it until then.

Chance has put in our way a most singular and whimsical problem, and its solution is its own reward.

—The Adventure of the Blue Carbuncle

Chapter 16: Holmes

Inspector Graves and Sergeant Chipping arrived as quickly as Holmes had expected. Behind them, Simms drove Irene's wagon, but crowded in with The Woman were Edith Phillimore, Julia Rayburn, and an unhappy Mrs. Merriwether.

The first thing out of anyone's mouth was Edith Phillimore's hasty cry of "Where's Eliza?"

"Right here, Love," said Miss Rose, who'd stepped into the open door of the butcher shop with her precious bundle once the fire was out and the crowd dispersed. The child was still drowsy, but she was awake enough to smile at her mother and cling to her neck.

Meanwhile, Inspector Graves and Sergeant Chipping came over to the Winking Tree, where Holmes was still holding Clarke's handgun on the woman and the doctor. "You're sure, are you?" Graves asked, as if he half hoped Holmes might not be.

"The man confessed as much," said The Woman, coming up behind him, short and determined. "He tried to force Holmes to implicate Charles Stevenson."

Holmes's eyes scanned the group that had gathered around and noticed that Julia Rayburn was extremely pale. "Perhaps," he said, "we might discuss this further inside."

"My parents' home will suffice, I think," said Julia.

"Clarke's no longer will, I fear," said Holmes. "The damage was extensive." Irene, who was at his elbow, looked vastly pleased.

The group made its way into the Stevenson home and were set up in the drawing room.

In his pompous way, Inspector Graves began to question the suspects one by one—first Mrs Parkfield, then Clarke—taking them from the room almost ceremoniously. Meanwhile, the Stevensons' cook managed to produce enough tea for the impromptu guests, though the footmen looked as if they thought those they served were beneath them.

Within a short time, a tall, elegant figure appeared. Charles Stevenson, barrister, arrived home to find his house overrun with all manner of people and glowered at them all.

He came toward the detective, who was seated on a sofa with The Woman and Edith Phillimore, who held her sleepy daughter in her arms. "You'll never convict my friend," he said sharply. "The case will be fought at every turn."

"I highly doubt it will be so difficult," said Holmes mildly. The barrister's rancor, he thought, stemmed from his realisation that he had been a strong suspect. The detective wondered what he knew of his daughter's situation and concluded that he seemed to know nothing at all.

After a long time, Sergeant Chipping emerged with Clarke; behind them was Inspector Graves, whose eyes blazed. He pointed a long finger at the cowering Mrs Merriwether who, during the proceedings, had tried to seem as if she was invisible. "You," he said, "come with us." Mrs Parkfield, restrained under many watchful eyes, looked slightly triumphant as the corpulent woman was led away to be questioned.

Under cover of the excited and speculative conversation that followed, Irene turned to Holmes and spoke softly. "What has she to do with it? She helped the Phillimores with their plan, but Clarke would have no knowledge of that. I thought you took her admission of Phillimore's unfaithfulness as proof of her innocence."

"I suspect," the detective answered, "that she had nothing to do with the murder itself, but anything else would not surprise me. Phillimore was a small man."

The Woman looked irritated at the incompleteness of this speech, but Holmes turned to Edith and reassured her that if the cook was innocent, he would see to it that she was found so. The fact that he thought her far from innocent did not change the truth of the statement.

The final person Sergeant Chipping fetched was the white-faced and shaky-handed Julia Rayburn, though he did not return Mrs Merriwether to the gathering. As the girl walked across the plush carpet, all eyes in the room followed her, most with surprise, but a few with understanding. Holmes had noticed that she had neither spoken to her husband nor taken her seat with him.

Predictably, the barrister exploded at the perceived injustice. "What do they mean taking my Julia? What could she possibly have to do with it?"

"She's the reason for the whole thing," said Mrs. Parkfield, insinuating nastily.

Suddenly, Edward Rayburn rose to his full height and looked her in the eyes. "That's my wife you're talking about."

"Wife," she replied with an ugly laugh, but at the same time, she retreated into herself and held her tongue as if his vehemence frightened her. Characteristic, Holmes thought, of the sort of person so under another's spell that she would do what Mrs. Parkfield had done that day, the kind of person who only felt strong with gun in hand. Clarke sat silent, as he had the entire time he was not being questioned.

After a very long time, Julia finally emerged, and it was obvious she had been weeping. Edward went to her and took her hand. She did not pull away, and she did not speak.

The Inspector, the Sergeant, and Mrs Merriwether came out at last, and Graves went over to Holmes and held out his hand. "I'll shake your hand, Sir," he said. "You know I'm not fond of you from way back, but I acknowledge our indebtedness."

Recognising the immense effort it took for the man to swallow his pride, Holmes stood and took the hand that was proffered, shaking it firmly. Sergeant Chipping beamed like a large, slow sun, and as Holmes sat down, Irene gave him an ungenteel look that he could only interpret as a wink.

—

If the proceedings had begun dramatically, they ended without much fanfare at all. The policemen took Mrs Merriwether, Mrs Parkfield, and Dr Clarke with them, and the rest dispersed slowly, leaving the barrister's house as if bidding goodbye to a ceremony. Irene, Holmes saw, spoke quietly to a few people, though he did not know her purpose. Once outside, she slipped her hand in his arm.

"Holmes," she said, as they made their way back to the cottage, "you are a braver man than even I realised."

"What do you mean?" he asked. "You were calm enough in peril. Never lost your nerve."

"I mean—I mean the fire. You could have been injured or killed very easily."

"That was no matter," said the detective. "I was thinking of the child."

"But how did you do it? I confess my observational skills were eclipsed by my shock and panic."

"A white phosphorous match and alcohol are not the best of combinations at any time," said Holmes. "With a bit of a nudge, they are lethal. Nevertheless, I don't think Clarke was terribly sorry to be found out. For all his posturing, I think he's proud of his work."

"But why do it?" asked The Woman. "What did he have against Phillimore? Stevenson's potential motive was far more penetrable."

"Indeed," said Holmes. "My observation tells me that his decision had to do with Julia Rayburn."

"Does the whole world revolve around Julia Rayburn?" Irene exploded. "The poor girl seems to be at the centre of everything."

"Not, perhaps," said Holmes, "the actions of Mrs Merriwether."

"No?" Irene enquired, "After the past few days, I would believe any connection."

"I believe we will find," said Holmes, "that her complicity sprang from an unhealthy devotion to Edith Phillimore."

"Not unlike Mrs Parkfield's to the doctor, then."

"No, I believe Mrs Parkfield is in love with her employer, while at the same time deploring his hold over her. She's an interesting specimen. The psychologists of London would find her an engaging study."

"I am sorry," said Irene, "that your old friend is the guilty party."

"One can hardly call a man one only knew before the age of twelve to be an old friend, however much he wishes it. I see now that his kindness was meant to forestall discovery."

"Abominable," said The Woman, and her tone of voice made Holmes afraid that she might wrap her arms around him as she had done once during the Florida case. Fortunately, propriety reigned, and she simply gave him her most brilliant smile, a gift, he knew, that most men found priceless.

"The truly abominable thing," said Holmes, "is that I trusted him. It was unforgivable."

"You didn't ultimately trust him," said Irene. "Your instincts led you to the answer." But Holmes was unable to take such a sanguine view of his own behaviour.

"His assessment of the body gave no reason to doubt him," said the detective with irritation. "The preposterous nature of Edith Phillimore's tale prejudiced me against the man as a suspect, and my association with him finished the job."

"I don't suppose it helps any," said The Woman, "but Julia's part in the tale had me looking in other quarters. At one time, the thought even crossed my mind that Edward Rayburn might have done it to avenge Julia's honour."

"It was to your credit," said Holmes, "that you did not disqualify a man you obviously admire."

"Nevertheless," she rejoined, "I cannot think ill of you for taking longer to impute the guilt of a heinous crime onto someone whose methods and kindness were significant to your boyhood." Holmes didn't answer because they were at the cottage, and music was issuing forth from it.

The detective and The Woman found Watson sitting in a chair by the piano, clapping enthusiastically to the merry tune Mrs Turner played. She had on a long, violet dress, the likes of which Holmes had never seen her wear in his long years of association with her, and her hair, which was usually pulled back tightly, was softer this evening and framed her face like a halo. Her fingers ceased moving across the piano keys as they entered.

"Good evening," said Watson, smiling with colour in his cheeks. "Have you been able to advance the case?"

"Upon my word," said Holmes, "where have the two of you been?" He looked over at the housekeeper and saw her simultaneously blush and smile.

"We took a long walk on the Downs," said Watson. "The weather was nice, and we lost track of time. We've only been back a half hour."

"Obviously," Irene interjected. "I'm afraid, Mrs Turner, that I shall have to ask for your assistance. I've done something a bit impulsive and invited guests for an evening meal."

Mrs Turner looked surprised for a moment, and then she stood up with resolve. "As you know," she said, "I am more than equal to the task."

"I believe you," said Irene, "but I insist on helping, just this once. I was in peril for my life a short time ago. You might take pity on me." She grinned saucily at the older woman.

"As you wish, Miss Adler," the cook and housekeeper answered as her mouth tried to curve into a smile. Holmes realised then what Irene's whispers to various and sundry had been about.

The two women disappeared into the kitchen, and Holmes took his place in the wing chair opposite his flatmate, who had moved to the sofa. "Well, Holmes," said Watson, "I had no idea things would erupt in this manner. I apologise for my absence."

"No need," said the detective. "Miss Adler was adequate, though she lacks your physical instincts."

"A woman of her appearance needs no physical instincts," Watson answered, "so capable is she of engendering them in others on her behalf."

"Perhaps," said Holmes, "though I deduce that you are unaffected by her."

"My attentions go another way," said the doctor placidly, "but that is hardly important at the moment. My own limping effort at deduction finds from your manner and Miss Adler's that the case is solved."

"It is," said Holmes, "though it reflects little credit on my career."

"I doubt that," said Watson.

"Well," said the detective, "dinner will assuage your curiosity."

“That process,” said I, “starts upon the supposition that when you have eliminated all which is impossible, then whatever remains, however improbable, must be the truth.”

—The Blanched Soldier

Chapter 17: Irene

The surpassing simplicity of the instructions Mrs Turner gave me as we cooked and set the table had the effect of making me feel like a slow-witted child. "I'm not a fine lady," I finally said to her. "I've done these things for myself before."

"You've never been in service," she retorted.

"Very well," I acquiesced. I might be able to keep my wits about me when a gun was pointed in my direction, but I was hopeless in the face of my housekeeper's endless determination. I couldn't blame her when I saw the spread that she somehow managed to produce, consisting of sausage pies, potatoes, cabbage, and several other bits and bobs that made my mouth water. Sometimes, I was very glad I'd left the life of a professional touring singer behind.

My small party of guests arrived on time for our late meal. Edward Rayburn and the vicar came in together, followed by Simms, and finally Edith, Eliza and Julia. Edith and I quickly took Eliza and put her to bed in the housekeeper's room, where she had previously spent the night. Her ordeal and drugging, which turned out to be via a non-harmful sedative, had made her extremely tired, and she was delighted to fall asleep with Charles the rabbit in her arms.

When Julia saw her husband already present, I thought she might refuse to stay, but as I had hoped, she dreaded a scandal too much to run away. Perhaps it was unforgivably high-handed of me, but I could not resist a last effort to unite the couple. I knew that Julia intended to leave the village as soon as the police told her she might, and I couldn't stand the idea. Edward, I thought, had come to town expressly to plead with her; he'd have had no other reason to leave his farm. Judging by their looks at one another, it seemed that he had not succeeded in seeing her.

So far, I thought, Julia's predicament was known to only a few. How it could continue to be concealed, I couldn't fathom, but I trusted that Holmes would do his best to see that it was. My friend had no aversion to seeing the guilty punished to the full extent of the law, but he was always careful to protect those who had been brought into cases through the crimes of others.

My small table was hardly big enough for the eight of us to sit around while Mrs Turner served us, but we managed it, and the close quarters seemed to contribute to a more convivial atmosphere. There was a certain air of relief that pervaded the company at knowing, come what may, that the man responsible for the death of James Phillimore was in the hands of the police. The man's disappearance had hung like a spectre over the village, and it was as if Holmes's fire had been a cleansing one, ridding Fulworth of its confusion and fear.

I wasn't consciously thinking these things, though, as we sat down to Mrs Turner's sumptuous meal. I was merely thinking of how famished I was, and I didn't seem to be the only one. For the first time in days, Holmes really ate, and I relished the sight. Watson, too, showed his appreciation of Mrs Turner's cooking by partaking of a great deal of it. Simms was the most openly appreciative, remarking constantly about how wonderful everything was. I doubted that, as a shop boy, he was used to being invited out very often, and he seemed determined to savour the occasion as thoroughly as possible. I knew that he enjoyed my company and, perhaps, fancied me a bit, but I didn't mind.

"I would like to propose a toast," I said after a while, "to our friends, who helped us solve the case."

"The credit goes to Mr Holmes, surely," said Edith.

"In this instance, I believe Mr Holmes is happy to share it with all of you." I couldn't help the slight smirk that reached my face when I looked across the table at my friend.

"Certainly," he said. "You have all been exceedingly helpful." He was relaxed, I could see, far more so than he had been since his arrival in the village.

"To all of us, then," said the vicar, and we drank. As I looked around the table at the strange assortment of people I'd collected, the warmth I felt surprised me. For the years I had been in Fulworth, I had kept mostly to myself, only coming to know people as I encountered them in my official capacity as musician or in my daily errands.

The trust Edith Phillimore and Julia Rayburn, even Julia's husband, had placed in me during the case had proven to me that I had not made as little impression on the village as I'd supposed. Holmes was fond of saying that when one gets rid of the impossible, whatever remains must be true, no matter how difficult to believe. It was now impossible for me to believe that I meant nothing to the village of Fulworth, and it had begun to seem as if, no matter how much I might deny it to myself, the truth was that Fulworth was also important to me. Perhaps, I thought, I needed people after all.

—

The late hour meant that the guests were not inclined to linger. The vicar left first, with many expressions of thanks and good will, to return home, where he cared for his ailing mother. Edith soon made to follow, and she went to retrieve her sleeping offspring, who waved to us all from her mother's shoulder and smiled as if she'd never had a care in the world. Simms would have stayed to eat and drink all night, I believe, except that the family for whom he worked kept strict hours, and he did not wish to upset them. He kissed my hand as he left, slightly overcome by the atmosphere and his overconsumption of my highest quality wine, opened especially for the occasion.

Finally, Julia and Edward were the only ones left, and it was obvious that neither wanted to be the first to leave, for which I was glad. "Julia," I said as we sat together on the sofa, "I am curious if you know more about the case than I do. I understand who is responsible, but I don't know how it was done."

Julia looked around at the small, informal gathering sitting on sofa and chairs pulled from the table to accommodate our extra visitors. It was just me, Holmes, Watson, and Edward to listen to her now, and I saw a decision cross her face.

"I expect everyone here already knows my—situation, since you have all been assisting the police. I believe it will be good for me to tell what I know, and it's the least I can do. The police were able to piece together most of what happened from the stories of the two women and the doctor." I patted her hand as if I was her aged grandmother. I couldn't help myself. Meanwhile, Edward watched her with one of the most intense gazes I have ever seen coming from anyone other than Sherlock Holmes.

"As you know, Miss Adler," she said, looking at me as if for support, "I have an unusual relationship with the servants at my childhood home. I think, perhaps, you did not think my behaviour was entirely wise, and experience bears you out. One of them, I don't know which, saw me speaking with James Phillimore outside the servants' entrance to the house. The encounter so inflamed her with curiosity that she followed us and found out that we—the character of our relationship." I shuddered internally at the implication, and Edward Rayburn looked as if he was in pain so acute he could no longer keep it from showing on his honest face.

"This person," Julia continued, "had a friendship with Mrs Merriwether at Oakhill Farm, and she took the tale to that lady, who was furious on account of her love for Edith Phillimore, whom she saw as a wronged woman. She's the one who told Dr Clarke." I had been listening intently, but this piece of information piqued my interest in the extreme. Now, I thought, we would find out if Holmes was correct in his surmise that Phillimore's murder had had something to do with Julia Rayburn.

Julia took a sip of her drink and waited a moment to continue. "I don't suppose it should bother me to tell the rest," she said, "since I've no reputation left anyway, but it still pains me to say. When I first returned from school, I noticed that Dr Clarke paid special attention to me. I thought it was just the affection of an old man, since he had always been fond of me when I was a child. However, before James had even spoken to me, the doctor approached me after church. He was a widower, he said, but he wanted—someone to share his life again, perhaps to give him the family in his old age that the wife of his youth had not been able to produce. You may imagine the effect of his words. I felt dreadful and filled with pity that I couldn't entirely conceal. As gently as I could, I told him that I did not consider myself equal to what he asked. I was barely past being a child, I said, and couldn't think of fulfilling his request. A month later, he asked again. That time, I told him more strongly that while I respected him, I did not care for him in that way. He never spoke to me again."

"I never told my father or anyone else because I wanted to spare the man's feelings, but his attentions had not gone entirely unnoticed. I did not know it then, but Mrs Parkfield was aware of his regard for me, and she was angry because she had long dreamed of becoming the second Mrs Clarke. She, too, was friends with Mrs Merriwether, who seems to have been apprised of any and all gossip among servants in the area. Mrs Parkfield told her friend what Dr Clarke's intentions were toward me."

"Mrs Merriwether held onto the information, as she must have held on to all sorts of scandal and gossip that might be embarrassing or damaging to a great many people. When she heard about James and me, she decided to make use of the knowledge. She went to Dr Clarke under guise of subservient friendship and told him that the object of his affection was being tampered with." Julia said this last part as if it was difficult for her to form the words.

"She had judged her man accurately. I had thought Dr Clarke had accepted my choice as a gentleman, but he was secretly obsessed. I have heard it said that he was possessive and unusually jealous where his first wife was concerned, but I was too young then to know for sure. In the months since I'd refused him, he'd grown increasingly unbalanced, and Mrs Merriwether only had to push him slightly to get him to act. She didn't intend to push him into murder, or so she claims. She only wanted Phillimore to leave so that she could convince Edith to rid herself of him. She suggested blackmail."

I looked at Holmes, who was as intent on the story as I was. "The blackmail was real, then."

"Yes," said my friend. "It was simply the subject that Phillimore fabricated."

"Clarke told him he must leave the village, or all would be known," said Julia.

"Not about money, then," Holmes murmured. "I thought that was the least plausible part of Edith's story."

"According to Mrs Merriwether," Julia continued, "Phillimore sent a letter to Clarke agreeing to leave, and then, of course, he convinced his wife to help him, with the object of rejoining him later. The cook thought she could dissuade Edith from this once she disclosed the truth. Clarke, however was not satisfied with the man merely leaving Fulworth."

"He had—seen what my husband saw. After all, he has been a doctor for many years, and he watched me. He began to suspect the truth about the baby, and it filled him with jealousy. On the pretext of making Phillimore prove that he was actually leaving, he asked for the particulars of the man's plan. Phillimore, who was terrified that his actions would become known and that he would lose his wife and daughter, complied."

"On the day of my wedding," she said, pausing a moment and breathing heavily, "husband and wife followed the plan to the letter. James went inside to fetch his umbrella and never came back. Edith followed, but she did not look through the house, since she knew her husband was simply lying in wait. They had arranged for the property to be deserted after Edith's departure, so James lingered and then made his escape."

"Dr Clarke was aware of the details of the plan, so he had already circulated the information that he was laid up with gout and would be unable to attend the wedding. He and Mrs Parkfield waited for James on the road outside the village, and they drugged him and brought him back to Clarke's house, where they kept him sedated for several days. The doctor, of course, has access to all manner of drugs."

"Mrs Merriwether faked the posting of the rabbit both ways. She apparently tried to extricate herself when Clarke told her that he had kidnapped Phillimore instead of letting him leave as they'd agreed, but he threatened to bring her down with him if she did not do as he asked."

"Finally, when the police had begun to talk about ending the investigation because of insignificant evidence, Clarke shot James. I do not—I do not know exactly how or where he did it. The police believe he took him out on the Downs."

"Horrible," I said.

"Yes," said Julia. "I would not have wished such an end on him."

"Clarke was then," she added, "faced with the task of what to do with the body. He was highly unbalanced by this time, and he wanted to display what he had done as revenge against the man he believed had stolen the woman he loved. He could not contrive a way to do it himself, so he called on Mrs Merriwether again. This time, she claims, she very nearly refused, but she was terrified that Clarke would convince the police that she had killed Phillimore, since the plot had originated with her. Of course, Clarke would probably have gotten away with it if he'd just discarded the corpse somewhere on the Downs, but he could not be satisfied with that."

"The night before the body was found, Mrs Merriwether went to Clarke's house in her husband's wagon. Mrs Parkfield helped her load Phillimore's corpse into it, covered by a blanket and then various edibles, so that if pressed, she could claim she was taking supplies back for the big house."

"She had told her husband that Edith Phillimore wished her to remain at the house later than usual, so under cover of night, she placed the body on the carriage and then went home and to bed. Clarke had told her that the police would never suspect that a woman had done it, which was true. Only one as strong as she is could have managed it, aided by the fact that James was a slight man."

"Mrs Merriwether received quite a turn the next morning when Edith Phillimore told her the body had been found by Eliza. She'd hoped that the location of the carriage house would lead to its being found by one of the men and that Warren would be suspected. She convinced Edith, who was shocked and fearful because of her own duplicity, that it would be better to wait and let him be found by someone else, which soon happened."

"There you have it," said Julia, sitting back wearily. I almost laughed. It was such an oddly anticlimactic end to a tale of horror. We sat silently for a few moments, thinking about the ending of a man's life and the sad circumstances that had led him to it, not that none of them were of his own making—far from it.

After a while, Dr Watson rose, rubbing his eyes. "Thank you for enlightening us so fully," he said to Julia. "Forgive me, Miss Adler," he continued, "but I must retire, or I will be snoring into my cups." I nodded and stood up, and Holmes and the Rayburns followed suit. "I'd better go, too," said Julia.

"Jule," said Edward, and he put out a tentative hand to touch her hair. She flinched. I gave Holmes and Watson meaningful looks, and they disappeared into their rooms. I, too, retired, but instead of disappearing altogether, I sneaked into the shadows of the hallway and ducked behind the chaise longue with my head just peeking up enough to see what took place. I am not proud of this, but I'm not terribly sorry, either. I simply could not resist.

"Where are you going?" Edward asked, once they were alone.

"I'll stay one more night with my father and mother and then leave for London tomorrow."

"Do I get no say?" he asked desperately. "I feel—the same for you that I've always felt."

"How is that possible, Ed?" she asked. "Do you understand what this means? I courted you on purpose just so I could marry you quickly and cover my shame. I used your love for me as a means to an end." She spoke vehemently, as if she was determined to condemn herself as fully as possible.

"I know all that, Jule," he answered, "but I think you love me. Look at me and say you don't."

She made a valiant effort, and I was afraid that if she succeeded, she might very well have gotten her way that night. As it was, she couldn't meet his eyes and tell the lie. "I can't," she said in a short, brittle voice.

"I thought not," he said, sounding more hopeful.

"What is the matter with you?" Julia asked. "I'm carrying a dead man's baby."

"It could be our baby," he said.

"Are you insane?" she asked. "You know what they'll say about us, about you."

"I don't care," he answered calmly.

"Why?" she asked, finally exploding. "I'm not worth this, Ed. I've never been worth all of your love and faithfulness and kindness." She spit out the words as if they were pejorative rather than complimentary. "I've never done anything but stomp on them."

"But you love me, Jule," he said. "Can't you see it in yourself? You love me so much it's nearly killing you to let me go." His eyes shone with tears.

Julia let out a pained cry and buried her face in her hands, though she did not weep. She simply stood silent and refused to look at her husband. "Why?" she finally said. "Why must you be so right and know everything?"

"I know you," he said. "That's all."

"I want you to love someone else," she said stubbornly.

"I've never loved anybody else," he said. Julia turned away.

Edward cried. I have seen men cry for effect, and I have seen them cry like lost children. He did neither. He cried like someone who hurts so deeply for another that the pain cannot be contained.

"Ed—stop," said Julia, finally sounding desperate instead of resigned. "I can't bear it."

"Do you think I can bear it?" he asked, talking to her back. "Do you think I can stand to watch you sacrifice yourself, alone without anyone to help you? We can live like brother and sister if you wish it. I will give up every other dream I've ever had if you'll just let me take care of you and the baby."

For a long, horrendous moment, I was afraid that Julia was going to run away. Her internal conflict was excruciatingly visible, but Edward was wise enough to let her make the decision on her own terms. She finally crumbled, collapsing into herself and sobbing so hard she bent double. The farmer recognised her choice for what it was, and he came to her in an instant, catching her and pulling her close. "I've got you," was all he said, but in spite of his tears, he looked happier than I had ever seen him. He held her for a long time, only stopping when her sobs subsided, and even then, he only let go so that he could take out a red handkerchief and wipe away her final tears. His wife, in her turn, took the piece of cloth from him and wiped his face.

"Julia," he said, cupping her face in one of his broad hands, "will you really come home with me?"

"If you want me to," she said.

"I want—I want you to come home more than I ever wanted anything in my whole life," he answered, and I was afraid they were both in danger of weeping again. Instead, Edward put a big arm around Julia's shoulders and led her out into the night.

I watched the Rayburns leave my cottage with no idea what lay in store for their future. I have not always been a hopeful person, but I hoped for them. Julia did not deserve Edward after everything she had done to him, but, as I pondered then, life would be a terrible thing if we all received our just deserts. Holmes would disagree on principle, I thought, but that would make him the greatest of hypocrites. He was, after all, the man who had given a cottage to his enemy and made her his friend.

They can go everywhere, see everything, overhear everyone.

—The Sign of Four

Chapter 18: Holmes

The detective slept all night, finally giving his body the rest it craved. When he awoke, he realised it was late morning, and he heard the voices of The Woman and the doctor in the main part of the house.

"Good morning, Holmes," said Irene when he emerged. She looked fresh and rested, though he knew that the case had taken a toll on her as well, a toll that was now evaporating in the aftermath of success. The detective sat down beside her at the table and proceeded to avail himself of the large brunch Mrs Turner had provided. Far from being averse to a good meal, he simply found food a largely irrelevant distraction when a case was on. Now, he was free to fill his stomach.

His mind, however, was not entirely engaged in pleasant matters, and he sank into silence as he pondered his failure to put together the details that had implicated Dr Clarke as quickly as he believed he should have done. He had seen the tobacco and the man; that should have been enough, without the kidnapping to serve as a catalyst.

"You are very quiet, Holmes," said Watson after a while. The detective was surprised his flatmate had noticed, so taken up as he seemed with watching Mrs Turner bring food and drinks back and forth from the kitchen. "I'd have expected," the doctor continued, "to hear about Brahms or Greek sculpture or some other obscure topic."

"Brahms is hardly obscure," said Irene, and the detective cast an approving eye on her.

"I committed an error of judgement," said Holmes. "That is all."

As if she knew that nothing could really ease the blow but couldn't help saying something, The Woman said, "You did something perfectly natural. You trusted someone you had trusted in your youth."

"Natural, perhaps," he rejoined, "but not forgivable."

"Still," she answered, "I don't see that there's any harm done. The murderer is behind bars, and Eliza Phillimore is safe. The loss of the man's house seems more like poetic justice than anything else. As they say, all's well that ends well."

"Convenient platitudes or not, my blundering has wasted time and put a great many people in danger," Holmes lamented.

"I am determined to see the bright side," she retorted. "The case is solved, and your bravery has restored a child to her mother." She smiled wickedly. "You are a hero whether you wish to be or no."

"Frailty, thy name is Sherlock," said the detective, sardonically misusing the words of the Bard.

"I agree with Miss Adler," said Watson gallantly. "You can hardly call a case a failure when it yields a conclusion as excellent as this one." Looking at the glow on the doctor's face, it was obvious that the perceived positive outcomes of his visit were not only related to the case. Holmes grew silent then, but he did not entirely deplore the praise of his friends, however much he might wish to appear that he did.

"Clarke is a fool," Irene said.

"Not a fool," Holmes rejoined. "He miscalculated. Without me, he'd probably have gotten away with it."

"I'm sure Inspector Graves is delighted to have to confront that reality," The Woman answered.

"I can't help feeling a small amount of pity for the doctor," said Watson. "He really seems to have loved the girl, however misguidedly."

"I don't," Irene answered, more sharply than he deserved. "Clarke's love is the sort that holds so tightly it chokes, rather than letting the object of its affection grow and thrive." As the detective watched her, he understood. When she saw Clarke in her mind, Holmes thought, instead of his own, he wore the face of Godfrey Norton, her late husband.

"What I don't understand," Watson added, "is why Stevenson went to the Merriwether home at all. You considered it highly suspicious at the time."

Holmes smiled sardonically. "The answer is quite prosaic. The barrister's wife suffers from chronic headaches, and Mrs Merriwether is known to dispense herbal remedies, which Mrs Stevenson does not trust the servants to procure for her."

"It's satisfying to know the answer, at least," said The Woman. Watson nodded complacently.

"Will you add this story to your collection of tales, Dr Watson?" Irene finally asked.

"I think not," he replied, "though the sensational nature of the case is appealing, purely from an objective standpoint. Nevertheless, I would not like to offend Edith or Eliza by providing a written reminder of their tragedy. If I ever do write it, I will change the particulars of the case, something I have been known to do before that never fails to irritate my friend." Holmes shook his head.

"I will," continued Dr Watson, "treat the case as a disappearance that was never solved. I can't think that it is bad for my friend's vanity to be thought fallible on occasion."

"In this case," said Holmes glumly, "you could hardly paint me as more fallible than I have been."

"Nonsense," said Watson.

Holmes lingered at the table for a long time, letting himself enjoy the company of The Woman, his flatmate, and the housekeeper. He thought he might stay one more day in Fulworth, enjoying the air and companionship, before returning to the equally desired smells and sights of London, where the police could contact him if they desired his evidence. He had begun to think that he might retire some day. When he'd bought the cottage, the idea had been so far off as to be almost unreal. So, too, when he had given the property to Irene Adler after the case that had made them friends. Now he could begin to see an end to his career, though it did not yet beckon him. He was still intoxicated by his metropolitan mistress, and he could not bear to cease savouring her delights just yet.

The detective's pondering was cut short by a ring of Irene's bell. Mrs Turner opened the door to reveal Eliza and Edith Phillimore, who held out a cake wrapped in brown paper. "I don't know how to thank you," said the mother, "but this is Lewis's special recipe. She's turned out to be quite a cook, now that Mrs Merriwether is gone."

"Thank you," said Irene, taking the parcel and smiling at the sweet smell that issued forth from it. "I'll make sure Mr Holmes has a bit."

"Eliza has a different gift for him," said Edith, pushing her daughter forward gently. Holmes rose and stood in front of her,

With an intensely serious expression, Eliza held out her rabbit, her one prized possession in the whole world, toward Holmes. "You take him," she said.

The detective stared down at her for a long moment, unable to assimilate the immensity of her offering. Finally, he knelt down in front of her and took the toy from her hand. He held it to his ear. "I'm afraid I mustn't take Charles," he said. "He doesn't want to move to Baker Street. He'd rather stay with you."

Eliza stared hard, then took the rabbit back and held it to her own ear. "He says his name isn't Charles any more," she said firmly. "He says his name is Mr Holmes." With that, she wrapped her arms around the neck of the still-kneeling detective and kissed his thin cheek. His smile revealed that he did not mind.

"Eliza," he said after a moment, "would you like to be a Baker Street Irregular?"

"What is that?" she asked, staring at him intently.

"A group of very clever children who help me solve crimes," he answered.

"But I don't live on Baker Street," she said, perplexed.

"No," said Holmes, "but you can be an Irregular wherever you live."

"How?" she asked, clearly excited.

"By keeping your eyes and ears open and learning as much as you can about the world around you," said Holmes.

"Oh," she said, as if this wasn't quite as enthralling as she'd anticipated.

Holmes touched the tip of her nose with his long index finger. "You have much to learn, and if I ever see you again, I expect to find out that you've made good use of your time." He leaned toward her conspiratorially. "After all, Miss Eliza, you never know when the smallest detail will solve the biggest case." This statement produced a delighted grin on Eliza's face. The detective took her hand and kissed it before standing to his feet once again.

Few people ever credited Holmes with such sentimentality. Then again, if they had read Dr Watson's description of the ragtag group of children he employed, children who followed him year upon year, they should have known.

The Woman installed the mother and child on the sofa, and Mrs Turner brought tea for Edith and milk for Eliza, who lapped it up as eagerly as a kitten and seemed very well pleased. "I cannot fail to tell you, Edith, how grateful I am at your reception of Julia Rayburn," said Irene quietly. "You would have been justified in a much different response."

"Perhaps it was stupid of me," said Edith, staring down at her hands, "but I forgave her immediately. She's so pale and so young and afraid. I think she's terrified of what will happen if her father finds out. So far, the police have agreed to conceal as much of the matter as they can, and I hope, for both our sakes, that they will be able to do so."

"You are a far from ordinary person, Mrs Phillimore," said Holmes.

"Thank you, Mr Holmes," she answered. "I am proud of my actions, even though they must never be known. I am not, however, proud of the deceit that began the nightmare," she said, "and I thank you for keeping it hidden."

"No reason to reveal it now," said Holmes, "since it has nothing whatsoever to do with the outcome of the case, and Clarke had no idea James had brought you in on the matter. I am only sorry it took me so long to solve the case that Eliza was put in peril."

"It's all right," said Eliza, suddenly looking up from her cup. "I had Mr Holmes to protect me," and she hugged the bedraggled white rabbit delightedly. A stuffed rabbit might have limitations of ability, Holmes thought, but it was hardly deficient in loyalty and faithfulness. In the main, he was pleased by the comparison.

Edith continued a moment later, "We'll be leaving Fulworth soon. I don't believe it's fair to either of us to remain. I have a sister in London, and we'll sell the farm and join her. That will also help to keep—Julia's matter from becoming as widely known, I think, but don't imagine that I'm being ridiculously self-sacrificing." She smiled at the detective. "Mr Holmes, you've had no occasion to see me as I usually am, but I dearly love a party, and Louisa promises me she'll quickly get our minds off our troubles."

The Woman hugged both mother and daughter before they left, and Holmes saw tears in her eyes when she straightened back up.

They suited her, he thought, and gave her a softness she did not always possess.

He continued to watch her as she stood in the doorway and waved to the retreating figures, and he realised that he had been mistaken. The softness was always there now. He had observed her since his arrival, but he hadn't really looked at her, not enough to consider the implications of how she now appeared. His first visit to Sussex had shown a change in her, a freedom and peacefulness that had been alien to her previously. That transformation had continued. She would never be identical to other women in the village of Fulworth. She was far too American and too much herself for that, but she had a place there now, and within it she was content. Holmes enjoyed watching her.

"It's pleasantly chilly today," she said, finally turning back and closing the door. "Would you like to greet the bees?"

"Certainly," he answered, retrieving his coat. He followed The Woman to the hives and watched her interacting with the bees. She was filled with calm and intuition, perfectly at home among them. That made sense, he thought, for she was one of them. No, not a drone. She was the queen. He had seen through the days of his visit how often the people of Fulworth came to her, consulted her, even loved her. The small cottage on the hill was fast becoming the centre of all things. The charming thing about Irene Adler was that she had no idea. She was a queen who was totally oblivious to the fact that the kingdom was hers.

—

Holmes spent the afternoon reading the London newspapers, which Mycroft had contrived to have delivered to Irene's doorstep. He was glad at such times that he and his brother were at peace with one another. He was frightened by few things, but he did not like to contemplate being in the disfavour of someone so powerful. The detective, of course, had no such desire for power himself. He was quite pleased with his lot.

Finally, when it was nearing time for the evening meal, Watson rose from his place on the sofa, where he had been reading the description of a new discovery called X-radiation, which some were predicting might have vast medical implications in the future. "Holmes," he said, "I've a mind to go down to the inn in the village. Mrs Turner says the apple pie is outstanding. I thought you might wish to accompany me."

"Very well," said Holmes, extracting his long limbs from the wing chair. "I wouldn't object to a drink in your company if Miss Adler doesn't mind us deserting her for the evening."

"Certainly not," said Irene saucily. "I welcome the solitude; it's been hard to come by these past days."

As he closed the cottage door, Holmes heard the sound of a body sliding onto a wooden surface, and the sound of piano music followed. He almost wished he had not agreed to leave.

And when he speaks of Irene Adler, or when he refers to her photograph, it is always under the honourable title of *the* woman.

—A Scandal in Bohemia

Chapter 19: Irene

The two men came back very late in the evening from their visit to the Mountebank Inn and Pub. Watson went to bed immediately, but Holmes joined me, relaxing into the black chair and taking out his pipe. I could finally see the toll exhaustion and hunger had taken on him, and I knew that one day had not been enough time to assuage his body's demands. I wished he would give himself more time to recover from the strain of the case, but I very much doubted that he would do so.

"You must be pleased," he said, closing his eyes and enjoying his tobacco. "You played through your entire repertoire of Bach this evening. Your pleasure, I expect, is due to your success in reuniting the Rayburns." I smiled. Holmes's deductions had become comfortable to me, like an afghan or a pair of old Wellington boots. I liked knowing how they were done, but I could trust him even when he didn't explain his conclusions.

"It was as successful as it could have been, I suppose," I said. "They have a great deal between them."

"Any two people have a great deal between them," Holmes observed. "Some of the most lurid crimes I've ever encountered were between people who appeared to be in simple, straightforward relationships."

"Nothing is straightforward about relationships," I added, smiling. And yet, as I sat opposite Sherlock Holmes, I felt as if we two were the exceptions that proved the rule. We had weathered being enemies, lying to one another, and fighting for our lives. Somehow, we had come out of it all as friends. To the outside eye, it might seem complicated, but it wasn't. He was the detective, and I was The Woman, and it was all, and it was enough.

—

The following morning, Mrs Turner cooked a hearty breakfast to prepare our friends for the journey back to London. As we waited for the table to be set, I sat down beside Dr Watson and could not resist teasing him a bit.

"I take it you and I are likely to be enemies soon," I said.

"Whatever do you mean?" he asked, his kind face turning suddenly pink.

"I refer to the fact that you seem to be on your way to parting me from the best housekeeper and cook on this side of the country."

He smiled beatifically. "I won't deny my intentions. When my Mary died, I never thought I would meet a woman as capable and sensible as she was, and the London girls have proven me sadly right. Unstable, I'm afraid. Mrs Turner is—she's strong and able and quiet, just the sort of woman I'd like to sit with in the evenings by the fireside and talk over the events of the day. A comfortable woman, you understand."

I did understand. Though Mrs Turner was not to every man's taste, she was all the things he said, along with possessing a gentleness of spirit that she took pains to conceal but could not keep from expressing. I approved of the man's choice. Of course, sedateness had never been a quality that particularly attracted me, but I could allow for human differences. It pleased me to think that the easier life the doctor would provide for her would allow for more and more days of violet dresses and handsomely arranged hair and none of having to wait on a flighty singer with eccentric acquaintances. She might, I thought, find the leisure slightly trying, but she would have to work that out with Watson.

—

"Lewis told me how the Winking Tree got its name," I said as I walked Holmes to the train station later in the day. Mrs Turner and Watson were far behind, deep in congenial conversation with one another, as they attempted to prolong their time together.

"Yes?" said my friend after a while. "I take it you intend to share this information."

I smiled. "You needn't be cross. It's a local story about a beautiful farmer's daughter who fell in love with the son of the richest man in the village. His father forbade him to see her, but the two left each other letters in a hollow of the tree. Others in the village would help the lovers by passing on the message that the tree was winking whenever it contained a note. Finally, after the girl almost died of a fever, the young man's father relented and let him marry her."

"I must say," rejoined my friend drily, "I was expecting something more ancient and tragic than that."

"As soon the young man was married, the young girls of the village began to view the tree as a symbol of passion and to whisper that if a person in love touched its bark, her romance was sure to have a happy ending."

"Villages are hotbeds of such nonsense," said Holmes.

—

It was twilight when I returned from the train station, and everything in the village was closed, with most of the homes shuttered and quiet for the evening. As I passed the green, I stopped and looked at the Winking Tree, the place where Eliza had spent happy hours with her father and lost her rabbit, the clue that had sent Holmes along the pathway toward the conclusion of the case. The outline of the branches was magnificent against the night sky, and I could almost imagine how the villagers had begun to regard it as lucky or even magical.

The slight breeze through the leaves whispered my name *Irene Adler* on the wind, and I thought of who I was: The Woman, who had known few good men and loved even fewer. I slipped off my shoes and stepped onto the grass, enjoying the sensation on the bottoms of my feet.

I am not normally a fanciful person, but as I walked toward the Winking Tree, its branches seemed like open arms welcoming me into its green and vibrant embrace. I reached forward and touched the tips of my fingers to its rough trunk, and my mind was filled with the face of my friend, the best man I had ever known.

Epilogue: Holmes

The detective read the London papers on his way back to Baker Street, but he silently perceived, as he had before, the look of joyful preoccupation in his flatmate's face that denoted the presence of a strong attachment. It had been that way with others, but never as strongly as with Mary Morstan, as if a part of John Watson's heart had been permanently buried along with his wife's silent form.

This time was different. Holmes considered himself neither a psychologist nor a romantic, but he was a student of human behaviour. He steeled himself for the eventualities of a half-empty flat and evenings spent smoking alone by the fire.

He understood not one whit why a man would voluntarily surrender his freedom to the fragile but iron-willed fingers of a woman. Even Mary, who had been, by most comparisons, an understanding wife, had required Watson at times when Holmes had needed his presence. No woman wanted to be married to a detective, not really.

Women in general, he thought, were different from *The* Woman. She was no less infuriating than any of them, but she was clever. She played The Game, and there was something to be said for that.

Epilogue: Irene

Edith Phillimore sold Oakhill Farm to Peter Warren, who cried when he signed the papers that made it legally his. The widow took her daughter to London, where they were able to settle comfortably on the money she'd made. I received a few letters from her, but they stopped after several months. I heard nothing more of Eliza for many years, until the day that the papers reported her name as part of a group of women who were the first to cast feminine votes in a national election. Holmes, who was beside me when I read the story, declared that it surprised him not at all.

Edward and Julia Rayburn remained at their farm outside Fulworth. In the eyes of all in the village, Julia's baby, a son named Steven, belonged fully to Edward, and her father's reputation did much to counter the few stories that claimed otherwise. Tongues wagged about the exact date of the birth, as they always do in a village, and Edward bore the brunt of all suspicion, as if any shame belonged only to him. Still, I had never seen a man so happy with his lot in life. In time, with the help of a son whose laugh was like music, his wife began to smile again.

The Detective The Woman and The Silent Hive

Book 3

The Beginning

"The bees are dead," I said. That was hardly the way I'd planned to greet my friends, but I could find no other words when I had finally reached Baker Street.

"Please sit down," said Dr Watson kindly, putting a solid hand under my elbow and guiding me to a chair near the cheerful evening fire. It seemed to me the flat looked just as it had when I'd impersonated a maid to gain entry to it years before, though my own recollections had been dimmed by time and were inextricably entwined with the doctor's descriptions of it in his stories.

Holmes had stood upon my admittance by Mrs Hudson, but he immediately took his place in his chair opposite me, his eyes taking in every detail of my appearance and expression. I knew that he was deducing me, learning where I had been, how I had travelled, and probably even the frayed state of my nerves. I was used to his ways by then, and I did not speak until he closed his eyes and leaned back, his assessment complete.

"My bees are dead," I reiterated.

"How?" One word, one question from the lips of my friend, but it was like a candle at midnight. I knew that if Holmes was listening, all could not be lost.

"Foulbrood," I said, spitting out the word like a bad taste.

"That's certainly distressing," Dr Watson said kindly, though I could tell that the disease was unfamiliar to him. Holmes did not appear to share his confusion.

"I know why you're here," he said. It was my turn to be perplexed.

"What do you mean?" I asked. In my defence, I was weary and unhappy, and the speed of my thoughts was somewhat inhibited.

"You know the cause of the malady. That means you've already consulted an expert in beekeeping. If the disease had a likely origin on the Downs, you'd have no reason to be here. Therefore, I gather that you cannot divine the origin of the disease and have come to seek my advice." Holmes rattled off his deductions without a pause, but his tone was not unkind.

Hearing my reason put in such simple terms, I began to feel as if my errand was foolish. "I—was, perhaps, impulsive in my decision to travel here," I said, "but I confess that I was somewhat emotionally affected upon seeing the demise of my hives and did not wish to wait for a letter to reach you and its subsequent response to reach me. A telegram seemed insufficient to convey the peculiarity of the situation."

—

Sherlock Holmes looked at the woman in front of him as he looked at everyone—with eyes that took in the physical details of her muddied green skirt and haphazardly arranged hair, as well as the desperate tone of her voice and downcast expression. Clearly, the length of the entire journey from Fulworth to London had not been sufficient to relieve her distress.

Those who did not know her might have thought Irene Adler's grief strange or misplaced, but the detective understood it instantly. Ever since her retirement from the world, The Woman's life work had been her bees. Their order was her order, and the systematic patterns of their lives had become her own. In her eyes, he saw grief for the death of innocent creatures, but there was something more, a deep agitation, as if the failure of the hives indicated her own failure to exert control over the chaotic forces of the world.

"I will take your case," he said. He saw instant relief on her face, and it pleased him.

We heard of you as living the life of a hermit among your bees and your books in a small farm upon the South Downs.

—His Last Bow

Chapter 1: Irene

I knew I must give an appearance of being woefully bedraggled, judging by the pitying look on Dr Watson's face, the force with which Mrs Hudson pressed tea upon me, and, most tellingly, Holmes's concerned expression. I grieved, to be sure, but some of my dishevellment was simply a result of the unplanned nature of my journey.

I would have liked to remain where I sat as afternoon turned to dusk, but even my low esteem of propriety did not quite admit for a night spent in the flat of two bachelors. Besides, I'd heard that the Savoy Hotel, which had been completed during my absence from London, was a marvel to behold. My preoccupation did not prevent me from wanting to see it.

Dr Watson offered to arrange transportation, but my feet itched to walk the London streets once again. The doctor and Mrs Hudson were slightly horrified at this, but Holmes understood and walked me to the door without a word.

"Good night," I said. "I promise to return tomorrow with a clearer head for details."

"I have business with my brother," he said, "but Dr Watson will receive you if I am absent." We parted ways, and I had the satisfaction of knowing that as Holmes watched me disappear down the street, he experienced not one instant of worry for my safety.

I had forgotten what it was like to step into a morass of people. We didn't have morasses of people on the Downs—more like trickles of people, or, oftener than not, one odd person here and there. My body no longer recalled the feeling of being whisked into the world of London, that seductive, beautiful, grimy place. I passed beyond Baker Street, and a surge of nostalgia filled me. I'd never intended to return, but since I had, I couldn't claim to be unaffected by excitement. My bad memories were mostly tied to other places, and the city was like an alluring dream.

When I finally reached my objective on the Strand, I was quite satisfied with myself and with the fact that my long walks on the coast had made me more than equal to a lengthy city stroll. I was particularly grateful that I had escaped having a load of cabbages dropped on me or a bucket of sewer water splashed across my clothing, both imminent dangers I had avoided with great effort.

If my walk had reminded me of my previous life, the Savoy Hotel reminded me that London never stays the same for two days together, let alone decades. In previous years, I had visited the Savoy Theatre many times and admired its electric lights, but the hotel that now stood next to it eclipsed it in size and grandeur, a white edifice with twinkling lights peeking out of over a hundred rooms.

I stood still in front of it for some time, one woman against a backdrop of carriages and grand personages in brightly-coloured clothing and gleaming jewellery leaving for evening engagements. I had been one of them, once, but as the half-light of evening gradually diminished, I felt as though everything around me was an elaborate theatrical production with me as the lone member of the audience. Or perhaps it was the opposite; I was the play, and the world my audience. I only know that I would not have been surprised to see the Irene Adler I had once been emerge from the immense doorway on the arm of a stylish gentleman. I felt far enough removed from her that the idea of her as a separate being still living a mad, whirling, city life was almost believable.

"Do you need help, Miss?" The man at my elbow was under twenty, with short, shiny hair and a crisply starched porter's uniform. His determined cheerfulness recalled me to the literal world.

"I need lodging," I said, as sweetly as I could, handing my suitcase to him. I was aware that my position as a female travelling alone would seem unusual, but I was also well aware that liberal quantities of money tend to lower raised eyebrows and engender cooperation.

The porter led me between the tall columns that framed each entrance, and I looked around me in amazement at the blindingly white ceiling, gold chandeliers, and plush carpeted floor that adorned the huge room.

"Are you all right, Miss?" I realised after a moment that I had inadvertently stopped to admire my surroundings and been left behind by the porter, who'd doubled back to fetch me.

"Forgive me," I said, handing him a coin. "It's been quite a while since I've been inside a hotel."

Unexpectedly, he broke into a smile. "Between us, Miss," he said, "it's my first week here."

"What's your name?" I asked.

"Billy," he answered.

—

Billy proved as useful as I could have hoped, and he deposited me in a room on the hotel's second floor in under a quarter of an hour, using one of the establishment's ascending rooms that carried one from the ground floor to the higher levels. I had never seen such a thing.

My suite itself was large, inviting, and beautiful in every way. A floral sofa sat beside a large window, and the bed was covered with blue satin. I was most shocked by the private bathing room, a tiny marble palace with water that ran hot and cold at all times.

As soon as Billy had left me, I was joined by a maid, who offered to unpack my suitcase. I thought of declining, but I was tired, and I liked the prospect of stretching out on the bed and gathering my thoughts.

The girl was young but diligent, and she had my clothes put into drawers and closet within ten minutes. "Here, Miss," she said, showing me a metal tube situated in the wall above the ornate side table. "If you speak into this, the floor waiter or I will fetch you anything you need."

"Thank you," I answered, possessed of a sudden desire to use the contraption just to see if it worked, which I did as soon as she'd left the room. "Excuse me," I said, feeling foolish as I held the tube close to my mouth and inhaled the aroma of tarnished metal, "is the waiter there?"

"Here, Miss," said a voice with a Cockney accent.

"May I—I'd like a poached egg and perhaps a few slices of toast," I said, rather weakly, realising I wasn't entirely sure of the etiquette of how to communicate using a metal speaking contraption.

"And a pot of tea, Miss?"

"Certainly," I answered.

“I’ll be up in a moment, Miss,” the voice finished, and I returned the tube to its place in the wall. I began to think I would go mad if anyone else called me Miss.

Left alone, with only my thoughts to accompany me, I opened the lace curtains and looked out at the Thames. I felt less displaced than I expected. London’s pulse was the same as ever, even if her face was made up differently.

Within fifteen minutes, the floor waiter appeared. He was a man of middle age, with a round, red, smiling face, wearing a grand uniform that seemed to suit him not at all. “Here you are,” he said, bringing in a tray with china dishes and a silver tea service upon it. I watched as he placed everything upon the room’s larger table, which also doubled as a desk. Before I was allowed access to anything, it must be opened, approved, and placed in what the hotel considered to be the most convenient arrangement possible for my dining pleasure. Woe betide the waiter who made his guest take any extra movements in the service of her own comfort.

The smell of food in my nostrils had me practically starving by the time the man finished. “Thank you,” I said hastily, handing him a mess of coins that was probably excessive compensation for his pains, but which I hoped would hurry him out of the room. He was far too well trained to betray surprise, but I thought I detected a gleam of satisfaction in his blue eyes.

Once blessed solitude had finally descended again, I let my hair down. I divested myself of each hairpin one by one, sighing as my heavy locks fell down my back and gave my aching head the relief it desired. I would have liked to undress and bathe, but the piping hot egg beckoned, and I could bear to wait no longer. I ate, savouring each bite as if it were the first I’d ever taken. Indeed, the Savoy’s toast was crisped to such perfection that I began to wonder if I could ask for the secret of it. I’ve never laid claim to any measure of asceticism, and the reason for my journey did not inhibit my enjoyment of sensory comforts.

By the time I had finished eating, it was completely dark, and I turned on the gold electric lamp that stood on the bedside table. I had been in the presence of electric light before, but I had not experienced the power of a lone electric bulb against the falling night of London. It was grand. I was never one to feel sentimental attachments to the obsolete past. As far as I was concerned, electric lights could not take their rightful place in the world soon enough.

I drew a bath, marvelling at the warm water that instantly filled it. Even in the bathroom, electric lights brightened the gleaming white marble, and I contemplated the possibility of reading a book whilst soaking in white bubbles. In the end, I decided to force myself to arrange my thoughts, knowing that when I encountered Holmes again, I must have a far more coherent narrative to recount than I had already given.

Until a month prior to my visit, I had experienced no serious threats to my hives or problems with my beekeeping, save a few lost larvae here and there. I'd come into the practice gradually, first vicariously, as a reader of beekeeping journals, then, once my curiosity had got the best of me, as a literal keeper of hives—one, then three more had joined it.

I had not realised, when I began, how consuming beekeeping could become. I'd had very little to demand my time during my first days in Sussex, and I had welcomed a hobby that required regular attention. As the years had progressed, my musical engagements in the village had grown in frequency, but they did not encroach on my day-to-day freedom. The bees continued to be my favourite responsibility.

I let my body sink deeper into the warm water and my thoughts sink with it. The bees, truthfully, had become more than a hobby. They had become my refuge when darker memories of my life insisted on asserting themselves. Time after time, I had found satisfaction and relief by rushing to the hives and finding them as calm and productive as ever. The disordered thoughts in my mind had found clarity there. The determination of each worker to complete her tasks, each queen to rule her kingdom, returned to me a sense that order exists in this strange world. That was why my horror had been so great the day I'd gone to check the hives four weeks previously and found many darkened, dying larvae, as if all the love and care I'd given the hives had turned to death and decay.

I'd forced myself to rein in the violence of my first reaction. After all, I had been a beekeeper for some time, and I knew that hive maladies were not uncommon. I consulted books and journals, and I sent for the remedies they suggested, but nothing worked. Finally, I consulted the village veterinarian, who recommended an associate who was also a beekeeper. By this time, three of my four hives were affected, and I was frantic. The man diagnosed foulbrood, a bacterial malady, and assured me that since the hives had been previously healthy, they would survive. He was wrong; within weeks, my hives were nearly dead. The man returned, perplexed. He had never seen foulbrood that severe. The morning after his second visit, I went to the hives alone. Instead of the joyful buzzing of health, there was only silence. A few remaining bees went about their tasks, and I wept for them.

I went back to my cottage and wrote a letter to an American apiarist, a man named Robert Holekamp, whose name I had seen in a beekeeping journal. I had not consulted him previously because I'd recognised the impracticality of expecting letters to proceed across the ocean and back rapidly enough to be helpful, but I was determined now. I had not been able to save my bees, but I would discover why they had died. The reason I chose an American was that I had read that certain maladies affecting bee populations had arisen in the United States that were rarely seen in England, and the fruitlessness of my research had made me begin to suspect that something more rare had afflicted my hives.

In my letter, I described the darkened larvae, the speed with which the disease had travelled between hives, and the dry scales that remained once the bees were dead. Holekamp replied promptly, the letter addressed from his farm in Annapolis, Missouri. He suspected, he said, that foulbrood was the culprit, but not the variety with which my veterinarian's associate had been familiar. No, he said, there was another strain of foulbrood, a bacterium that had been discovered in America and produced the exact effects I'd described. As a fellow apiarist, he offered his sympathies and his hopes that the two strains of foulbrood would soon be differentiated for the sake of more effective treatment. The end of his letter, a single question, was the thing that had brought me to Holmes: *How did an isolated hive of bees on the Sussex Downs acquire such a severe strain of foulbrood?* Upon receipt of his letter, I had travelled immediately to London.

Again and again I have taken a problem to him, and have received an explanation which has afterwards proved to be the correct one.

—The Greek Interpreter

Chapter 2: Holmes

Sherlock Holmes stepped into the Stranger's Room of the Diogenes Club. He always enjoyed his visits there, as if he was taking a holiday to a foreign but highly pleasurable land. He did not share its members' rigorously religious devotion to silence, but he paid it reverence and enjoyed its serenity nonetheless.

He had just seated himself when the immense frame of his brother Mycroft hove into view and took its place opposite him, dwarfing any and all furniture in the room. "Good morning, Sherlock," he said drily. "I'm surprised you found time to leave your fair guest and visit me."

"My fair guest?" the detective asked.

"Oh, yes," said Mycroft. "If I'm not mistaken—and of course I am not—the charming Irene Adler yesterday debarked in our fair city with the intention of visiting you. The latter is, of course, a deduction based upon her likely behaviour, but of the former I have proof."

"Quite right," said Sherlock, "but she's currently lodged at the Savoy Hotel and is far from reliant on me for her comforts."

Mycroft smiled. "You've come to see me about the stolen key, have you not? Any moment now, it would have occurred to you that the red gloves are the answer to the whole thing."

Sherlock Holmes nodded to his brother, stood, and left the club to return home, stopping only long enough to send a telegram concerning the gloves in question and the solution to the mystery. He did not intend to tell The Woman of his sacrifice of dignity—the fact that he had consulted his brother rather than concluding the case himself because he wished to give her problem his immediate attention. Of course, he could not deny that the prospect of poisoned bees interested him far more than a careless peer's missing key.

Upon his return to Baker Street, he was rewarded by obvious evidence that Irene Adler was inside. He saw her shoe prints in the dust leading to the door, and he smelled the faint aroma of her perfume, which reminded him of cut grass.

Sure enough, upon his entrance, he found The Woman enthusiastically reducing the number of scones on a tea tray and laughing at Dr Watson, who blushed and seemed inordinately pleased at something.

"Good day, Holmes," said Irene, and he noticed that she looked far better rested and in better spirits than the previous night.

"Good day," he answered, unceremoniously taking the plate from her hands and divesting it of two remaining scones before returning it and taking his seat in his chair.

"I've just been telling Dr Watson that Mrs Turner intends to visit her sister in Dartford next month and is eager to see him as well," Irene continued. The detective did not respond, which elicited even more laughter. Truthfully, he was far from surprised. It was only a matter of time, he knew, until Watson had his way and convinced The Woman's housekeeper to marry him. Still, he did not intend to look as if he approved.

"I am prepared to tell you the full tale of why I've come." Irene's face turned serious as she changed the subject. "If, at the end, you believe that I am unreasonably concerned, I will accept your judgement in the matter."

"I'm certain that won't be the case," said Watson in his usual gallant manner. Holmes did not answer, though he was no less sure that he would not find The Woman's suspicion ridiculous. He knew her too well and trusted her instincts too thoroughly for that.

"It began two months ago," said Irene, leaning forward in her chair. With that, she spun a story that began with the appearance of an unexceptional though unfortunate beekeeping mishap and ended with the immensely perplexing question of why someone might seek to poison bees, or how the malady could have been contracted naturally, which was highly improbable. Both alternatives seemed preposterous. Had Irene been less reliable, he might have questioned her assessment of the disease and postulated an easier solution—perhaps a more common disease that had been misdiagnosed. However, he knew that The Woman was intellectually knowledgeable and a meticulous beekeeper. He could not blame the strangeness of the case on her possible mistake. She was too rigorous.

"I am well aware," said Irene, after she had been speaking for some time, "that it is highly unfortunate that the hive was infected a month ago, and any evidence of how it might have been done is almost certainly destroyed. I had no idea anything unusual had gone on."

"It is certainly lamentable, but hardly preventable in this case," Holmes answered, thinking to himself that if a crime had been committed, the perpetrator had done an admirable job. Of course, if nature itself was the criminal, there would be no evidence to discover.

"I am at a loss, Holmes," The Woman admitted. "I had ample time to consider the matter on the train, and I can think of no facet of it that is not intensely perplexing."

"It has, of course, occurred to you that someone might have introduced the bacterium on purpose in an effort to distress you," the detective answered.

"Yes," said Irene, but the shake of her head belied her affirmative answer. "I simply cannot comprehend the reason for such a thing. If I have an enemy, why should he not attack my person? It's certainly a wildly indirect way to get at me."

"And yet," said Holmes, "very effective in provoking you to act."

"Might some piece of evidence be recovered from the hives, Holmes?" Watson asked, pulling at his moustache in a concerned manner.

"Doubtful after this lapse of time, since the hives are out in the elements," the detective answered. "I must take time to consider how best to proceed." He stretched out his long legs and fixed his gaze on The Woman. "I thank you for providing me with an intriguing puzzle. I may require more information from you soon, but for the time being, I desire quiet."

Irene obviously considered herself dismissed, since she rose and bid good day to both flatmates. Watson accompanied her to the door, but Holmes was already lost in thought by the time she reached the street.

The detective had known little of beekeeping before his visits to Sussex, though the idea had always held a certain fascination for him. He had come to enjoy his walks to the hives and the endless opportunity for observation they afforded, and though he had not been attached to them in the same way The Woman was, he understood her dismay. Dismay, however, did not solve cases or illuminate the obscure. He put his mind to considering the mystery and eliminating what he could.

The fact: Irene Adler's bees had died, and the disease was recognisably American in origin. The possibilities: Either the disease had been contracted naturally, or it had been introduced in some intentional manner. He did not waste time musing on the obvious unlikelihood of either being true; the world, he knew, was filled with things that seemed improbable until their perfectly logical cause was discovered. If that cause was criminal, well, so much the better, for then it came within Holmes's purview.

The first line of enquiry, he decided, would be to acquire further information about the American strain of foulbrood. He would have considered it unlikely for Irene's bees to contract even the European strain, given their location and isolation, but he did not trust his own limited knowledge enough to be absolutely sure. He was aware that Irene's appealing to him meant that she had already made this deduction, but he did not wish to embark prematurely on an investigation in which there was no perpetrator. He determined to consult a London expert to confirm what the American apiarist had told Irene.

As Holmes finished formulating his plan, Watson returned, looking flushed and hearty. "It's a beautiful day," he said. "It would do wonders for your health to take a stroll outside. I could hardly force myself back in."

The detective shook his head. "You know very well that I am in excellent health, and I have neither the need nor the desire for fresh air when my mind is engaged."

"Ah, yes," said the doctor, taking his customary seat and lighting his pipe, "I gather you appreciate Miss Adler's problem."

"I judge by your tone that you disapprove of my enjoyment," said Holmes.

"The loss of such fine honey is not a matter for amusement," said Watson sharply, "however intriguing the mystery of it, and I cannot help being distressed by Miss Adler's obvious unhappiness, in spite of her efforts to keep her spirits high."

“The way to raise all of our spirits will be to solve the case once and for all,” said Holmes drily, rising and preparing to leave the flat.

“I can’t imagine that you’re taking my advice and engaging in a constitutional for your health,” said the doctor, “therefore, I gather that you embark on an errand related to the case. Shall I accompany you?”

“A capable deduction,” said Holmes. “I go forth to visit Charles Ward and would be very glad of your company if your previous walk has not entirely depleted your strength.”

“Certainly not,” said Watson stolidly. The two men set out, and their shadows against the wall of Baker Street formed as amusing a contrast in every physical respect as did their personalities and intellects.

So perfect was the organisation of the society, and so systematic its methods, that there is hardly a case upon record where any man succeeded in braving it with impunity, or in which any of its outrages were traced home to the perpetrators.

—The Five Orange Pips

Chapter 3: Irene

I left Baker Street with one clear objective, which was to visit Briony Lodge, the home I had previously called mine when I had been resident in London. This did not seem to me to be an unusual desire. As I drew close to it, the feeling I'd had the previous night, that some other Irene Adler might still be living my old life, overtook me.

In my mind, I saw scenes of former days—the carriages, the laughing people, the face of the handsome, coarse man who had won my heart before tearing it to pieces. I smiled to myself when I recalled the day I had purchased a suit of clothes from a street peddler, forced my hair into a boy's cap, and fooled Sherlock Holmes into thinking I was male. I couldn't deny the thrill of pride I still felt at the memory. At the time, it had felt like besting an enemy—an honourable one, but an enemy nonetheless. Thinking back, it felt sweeter, like a game of chess won against a dear friend.

Though I had made the decision impulsively, I now realised that friendship was what had assured me that I would not be disappointed if I traveled to Baker Street. My certainty, though perhaps precipitate, had not been misplaced. Nevertheless, as my feet took me up the walk to the house that had belonged to Irene Adler, celebrated opera singer, I could not help marvelling that the detective and The Woman—as Dr Watson claimed Holmes referred to me—had managed to find themselves friends.

I suppose I shouldn't have been as surprised as I was. The turns of mind that had made us formidable opponents were the same ones that made us congenial associates. I say *congenial*—we argued and disagreed quite regularly, but I enjoyed it immensely, and I believe Holmes did as well, for by the time my bees had died, he had made many visits to my little cottage.

I did not expect to enter my former home, for it had been purchased by a widow of high social standing when I had vacated it, and she continued to inhabit it whenever she resided in England, though much of her time was spent on the Continent. I had no wish to disturb whatever household staff she might retain to care for it. I simply stood and watched the vast windows for a time, thinking about the Irene who had been and thinking that I was glad, in the main, to have become the Irene Adler I now was. The bridge between us, of course, had been Irene Norton—unhappy woman, deceived out of the life she'd desired. During the Florida case, the occasion of the beginning of my ongoing association with Holmes, I'd still been chained to her. My clutching at the name of Adler had been a desperate attempt to regain my sense of self, the assurance of my own autonomy. Without meaning to, Holmes had helped me to understand that no good could come of trying to claw my way back to the past. Even as we began to forge a friendship out of the fires of animosity, I chose to become myself again—a newer, stronger self. It had taken time and effort for me to fully understand and inhabit that self, but bolstered by the Sussex air, the detective's friendship, my music, and my bees, I had succeeded.

I was so lost in thought that an elderly woman in a yellowed shawl nearly ran into me as she made her way down the street. "They said you would be here!" she cackled gleefully as she brushed my shoulder. I turned around and watched her walk away, more annoyed than disturbed by the encounter. I searched for the telltale signs that she was not what she appeared to be—concealed height, padding on the body, unnatural hair—things that might have alerted me to the fact that I had just been accosted by Holmes in disguise. However, she seemed perfectly genuine.

I turned away from my old house, the spell broken. From the outside, it looked much as it always had, and I was content to remain ignorant of the changes that might have been made on the inside. I tried not to dwell on the encounter with the old woman, but it had been so long since I had been intimately acquainted with the oddities of London that I could not put it out of my mind as easily as I would have wished.

I had eaten a late breakfast at the Savoy and my fair share of the delicacies on Mrs Hudson's tea tray, but as afternoon wore on, I realised that I was hungry. I eagerly returned to my hotel, lured by the promise of a magical speaking tube that would allow me to request whatever food I desired.

When I arrived at the Savoy, the crowd of people about was equal to that of the night before; only the costumes were different, and the atmosphere was more businesslike and less convivial. As I made my way inside, I suddenly heard a voice booming out my name. I looked around me, disorientated, and finally found the source of the noise—a man behind one of the hotel's marble desks. I watched him curiously as he made his way over to me.

He was dressed in the well-made suit of male Savoy staff, and he smiled. "We received this in your absence," he said, handing me an envelope. It contained a folded piece of notepaper.

I took it and stepped aside to see what it said: *Tell him we know you're here. K.K.K.* I felt the same annoyance I had when the old woman had spoken to me. I could only suppose the note meant Holmes, but if someone was intending to frighten me, they were certainly doing an obscure job of it. I'd intended to spend the evening alone in my room unless my friend contrived to send for me, but I changed my mind and turned for Baker Street instead.

—

I found the flat empty save for Mrs Hudson. "They've gone out," she said, "and left no indication of when they might return, as usual."

"I'm not expected," I said.

"No, I'd say you were quite unexpected, as a rule," she answered. I was slightly astonished at this burst of wit.

"I must thank you for your kindness to me," I continued, glad to have her alone.

"Not at all," she said. "You're one of Holmes's."

She installed me in the flat and took pity on my pallor by bringing me a cold meat pie and a cup of tea. She left me alone, and I was pleased by what she'd said. I didn't mind being "one of Holmes's," because Holmes never tried to own anyone. He simply collected them, like his books or his chemistry set, and appreciated each for what they were.

I waited three quarters of an hour before the tramp of feet signalled the return of Holmes and Watson. Unlike my friend, I did not have the ability to instantly divine where someone had spent the past three hours based on his clothes or the mud on his shoes. I was forced to rely, like the majority of humanity, on verbal enquiries. Thankfully, Holmes anticipated me.

"We've been to see Dr Charles Ward at St. Bartholomew's. Aside from being a medical doctor, he takes the study of animal disease quite seriously. I have consulted him about foulbrood."

"Yes," I said, wishing, as usual, that he would reach the point of the narrative more quickly than he was likely to do.

"Dr Ward is familiar with the malady and agrees with Holekamp that science has not yet distinguished the types of the disease adequately. Unfortunately, his information may complicate the facts. Namely, foulbrood of the sort your bees contracted is not limited to the American continent, but has been widely documented all over the earth. The American distinction Holekamp used refers to its origin; it was first discovered in America, but its presence is felt everywhere."

By this time, Holmes and Watson had taken their seats and each lit his pipe, filling the flat with smoke. They would not have smoked in front of many female clients; I was glad they felt free to do so in front of me.

"That is unfortunate," I said, my heart sinking.

"Perhaps," said Holmes, "but even if both strains of the disease are found generally, that does not provide an explanation of how a hive of your bees managed to contract it. My scientific pursuits generally run in directions that advance the detection of crime, but I am cognizant of the fact that the sort of bacterium that causes either type of foulbrood must be acquired in a specific way, through contact with the bacterium itself or other diseased bees."

"Yes," I answered, "but there are no other hives within ten miles of my cottage, which is further than the bees ever forage."

"I am aware of this," said Holmes in a measured tone. "We cannot now know if we seek an American source or not, but I believe we may reasonably eliminate the possibility of contraction of the disease by natural means, since your bees were almost certainly too isolated to have come into contact with it."

I breathed deeply and felt something like relief. I had come to London because I suspected what Holmes was now telling me he believed, but the sheer preposterousness of the concept had made me frightened that my thoughts were unreasonable. Hearing them confirmed aloud by my friend was immensely comforting.

"Perhaps I have an unknown enemy in the village," I murmured speculatively, my mind leaping to find explanations for the implication.

"An enemy with enough knowledge of the science of beekeeping and enough resources to poison a hive of bees with a specific infection?" I had to agree that it seemed highly unlikely. The only person in the village I could have imagined contriving such a thing was Dr Clarke, who had been helped from this earth at the end of a rope a few months previously after the murder of James Phillimore. He had been replaced in the village by young Dr Palmer, who was as harmless a creature as I had ever encountered.

Dr Watson had been silent all this time, listening and smoking and shaking his head sympathetically whenever the conversation warranted. He now proceeded to clear his throat loudly. "Holmes, it's lamentably rude to keep a lady waiting to dine in this manner. Miss Adler, you must be starving. Just because he loses his appetite whenever anything interesting happens doesn't mean we mere mortals do."

I smiled. "Mrs Hudson was kind enough to furnish me with something earlier, but please don't feel constrained on my account. In fact, I intend to leave presently, but I have news of my own to report first."

"Yes?" Holmes had not responded to his flatmate, but he showed interest at my statement.

"I was mystified by two curious incidents today. They may prove to be of no consequence, but I feel I should recount them. I walked in the direction of my former home, Briony Lodge, earlier, and an elderly woman nearly knocked me off my feet, as if she hadn't seen me. However, as she passed me, she asserted that someone had 'said you would be here,' exactly as if she knew who I was, though, to my knowledge, I had never seen her before. I thought perhaps I might be looking at you in disguise, Holmes, but to my eyes, she appeared to be just as she seemed.

"And the second incident?" I could tell by Holmes's clipped tone that he was becoming impatient at the length of the tale.

"Here," I said. "See for yourself." I handed him the note I had received in the lobby of the Savoy. He perused it for a moment.

"Oh, you've got more direct with a decade more behind you," he said, staring at the simple missive. Before my eyes and those of Dr Watson, Holmes's face grew animated, his eyes illuminated with the fire of purpose. "But why here? Why now?"

I looked over at the doctor, but he seemed as mystified as I was. "What have you discovered?" I finally ventured.

"This!" said the detective, pointing to the three letter Ks, which I had assumed were the initials of the letter writer. "It's the signature of the Ku Klux Klan. The old crone must have been hired to watch for you," Holmes continued. I'm afraid I stared at him rather stupidly for some moments before the incidents Watson had recounted in his story about the unfortunate Openshaw returned to my mind. I suppose I should have made the connection more quickly, but the idea seemed so fantastic to my mind that it had not yet occurred to me to relate my encounter to Holmes's old case.

"You contended with them once before," I said, hoping that Holmes, whose mind was engaged in considering this unexpected new development, might nevertheless be prompted to articulate his thoughts.

"Yes, of course," he said, "and I would have had them if nature had not meted out justice instead."

"But why should they have anything against you," I wondered, "or me, for that matter? And what can this possibly have to do with my hives?"

"The second question is answered simply enough," said Holmes, speaking rapidly. "I know from my prior experience and knowledge of the organisation that it is a vast one with ties to many men in high position. Its initial wave of power was hindered by laws intended to curb its activity, but, unfortunately, it quickly regained footholds throughout the southern part of the United States of America. At this time, it is supported by the political structure of several states. As to your hives, it is not difficult to deduce that one of their number was somehow sent to introduce the bacterium in order to lure you to London."

"Whatever for, and how could they possibly know I would actually come here?"

"I have no reliable information to tell me the purpose as of yet. As for you coming here, if they have watched my activities over the past few years, they will be aware of my visits to your home. It was not a wild leap to imagine that you would appeal to me if a mysterious malady destroyed your beehives. Knowing their modes of behaviour, I believe they are trying to taunt me," said Holmes, his face dark. "They wish to show me their power, to prove that their reach extends to Sussex and beyond."

"You have not answered the reason for their animosity," I reminded him.

"I despise the practice of guessing," Holmes said, "but it is allowing of too much coincidence to believe that this has nothing to do with my previous case." He looked over at me then and stared at me so intently for a moment that I was confused as to his purpose. Finally, he spoke again. "I am—sorry for the loss of your bees; it appears that their demise must be laid at the door of your association with me."

A host of different feelings flooded into me, but the chief among them was anger, both on behalf of my bees and on behalf of my friend. "Don't be ridiculous, Holmes. The fault is that of the man who did it and the man who ordered it. You have nothing to apologise for." He smiled.

Dr Watson fairly bristled in his chair. "Holmes, you can't possibly expect Miss Adler to go back alone to her hotel this evening with some sort of vague threat wandering around London." I had the greatest urge to kiss his cheek, but I restrained the impulse, fearing that it might be overly disturbing to his dignity.

Holmes was, by this time, sitting curled into his chair with his eyes closed, no doubt pondering the latest, cataclysmic development that had occurred. His eyes fluttered open. "I'm quite sure Irene is capable of defending herself if the need arises. I've observed that she is carrying a firearm in her handbag, as is her usual practice. Once at the hotel, Billy will look after her, of course, but if you wish to accompany her there to see that she arrives safely, there's no harm in it."

"Is Billy in your employ, then?" I asked curiously, remembering the bright green eyes and wide smile of the porter who had helped me into the hotel.

"Yes," answered my friend. "I sent him there a week ago to watch a guest who was a suspect in a theft that has since been proved to be someone else's handiwork. I had expected to recall him hence, but his employment is convenient for the time being. He has keen eyes and will send word to me if anything unusual occurs. His instincts are to be trusted." I wanted to ask Holmes more about the boy, but I realised that my enquiries would be fruitless, and I did not wish to distract him. I determined to ask Dr Watson as soon as I could.

"You may go," said my friend, with finality. I would have laughed at his dismissal if the occasion had been less serious. As it was, I simply rose and let the doctor walk me to the street.

"Are you certain you wish to risk a night spent in the Savoy?" asked Watson. "I'd be happy to see about arranging private lodgings for you."

"That is most kind," I answered, "but I agree with Holmes."

"You're a pair, the both of you," he groused. "I believe Holmes would have us all sleeping in the street if our comforts depended on his concern, and you appear to have endless confidence in your safety, regardless of the evidence."

I laughed, but consented to take the doctor's arm. "I had no idea Billy was one of Holmes's brood. Is he a former Irregular?"

"No," said Watson. "Holmes employed him when my absences from the flat grew more frequent." He was, of course, alluding to his courtship of my housekeeper. "He seems very reliable, and Holmes trusts him more than he trusts most people."

"I see," I answered.

The doctor was silent for a while, and I imagined that his thoughts were taken up with Mrs Turner. He had visited many times since the Phillimore case, sometimes with Holmes and sometimes without. It amused me to act as chaperone at these times, legitimising in the eyes of the world the association of two of the most respectable people I had ever known, both of them far more respectable than I had ever laid claim to being. I knew that it would not be long before

Mrs Turner left me, but I could not find it in myself to lament the loss, since I was excessively pleased for her. Besides, I knew that her leaving would also mean the probable departure once again of the doctor from Baker Street, and my friend would, I supposed, suffer more than I.

I was pulled from my thoughts by the soft scrape of Watson's foot on the dirty ground. He was tired, and I had no wish to explain to my housekeeper that I had allowed him to overexert himself. She would certainly get it out of me; I expected her to resemble the Spanish Inquisition when I returned home, so eager would she be to hear all about her doctor. I turned to him, attempting to be tactful.

"Dr Watson, I can see the lights of the Savoy in the distance. I would be very pleased to walk the rest of the way alone. As you know, I had a long journey to get here on a train filled with people, followed by my immediate re-entry into the melee of London, and my head is still spinning. I would love to enjoy the night air on my own."

"You and Holmes," he mumbled, "with your odd notions." He patted my hand kindly. He'd always been courteous to me, but ever since he'd begun courting my housekeeper, he seemed to think of himself as a fond uncle. "I don't like it, but if you insist, I will acquiesce."

"Very good," I answered cheerfully. He turned back, and I went onward. Everything I'd said to him was true. I could see the hotel in the distance, and I enjoyed the breeze on my face. I'd forgotten how claustrophobic London could feel compared to the open spaces of the Downs. When I'd lived there, I'd learned to disregard the crowds that were everywhere, but now I had become re-sensitised to them. I felt as if, everywhere I went, I was being watched, by mostly indifferent eyes.

One of their number, taller and older than the others, stood forward with an air of lounging superiority which was very funny in such a disreputable little scarecrow.

—The Sign of Four

Chapter 4: Holmes

Holmes barely noticed when the doctor and The Woman had departed, so consumed was he by his thoughts. He wondered, at first, why the remaining Klan members had not simply sent him his own envelope filled with five orange pips. No, that had been the calling card of a previous generation. Those who remained were obviously imbued with their own brand of hatred.

The detective rose and went to his shelf, taking out the book with its entry about the Klan and his notations on the Openshaw incident, but nothing he saw illuminated the present situation. Many of his cases through the years had contained unusual features, but this one was shaping up to be one of the most surprising he had ever encountered, provided his deductions were accurate.

He had erroneously supposed that Openshaw's death was an anomaly, a vendetta by those who wanted proof that none of their misdeeds would be remembered by the law. Their deaths at sea had seemed like justice, and Holmes had not pursued the matter any further. The state of the Klan at that time, when it had been weakened by law and softened by public opinion, had made him think its hold would loosen in America, and he had not thought the members organised enough at the time to even realise his involvement with Openshaw, let alone pursue a years-long quest based on it. He thought, in passing, that he might be mistaken in considering the past case linked to the present one, but the coincidence was too great to treat them as separate instances.

He took up the note once again to gather what evidence he might from it. The handwriting was neat, the ink black, and the intention clear. He looked for signs of particular colouration by mud, burning of the edge as by a candle, or characteristics of the paper that might reveal something about the writer, but the paper was white, unmarked save for the message, and might have come from any one of several printers of stationery in London, or elsewhere, for that matter. The envelope was unmarked, and it too was not unique.

The detective experienced a moment of annoyance, both at The Woman and at the conveyor of the note—first, at Irene, because she was not him, and therefore had not thought to ask the member of the Savoy staff who had given her the letter for a description of its deliverer. Second, at whoever had written the note, for having the sense to send it to him indirectly, thereby lessening the chance that he would be able to trace its origin. One thing was certain; if the remaining members of the Klan were attempting to irritate him, they were succeeding.

He did not dwell on his feelings of annoyance. The Woman, though clever, was not a detective, and the events of the day had surprised her. Holmes had learned, long ago, that few people could be expected to act perfectly rationally when confronted with the unexpected. He wished it were daytime, so that he could investigate without further delay, but evening had its own uses.

Just then, Watson returned. The detective could tell, from the sound of his steps in the passage, that he was limping. When he finally opened the door, Holmes saw that he was panting with slight weariness. "She sent me back halfway," he said crossly. "I didn't want to leave until I saw her to her room."

"She is sensible enough to reach it safely," said Holmes calmly. "I must go out, Watson."

"So late, Holmes? You haven't dined."

"I have no wish to dine," said the detective, rising abruptly.

—

A half hour later, Holmes found himself on the corner of a small alley in one of the more disreputable sections of London. Dusk was falling, and few were about in the half light. No one paid him any attention except an extremely comely young girl in a tattered dress, who held a crying baby, and an old man deep in the bottle of gin he carried. "It's you," said the girl, staring at him pointedly.

"Yes," answered the detective, handing her a coin.

"You've no cause to give me anything," she said sourly. "I don't work for you no more."

"Not entirely of your own choice," said Holmes nodding towards the tiny infant.

"Not forced upon me neither," she retorted, but she kept the coin and almost smiled. Meanwhile, the elderly drunken man pointed at the detective and sang an unintelligible song of former days.

"Go and buy your child something to eat, Anna," Holmes ordered.

"It don't go easy for you to stop giving orders, does it?" she asked saucily, but she turned on her way, clutching her baby to her chest.

When she was far enough away for her child not to be disturbed, the detective did something that would have astonished many who knew him, though perhaps not those who knew him well: He put his thumb and forefinger into his mouth and uttered a whistle so ear-piercingly loud that it sounded as if it would raise the dead.

At this, the inebriated man ceased singing and stared open-mouthed at Holmes, while a few workmen who had been loitering nearby glanced in his direction. He took no notice of them and waited calmly for another three minutes, until a grinning boy of fifteen years peeked his head around the wall of a dilapidated shop at the opposite end of the alley. Apparently satisfied, he brought the rest of his lanky body into view and proceeded quickly in Holmes's direction.

Wiggins was, by this time, no longer a child. Instead, he had proceeded into the phase of life generally referred to as awkward, and as he approached Holmes, his long arms hung loosely at his sides as if he did not know what to do with them when they were not needed.

"Evening, Sir," said the lad, touching his cap.

"Good evening, Wiggins," said the detective. "I'd like to discuss my business with you in a more secluded setting. I assume a morsel of food will not be taken amiss."

"Not at all," the boy answered, beaming once more. For all his bravado, Holmes could see the darkness under his eyes and the hollows in his cheeks, signs no lad in stages of rapid growth should display. Holmes knew that after their long association, Wiggins would have been highly offended by compensation that was any greater than the usual rate, but the detective reasoned that if he fed the boy as part of their meeting, he could also pay him without giving offence.

The two passed a few streets over, where the detective knew of a public house that served passable meals. The establishment was small but busy, and Holmes was able to bury himself and the boy in a corner near a grimy window, their speaking masked by the sounds of the rowdy men who were celebrating the end of the day by growing increasingly louder and more raucous.

Once Wiggins had a few mouthfuls of soup in him, the detective leaned close. "I have something for you to do that's a bit more difficult than usual. I'll add an extra shilling a day for the others and a guinea a week for you above the regular rate." Even the distraction of edible nourishment did not keep the boy from looking up at this and fixing Holmes with an interested stare.

"That's generous, Guv'nor. Is it dangerous?"

"Not to you. I need you to follow a lady." The detective had asked his Irregulars to follow any number of personages great and small during their time of employment, so he was not surprised that Wiggins looked confused at the idea that there was anything unusual in such an assignment or that he should specifically be the one to carry it out.

"I don't want you to follow her for her own sake. That's the material point. I want you to take note of anyone who takes interest in her. I don't mean incidental interest. She's an unusually beautiful woman who attracts attention wherever she goes. No, I want you to note anyone—man, woman, or child—who lingers near her or seems inordinately interested in her movements. You will report to me in the usual way. The lady will be aware of your mission, but you must act as if she isn't, so that anyone who wishes to follow her will be unaware of you. Two things require that you contact me immediately—if you become aware that someone else is following all of her movements, or if someone lingering around her speaks with an American accent. If either of those things occurs, send word to me instantly. I trust you know an American accent when you hear one."

Wiggins nodded emphatically. "Yessir, all flat vowels and strange ways of saying words that make them sound like something else until they get to the end."

Holmes smiled. "The lady's name is Irene Adler. She lodges at the Savoy Hotel." He handed over a photograph, and Wiggins's eyes grew wide at The Woman's appearance. "I will call on her in an hour. You will be situated outside. She will walk out with me, and you will note that as the beginning of your assignment. During the time that you're engaged in this assignment, leave Lewis to do any of your usual duties that you're forced to neglect. You may consider the end of each day to be when Miss Adler retires for the night. I have another set of eyes within the hotel itself."

"What about the others?" Wiggins enquired, coming to the end of his bowl of soup and looking as if he'd have liked it to be three times its size.

"As for the others," said the detective, "Ayers must shadow Dr Watson with the same instructions as yours; put three of the most observant around Baker Street, looking for anything out of the ordinary, two at the docks, and two at the train station. They can all report to you or to Lewis, unless they discover something of particular importance. Keep watch for groups of Americans or anyone out of the common way—you know what sorts. I will give you more specific instructions in the near future when I am able. You and Ayers must take extra care to be vigilant but not obvious."

Wiggins had finished his drink by this time and sat back in his chair, nodding with satisfaction. "We'll do it, Sir."

"See you do," said Holmes, getting up and leaving the boy with payment for the food—and enough for another bowl of soup or piece of bread if he should choose to use it for that purpose.

From the public house, Holmes went out to the now-dark street and hailed a cab. The driver was young and smiled widely, but the detective found himself distrusting the appearance of everyone he met. He did not consider the Openshaw case a failure, not completely. The man had made his own choices, and Holmes did not feel responsible for his death. He did, however, retain a sense of dread when he considered the elusive KKK. Those who had actually killed Openshaw had met their fate, but their associates had escaped, and it had never been as neat a solution as he preferred his cases to have. On the other hand, he had acknowledged the logical impossibility of personally eradicating all forms of institutional prejudice, and he knew that the surviving elements of the Klu Klux Klan were examples of an attitude that still pervaded the American South. Apprehending Openshaw's killers would have been satisfying in its way, but it would not have eliminated the problems that had created them. He had hoped time would do that, but in the last decade of the nineteenth century, it had not yet done so.

Once he'd reached the Savoy Hotel and paid the cabdriver, the detective found his page very quickly. The unfortunate Billy was standing in front of the entrance, being soundly and loudly abused by a large, red-faced woman in a vast black hat. "You've broken my handbag!" she shrieked, while a small, mouse-like personage who was obviously her maid skulked behind, and Billy stood resigned and listened to her hysteria without response.

"Madam," said Holmes, inserting himself between members of the gathering crowd of onlookers, "I am in charge of this young man. He will certainly be sacked immediately." Without another word, he seized Billy by the arm and pulled him away from the crowd.

"Your timing is as excellent as ever," said the page, once they had rounded the corner of the building.

"Fortunate," said Holmes.

"I don't suppose you're here to relieve me of my assignment."

"Not yet. There's a possible threat against the lady—Irene Adler—that I told you about."

"She's very pretty," said the page, with extreme solemnity. His manner of utterance was as opposite to what Wiggins's would have been as it was possible for it to be.

"Quite so," said Holmes, wondering to what the comment tended. Billy was not given to pointless musings.

"I thought perhaps—I wondered if Dr Watson might be—interested in her. I gathered that was the reason for watching her. I know how he likes a pretty face." Billy finished, as if the delicacy of the matter gave him a certain amount of discomfort.

Holmes laughed. "You may be assured that Watson's interests lie elsewhere at this time."

That matter settled, Holmes tasked himself with explaining the present condition of the case and reiterating the necessity of vigilance.

The landlady stood in the deepest awe of him and never dared to interfere with him, however outrageous his proceedings might seem.

—The Dying Detective

Chapter 5: Irene

The London streets did not frighten me, but I succumbed to paranoia when I reached the hotel. No one accosted me or called my name as I stepped through the wide entrance and into the carpeted vestibule, but I looked around me at every lodger and every member of the hotel staff as if each might be waiting to interfere with me in some way. Perhaps the claustrophobia of the streets had affected me more than I'd realised.

I would not have travelled to London if I had not suspected that the death of my bees had been intentionally inflicted; however, the confirmation that a threat existed, and, even more, that it was, for the moment, without name or face beyond that of a supposedly-defunct American organisation, unsettled me. I was not overly worried for my own immediate safety. The feeling was one of general discomfort at the idea that anything in the whole of London existed that was not under Holmes's jurisdiction in some way. Perhaps it was a silly way of thinking, but I had come to regard Fulworth as my domain and London as Holmes's. That I had once been able to fool him did not negate his power. He described his brother Mycroft as the whole of the British government, and I thought of him, perhaps wrongly, as the whole of detecting. It seemed to me that there was nothing in London worth knowing that my friend did not know. The revelation that a network of malevolence existed of which he had been unaware was deeply troubling—it was as if the rock solid ground had been shaken beneath my feet. Finally, in spite of my morbid thoughts, I reached my room in safety. I did not bother to call the maid, wishing to absorb the tranquility of solitude.

I was settling down with Boswell's *Life of Samuel Johnson*, a personal favourite, when a knock at my door set my heart pounding. "Who is it?" I asked sharply, ready to reach for my pistol if need be.

"Sherlock Holmes," said the unmistakable voice. I opened the door in high dudgeon. "Feel free to dress yourself," he said coolly, striding in and taking his seat on the sofa. In my alarm, I had failed to recall that I was barefoot and clad in a robe.

"How did you get inside the hotel?" I asked, going into the bathroom and closing the door.

"I acted as if I was a guest," said Holmes loudly. "The lack of security is shocking."

"I don't want to know how you knew which room was mine," I said.

"Nothing complicated," he answered. "Billy told me."

"Whatever you pay him, it isn't enough," I retorted. "He's like Satan, roaming to and fro across the Savoy Hotel." I emerged, dressed once again, but not bothering to re-pin my hair. Holmes had, after all, seen it in various states of disarray plenty of times when he was a guest at my cottage.

"Why are you here?" I asked, sitting on the other end of the sofa from him. "You had better have a good reason for making me dress myself and risk all attempts at propriety by letting a bachelor into my hotel room this late in the evening." At such times, I felt that teasing was my last defence against the ridiculous rationality of my companion.

"I have come to explain my plan to you," he said.

"A plan that could not have been told when I was in Baker Street three hours ago, or waited until a decent hour of the morning?" I asked irritably, thinking of the long, tranquil evening I'd anticipated.

"No," he said simply. "I wished to arrange things before I brought the information to you, and if anyone is watching your movements, I wanted them to see you return here at a reasonable hour."

"If they're watching me, they'll have seen you," I observed.

"Unlikely," said Holmes. "Billy admitted me by the staff entrance, and I made sure to intermingle with a large party of guests."

"What is your plan, then?"

"I've instructed Wiggins to shadow you. He's the leader of the Irregulars, a boy of fifteen, with a very keen mind."

"Perhaps my mind is slow this evening, but I hardly see how following me will solve the mystery, unless you believe I am the perpetrator, in which case telling me would hardly be prudent."

Holmes did not respond to my teasing. "You are to act as if you don't know he's there, so that anyone else who may be watching you will think you lack vigilance. Wiggins's purpose is to observe everyone around you. Of course, if you see anything unusual, come to me. The perpetrators already know we are in contact with each other. I have also placed Irregulars around Watson and Baker Street. I intend to cast a net that will choke anyone who comes into it with evil intent. Unfortunately, I do not yet know what their full purpose is."

"Sometimes I feel that I should be writing down everything you say, like a schoolgirl transcribing a lecture," I answered, irked at his pedantic tone.

He looked at me oddly for a moment. "Sometimes I forget," he said, "how different you are from Watson."

I laughed, but I was interrupted by the sound of heavy feet in the hallway outside my room, followed by excessively loud knocking. I opened the door, glad I had dressed after all.

The unexpected sight that greeted me was a uniformed policeman who was tall and slight and seemed extremely nervous, judging by the shake of his hands and darting eyes. "I'm Sergeant Keating. Is—is Mr Sherlock Holmes with you?" he asked.

"Yes," I answered.

"In—inspector Lestrade sent me to fetch him. There's been a murder."

"There are murders every day," said Holmes, coming to stand behind me. "Why this one in this haste?"

"It was—she was found with a note the inspector wanted you to see," the policeman answered.

"Very well," said my friend, following him out into the hallway, while I hurried to keep up with the two men and rearrange my dishevelled hair. Several other guests had opened the doors of their rooms and stared out at us like startled rabbits as we passed. No doubt the Savoy was unused to having its guests rousted out by the police at late hours. Keating made no comment on my presence, and Holmes helped me into the police conveyance before climbing in himself.

—

A drive of fifteen minutes brought us to the place where the body had been found—an alley in central London, which was crowded with policemen and onlookers. As we approached, I felt Holmes's body tense in the seat next to me, and I looked over at him, but his face was as inscrutable as ever. Sergeant Keating was stiff and said nothing until we stopped.

As soon as we alighted from the carriage, Holmes was approached by a short, slight man with dark brown eyes and pointed features. "Lestrade," said my friend, from beside me.

"Holmes, thank goodness you've come! You should leave information about your whereabouts at your flat. Dr Watson's list of possible places has lost us three quarters of an hour finding you."

My friend stared down at him. "I don't believe you've met Miss Irene Adler." Lestrade stood barely taller than I. "Good evening," he said tersely, obviously less pleased than his associate that Holmes had brought me along. He handed Holmes a sheet of paper, originally white, but covered in dirt. I stood next to my friend, overcome with curiosity about what it said.

What I saw was a drawing—six-pointed shapes, some coloured in with dark ink, others empty. I immediately recognised it as the representation of a beehive infected with foulbrood. Below, it simply said *Holmes K.K.K.*

"Nonsense, isn't it?" said Lestrade, "but I thought I should contact you in any case."

"Quite so," Holmes murmured. I had no idea what he was thinking, but I knew he'd understood the message, just as I had.

"Dr Watson is with the body." Lestrade turned, and we followed him through the mass of people. My slippers crunched on the dirt of the street below, and I felt like I was in a nightmarish dream.

The victim was a girl of no more than seventeen at my estimation. She'd been pretty, in spite of her matted hair and the pinched look of hunger on her face. The reason for her death was obvious—a knife wound to the chest.

I had never seen Holmes look as he looked then. Intense shock, horror, and anger flashed across his face in succession, their origins unknown to me, though Dr Watson looked as if he was less mystified.

"What about the child?" Holmes asked suddenly. "She had an infant." In spite of his face, his voice betrayed none of his agitation.

Inspector Lestrade stared at my friend as if he had uttered some foreign tongue. "I suppose you have some way to divine such a thing by looking at a girl, but goodness knows I've no idea how you do it. The officers who first came to the body heard a baby crying nearby and found the little lad tucked under an old newspaper a hundred feet away. No one knew he belonged to her until now."

"Show me the place," Holmes said, and he and Watson followed Lestrade. I trailed behind, conscious that I did not belong.

"Miss Adler, Sergeant Keating will accompany you wherever you wish to go," said the inspector, stopping for a moment to look back at me. For once, I did not mind being dismissed, as reluctant to accompany them as he was to have me. The only thing I regretted was being parted from Holmes.

Once before, after the murder of James Phillimore, I had seen my friend in the presence of the dead. He had been like a doctor or a policeman then, clinical and detached as he went about his work. This was something entirely different. I knew that Holmes was not without compassion and feeling, but he usually regulated them strictly, allowing them free reign only through his music, keeping tight control over his passions whenever he was engaged in his profession. I had never before seen him so visibly affected by emotion.

During our acquaintance, I had touched Holmes once in a way that went beyond the common courtesy of a hand under the arm or accidental brush in a crowded space. At the end of the Florida case, my feelings of gratitude had led me to embrace him, a man I had only known as more than an opponent for a matter of days. I now wished to embrace him with the comfort of a friend.

I had Keating take me to Baker Street instead of the Savoy. It was, by now, nearly eleven o'clock, but I no longer cared. All I wished was to be waiting when the flatmates returned. I did not know if it was for their sake or for my own.

"Please go to bed, Mrs Hudson," I said, when she came in for the third time to ask if I wanted a pot of tea or something to eat. She looked tired. The beginning of her acquaintance with my friend had come in her middle age, but now she was elderly, and I was concerned that a sleepless night would be needlessly taxing to her.

"Nonsense," she said. "I'm always unsettled when they're away at this hour. I feel a little uncomfortable taking liberties in 221B. Would you like to come into my flat?"

Somewhat shocked by this unexpected offer, I complied. She led me upstairs and into a set of rooms that was exactly the same as Holmes's, with, from what I could tell, two bedrooms, sitting room, kitchen, and bathroom. "Please sit down," she said, and I did so, on an overstuffed blue sofa with a white crocheted doily upon it. The carpet was worn and the curtains faded, but the place was scrupulously clean and did not show signs of want.

My hostess disappeared into her tiny kitchen, and I thought with amusement of the horror my housekeeper, Mrs Turner, would have experienced at the thought of me taking my ease in the camp of the enemy. I did not know of the origin of her distrust of Mrs Hudson, but I suspected it originated from a fear that her cooking or housekeeping would be deemed unworthy by comparison, an entirely unfounded worry, given how meticulous she was. She had often expressed a wish, since the Phillimore case, that she might rescue Dr Watson from Mrs Hudson's clutches, and it seemed to have an expediting effect on her willingness to accept his advances.

After a few moments, I heard the hum of a boiling kettle, and Mrs Hudson soon emerged, carrying a teapot that looked to me like it had come from somewhere in the Far East. It was made of deep brown porcelain, accented with golden designs of flowers and birds with broad wings. I stared at it in fascination, wondering why she would be in possession of such a thing.

"That was a gift from my Frederick," she said wistfully. "He was in Kyoto, Japan, when Admiral Stirling signed the first friendship treaty. He was part of all the diplomatic missions to Japan after that—until he died. He always said Mycroft—Mr Holmes's brother, you understand—was the cleverest man in England. He knew him through his work in the Foreign Service. I don't think anyone could be cleverer than our Mr Holmes, though I've nothing against his brother. He's the one who helped get the money from

Frederick's estate handled quickly so that I could purchase these flats."

This was the most I had ever heard her say, and I was grateful for the distraction from the sadness of the evening. "Thank you for your kindness during my stay in London," I said simply, taking a sip of the tea, savouring the bitterness of the black leaves and the feeling of the warmth coursing through me. "I had not—well, recalling that the last time I saw you, you were putting me out of the house, I was not sure that we were on friendly terms," I finally ventured.

Mrs Hudson laughed, rather more loudly than I would have expected. "I can't deny that I was gratified when Mr Holmes came back from the dead—his journey, I mean—and told me that my suspicions about the new maid had been proved correct. I'd forgotten all about it, but he made sure to tell me. You were a very believable maid, you know, just an untrustworthy one." At this, I laughed with her.

"I did not think I would ever return to the city," I said.

"I've never thought I could leave it," she replied, "but I'm getting old, and some of Dr Watson's descriptions of his visits to Sussex make me quite envious. Mr Holmes, of course, never utters a word except to say things about the most random of subjects."

"I can imagine," I answered. "There was a time when I thought country life would bore me to tears, but it has suited me far more than city life did. I was born in a city, but it's not where I belong, not any more."

"It's good to understand that at your age," she said. "You're still young enough to enjoy it. But I don't regret my choices, either. Frederick made my life interesting, and that's what I wanted. I suppose that's why I'm daft enough not to mind Mr Holmes's ways."

"All of us who know him are a little bit daft, I think," I said, laughing, "even Dr Watson."

"Make no mistake," she answered, "the doctor is the daftest of all."

It becomes a personal matter with me now, and, if God sends me health, I shall set my hand upon this gang.

—The Five Orange Pips

Chapter 6: Holmes

The detective surveyed the place where the child had been found, which was a few paces from the body. He saw evidence that a man's boot had displaced the dirt between the corpse and the pile of newspapers where the tiny infant had been discovered, and after a few more moments, a gleam of something shiny among the crushed papers caught his eye, and he bent down to retrieve it. It was a button, small and silver, with the imprint of the letter C upon it.

"I'll have that," said Lestrade's grating voice, and the detective stood up and found the inspector standing uncomfortably close to him. He handed over the object readily, content with the fact that he had memorised its appearance. Without a word, he went back to the girl's body, conscious that the attention of all at the scene was fixed on him.

He stared at Anna Mason's lifeless form, the note folded in his right hand. For the first time in a great while, perhaps years, fury threatened to overtake him and destroy his ability to reason with clarity. With difficulty, he forced himself to begin to make the deductions that were usually natural to his mind.

The knife that had made the wound had obviously been small, and its edges had been smooth. The killer had known how to dispatch a victim efficiently, someone who had killed before or was perhaps an accomplished hunter of animals. A knife could be a more difficult way to end someone's life than killers in the heat of passion realised, but Anna's body showed no signs of either clumsy failed attempts or violent anger. The wound had been intentional and effective.

There was no sign of a struggle of any kind, either on the body or around the area, which suggested the girl had been drugged before the murder had taken place, most likely in order to keep her from calling out and attracting attention. As he leaned down, his theory was confirmed by the lingering odour of diethyl ether. That, at least, was merciful.

Holmes finally spoke to Lestrade, who hovered at his elbow, practically hopping up and down in his desire for the detective to communicate his observations. "I spoke to her earlier this evening."

"Who? The girl?"

"Yes, the girl," Holmes answered with annoyance.

"What has the note to do with it?" asked Lestrade.

"A great deal," said Holmes shortly. "Go to your office. I will meet you there in an hour and a half."

"What?" asked the inspector, but Holmes had already turned and walked away, followed by Watson, who looked as confused as Lestrade but dutifully accompanied his friend.

—

The detective heard The Woman before he saw her. As he entered his flat, the unmistakable sound of feminine laughter could be heard through the walls, which had never been impervious to noise. "Miss Adler isn't here. I thought she'd have wanted to know the end of the business, since she was dismissed so impolitely," said Watson, opening the door of 221B and turning on a lamp. "Do you suppose something happened to her?"

"Nothing more than a late-night visit to Mrs Hudson, I believe," said Holmes. "I will go and let the ladies know of our arrival." As irregular as the action was, Holmes climbed the stairs to his landlady's rooms and knocked twice.

"Oh, it's you." The relief on her face was apparent as soon as she opened the door and saw him. Irene was behind her, and she stepped around her and into the passage.

"Thank you for your hospitality, Mrs Hudson," she said.

"Think nothing of it," said the older lady. "It's a nice change to have a woman around to speak with." Holmes and The Woman trudged the short way back to the detective's rooms. Irene looked tired, and he regretted, for a moment, what he was about to ask her to do.

"I'm glad you're still here," he said. "I have something important to talk over with you before you return to your hotel for the night."

"You look very serious indeed," she answered, following him inside. Watson had gone to his room, excessively weary, and Holmes was glad. He did not think the doctor would approve of his plan, and he wanted to have The Woman's support before he presented it to his flatmate and the policemen.

The friends sat down, and the detective began. “I need your help.”

“This is quite different,” said The Woman, smiling. “I prefer this method of you explaining things to me beforehand to being an unwitting player, as I was in Florida.”

“It hardly needs saying,” Holmes continued, “that my trust in you is greater now than it was then.”

“Quite right,” she answered, “but if I must do something for you, then explain one thing to me: Who was the young woman?”

“Her name was Anna Mason. She used to be one of the children who gathered information for me, until she became a mother. I spoke with her earlier today, and I can only assume that is why she was killed.”

“I’m sorry,” The Woman said.

“She will be avenged when we catch them,” he answered simply.

“Now,” she continued, “what do you want me to do?”

“I must speak quickly,” he said. “I have an appointment with Lestrade in a few moments’ time. Tomorrow, an inquest will be performed. The jury will return a verdict of murder. I will present evidence against you, and the jury will recommend that you be arrested—highly irregular, but all for the sake of appearances. Soon after, Lestrade will arrest you, conveying you to Newgate Prison. The following morning, *The Daily Telegraph and Courier* will carry a story reporting your arrest for the murder.”

“Newgate! I will be famous indeed. I take it you wish, in as flamboyant a way as possible, to make the Klan think that you do not credit them with the murder to provoke them into showing their hand,” she said.

“Exactly so,” he answered. “You will, of course, be released as quickly as possible. Do you consent?”

The Woman fell silent for several moments, her gaze seeming to light on everything in the room before coming back to his face. “I do,” she finally replied.

“Excellent,” he answered.

—

"I want you to arrest Irene Adler," said Holmes, sitting on the edge of a chair in Inspector Lestrade's spartan office at Scotland Yard. The policeman's small eyes managed to open very wide at this.

"Whatever for?" he asked.

"For the murder of Anna Mason," said Holmes.

"She's the murderer, then?" said the inspector, looking like an animal of prey with the scent of meat in its nostrils.

"Of course not, you utter fool," said Holmes. "I wish the real murderer to think you suspect her."

"I confess I share the inspector's confusion," said Sergeant Keating with a slight stutter. "Whatever purpose could this serve?"

"The Klansmen are watching my movements," said Holmes, "and trying to taunt me with their reach and inaccessibility, absolutely insistent that I be made aware of their power. I intend to raise their ire by acting as if credit for the murder is laid at another's door."

"That seems unfortunate for the lady," said Keating. "Couldn't someone else do it?"

"Impossible," said Holmes. "Judging by their actions, they're not stupid enough to believe that I would suspect Watson, and I wish it to be someone who might conceivably have a grudge against me—someone I would be likely to suspect."

"And she consents to this?" Lestrade asked.

"She does," said Holmes. "She wants to catch them as much as I do, and besides, she'll be locked away from them in prison, which could be seen as an advantage at this point. We do not know if they intend to take my associates as their next targets, but they may very well attempt to do so."

"I don't like it," the inspector continued, "but I'll try it if you insist it's the only way."

"I do," said the detective with irritation, tired of having to justify his plan.

—

The next day, an inquest was conducted. The earnest-faced jurors heard the evidence with all the gravity of a funeral mass. Holmes studied each of them with interest. If he had not known better, he would have thought they were ordinary people of the city, just as they were supposed to be. None of them betrayed in any way that they were actors paid for by Mycroft Holmes and gleaned from the vast roll of individuals he had at his disposal for various purposes. Even the coroner, a sharp-eyed man of middle age named Malmsley Tompkins, seemed in no way aware that something was amiss. The policemen acted with exactitude, and the discoverer of the body, a dustman, was so awed by it all that he burst into tears on his wife's shoulder after giving his evidence.

Irene and Watson were called, and they were questioned routinely and gave their versions of how the body had been found. The doctor's statement was predictably medical, The Woman's filled with emotion. Holmes mentally applauded her for being dramatic—all the better to make it seem as if she were overdoing her effort to appear innocent.

When it was finally Holmes's turn to speak, he squared his shoulders like an actor about to burst onto centre stage and prepared to lie convincingly. He knew that the verdict did not depend on his ability to persuade the jury, but he also did not want to leave any loose ends to signal that he was not completely persuaded of his own statement.

He spoke about the note, about the body, and about the button he'd picked up. Finally, he mentioned The Woman. Beginning with subtlety and gradually moving towards the obvious, he made connections between her arrival in London and the timing of the murder. He spoke of her knowledge of bees and how it would have enabled her to produce the note found on the girl's body. Finally, he suggested that the button might belong to her. Had Holmes heard anyone else make such unfounded assertions at an inquest, he would have grown apoplectic with outrage, but they were just the sorts of statements that he knew persuaded juries every day.

After he'd finished, the jury returned the verdict it had been instructed to produce. The coroner seemed slightly dazed at the speed and direction of it all, but Lestrade behaved exactly as if nothing were unusual.

"Miss Adler," he declared solemnly, "it is my duty to inform you that anything which you may say will be used against you. I arrest you in the Queen's name as being involved in the death of Anna Mason." The inspector played his part remarkably well. Perhaps, Holmes thought, the man's lack of imagination could be an asset in some situations. The Woman, too, managed to look sufficiently discomfited to befit the occasion.

The subsequent morning, the *Daily Telegraph and Courier* carried the story of the sensational arrest of former opera singer and socialite Irene Adler for the murder of a street urchin. The motive, it said, was unclear, but the police were considering the question of whether or not Miss Adler might be mentally unbalanced. Mycroft Holmes had arranged the article, and his brother was satisfied.

The detective dressed and readied himself to visit Newgate Prison to see The Woman and ascertain how she was bearing up under incarceration. He did not believe in guessing, but based on what he knew of her, he predicted that she was rather enjoying the drama of her predicament. She had proven herself a good actress more than once, and he had no doubt that she would carry it off.

"Shall I accompany you?" asked Watson, emerging from his room dressed impeccably in brown.

"Certainly," answered his flatmate, rising from his chair. "We wish to appear as if we're quite serious about investigating the murder. A visit to the supposed murderess is quite within our normal sphere, and it would be stranger for you to fail to accompany me than otherwise."

Watson beamed at this, obviously pleased, but after a moment, his face fell.

"I feel for her, Holmes. It's a very hard thing for a lady to be falsely accused and thrown into prison, especially one as refined as Miss Adler."

The detective laughed. "I hardly think it's any more of a hardship for her than it would be for an unrefined gentleman. But do not fear. She is well aware of my intentions and knows the importance of her part."

The two men left the flat and hailed a cab, ignoring the strange look that passed over the driver's face at the declaration of their intended destination. All the better for as many people to know about it as possible, Holmes thought. He wanted there to be no question whatsoever that he was treating Irene Adler's case as seriously as he treated any other.

Newgate Prison was as bleak as it had ever been, complete with darkly ponderous walls and imposing gates that denoted an oppressive atmosphere. Holmes and Watson were shown inside and granted their request for a private audience with the prisoner, their way having been smoothed by a judicious note from Mycroft. They were seated in a tiny room with a policeman at the door. By design, that policeman was Sergeant Keating, assistant to Inspector Lestrade, whose presence had been insisted on by the inspector and enforced by edict of the Yard. The only furniture was a table and three chairs. As The Woman was led into the room, the detective mentally commended her for her thoroughness. If she hadn't been an actress, her condition would have been alarming. Overnight, her eyes had become red and swollen from weeping. Her hair was tousled, and her hands showed signs of having been scratched by her own fingernails. So convincing was she that Holmes heard his flatmate gasp.

Irene was seated on the opposite side of the table from the two men, and the door clanged shut, leaving them and The Woman alone with the policeman, who forsook his post and came over to take part in the conversation. "Are you all right?" asked Watson, provoking Holmes to smile.

"Of course," said Irene, speaking low and grinning broadly. "I haven't enjoyed myself this much since I sang the part of Ermine on stage."

"You're right, Holmes, very good indeed," said Watson.

His flatmate nodded, but spoke quickly. "No more nonsense. We must confer quickly, for Sir Lloyd Allen is to join us in but a few moments. Sergeant, what have you observed?"

Keating answered, "I've seen nothing out of the common way. There have been no American visitors. That doesn't preclude the possibility that there may be an informer watching Miss Adler from the inside, but given that her arrest was only last night, it seems unlikely."

"And you?" asked Holmes, looking at Irene.

"I have seen nothing I would not expect to see here, either, though admittedly, I have little prior experience of the routine of prison existence." She smirked.

"Well, that is hardly surprising," said the detective. "We must continue this charade a bit longer."

"I have noticed a young man hanging about," the policeman added. "He looks like any of the others, but I've seen him several times since Miss Adler's arrest. He's a tall lad, not eighteen, I'd say, with a cheeky sort of face."

"Wiggins," said Holmes. "He was sent by me. I will caution him to be less obvious in his vigilance. He's a very keen watchman, but he mustn't let his enthusiasm get in the way of his subtlety."

"Poor lad," said Irene. "He's nearly as imprisoned as I am, then."

"For a time," the detective answered.

Just then, very loud voices could be heard outside, and the door burst open to reveal two guards and an extremely irate Lloyd Allen, an imposing man with broad shoulders, a large grey moustache, and enormous hands, who proceeded to smash one of those hands onto the table and demand why he had not been summoned sooner.

He played his part well. Holmes had nothing whatever to complain of, and the noise, he was sure, had carried through the prison. The detective rose and extended his hand. Sir Allen had been the Holmes family solicitor for many years, and as such had an expected familiarity with the younger Holmes, though he ignored the proffered hand distractedly.

The lawyer finally calmed himself and turned to the detective with perfect gravity, taking his hand solemnly. "This is a ridiculous business, Holmes, but I am very glad to see you."

"I'm sure we're after the same thing, Sir Allen, the truth of the case."

"Perhaps we are, and perhaps we're not," he answered. He was not a trial advocate, but he had a vast reputation for the utmost tenacity when it came to protecting his clients' personal matters.

"Miss Adler, I am at your service," said the solicitor, turning to Irene, who, Holmes could tell, was having to make a valiant effort not to look as if she was heartily enjoying the whole thing, since the door to the room was open, and the commotion had attracted the attention of several guards.

"I am sure you will engage the best possible advocate," she said in an extraordinarily subdued voice, one that, Holmes thought, masked the laughter that wanted to escape from her throat.

"You look dreadful," continued Sir Allen. "I will immediately insist that you receive medical attention."

"I would be—very grateful," Irene answered sweetly.

You do not know her, but she has a soul of steel.

—A Scandal in Bohemia

Chapter 7: Irene

I hadn't foreseen enjoying myself quite so much. Between Holmes's impassiveness, poor Dr Watson's belief that one night in gaol had somehow utterly wrecked my constitution, and Lloyd Allen's convincing performance as my irritated solicitor, I felt like I was starring in England's most entertaining theatrical production. I could see the posters in my mind: *Thrilling detection! Angry solicitors! Gullible men of medicine!*

Even Keating played his part with panache (*Young men of the police!*), giving a very believable impression of a slightly bored prison guard, which was surprising, given his earlier nervousness. He performed well under pressure.

I felt that it was all going very well, but whenever I was in the presence of outsiders, I managed to hide my buoyancy of spirit underneath a veneer of cowed distress. Prison itself I did not mind, since I knew that my residence there would be temporary.

Holmes and Watson soon left me with the policeman and Allen. The solicitor and I had never met one another in person before. After the events of the Florida case, Mycroft Holmes had helped to secure my assets by placing my legal concerns in Allen's hands; since then, we had exchanged lengthy correspondence, but our paths had not crossed.

Once the door of the room was closed again, my solicitor sat down opposite me. "Are you all right?" he asked.

"I am very well," I answered. "Thank you for coming. I am sure Holmes was very pleased by your performance."

"Not all performance, my dear," he said looking at me from under his large white eyebrows. "I am less than comfortable with any of my clients in gaol, no matter how good the reason. If you, at any point, do not wish to go through with this, you have a friend in me."

"You are excessively kind," I said, meaning it.

"I am, I am," he answered. "I make it my business to be. I suppose I will go through the motions of attempting to secure a trial advocate. I thought I might write to Charles Stevenson. Were your predicament real, I would want to approach him immediately."

I wrinkled my nose at this, which he noticed. "I see that you are uncomfortable, my dear. You must not keep me in darkness. Do tell the reason for your nose-wrinkle, delightful though it was."

In spite of myself, I smiled. "I know Charles Stevenson. His family resides in the village where my cottage lies."

"Ah," he said, nodding. "You are acquainted with the man—always most unfortunate for anyone, and I certainly wouldn't wish it on a lady as lovely as yourself." At this, he twirled the edge of his moustache so comically that I laughed aloud. "And yet," he added, "Stevenson is a most capable barrister. It is fortunate that his talent does not become acquainted with his personality and flee like the rest of us are inclined to do. Nevertheless, I would not want to complicate your charming life in the village by alarming your neighbours, so I will find someone else."

At this, I felt a bit sick. I hadn't for a moment considered the impact my arrest would have on the village of Fulworth. My mind conjured images of a vindicated Irene Adler returning home and nevertheless being branded as a murderess by all and sundry.

"I wouldn't worry too much, my dear," said the solicitor, understanding my distress. "Once the real murderer is brought to justice, you will no doubt be branded a celebrated victim of the overzealous police. It may increase your notoriety in unpleasantly invasive ways, but I would expect it to augment your neighbours' regard for you, rather than the opposite." The man's peculiar blend of cynicism and optimism amused me.

"Well, there's nothing to do but go through with it now," I answered. "My reputation is hardly one of conventional respectability in any case."

"No," he said, his eyes twinkling, "I shouldn't imagine it was."

He took his leave, standing and walking out with great dignity of manner. I was taken back to my cell, and the guards around me complained at the inconvenience of having a prisoner whose case had been noticed by important and troublesome personages.

I'd expected to spend the rest of the day immersed in the monotony of prison life, but after about two hours had passed, punctuated only by a meagre and distasteful lunch primarily consisting of a nearly inedible brown bread, a guard came to my cell with a bundle of the objects I'd been carrying when I'd been arrested. "You're to come with me," he said, and I followed curiously, the eyes of the other prisoners boring into me. I was taken to a tiny office with nothing but a desk, and the bundle was placed in my hands. I unfolded it to find that my small bag was as I had left it, except lightened by the absence of the few coins it had contained. I placed its strap back around my wrist, anticipating imminent freedom.

From there, I was led outside the bleak grey building and into the steady, drizzling rain. Beside me, the guard murmured discontentedly *irregular, highly irregular* the whole way until we reached the gate, which another guard opened wordlessly. I walked through it, feeling as if I was in some kind of daze, and no one followed.

Once the gate had clanged shut behind me, my mind awakened, and I realised that I must present quite a dreadful picture, with my hair tousled and my dress dirty and wrinkled beyond recognition. I walked out towards the street, trying to imagine what I might do and wondering why Holmes had not contacted me.

"Miss Adler!" I looked sharply to my left and found that the voice hailing me belonged to a boy who had seemingly materialised out of nowhere. He grinned impishly. "Startled you, did I? I'm good at not being seen when I don't want to be."

"You're Wiggins," I said, and relief flooded me.

"The same, My Lady," he said, bowing low and removing his cap with facetious flourishes. "I am instructed to convey you to your hotel without letting you out of my sight. There's a cab waiting."

"Was this part of the plan, then? I hadn't expected it to happen so quickly," I said.

"Mr Holmes didn't say," Wiggins answered, growing more serious. "He wired me an hour ago to wait for you. I've been watching about the whole time you've been here."

"I'm very grateful," I said.

When we reached the cab, I was concerned that the driver might not wish to convey someone in my state of dishevellment, but he smiled and tipped his cap. "One of ours," Wiggins murmured, indicating another member of the vast network Holmes had throughout the city. London was drab and wet as we passed through it, but it looked beautiful to me. I had been in gaol by my own choice, but I was glad enough to be out again, even if the speed with which it had all happened confused me greatly.

When we neared the Savoy, I did my best to smooth my hair, but I knew that no amount of effort was going to make me look respectable. "Don't worry," said Wiggins, "I've told the driver to take us to the staff entrance. Billy will meet us there."

Just as he said, the man conveyed us to the back of the vast building. Billy stood, in uniform, just outside a door that was small and insignificant compared to the ones at the front that were intended for the hotel's guests. He seemed very ill at ease. Wiggins and I both alighted, and the driver left without a word or request for payment.

"Here's the delivery," said Wiggins to Billy, indicating me with a jaunty toss of his head.

"Very well," answered Billy, his eyes darting about. "You can go." Wiggins took his leave with another bow. Wordlessly, Billy inclined his head towards the door and took light hold of my arm, pulling me inside.

The entrance led to a tiny, dark room that seemed to exist only as a way to access the steep staff staircase that nearly filled it. As we passed through the doorway, I heard the sound of voices from above, and they grew gradually closer as their owners came down the stairs towards us. Before we could be seen, Billy grasped my hand and dragged me into the tiny room underneath the stairs, which was filled with dust and cobwebs and smelled of decay. Pressed against the boy's back, I suppressed the coughs and sneezes that threatened to fight their way out of my tortured throat. Thankfully, the agony lasted a mere five minutes before the voices disappeared once more. Billy did not open the door for another minute or two to make sure that no one intended to return, and when he finally did so, we nearly fell out on top of one another.

Still silent, he led me rapidly up two flights of stairs, motioning for me to remain in the stairwell until he could make sure no one was in sight. My heart raced, and I fought the fear that someone would come up the stairs at any moment. Thankfully, no one did.

Billy returned within ten minutes and motioned to me to follow him. It was excessively strange, after what we had just experienced, to be thrust into the gleaming world of the second floor. I suppose we made a comical sight—a bedraggled woman and a smartly-dressed porter practically running down a hotel hallway. Finally, we were in front of the door with the number eight upon it—glorious eight!—and Billy let me in using the key I had given Holmes before my arrest, entering after me.

I collapsed onto the sofa, but the boy paced in front of me, as if he thought he should not sit down. "Please take a rest," I said, when I had collected myself enough to manage words. He did so, on the opposite end of the sofa, where Holmes had sat during his visit.

"I—hardly know where to begin apologising for all the liberties I've taken," he finally ventured, looking frankly horrified. Even though I was sensible of the acuteness of his distress, I could not stop myself—I laughed in his face. I'm sure some of my mirth was the result of relief, but a good bit of it resulted from the absurdity of the situation.

"I do not intend to complain at the man who is responsible for helping me to reach this room safely and without arousing suspicion," I said.

"Thank you," he answered, simply and seriously. "I have several things I must tell you."

"Please do," I answered.

"After Mr Holmes left you this morning, he received a wire from his brother—Mr Mycroft Holmes—to the effect that a journalist had been found dead. He was the gentleman who wrote the story in *The Daily Telegraph and Courier* about your imprisonment. He'd been stabbed in the same manner as Anna—I mean the young lady who was murdered. Mr Holmes went to see his brother, and then he sent Dr Watson to see me. Mr Mycroft had been notified about the murder right away because he was the one who'd commissioned the story the man had written. He has connections, you understand." I nodded.

"The body had a dead bee with it," he continued. "Dr Watson didn't say what that meant, but he said you would understand. He came to me to say that Wiggins would be delivering you and to keep you in my sight until you were in your room. Sergeant Keating of Scotland Yard explained to the hotel that you had been released and cleared of all wrongdoing, but the doctor said I shouldn't let anyone see you who might recognise you. He says you're to keep to your room until Holmes comes and to stay on your guard."

My head spun with all of this new information. "Did he say when Holmes intends to come here?"

"No, Miss. He said you'd ask that and to tell you that Mr Holmes wouldn't insist on your staying in if he didn't believe it was absolutely necessary, but that he is sure it is necessary and does not know how quickly he will be able to come." He was earnestly breathless after this, like a schoolboy finishing a recitation.

"You must get back to your duties," I said, realising suddenly that Billy would be putting his job in jeopardy if he remained with me.

"Yes," he said, "but I'm to look after you first and foremost. I work for Mr Holmes before I work for the hotel."

"Quite right," I said, "but as I am now safe and sound, I don't wish to keep you."

"Thank you," he said, taking his leave quickly.

I sat motionless for a few moments, trying to make sense of my thoughts, but finding that they ran around in circles and could not seem to line up in any logical progression. I understood that Holmes was worried for my safety and that a second murder had occurred that somehow related to my bees, the poor dead face of Anna Mason, and a newspaper article that had implied I was a murderess. I tried to understand all these things, but I really just wanted to bathe and have a proper meal, so I did. I found that even the jovial face of the man who brought my food—I did not think it would be overly imprudent to order a meal—seemed sinister, and any noise in the hallway made me wonder if Holmes's enemies were coming upon me.

If the art of the detective began and ended in reasoning from an armchair, my brother would be the greatest criminal agent that ever lived.

—The Greek Interpreter

Chapter 8: Holmes

Sherlock Holmes sat motionless in his chair, his eyes closed, but as far from sleep as anyone could be. Opposite him sat Watson, scribbling in a notebook, and filling up the other chair was the immense magnitude known as Mycroft Holmes. The younger Holmes had been surprised at his brother's insistence on coming. The man who rarely moved from his post at the Diogenes Club had nonetheless viewed the corpse of the journalist, Thomas Matthews, and then repaired to Baker Street in the company of the flatmates.

"Too fast," said the elder Holmes.

"Quite right," answered his brother. "Either someone informed on us, or a stray word was heard in the prison. If the second possibility is the case, then they moved with extraordinary alacrity.

"It can't be ruled out," Mycroft answered, "but the first possibility seems more likely."

"What do you mean?" asked Watson.

"The journalist was obviously killed in order to signal to me that our enemies knew the true nature of the deception concerning Miss Adler," answered Sherlock.

"Poor man," the doctor murmured, shaking his head. "It's not as if he did anything to deserve to be mixed up in it."

"No more did Anna Mason," his friend rejoined, "which is why we must bring those responsible to justice."

"You insist on there being more than one of them," Mycroft put in.

"I do," his brother confirmed. "The idea that the bee poisoning and both murders were committed by the same person stretches credibility, particularly in the case of Matthews. The lack of time between the devising of the plot, the publication of the article, and the murder strongly suggests at least two people, working in tandem to provide information to one another."

"Quite right," said the elder Holmes.

Mycroft was not given to displays of emotion of any sort, but Sherlock realised that his willingness to engage in the kind of precise work he hated dearly and usually avoided at all costs was the strongest possible indication of the level of responsibility he felt for the journalist's death. As repugnant as the idea was to the detective, he knew that it was not unusual for his brother to arrange press articles skewed in particular directions or, as in the present case, to completely falsify a story for the supposed greater good. In addition, when it came to Mycroft's own people—that vast, seemingly hazy network he always described as his *department*—he could live with a certain amount of dangerous uncertainty; after all, his subordinates had made their own decisions to join his employ. He was not, however, accustomed to losing innocent pawns, and Sherlock could see that he was keenly aware that it was his direct order that had led to the man's demise.

The detective was uncomfortably conscious of the fact that the two murders had struck at him and his brother in particularly specific ways—the girl had been slain simply because she had been seen speaking to him and the journalist because he had carried out Mycroft's order. Even if the murderer had not known that the command originated with the older Holmes, he or she was clearly aware that the plot that had produced it belonged to the detective. Sherlock's current concern was whether or not the murderer would decide to strike even closer to the target—to make an attempt on one of the people he valued most in the world.

"Miss Adler will need more security than your Irregulars can provide her," said Mycroft, as if he'd read his brother's mind. "I will assign a man to the hotel grounds. If Lestrade tries to offer something similar, accept. It would be better for the murderer to be distracted by the presence of an obvious policeman than to risk her safety."

"As for you, Dr Watson," he said, "you must stay close to my brother and not go out without accompaniment until this matter is resolved."

"What about Mrs Hudson? Is she in danger?" asked the doctor.

"I wouldn't like to tell her so," said Sherlock, "but she should be watched as well. The ruthlessness of our opponents is such that they seem willing to stop at nothing."

"Very well," answered his brother.

The matter of protection resolved for the moment, the three men subsided into silence once again. As afternoon turned to dusk, the detective thought through each facet of the case, and he brought to the forefront of his mind a suspicion that had been forming in his thoughts for some time.

The end of the Openshaw case had been an unusual one. Instead of having the opportunity to apprehend those responsible for the man's death, he had contented himself with the poetic justice of a ship lost at sea, the murderers supposedly lost with it. He now began to suspect that he had been mistaken.

Holmes's mind gave form and shape to his growing dread. What if, instead of dying, one or more of the conspirators had lived? What if his intention to implicate the three men aboard the *Lone Star* had become known to them without resulting in their apprehension? That began to put a different light on the matter. Motive, after all, played a part in any criminal act. Understanding the facts behind it was as important as any physical detail, and he had not yet been able to adequately settle in his mind the reason why remaining members of the Klan would express such hatred against him and his associates. There was no purpose in surmising. The detective rose, determined to ascertain, as quickly as he could, whether his suspicions had their basis in fact.

"Are you going out?" Watson asked.

"Indeed," said his friend. "Do not trouble yourself to accompany me. I only wish to send a wire, and then I must visit Miss Adler. Your presence would be a cause for needless concern."

"And needed defence," the doctor retorted. "They haven't hesitated to kill thus far. Who's to say they won't come after you next?"

"Judging by their pattern of behaviour," said Holmes, "they wish me alive to bear witness to their triumphs. As disgusting as it is, I'm unlikely to be in danger until their plan unfolds more completely."

"I suppose that's logical," groused Watson.

"I'm leaving too," said Mycroft, taking a considerably longer time to disgorge himself from the crevasses of his chair. "I will return to my flat. You know how to reach me if you should need me. I will inform you of any developments." The brothers left the flat together, their silence companionable in an abstract way—each knowing that the other occupied the same mental territory and made the same effort to map it as he.

—

Sherlock Holmes was acquainted with many Americans, but the one he intended to wire was the sheriff of a town called Fort Myers in southern Florida, the place where he had once spent several eventful days tracking a threat against Irene Adler while in disguise as her husband. His current enquiry had little to do with that incident, beyond recalling the rapport he'd developed with Sheriff Morris, an intelligent and capable man.

The wire itself was simple, a request for any information Morris could obtain about a man named James Calhoun, who had, at least once, been a ship's captain. He added a line asking for information on the man's family if he should prove to be deceased. His telegram sent, the detective made his way towards the Savoy Hotel.

—

Holmes blended seamlessly into the throng of hotel guests, taking care to attach himself to a party of revelers who were making for the Savoy's grand dining room, in order to avoid the watchful eyes of the staff. At the last moment, he peeled away and made for the ascending rooms. He was joined by a man and woman who were obviously under alcohol's influence, judging by their conviviality. Holmes was grateful for this, because they went their way without paying him any mind at all.

Once on the second floor, he waited a moment and went to Room 8, tapping lightly on the door.

"Who is it?" The Woman's voice was strong, but apprehensive, and he could tell that her nerves were acutely on edge.

"Holmes," he answered simply, and he heard the door open.

Irene was herself once again, dressed in a blue gown, with her hair arranged neatly atop her head. "Come in," she said, breathing quickly, with slightly heightened colour in her cheeks.

"Thank you," he answered, taking his place on the floral sofa.

"Would you like some tea?" asked The Woman. "I've acquired some."

"Indeed," he answered, realising that he had not eaten anything for a day and a half.

Irene went to the side table and poured a cup of the hotel's black tea. Her hand shook, spilling a few drops onto the table's white doily.

"I'm afraid the case is fraying me a little," she said. "I'm ridiculously paranoid."

"Watson would say that a good night's sleep will most likely put you to rights," said Holmes, "but I would prefer the conclusion of the matter and apprehension of those responsible."

Irene, to his surprise, smiled as she handed him his tea. "We are certainly in agreement about that." She took her seat. "I hope you intend to explain the day to me. Billy relayed only enough information to confuse me."

"I will explain," said the detective, "and I wish to know if you have observed anything helpful." Holmes closed his eyes and began his recollection.

"As you know, our coming to you this morning was entirely a fabrication for the benefit of those who may be watching. The death of Anna Mason indicates that my movements are being tracked, and I have no doubt the aggressors are aware that I am with you now. As I explained to Watson earlier, they obviously wish me alive to see their handiwork, so I do not believe my own safety is at issue for the time being. In fact, I wish to use what I know to our advantage. Your incarceration was, of course, meant to enrage those who would wish for us to consider them responsible for the murder, and when we left you, I believed the subterfuge had been remarkably successful."

"So did I," Irene answered. "Sir Allen stayed behind and offered me his help if I should wish to escape the plan, but I was immensely pleased at how things seemed to be progressing."

"I returned to Baker Street," Holmes continued, "the better to be where anyone who wished to contact me could easily do so. By that time, of course, the news of your arrest was publicly known, and I expected that the Klansmen would somehow contrive to communicate their anger at having their evil deeds attributed to another. I hoped they would come to me directly, but barring that, any communication would have revealed more about their threat."

"I assume neither thing happened," said The Woman.

"Indeed not," said Holmes putting a hand through his short dark hair. "Our deception was known. I received a wire from my brother about the journalist's murder a mere two hours after I'd returned home."

"You believe they overheard something in the prison?" asked Irene.

"Perhaps," said Holmes. "Unfortunately, there are other ways. It is never the most conducive to a plot for it to be known by as many people as were aware of this one. Lestrade might have been indiscreet, or someone might have heard a stray word in a public house. We do not know who the policemen may have told. The more people know of something, the more likely they are to discuss it, unfortunately."

"Surely, though, the possibilities are limited," Irene answered. "The doors were closed on anyone in the prison hearing us, and Inspector Lestrade hardly seems like the sort of man with a loose tongue, however slowly his mind may move. Beyond him, his sergeant, yourself, your brother, and Dr Watson, who was aware of the plot? Even the journalist was, I assume, unaware that what he wrote was part of a deception. An overheard word or two hardly seems like enough to bring the whole plot crashing down."

"Just so," said Holmes. "But it is still impossible to totally rule out eager ears overhearing more than was intended, an accident that has unfortunately led to a man's death."

"An accidental stabbing," said Irene drily.

Crime is common. Logic is rare. Therefore it is upon the logic rather than upon the crime that you should dwell.

—The Copper Beeches

Chapter 9: Irene

"What do you intend to do now?" I asked my friend.

"I have wired Sheriff Morris from Florida. Do you remember the man?"

"Of course," I said, surprised. I remembered him as a resourceful officer of the law, possessed of a great deal of nerve.

"I wish him to trace Captain James Calhoun, the man responsible, along with his confederates, for Openshaw's death."

"But he is dead," I answered, taking a drink of my now-cold tea, my hands curled tensely around the cup.

"Perhaps," said Holmes, "but I begin to doubt it. His ship was, apparently, lost at sea, but that does not mean he perished."

I stared at my companion in astonishment. "Have you suspected this before?"

"I have not," he admitted. "The Openshaw case, while not precisely a failure, was not unequivocally a success, and it contained no new method from which I learned for the sake of other cases. The features were sensational, perhaps, but that hardly concerns me. The Savannah, Georgia, police were alerted as to Calhoun's true nature, but he was never arrested, and logic suggested that his failure to reach his destination, coupled with the sighting of a piece of his ship's stern, meant he was no longer in this world. I did not let the matter concern me further, especially given the attempt of the law in the United States to put an end to Klan activities."

"I had supposed that our enemies were comprised of a new order of Klansmen who had contrived to take up Calhoun's mantle, but the facts fit this supposition less and less."

"I agree," I answered. "From my understanding of the Openshaw matter, I have been unable to understand why you would have come to the Klan's attention if the *Lone Star* party had been entirely lost. You have done nothing to pursue any of its members beyond those directly responsible for the murder."

"That is true," said Holmes.

"Thank you for informing me of your thoughts," I replied.

My friend smiled. "I have work to do, Irene, and I must ask you to remain here until I have a more specific course of action arranged. The hotel is being watched on your behalf, but I cannot guarantee a reasonable level of safety for you beyond its walls until I know more." I did not argue, and he left with his usual haste.

—

I considered my options, feeling that I was of two minds. On the one hand, I trusted Holmes, and I knew that if he considered the danger too great for me to be out of hiding, he was probably correct. My own assessment of the situation was similar. The enemy had made it abundantly clear that they would not spare anyone connected with the detective.

At war with that rationality was the impulse to fight, to join the fray. I was tired of being afraid, of sitting in a prison cell or my hotel room and letting my terror paint dreadful pictures on the canvas of my thoughts. I was not a woman who had ever avoided danger. I couldn't help thinking that the Irene who had tricked Sherlock Holmes would not stay holed up in a comfortable room while others braved danger. I might be different from her now—older and wiser, I hoped—but I did not wish to ever lose her nerve or let my fear keep me from doing what I thought was right. Much better to meet terror head on than to skulk in hiding.

As soon as I had reached a decision, I called for the maid, and she appeared promptly. "This may be a strange question, Louisa, but where do you get your clothes?"

"The hotel, Miss."

"And do you have more than one dress?"

"Two, Miss."

"What happens if you lose one?"

"I've never done that, but I'd have to pay for it."

"This would cover it, I believe," I said, handing her a sum of money that was at least three times more than a maid's uniform could be worth, even from a hotel as luxurious as the Savoy. She stared at the money and then at me, as if she had lost the power of speech.

"It's just for a silly lark," I said, attempting to sound conspiratorial, like a vapid member of the upper class, whose most pressing concerns were the style of her hair or the evening's entertainment. "I need something for a masquerade party."

She grinned. "I could—help you get ready," she said.

"That would be charming," I answered. "Come back in an hour. Mustn't tell anyone, though."

"Of course not, Miss." She said, sashaying out of the room in exceedingly high spirits. I hoped I could trust her not to provoke unwanted interest by revealing the arrangement, but it would have been as disadvantageous to her as to me for her employers to find out she had entered so irregular an agreement, so I trusted that she could hold her tongue for an hour. After that, I would at least have accomplished my goal.

While the girl was gone, I took my hair down and parted it in the middle, brushing it until it was flat, and then rearranging it on my head to be plain and severe. As I did so, I thought about what I had said and realised that it was not untrue, in a strange way.

My time away from London had detached me from the city, and I now saw what a mad, grotesque, beautiful, never-ending masquerade party she was. Her floor was always filled with dancers—the rich, glittering elite of which I had once been a part. The workers kept the music playing and the wine and food flowing, their roles often unseen but absolutely essential. Finally, along the walls stood the poor, ever watching, hoping someday to take part. Those with whom Holmes dealt, and whom I now sought, were none of these, or perhaps all of them.

There were the Charles Augustus Milvertons, those who skirted the dance, occasionally taking part, but only long enough to pickpocket the other dancers. There were the John Strakers, the workers whose hands hammered and nailed and cleaned and cooked, but whose minds were ever engaged in planning how they might also use those hands to grasp and tear and cheat and rob. Even the Isa Whitneys existed, who managed, while they tried to eke out an existence, to scratch others in their efforts to claw their way through life.

It was all of these, who masqueraded as part of the world, but whose defrauding of their fellow men kept them fundamentally on the outskirts, that were Holmes's purview. This night, I planned to make them mine.

The girl returned punctually, with a box in her hand, which she handed me proudly. “Oh, Miss,” she said, “you’ve done your hair so perfect!”

“Thank you,” I said, thinking that since I had modeled it on hers, it ought to be. I opened the box and found a full maid’s uniform, with its crisp white pinafore that contrasted with the inky black of the underdress. I almost laughed because it reminded me keenly of the maid’s uniform I’d donned long before in an effort to get a look at Holmes’s private papers. I had been unhappy then, but the memory was no longer an unpleasant one. The intervening years and the soft patina of friendship had aged it into something quite different, even nostalgic.

After a moment, I set about undressing. Louisa was more robust than I, but that simply meant I could keep all of my own undergarments on and still have a slightly ill-fitting, lumpy silhouette, which I desired. The girl helped me, tying and buttoning me here and there, a process I found strange, since it had been several years since I’d had a personal maid. With my means I could have afforded one easily, but after living with my husband, who had used my maid to spy on my every waking moment, I could no longer bear the idea of employing one. I’d become used to taking care of myself—at least as much as Mrs Turner, my indomitable housekeeper-cook, would allow.

“Oh, Miss,” said the girl, surveying me when she was finished tying a bow across the small of my back, “you look beautiful, just like a maid in a play at the theatre.” Her comment engendered less delight than she intended, since I desired to pass inconspicuously. I wished I had Holmes’s paint with me to somehow alter my features, but since I did not, I determined that alteration of attitude and carriage would have to do.

“Thank you for your help,” I said. “I am sure my friends will enjoy this costume.” I had begun to feel like I was speaking in some sort of code in which friends were enemies and enjoyment equated to trying to kill me.

I finally succeeded in ushering the excited maid out of the room. Once alone, I took my pistol and secreted it in a small purse, which I affixed at my waist underneath my overskirt, glad again of the extra space the girl's size afforded me.

I went to the window and opened it, staring out at the Thames, watching as the water sparkled and shone with the reflections of the hotel's lights. Tiny, radiant pinpoints darted across the surface like the fireflies I had loved to catch during my childhood in America. The beauty, I realised, was in the randomness. The lights reflected and bounced of their own free will, just as the fireflies had danced to their own incomprehensible music, no two following the same pattern. They were the opposite of my bees, whose hive existences had been orderly and predictable. I had found great comfort in the beauty of symmetry and routine, but as I looked out my window that night, I remembered that the beauty of unpredictability could hold its own wild charm.

I drew myself away, walking across the soft carpet to the door of my room. I knew that if I opened it, I would be making a dangerous decision that went directly against Holmes's wishes. I knew, and I did not care. I was mixed up in the case; my bees had met their demise at the hand of formidable enemies, and I wanted to do my part to catch them. I had done what Holmes had asked, and it had failed, not from any deficiency on his part, but it had failed nonetheless. In my day, I had been resourceful and more than capable of getting what I wanted, and I decided that my turn had come. I twisted the knob on my room door and stepped into the hotel hallway, knowing that I might very well be risking life and limb.

The second floor hallway was as bright as ever, its electric lights making night seem like day. To my relief, no one was about, but I knew that condition would not remain for long in a place as busy as the Savoy. I weighed my options. I could pass through the hotel and hope that no one recognised that I did not actually work there. The Savoy had many maids, and it was possible, I thought, that anyone I met might accept that they had simply never seen me before. However, I could not be certain that the floor maids were unacquainted with each other, and the risk of meeting someone who knew them all unsettled me. About the other guests I did not worry overmuch. They seemed, in the main, to be a self-absorbed lot who would dismiss me as soon as they saw what I was wearing.

The other option was to make my way to the servants' stairwell entrance, where Billy and I had made our furtive return earlier in the day. The risk of meeting hotel employees was higher there, but I also reasoned that I might be able to keep a lookout and avoid meeting anyone at all, which would be impossible if I brazenly made my way through the main part of the hotel.

I wished I had Holmes's brain, which would have, without a doubt, been able to weigh the two options and make a judgement about which was the safest. I was less confident in my own ability to do so, but I knew that I could not continue to linger suspiciously at the door to my room without someone passing by and wondering what I might be doing there in the garb of a maid.

With a sudden burst of inspiration, I went back into my room and surveyed the tray of food I had been brought for dinner, glad I hadn't called for its removal. I quickly put the silver covers on the plates and rearranged them on the tray, picking it up and again leaving the room.

This time, I made my way to the servants' stairwell with determination, ducking around a corner while a maid and butler passed. I listened carefully, but I could detect no further sound of foot or voice, so I stepped onto the topmost stair, took a deep breath, and walked.

I made it down the first flight without incident, but when I reached the first floor landing, a porter joined me. I kept my head down, and he was in such a hurry that he quickly outpaced me and made no effort to speak. My heart fluttered, but I finally reached the ground floor and the small room that would let me out into the world beyond the Savoy.

His eyes, which were of a peculiarly light, watery gray, seemed to always retain that far-away, introspective look which I had only observed in Sherlock’s when he was exerting his full powers.

—The Greek Interpreter

Chapter 10: Holmes

Sherlock Holmes never visited his brother at late hours. In point of fact, he rarely visited his brother at all, and he could count the number of his visits to the Pall Mall flat on the fingers of one hand. This rarity didn't spring from any animosity; rather, the temperaments concerned did not lend themselves to frequent socialisation. Furthermore, the scarcity imbued each instance with particular weight.

Mycroft's butler opened the door of the flat for the detective. He was an unmarried man of thirty-eight, excessively correct in every movement and inflection of voice, who was a professional card player in his two evenings off. The elder Holmes had deduced this secret soon after the beginning of the man's employment and had found it amusing enough to tell his brother. The younger Holmes had, on occasion, found the man useful and quick-witted, nowhere near as averse to practical labour as Mycroft was.

"Good evening, Parker, is my brother at home?" the detective asked

"Certainly, Sir," the man answered, every word enunciated to sublime perfection. "Please come in, and I will make him aware of your arrival." Everything about the flat oozed pure luxury, from the thick carpets to the mahogany furniture. Many of the pieces were gifts—relics of a job so secret that even Sherlock did not know the full extent of it.

After five minutes' wait in the comfortable sitting room, Holmes was joined by Mycroft, who came out of his bedroom wearing a midnight blue dressing gown of magnificent proportions. The detective knew that his brother had not been sleeping, for it was his usual habit to smoke cigars and read long Russian novels for several hours each evening before he finally took to his bed.

"Good evening, Sherlock," he boomed. "Have you dined?" Out of the corner of his eye, Holmes could see Parker blanching at the idea of having to produce food on immediate notice at such an hour.

"I have no need of food at present," he answered. "I am sorry to take you from your usual routine."

“So you should be,” said Mycroft, breathing heavily as he squeezed into an armchair. “You’ve forced me to abandon Tolstoy.”

“I hope my errand will amply repay you for that,” said Holmes, taking a piece of paper from his pocket and handing it to his brother. On it he had drawn the likeness of a button—silver, with the letter C etched upon it.

“I found the button near the body of the slain girl,” he explained. “Have you ever seen one like it?”

“My dear Sherlock,” answered his elder brother, “I am hardly omniscient.”

“And yet,” replied the detective, “I know that you forget nothing and are able, with effort, to recall anything with which you have come into contact.”

“That is true,” Mycroft answered. For a few moments, he pondered the picture. Holmes wished he could have produced the button itself, but it was of little matter. If Mycroft could not identify the drawing, he would not have been able to identify the object.

After a while, the larger man leaned forward, his chair creaking with the weight of his movements. “I have never seen one exactly its twin,” he said, “but it resembles the buttons used by the Confederate States of America during the American Civil War. I once had an American contact who retained a coat from his uniform that had similar ones upon it.”

“Why did you not show this to me sooner?” he continued.

“I was not originally certain that it would be needed,” his brother answered.

“This is certainly suggestive of the murderer being a former part of the Confederate army, or attempting to impersonate one.”

“Which,” said the younger Holmes, “makes it even more likely that he is an original member of the Ku Klux Klan, for it consisted of many former Confederates.”

“It still does,” answered Mycroft, “but behind closed doors and in clandestine political meetings.”

“Thank you,” said the younger brother, rising to take his leave. Parker opened the door to the evening wind, and the detective stepped outside.

—

The streets around Pall Mall were mostly deserted, which delighted Holmes. It was a truism of detection that following someone when there was no one else about was much more difficult than following someone in a crowd of people. Without looking behind him, he sped up, walked ten paces, then suddenly turned on his heel and doubled back.

Peering into the evening dark, he saw a figure disappear behind a corner. He did not see its face, but he noted the tall, wiry form and the back of a pair of black boots he'd seen before. Contented, he went on his way.

—

Upon his arrival at Baker Street, the detective found his flatmate dozing in his chair, but the doctor started up as soon as he heard his friend approach. "Steady on, Watson," said Holmes, "I've not come to kill you."

"You oughtn't to joke about such things," said the doctor, rubbing his bleary eyes. "I take by your keenly delighted expression that you've been successful in some way."

"In two ways," said Holmes, taking his seat. "First of all, Mycroft confirmed my suspicions that the button found near the body of Anna Mason was of American origin, most likely from the coat of a Confederate States of America uniform. This suggests several fruitful lines of enquiry. Secondly, I know who is tailing me, and almost certainly who is revealing our movements to the Klan.

At this, the doctor sat up straight. "For goodness' sake, Holmes, don't leave me in the dark."

"I have no intention of doing so," the detective rejoined. "It's none other than Sergeant Keating, Lestrade's young assistant."

"When did you begin to suspect him?" asked Watson, obviously shocked. "Or are you as surprised as I am?"

"After Irene's arrest," Holmes answered. "When it became apparent so quickly that the Klan knew of our deception, I began to believe someone must be informing them of our movements; it seemed overly coincidental to imagine that they had somehow overheard enough snatches of conversation in the prison to understand the whole plan. Keating was overconfident, I believe, and his associates put too much faith in him. Still, it was not enough on its own, and his nervous act was impressively convincing.

"Of course, the sheer scope and speed of everything that has been carried out had already suggested more than one person in collusion. I did not realise, though, that they had an informer so directly involved with us. They should never have acted to kill the journalist so quickly. If they had waited even a day or two, the signs would not have pointed back to them so clearly. As it is, their hubris got in the way of prudence, as it does with many murderers who have psychopathic inferiority."

"I'm surprised to hear you use that word," said the doctor. "It's largely confined to medical and psychological circles."

"You know my methods," Holmes answered. "I absorb any information that is useful for detection. I have recently studied the writings of the German psychiatrist Julius Koch, and I find his observations of moral psychological disorders most informative." The doctor simply smiled at this.

"What do you intend to do now?"

"I will tell Keating I know what he is and give him a choice between helping our case and being reported immediately without the amelioration of any of the charges."

"I supposed being turned in to Lestrade is a grave enough threat to encourage cooperation."

"The prospect of being turned into Inspector Lestrade should be a direly frightening idea for anyone," said the detective, smiling sardonically at his own joke. Watson simply stared at him, shaking his head in obvious disapproval of his mirth. "The young man is, of course, done for, whether he assists us or not, but I believe I may entice him with promises to speak on his behalf if he cooperates."

""'Have you eaten?" asked the doctor after several minutes of silence.

"Not today," answered Holmes. "I haven't need of anything."

"Well, if you will not be persuaded, I intend to go to bed," said his flatmate, rising. Holmes noticed that in spite of Watson's attempt to appear incensed, he was actually excessively pleased at the evening's success, as he always was.

Holmes remained in his usual place after the doctor had left the room. He took out a black notebook, and by the low light of the lamp, he looked at the two notes that were tucked in its pages. He had, with difficulty, persuaded Lestrade to let him keep them. He now looked at them again, comparing the handwriting. They had obviously not been written by the same person. The first, the one to Irene, had been penned, he thought, by a young person; its letters were very small and decisively neat, with even pressure. The second was in a spidery hand; its drawing had imprecise lines, and its letters were large and wobbly. If the policeman and Calhoun—if it was Calhoun—were the only two in league with one another, then he would have supposed the first note to have been Keating's and the second the American's. He could not, however, be sure that they did not have other compatriots. In fact, his supposition that they had, at one point, been tailing him, Dr Watson, and Irene at the same time indicated at least one other associate.

The detective was glad to recall that Irene was secure in her hotel, the doctor was asleep in 221B, and that Billy, whom he had seen on the day of Irene's return from prison, was known to be especially careful and had been instructed to tell Wiggins to remain on his guard. Holmes wished he could convene a meeting with all of the children in his employ, something he had not done in some time, but he did not wish for any of them to meet the same fate as Anna Mason. Depending on how thorough the Klansmen were, he knew that even speaking to Billy could be dangerous, but both he and Wiggins were well aware that their work for Holmes came with risks, and he had personally instructed them in how to be vigilant.

The information the detective had gained pleased him, but it was not enough. When Moriarty had been alive, the detective had lived with the constant awareness that the criminal might win in the end, in spite of his best efforts. He did not relish feeling the same way, especially since he knew the Klan's organisation could not be half as powerful as Moriarty's, not without attracting far more attention. No, they had struck first and struck hard, but he would answer them. Of that he was certain.

So silent and furtive were his movements, like those of a trained bloodhound picking out a scent, that I could not but think what a terrible criminal he would have made had he turned his energy and sagacity against the law instead of exerting them in its defence.

—The Sign of Four

Chapter 11: Irene

As I prepared to step off the bottom of the Savoy Hotel's servants' staircase and make my way into the outside world, I heard the footfall of others approaching above me. Cautiously, I scurried into the dark room under the stairs, just as Billy and I had previously done. Soon, the others passed me, and I heard what they said.

"I hope he's not gone for good. I thought he was handsome," said a young woman's voice.

"He'll be sacked if he doesn't give an awfully good reason for being away," said another girl. My brain registered, in a moment, recognition of her voice. She was my own maid.

"It isn't like porters to leave so suddenly," said the first girl, "and he'd only been here a week. He must be in the clover if he's willing to leave a job like this so easily."

The two maids lingered in the tiny entrance room, and my agony was as great as it had been before, this time because of mental rather than physical anguish. Neither Holmes nor Billy himself had told me that he would be somewhere other than the hotel. I tried to tell myself that it was possible that my friend had given him some other assignment, but in the case's present state of uncertainty, I could not convince myself. The maids finally uttered the name of Billy in reference to the gentleman who was the subject of their discussion, but by that time, I was more than resigned to its certainty. A scant ten minutes had elapsed since the beginning of my flight from the hotel, but it felt much longer, since I wanted nothing more than to burst out and alert Holmes.

When the speaking had finally died away, I emerged out of the door and into the London evening, leaving the tray in the cramped room. Thankfully, my maid's uniform caused me to be relatively inconspicuous to the usual crowd of glamorous guests who were constantly streaming in and out of the hotel. In a short time, I found myself in front of the street, ready to hail a cab. Before I could do so, I heard someone behind me, closer than normality would have allowed, silent and ominous. I did not turn around for a few seconds, trying to calm my breathing and reassure myself that with so many people about, I could not very well be hurt or abducted without someone noticing.

Finally, I spun about and found myself face-to-face with Wiggins, who grinned at me as if he was exceedingly proud of himself. I restrained a strong urge to slap his face. "How dare you—" I sputtered.

"I'm sorry, Miss," he said quickly, his eyes wide with surprise. "I just wanted to have a bit of fun."

"I'll thank you to save your fun for some other occasion," I snapped. "Billy is nowhere to be found, and I intend to tell Holmes as soon as I can."

At this, the boy was well and truly aghast. "Are you sure he's not in the hotel?"

"I'm sure," I answered. "I heard two maids saying he'd disappeared without telling anyone."

Wiggin's face fell even further. "Mr Holmes will be angry with me. I was supposed to keep watch for things like that."

I took pity on him. "I believe Mr Holmes has more than that to think about at present. Besides, we already know that the gang is very resourceful and skilled. Do not berate yourself. Billy knew to watch out."

"I've been skulking about in shadows all day," Wiggins continued. "Mr Holmes left orders to be as hidden as possible, but that means a harder time trying to keep watch on things."

Again, I reassured him. "You must not blame yourself, but we need to let Mr Holmes know." He nodded wordlessly and hailed a cab, for there were always many of them idling about the street in front of the hotel. As we stepped into it, I kept my hand on the place where my gun rested just under my skirt in case the driver should prove difficult. The idea that the gang had managed to abduct Billy from the hotel made me even more wary than I had previously been, and as we clattered towards Baker Street, I realised how foolish the idea of leaving the hotel alone had been. I'd wanted to prove to myself that I still possessed my former courage, but I'd chosen a foolhardy method.

The drive was uneventful, and we arrived at Baker Street within a quarter of an hour. I had the presence of mind to tell the driver to wait, thinking that Holmes might wish to use the cab. Upon banging at the door, we were met by the detective himself, who stared at us with surprise. It was difficult to shock my friend, and under pleasanter circumstances, I would have been delighted.

"Billy's missing," I said quickly. "Is it by design?"

"No. How long ago?" asked Holmes immediately.

"I don't know exactly," I answered. "Some time this evening. I heard two maids talking about it."

"No chance he's just gone off for a lark?" asked Wiggins hopefully.

"Certainly not," my friend answered. "Not Billy. Wiggins, I want you to stay in the flat until we return. There's no reason to have you along and in further danger." I was flattered that Holmes had chosen me to accompany him, but I pitied Wiggins, who looked supremely crestfallen; nevertheless, he followed his employer into the flat like a faithful spaniel.

"Wait here," said Holmes, turning his head back in my direction. After a moment, he returned with a small black case that he often brought with him. "Wiggins," he reiterated, "stay here and wait to see if Billy makes contact." The boy nodded obediently and did not voice his obvious disappointment.

Holmes and I went to the cab together, and I could tell that he was tightly coiled, like a Jack-in-the-Box that was ready to spring open.

"I deduce that you planned an expedition of your own this evening," he said, once we were on our way back to the Savoy, the scene of the supposed abduction. I nearly asked him how he knew, since I was so preoccupied that I had forgotten my unusual attire.

"You needn't berate me," I said. "I have already realised that it was a foolish idea."

"I have no intention of doing so," he retorted. "I merely wished to ascertain what steps you had planned to take."

"There's a public house near Bethnal Green, a den of iniquity sort of place, where unusual information used to be available for a price. I would have liked to don a costume even further from gentility to visit it, but this was the only thing at my immediate disposal."

"I know the place," answered my friend, "and you'd have been disappointed in your visit, for it was pulled down some time ago." I was glad, again, that my errand had been prevented.

"Is there no other establishment of a similarly squalid but forthcoming nature?" I asked.

"Oh, several," he replied. "The problem is, the information gleaned is more likely to be what the hearer wishes than the real truth, especially in cases where life is at stake." I had to concede the point. My own successful attempt to gain information, carried out several years before, had been related to something much less important. "I have made discoveries this evening that you ought to know," he continued.

"Yes?"

"The main one is that Sergeant Keating has been following me."

"Keating? Lestrade's assistant?"

"The very same."

I blinked hard a few times. "Have you confronted him?"

"Not yet. He should know by my peculiar behaviour this evening that I am aware that someone is tailing me, but he does not know that I am aware of his identity."

"Is it possible Lestrade put him up to it?"

"During the earlier part of our acquaintance, I might have thought so," said Holmes, "but though he has not become cleverer over the years, he has learned to trust my methods. Besides, this explains the link between our plans and the gang."

"I see," I answered. I wanted to ask Holmes what he planned to do, but we had arrived at the hotel. "I must go in the servants' entrance," I said. "It will hardly look right for me to be prowling around outside with you in this getup."

"That suits my purposes," said Holmes. "I wish to question the hotel staff. If Billy disappeared while working, there is a very great chance that someone saw something relevant."

"I don't—I acquired this dress from one of the maids. I don't want to get her into trouble," I said, as we walked back towards the hotel. There were fewer people than usual about, as most of the guests were inside for the night.

"I suggest a different course, then," he said. "If we enter by the main entrance, I will ask to be shown to the highest possible authority. I will create enough of a commotion that you can slip up to your room and then return in your normal guise. If anyone asks—did you not have a story for the girl whose dress you're wearing?"

"I told her I was attending a masquerade party."

"Then I suggest we say the same to anyone else who asks and refuse to disclose where you acquired the garment. The staff of the Savoy Hotel is used to dealing with the eccentricities of the rich."

"True," I answered, following him through the large doors and into the gleaming lobby, which was lit late into the night for the convenience of guests returning from raucous parties.

"Girl, why aren't you at your work?" I was barely inside before a shrill female voice stopped me.

I had hoped for less of a disturbance, but Holmes intervened. "Excuse this lady's attire. We have been attending a masquerade party and are only just returning." His tone was smooth and gentle, even charming.

"Excuse me, please, Sir," said the same voice in a more ingratiating tone. I now saw that it belonged to a crisply starched, matronly figure of middle age. "I meant no disrespect."

"Of course," Holmes murmured. "I would like to speak to whoever is in charge at this hour of night."

The woman's face fell. "I hope that your stay here has not been in any way inadequate."

"Quite the contrary," said Holmes, continuing his act of cloying cheerfulness. "I want to compliment the excellence of the staff."

In many contexts, such a request made at such an hour would have engendered raised eyebrows at the least and possibly even outright derision. The Savoy, however, was not like other establishments. Without betraying a single ounce of incredulity, the elegantly-dressed woman ushered us forward. "Follow me," she said imperiously. We were taken down a carpeted hallway and into a wing of the ground floor I had not seen. It was as opulent as the rest of the hotel, but it was far quieter.

The severe woman seized the golden knocker on a thick wooden door and tapped it one time before entering the room. Holmes and I followed her into what seemed to me to be an outer office. It was large and airy and contained several chairs and a table, along with a heavy wooden desk. A tired-looking man sat behind it, and I experienced a moment of pity for the fact that he was working at such an hour. Holmes presented an outward appearance of calm, but I knew him well enough and had learned enough of his methods of observation to realise that the stiff set of his shoulders and the clenched fists at his sides meant that he chafed against the inevitable delay.

"Wilson, these guests wish to compliment the hotel," said our hostess. The man raised his bleary eyes and stared at us in confusion.

"Thank you for your help," said Holmes quickly, turning towards the haughty woman. "Please return to your work. I'm sure you have a great number of important things to do." My friend did not often exert his social will in this way, but when he did, the combination of seeming courteous but imperiously determined was formidable. Without another word, the woman left the office.

A moment after she had gone, I followed, without looking back at Holmes. I could easily imagine the trajectory of events. He would use the tired secretary to gain an audience with the night manager and insist on questioning the staff. If he encountered resistance, the threat of a visit from the official police would encourage compliance.

As I made my way to the ascending rooms, I put my head down and stared firmly at the floor in order to discourage comment or communication. The idea had not escaped me that if Billy had been taken from inside the hotel, I might suffer the same fate, but I also knew, as, doubtlessly, did Holmes, that the perpetrators would have been fools to remain at the scene of the crime and risk exposure. For that reason, I forced myself not to worry. My mind was, instead, taken up with trying to push back thoughts of Billy's fate. I did not want to consider the possibility that his lifeless body might be lying somewhere with a stab wound through its heart.

When I reached my room, I entered quickly and set about undressing as rapidly as I could, exchanging the maid's uniform for a sensible brown skirt and white shirtwaist. My body was weary enough to make me desire to simply lie down and let my concerns pass into sleep, but I knew that I must not. Holmes's work would continue late into the night, and so must mine. I shook my head at the thought of my failed attempt at prowling London dressed as a hotel maid, but I re-emerged clad in Irene Adler's clothing and feeling her anger at Billy's disappearance.

Here I had heard what he had heard, I had seen what he had seen, and yet from his words it was evident that he saw clearly not only what had happened, but what was about to happen, while to me the whole business was still confused and grotesque.

—The Red-Headed League

Chapter 12: Holmes

The detective watched as more than twenty maids, ten night porters, and the ground floor butler lined up before him in the office of the Savoy Hotel's evening manager. He looked down the two orderly lines and deduced a love affair between a porter and a maid, the butler's overweening fondness for beer, and various other details, none of which suggested immediate relevance to the case at hand. Some of the faces were guilty, some calm, others annoyed at being called from work. Unfortunately for the detective's purposes, a guilty look could mean a myriad of things that had nothing whatsoever to do with lawlessness, let alone a particular offence.

"Do you find this satisfactory, Mr Holmes?" asked the manager nervously. Contrary to Holmes's expectation, he had not found it at all difficult to gain admittance to the man's office. By nature, he was obviously a friendly, gregarious individual, but the description of the gravity of the situation had dampened the high spirits with which he had initially greeted the detective.

"Perfectly so," Holmes answered, noting that the manager's cheeks were flushed and that his red hair clung to his forehead with the slight dampness of perspiration. The man's every action was intensely professional, but Holmes could see that he was unraveling at the edges.

With, seemingly, all the authority his thirty or so years could muster, the man cleared his throat and began to speak loudly over the hum of the voices of the gathering staff. "You have all been called to help give information about a serious matter," he said. "The police are not involved at present, but they may very well become so if anyone chooses to be uncooperative. Now, Mr Holmes, I'll let you speak."

As Holmes was about to open his mouth, the office door opened once again, and The Woman stepped inside. Her presence was welcome, because it would allow him to separate the staff into groups and question them more quickly. He trusted her to single out potential witnesses for his further examination. She took her place by his side, appearing assured and calm in spite of the attention of a room full of people.

“Thank you for assembling,” said the detective. “I am here to enquire about the disappearance, this evening, of a newly-employed porter by the name of Billy.” He could see, as he spoke, that the news was known to some but a shock to others. He noted those who looked excessively surprised, since their reaction proved that they were either uninvolved or trying hard to appear so. “I will now walk around and tap some of you on the shoulder. When I do, I would like you to follow Miss Adler into the office across the hall, where she will hear your stories.” With that, he went through the two lines and selected each of the shocked individuals. As Irene made her way for the door, he brushed past her and whispered *uninvolved or extremely guilty*, having faith that she would understand his shorthand. If Holmes had had his way, he would have liked to question each person individually, but he was ever conscious of the infuriating fact that each moment that passed might mean the difference between life and death for his faithful page.

The group that remained in the manager’s inner office was smaller than Irene’s. He had kept it for himself because of its potential ambiguity. These were the members of the staff who had shown no discernable reaction or had displayed signs of already having heard about the disappearance. The detective took his seat behind the manager’s desk, wishing to create an impression of distance and authority. Left to his jurisdiction were seven maids, the floor butler, and six porters. It made sense, of course, for a larger proportion of porters to have already known about the event since Billy had worked with them.

“Do any of you wish to make a statement?” asked Holmes. No one moved, and he looked towards the back of the office, where the anxious manager paced behind his employees. “Mr Evans, would you be so good as to send word to the kitchen and ask if anyone might have information they wish to add?” Obviously glad to have been given an errand, the man left immediately with a determined tread. The detective didn’t expect to receive much, if any, information, but he wished to ensure the manager’s absence while he interviewed the staff.

“Now,” said Holmes, “you may feel free to speak. As I understand it, Billy was working as a porter until about two hours ago. Is this true?" The detective noted that five of the porters looked pointedly towards one of the others, who appeared to be the oldest. He stepped forward.

"Yes, he had been here since morning. He was helping guests from the front lobby up to their rooms as we all do. About an hour and three quarters or two hours ago, I noticed that he had not returned for an inordinate amount of time. I asked, and no one had seen him. He might have disappeared before that. I haven't seen him for at least two hours. I had originally assumed he was with a party of guests." The man stepped back.

"Has anyone seen him since that time?" asked Holmes.

One of the maids hesitantly came half a step towards the desk. She was young, no more than sixteen to the detective's eyes. "I—saw him with a man and a woman. It weren't more than two hours ago."

At this, Holmes felt his heartbeat quicken. "Yes?" he said, forcing gentleness into his voice, since the girl looked like she might go silent at any moment. "Exactly what did you see?"

The girl blinked a few times. "He were—carrying two suitcases and taking them up to their floor. I don't know which one."

"What did these people look like?" asked Holmes.

The girl looked more confident. "Very rich! And she had on a beautiful ermine fur."

The detective breathed deeply. "How old were they?"

"Young," she answered vaguely.

"Thank you," said Holmes, feeling like he had exhausted his resource. "Did anyone else see this?"

No one came forward, but the detective used the moment to scan the faces before him to see if any of them showed flickers of recognition that they refused to share. He mentally singled out two of the porters and a maid who looked as if they might be hiding something. The butler, a distinguished-looking man of high middle age, appeared exceedingly bored by the whole thing.

"What is your name?" Holmes asked the maid who had spoken.

"Hattie Aldridge," she answered quietly.

"Very well, Miss Aldridge," he said. "You may be required to give a statement to the police." Her large, blue eyes filled with sudden fearful tears. The detective had hoped things would proceed in this manner. He had mentioned the police on purpose in order to try to engender sympathy in any members of the group who were fond of the young maid. She was comely enough, in a mousy sort of way, and he had seen some of the porters' eyes drift towards her several times.

To the detective's surprise, the butler suddenly snapped to attention as if he had been poked. "That won't be necessary," he said quickly. "If I may, I wish to speak with you privately."

"Certainly," said Holmes. "The rest of you may go into the outer office. Do not leave until I give the word." The others shuffled out as a group, but Hattie was the last to go. She gave a poignant look to the old butler before finally taking her leave.

"Now," said the detective, "what do you wish to tell me?"

"I also saw the couple in question," said the butler, "and I know the identity of the young lady in the ermine fur. It is not my habit to gossip about guests, but I suppose there is no help for it in the current predicament."

"Quite so," said Holmes. "Who was she?"

Speaking very low and bringing his head closer to the detective's, the butler finally uttered, "Lady Helen Dabney, daughter of the earl."

"Thank you. Do you know the identity of the man she was with?"

"He was American," said the butler, "no more than thirty, I wouldn't think. He seemed—like a gentleman, though I have little to say about a man who brings the unmarried daughter of an earl to a hotel, exposing her to public scorn. He spoke with an accent I have heard described as southern in origin."

"This has been very helpful," said Holmes, meaning it. "You've most likely saved Miss Aldridge from having to provide a statement." He could not resist saying this, as an attempt to better understand the obvious connection between the butler and the maid.

"I'm sure she will be relieved," said the man, his manner entirely professional. With that, Holmes rose and went into the outer office, where the rest of the group stood about in uncomfortable silence.

"You are all free to go," said Holmes, "but you may be called upon in the future." From there, he went into the office across the hall, which was smaller and less opulent than the manager's.

As soon as he opened the door, he saw relief come over The Woman's face. She was standing, and she looked agitated, as if she had just been speaking in an animated manner. The maids and porters were clustered around her, crowded together miserably.

"I now have the identity of the final guests Billy served before he disappeared," he said, without preamble. "Miss Adler, do you wish to question any of these people further?" he asked.

"Not at present," she said calmly, and Holmes repeated the speech he had given the others, assuring them that their statements might still be requested. Once the others had cleared out, he stood opposite Irene.

"The lasts guests Billy saw were an American with a southern accent and the daughter of an earl."

Irene's eyebrows shot up. "That seems extremely suggestive. I don't like to think through the full implication."

"Nor I," Holmes admitted, "but it largely rules out the question of whether he was abducted by guests or by someone who worked at the hotel. It would be a heavy coincidence indeed for the American to have nothing to do with it under the present circumstances."

"This is a mistake," The Woman suddenly observed.

"What do you mean?" Holmes asked.

"You have always said," she answered, "that even the most intelligent criminals make a mistake some time. By being brazen enough to walk into the hotel as guests, they have given away a vital part of their anonymity."

"Exactly so," said Holmes. "They mistakenly relied on the confusion that attends the constant influx of guests to protect them. As it is, on my side, at least, I could only come up with one maid and the butler who would profess to seeing them. Fortunately, he was able to identify the girl."

"No one I interviewed would admit to anything," said Irene, but there was one porter I did not completely trust. His name is Charles Ealey, and I would not put it past him to have been an informer of some kind, helping the kidnappers know the best time and place to carry out their work. The rest of the group seemed genuinely shocked by the event, but he was not a good enough actor to carry it off. He clearly knew about it, but took pains to look as if he did not. I would have encouraged you to interview him when you first came in, but since you already know the identity of the probable kidnappers, I thought it might be unnecessary. I also did not want him to know that I suspected anything, for fear that he would become even more tight-lipped when you spoke to him."

"Quite right," said Holmes. "I made that statement for show, because I assumed that you would have the sense to say no, and I wanted to give anyone you suspected the impression that I would not be pursuing them further at this time."

Just then, the harried manager joined Holmes and Irene. "I'm afraid no one else saw anything," he said breathlessly. "I've asked every other member of staff who was on duty and received nothing helpful."

"It is no matter," said the detective. "I have received helpful information."

"Does this mean you won't be engaging the police?" asked the man hopefully.

"Not at the moment," said Holmes, "but you must be aware that there is a chance the man's body will be found. If that happens, the police will comb every inch of the hotel for clues, you may be sure."

The manager was aghast, but the detective considered the warning to be analogous to splashing cold water on the face—unpleasantly bracing, perhaps, but helpful. He hoped that the prospect of having Scotland Yard on the premises to frighten and disturb the guests would permeate the hotel and encourage the divulgence of any information heretofore concealed.

"We will—aid you in whatever way we can," the man finally choked out.

"Excellent," said Holmes. "The hotel keeps records of the room numbers of guests, I assume."

"Yes, of course," answered the manager.

"I must see them."

—

For all his nervousness, the manager was extremely efficient, and it was clear that his word was absolute law in the Savoy at night. Without delay, he roused up sleepy office workers and produced a book with names and room numbers for each guest. While he perused them, Holmes spoke to the desk workers and was informed that several Americans had arrived that evening and that no one was able to match the particular American in question with a particular room. If, they said, he might have the gentleman's name, they could help him. Even using the name of the lady was unhelpful.

The detective was inclined to believe them, just as he had believed the butler. Even as night wore on, the hotel was active, and the staff was encouraged to studiously take no notice of the rich patrons. It was in the Savoy's interest to treat each guest as if he or she were the reigning monarch of England, all the while taking no notice whatsoever of whether or not he or she might actually be. The employees were paid for their ability to be discreet, and they had turned it into a creed. That was immensely useful for the purposes of the hotel, but it was maddening for the purposes of detection.

There is nothing more to be said or to be done tonight, so hand me over my violin and let us try to forget for half an hour the miserable weather and the still more miserable ways of our fellowmen.

—The Five Orange Pips

Chapter 13: Irene

Holmes finally declared that he was ready to leave the Savoy when night was nearly turning to morning. By that time, he had scoured the hotel's records and searched for clues on the ground floor and in the two ascending rooms, but the incessant tramp of feet and the presence of so many people had obscured whatever might have originally existed. I could see weariness and discouragement in his look. Our worries were unspoken between us, but we shared the dread that we might never see Billy alive again.

I thought about remaining at the hotel, but under the present circumstances, I did not think I could sleep anyway, and Holmes did not seem eager to leave me to my own devices after one of his own had disappeared from under its nose. I, too, felt even more unsettled than I had before. The Savoy had seemed like a safe haven, at least to some extent, and that feeling of security was now destroyed.

During the drive to Baker Street, Holmes was nearly silent, save for the moment when he turned to me and said, "The coming of night is always irritating, but in cases such as this, it is absolutely inexcusable."

"I agree," I answered. Normally, I was a great proponent of sleep, but for once, I could feel the desperation that underpinned an investigation when speed was of the essence. My mind kept returning to Billy, and it was only with great effort that I managed to keep from being paralysed by my anxiety. I did not know what was in Holmes's mind, but I was sure it was more productive than mine, which was fast becoming overcome by emotion, tiredness, and frustration.

When we arrived at the flat, we entered quietly to keep from disturbing Dr Watson. Wiggins, too, was asleep in the visitor's chair, with his legs curled up underneath him. He looked about ten years old, and I was reminded that he was still a child, no matter how much confidence Holmes might have in him. He slept heavily and did not stir.

I went to the small kitchen to make tea, which seemed a slightly absurd thing to do in the small hours of the morning, but I was thirsty and wished for an occupation. Holmes took his place in his chair and lit his pipe, as I had now seen him do countless times. I couldn't really understand it. I had tried to smoke one time and nearly vomited, but I could not imagine my friend without his pipe. It was like an extension of him. In an odd way, his lighting of it gave me hope. I believed that with it in hand, he could not fail to find the solutions that had thus far been elusive.

I took my place in Dr Watson's armchair and clutched my steaming cup of tea. I did not speak so as not to disturb my friend's thoughts, but I would have liked to do so. I wanted to hear him reassure me that all would be well, but that was not Holmes's way.

After a while, I opened my eyes and realised that in spite of my certainty that I never could fall asleep, I had managed to do so quite quickly once I had finished my fragrant brew. The sun was beginning to come up, and Holmes was still opposite me, sitting motionless with his eyes closed, but I knew that he was not sleeping. Instead, he was deep inside his own mind, mining for the ore he knew it contained. Wiggins, too, was still sound asleep, with his jacket over his head.

I yawned and smoothed the hair from my face. In spite of my stiff limbs and the feeling that I hadn't ever quite relaxed, I was glad that I had rested at the flat. If I'd stayed at the Savoy, I would have spent the night in fear. As it was, I'd spent a few hours feeling safe, even if my sleep had not managed to fully rejuvenate me.

Wiggins awoke soon after I did, and he greeted the world with a grin, as was his usual practice. "Morning," he said, rising and stretching his limbs. "I suppose I'll be off."

"No," said Holmes shortly. "I won't risk you out on your own. There's no need for you to look after Miss Adler, as she won't be on her own, either. You're to stay here today, and you can accompany me if needed."

The boy's eyes flashed. He was not of a placid temperament, and I doubted his association with Holmes had been without its conflicts. "I'm no child," he said, looking as much like one as anyone possibly could. Holmes simply looked at him.

Once, when I was very young, I had observed a Cherokee horse trainer with an unbroken horse. Seemingly by only looking at it and moving in the most miniscule of increments, he'd managed to convince the horse to let him put a rope around its neck within an hour or two. I was reminded of this as I sat in Dr Watson's chair and watched with no little amount of fascination as Holmes interacted with his own high-strung specimen.

For a while, Wiggins held his gaze, and the two were like fire and ice—Wiggins, young like an ember that has just begun burning, and Holmes, like an unmoving, ancient glacier. I knew little about psychology as a study, but I couldn't help wondering if the younger man truly sought to win, or if, like the young lions who spar with the old, he simply wished to test his strength against a more powerful combatant.

After a while, the boy's gaze dropped away, and he sat back down with a huff. Holmes did not respond, but I noticed a suspicious curling of his lip that looked as if it wanted to turn into a smile.

Mercifully, Dr Watson soon emerged to spare us further awkwardness. "Goodness," he said, "Holmes went out alone last night and has multiplied. Is there anything I ought to know?"

"Billy was taken from the hotel," I said. "It appears the Klan is responsible."

The doctor looked horrified. "Holmes, I assume you have a plan. What are we to do?"

"First," said my friend, "I intend to turn Keating. I will go to Scotland Yard, and I would be glad if you and Irene will accompany me. Wiggins will remain here in case someone tries to send word about Billy."

Wiggins looked discontented, but he did not comment. Holmes, I thought, was doing it on purpose to test the boy's willingness to follow orders. He could as easily have left me behind, unless there was something he wished me to do that I did not yet know about. I had not given it much thought, but I realised that in order to keep his army of children in order, Holmes would have had to exert his authority at least once in a while. I also understood, even if Wiggins did not, that Holmes was extremely concerned for his safety. Knowing my friend as I did, I was sure that the death of Anna and the kidnapping of Billy must have made him deeply worried for all others who were important to him. He would never let the feeling overcome him, but it would certainly inform his decisions.

"Very well," said Dr Watson, "but I, for one, would like something to eat before I embark on the day's tasks. I won't be much good otherwise." I looked at him gratefully, and Wiggins, too, perked up at this. I volunteered to rouse Mrs Hudson, for it was earlier than her usual hour.

I tapped at her door lightly, not wishing to alarm her, but she opened it in an instant. "Don't worry, I sleep lightly," she said. "I heard commotion last night. I thought more of you returned than had left."

"Yes," I answered. "Wiggins is here also."

"Very well," she said. "I'll be happy to have someone to cook for. Mr Holmes barely eats when he's engaged in the chase, and the doctor isn't particular."

"I, for one, would be delighted to consume a full breakfast," I said, "but I'm afraid there isn't time."

"I suppose not," she answered. "There never seems to be." In spite of her dismay, she followed me into 221B and set about making coffee and gathering fruit and ham, which I helped her quickly set out.

Wiggins, Dr Watson, and I ate rapidly, while Holmes gathered his notebook and magnifying glass in case he should need them. He was ready before we were, but all of us were conscious of the need for quick action. Breakfast seemed to improve Wiggins's unfavorable opinion of staying behind. His spirits visibly rose as he realised that he was to remain where food was plentiful and available.

—

We arrived at Scotland Yard without incident, and Holmes said that Keating had not been following us, making it more likely that he was already at the Yard, which suited my friend's purposes. As soon as we entered the imposing building, I caught sight of the young sergeant, who was standing over a desk near the door, deep in conversation with a fellow policeman. It took him a moment to catch sight of us, and for that short time, he was out of character, confident and relaxed instead of the nervous newcomer he had shown himself to be at the scene of Anna's murder. I wondered how he could explain such a discrepancy of manner to Inspector Lestrade, but knowing what I did of the man, I thought perhaps he hadn't noticed.

When Keating saw us, he immediately stood to attention and came over, taking care to blink and rub his hands anxiously. "Good morning," he said. "I'll let the inspector know you've come."

"That won't be necessary, for the moment," said Holmes. "I'd like to talk the case over with you, if you don't mind."

"Cer—certainly," he answered. "I will hear anything you have to say." He looked around as if he expected Holmes to speak right then and there, in the middle of the Yard. I could not tell if his nervous way of speaking was completely feigned, or if he might have begun to suspect that Holmes was on to him.

"We will speak privately," said Holmes, leading us to the back of the building. None of the policemen or the few disreputable-looking characters who filled the room made any sort of response, and it appeared that most of the occupants were used to Holmes's way.

The detective took us into a tiny, empty office with nothing in it but an abandoned wooden desk. The room was small for a group that included me, Dr Watson, Keating, and Holmes, and I thought that he had chosen it purposefully.

"Now, Sergeant, it will save time if I tell you what I know," said Holmes, speaking quickly. "You have been following me. You are affiliated in some way with members of the Ku Klux Klan, who are responsible for the murders of Anna Mason and a journalist named Thomas Matthews. They have also kidnapped a man by the name of Billy, who is in my employ. I have no idea how you convinced them to trust that you were on their side; I suspect they were desperate for someone with the ability to actually get at me, and they were so eager to use the information you gave them that they didn't question overmuch how vigilant you were, until you'd made too many mistakes. Of course, no murder is perfect, nor is any murderer. They were bound to err, and you happened to be the weak link in their chain. I'm sure you thought you were clever to follow me undetected for a time. Indeed, you have some skill there. If you'd stayed honest, it might have served you well as an officer of the law."

"I see that you would like to speak, but in order to save time, let me finish first. You will say that I do not have proof. The truth is that last night, you followed me to Pall Mall. I caught a glimpse of you when I doubled back. Your exact involvement in the other crimes I do not know, but I know that you informed the Klan of our plan regarding the arrest of Miss Adler, which led directly to the murder of Matthews. I am perfectly prepared to report this to Lestrade this moment. He may not always appreciate my methods, but he has known me for many years. He will not take your word over mine."

Holmes delivered this speech with extraordinary speed, and all the while, the young man's face grew redder and redder, and he sputtered more and more. About two thirds of the way through, I could tell that he knew he was beaten. He appeared, at first, to hope that he might find a loophole in what Holmes knew, but none existed. We held all the cards, and he finally realised the fact.

"What do you want from me?" he asked at the end.

"I want you to help us," said Holmes.

"Why should I do that?" he asked. "I'm done for already if you reveal my part in things."

"You have a choice, right this moment," said my friend firmly. "If you agree to help, I will speak for you. I give my word that I and my friends will testify on your behalf at trial, and I will do what I can to secure an offer for you to testify against others in exchange for a lesser sentence. I cannot guarantee that our word will carry weight, but if you refuse, you will certainly swing for your crimes, and there will be no one to defend you, make no mistake of that."

"What do you want me to do?" Keating asked, clenching his fists at his sides.

"I want you to tell me with whom you are working and why. Then, I want you to bring me face to face with the ringleader of the gang without him having any warning. That will require you to act as if nothing untoward has happened. You will contact him in your usual way."

"If I do this," he asked, "you will not tell Lestrade right away?"

"For the moment, it will serve my purpose for you to continue in your present occupation," said Holmes. "I am curious, however, how you convinced him to let you out on your own for enough time to follow me."

"He's not the cleverest man," said Keating sullenly, "but he treated me well enough. He thought I had a bright future and encouraged me to take more responsibility."

"I suspected as much," said Holmes. "And now, make your choice. Either help us and secure for yourself what help you can, or take your chances in court alone. You have no way out of this." My friend could be excessively intimidating when he chose, and he used his entire force of will to push the young man's mind as far as he could.

We stood silent for a few moments that seemed, as everyone always says, to be much longer than they really were. Keating stood with his back to the desk, and we all faced him, a tribunal that was ready to convict. He looked at each of us in turn, and I thought he intended to gauge whether one of us was more sympathetic than the others, but he found no mercy in our eyes. He had forfeited it the moment Anna Mason had left the earth.

"Very well," he finally said. "I am in the employ of a man named Roy Calhoun."

"The most important matter for the moment is, where is Billy being held?" Holmes spoke eagerly, and I would not have wanted to cross him at that moment, so intent was he on the scent of the chase. Now that he had cornered Keating, I could tell that he had the end in sight.

"I don't know," the policeman answered.

"Don't toy with me," said Holmes, very sharply. "You have nothing to bargain with."

"I truly don't," reiterated Keating miserably. "I've never even met Calhoun directly."

"How do you get messages to him?" My friend, I could see, was losing what little patience he had left.

"Through Lady Helen Dabney," he said.

"I know about her," said Holmes. "Was she part of the scheme?"

"She only took messages," he answered. "She didn't like it, but she was set on Calhoun."

"When is your next meeting?"

"Tonight," Keating answered, "at Lady Colesworth's party."

"I wish to speak to her sooner."

"There is no way. She spends her days with the American. I don't know where they go."

"How did you secure an invitation for this evening?"

"My mother is the earl's distant cousin. We've never been close, but Helen used the connection to convince her mother to invite me."

"Will Calhoun be there?"

"No, he is unknown to Helen's parents. She meets with him under the pretext of calling on a friend. Her maid is very amenable and can be paid off to keep quiet."

"I see," said Holmes. "It will not serve my purposes for you to go alone this evening. Miss Adler, Dr Watson, and I will also attend."

"How, Holmes?" asked the doctor.

"Irene will secure the invitations," he said. "She was once a great friend of Lady Colesworth, Helen's stepmother."

Having gathered these facts, Watson, I smoked several pipes over them, trying to separate those which were crucial from others which were merely incidental.

—The Crooked Man

Chapter 14: Holmes

The Woman stared at Holmes as if he'd sprouted a second head. "Me?'

"Yes," said Holmes. "Do you remember a Miss Filcher?" Irene stared at him in incredulity.

"She was a barmaid."

"Yes," said Holmes, "and apparently a very charming one. It was a great scandal when the earl married her, though the intervention of years has somewhat dulled the acuteness of it. Their union occurred just after your marriage. Helen is the earl's daughter by his previous marriage. I am unsure of her exact age, but something under twenty. The tale of how she came to be mixed up in this is an interesting one, I'm sure."

"You will write to the former Miss Filcher and play on the heartstrings of friendship or whatever nonsense you choose and ask for an invitation to tonight's party for yourself and three gentlemen. I am not unknown to the earl, and as irregular a breach of etiquette as this may be, I do not believe you will be refused."

"Yes," echoed Watson. "A great many people would like to get a look at Holmes. He refuses party invitations as if it were sport."

"Very well," said Irene. "I might disagree, but I remember Jane Filcher as an extremely generous soul. I am willing to make the attempt."

"Very good," said Holmes. "Now I will go to Lestrade and explain that I require Sergeant Keating's services for the day." With that, he got up and proceeded to the inspector's tiny corner office, where he found the small man rooting around in the pile of papers that covered his worn desk.

"Good morning, Inspector," he said.

"It would be," said Lestrade, "if you had anything to tell me about either of the murders."

"I hope to, very soon," said Holmes, looking pointedly at the sergeant, who had enough sense to stay silent. "I would be very grateful," the detective continued, "if you would allow me to have Sergeant Keating at my disposal today. His expertise would be very much appreciated."

"Whatever you wish," said Lestrade shortly. "I don't know what Keating can possibly do for you, but I have no better use for him at the moment. I'll let you have the whole force at your disposal if you can solve these cases. I can get no rest from my superiors and the press hounding me."

"Don't worry," said Holmes. "I will have the solution very soon." Without another word, the detective led his small brood out of the Yard, paying no mind to the tongues wagging around them. His first objective was to get rid of the miserable Keating, for whom he did not wish to be responsible until evening.

"Miss Adler, you and Watson may return to the flat," he said, "and I will take the sergeant somewhere that will keep him from bothering us further until he's needed again. Watson, may I trouble you for your revolver?" The doctor eagerly complied, then gave his arm to The Woman, who left with him to take a cab back to Baker Street.

Meanwhile, the detective was left with Keating, who seemed to be alternating between abject defeat and a desire to attempt escape. Holmes did not fail to appreciate the irony of the fact that the hunter was now the hunted; after following the detective for several days, the sergeant was now trapped, and since he had no chance to alert his compatriots, there was no one to attempt a rescue. For the first time in some days, Holmes felt confident that he was gaining the upper hand. He had never doubted that he could eventually prevail, but he began to think that he might do so without more loss of life.

"Come along, Sergeant," he said. "I am going to take you to a place where you will be well looked after until I collect you again, but on the way, I'd like to hear about Roy Calhoun's manner of convincing you to join his outrageous cause. In all of this, I'm at a loss to understand what he offered you that was more attractive than an advancing career at Scotland Yard."

Before Keating could answer, Holmes herded him into a hansom cab with the aid of Watson's gun, held surreptitiously so that only the miscreant could see it. He looked daggers at the detective but climbed inside.

He was silent for several moments, but finally deigned to speak. "Calhoun promised me half of his estate in America."

"Greed is a cruel mistress," said Holmes.

—

Several minutes later, the cab reached a prim building with half-shuttered glass windows. The detective forced his prisoner inside and down a hallway to a small, nondescript chamber that contained a sofa and a chair.

Holmes rang the bell, and in a moment they were joined by an excessively small and very old man in a black suit of ancient design. "What may I do for you gentlemen?" he asked in an extremely quiet, reedy voice that had become so by modulation and practice rather than nature.

"If you will be so good as to fetch my brother, Mr Mycroft Holmes," said the detective.

"Very good, Mr Holmes," said the tiny servant, taking himself away with impressive dignity.

"We will be joined by my brother in a moment," said Holmes. "I'm afraid I shall have to leave you to his company, but I will see you again this evening. If you try to run, I will withdraw my promise to testify on your behalf, and you certainly will not make it far. This club may seem an innocuous place, but it is far from being so." He spoke briskly, but the young man refused to look at him and instead kept his eyes fixed on his boots.

Another five minutes brought Mycroft, whose eyes quickly darted from detective to policeman and back. "I see you've found the informer," he said.

"Yes," answered the younger Holmes, rising. "I trust you will look after him. I don't wish for him to be arrested until after this evening."

"Indeed," said Mycroft. "We are well able to do so here."

"I assume you won't want something so unrefined as Watson's gun," said the detective, rising to his feet.

"Certainly not," said Mycroft. With that, the brothers parted, and Holmes walked out of the sumptuous haven of the Diogenes Club, thinking that someday, if he became too tired of the irritating ways of the world, he might become a member.

—

When the detective returned to Baker Street, his entrance was blocked by a deliveryman who tapped insistently at the door. "Oh, Mr Holmes," he said, "I have a wire for you."

"Very good, Tyler," said the detective, paying him off and coming into the flat, eagerly perusing the message.

"It's a wire from Sheriff Morris," he said loudly, opening the inner door. "Excellent man! He was able to discover that James Calhoun's death was never reported and that he was suspected to be living in Mississippi under a false name. Roy Calhoun is the man's nephew, and he travelled to England with two friends several months ago. Such is the limit of what his message conveys," he said, "but it is vastly helpful."

"I begin to understand the shape of the thing," he said. "I had supposed Roy might be a son, but a nephew may easily be like a son, especially in the southern United States, where family ties are very strong. The absence of the elder Calhoun from the current expedition suggests ill health or perhaps even that the man is deceased. It is a simple matter of revenge, then, though the younger Calhoun is clever enough to have partially succeeded at it."

"Revenge against what?" Watson asked. "If James Calhoun neither died nor was captured as a result of your encounter with Openshaw, what injury would his family have to resent?"

"Exile, I should think," said Holmes. "If the captain was forced to relocate to another state, his family must have either relocated with him, enduring the uprooting of all they held dear, or endured his absence from their lives, with the additional possibility that the aura of scandal has followed them about ever since. If he is now a young man, Roy would have been at an impressionable age back then—young enough to idolise his uncle, but too young to have the proper judgement to temper his feelings."

"This waiting is more than I can bear. I wish it were tonight!" said The Woman. Holmes looked up from his examination of the telegram, which he had been re-reading to ascertain that he had not missed any hidden meaning in its contents. Irene had risen and was standing at the window. The light of the sunny day streamed in across her chestnut hair, and her eyes, which were always bright, sparkled with anticipation. She looked to him as Debussy sounded—all colour and light and movement; logical, but never contained; and beautiful, but never safe.

"It will be time soon enough," he said, "and I very much hope that you will have no trouble convincing the girl to assist us."

"You play your parts, and I will play mine," she retorted. "Mrs Hudson secured an errand girl for me, and I have sent her to Lady Colesworth with a note and instructions to await her answer. Wiggins wanted to take the note himself," she continued, "but I did not think that you would consider it safe for him to go alone." The detective had not asked about Wiggins, for he could hear the boy's laughter coming from the kitchen. It mingled freely with Mrs Hudson's, and he supposed the lad had not found his imprisonment in the flat as unpleasant as he'd expected. Truthfully, the detective disliked the wait as much as The Woman did, though he spent it sitting silent in his chair instead of pacing about the room as she was wont to do.

Irene's message was returned within the hour by the errand girl, a rosy-cheeked child of ten, who stood at the door and handed it in with a flourish, her golden curls bobbing. "Here you are, Miss, and you needn't give me anything, for they paid me over at the other house, and Mr Holmes says we must never take payment for the same thing twice."

"That is very honest," The Woman replied, her tone serious. "Are you one of Mr Holmes's Irregulars?"

"I don't know any name like that," the child answered, "but I do some looking about." She pushed her front half through the door and waved at Holmes and Watson. The detective nodded politely, but his flatmate waved his hand to her.

"Well," said Irene, "if I cannot pay you for taking the note, then I will pay you for the time you had to wait."

The girl looked contemplative for a moment, as if weighing whether or not her moral code would accept such a compromise. "All right, Miss, if you say so." She pocketed the coin she was given and ran away, her skirts flying helter skelter around her.

"What does Lady Colesworth say?" asked the detective, once Irene had taken her seat with him and the doctor.

"She will be glad for us to come and is honoured to welcome the great detective to her house. I'm happy to say she still has the spelling of an East London barmaid, for all her finery."

"Excellent," said Holmes.

"Yes," said The Woman, "but I am in sore need of something to wear." Holmes stared at her a moment, for the idea had not occurred to him.

—

There is nothing quite like the look on the face of a French dressmaker upon seeing a beloved customer after an absence of several years. Holmes followed The Woman into a tiny establishment that was on a quiet street in the most fashionable part of the city, and he was immediately greeted by the beaming face of a trim, elegantly-dressed man with a luxurious moustache.

"Miss Adler, you are unchanged!" the man beamed. "And Mr Holmes, you come with a lady this time. I would much rather dress her figure than yours," he added slyly, but the detective did not deign to reply.

Francois's assessment of The Woman was flattering, but it was also true. Her unhurried Sussex life had enabled her to retain her face and figure; she was still the petite, fair-faced singer Holmes had met many years before, with few alterations other than a look of greater contentment.

"I need a dress," she said quickly, her eyes lingering on bolts of cloth, imported from the far corners of the world. "I have a party to attend, and I need to be noticed."

"Pardon me, but Madam has never had any difficulty attracting the attention," said the man, rubbing his sharp nose gleefully.

"Perhaps not," she admitted, "but I need to be sure this time."

"You have come to the right place," he answered, bowing slightly. "How soon would you like this cloth confection?"

"Tonight," she said quickly.

The dressmaker was aghast for a single moment, but he quickly brightened. "This is why Madam has come to me," he said.

"You know that I will not disappoint you. Come again late this afternoon, and I will have what you seek."

"Very well," said Irene, smiling. "I had absolute faith in you."

"It would be better for you to come to us," said the detective. He took out his notebook and wrote the address of the flat on a piece of paper, which he handed to the Frenchman. He said nothing of financial compensation, knowing the man would find it indelicate.

"Very well," Francois answered. "You English will have your discretion." The Frenchman smiled knowingly, though Holmes thought he could not possibly be imagining anything close to the truth of the situation. However, the dressmaker was apparently used enough to the detective's strange ways by this time that he did not protest the arrangement.

"Good day," said Irene. "I will look for you this afternoon."

"The arresting nature of your ensemble is assured, then," Holmes commented, following Irene out of the shop.

"Yes," she answered, "I trust by Francois's manner of greeting that you are acquainted with him."

"Certainly," said the detective. "I've engaged him on occasion, when women's dress was required."

"Perhaps you should play my role at the earl's party," Irene teased.

"I would, if nature had given me your face," he retorted, which was very true.

She has the face of the most beautiful of women, and the mind of the most resolute of men.

—A Scandal in Bohemia

Chapter 15: Irene

With his usual reliability, Francois arrived before five o'clock, with several boxes and bags in his arms. Mrs Hudson admitted him excitedly, and, I confess, I was no less excited. We ushered the dressmaker into the landlady's flat, and he began to remove the contents of his packages. The largest contained the gown, which took shape before my delighted eyes and was far grander than I had expected on such short notice.

The styles had changed slightly since I'd lived in London. This dress, unlike the ones I had worn before, had a glorious simplicity about it. The waist was dropped to where mine naturally cinched in, which would accent my figure, and the skirt did not exaggerate the lower half as much as its predecessors had. It was a cream coloured, heavy satin, covered about with small gold stars, and accented with golden lace. I knew, as soon as I saw it, that I would look well in it.

"I haven't seen anything so beautiful since I was in Japan at the court of the emperor!" said Mrs Hudson, in thrilled awe.

"Its equal does not exist," said the Frenchman in a humorously businesslike way. "It was a creation of my own mind, not requested by anyone. I was saving it for a special lady, and I have made a few alterations to it to suit this one. It is most kind of Madam not to have changed in her measurements," he said, smiling at me as if my figure were a surpassing moral virtue.

"Mrs Hudson, will you help me put it on?" I asked. I hoped that she would not be offended by the request, but she looked pleased and took me into her bedroom. It was furnished neatly and frugally like the rest of her flat and smelled faintly of lemon verbena, which I liked.

"It's been a good many years since I wore anything like this," she said, but her tone was not wistful. She assisted me in putting together the underthings, which Francois had been kind enough to bring along but too delicate to mention, and then slipped the beautiful fabric around my body. Like the most diligent of maids, she fastened me in and went around to arrange the train of the skirt. Finally, she stepped back and breathed in sharply. I had my back to the mirror, but I could not help smiling at her response. Slowly, I turned and faced the small glass that hung on the wall, and I nearly gasped myself. I had not worn something so fine for many years, and I had forgotten how I looked in such a dress.

I had also forgotten how wearing such a thing naturally affects one's carriage. I left the room with a special confidence I had not felt in some time, my head high and my gait sure. Even with my hair done sensibly for the day and plain shoes, I felt like a queen.

Francois did not react right away. He stood, with his hand under his chin, and surveyed me like a scientist observing a specimen. Finally, he clapped twice and nodded. "Yes," he said. "That is precisely what was intended."

He went to Mrs Hudson's table and opened two other boxes. One contained a delicate pair of lace gloves and a hat. "Seeing that Madam was pressed for time, I thought I might secure these items to accompany the ensemble."

"Thank you," I said. I hated to mar the atmosphere with the mercenary, but for all of his art, Francois needed to eat. I did not know his terms, but I gave him what such a dress would have cost during my previous tenure in London, then doubled it for his time and effort and the natural increase in cost that comes with time. For the smaller items, I also gave their previous worth, doubled.

The Frenchman nodded once, then pocketed the notes without comment, as if it pained him to have to accept them. He took my hand and bowed over it. "Bon courage," he said, and Mrs Hudson showed him out.

—

By the time evening came, my anticipation was at a fevered pitch. The day had given me a new appreciation for the inevitable periods of inactivity Holmes had to endure during his cases. A few hours of waiting to find out a friend's fate were intolerable. Wiggins had certainly had the hardest time of it. I doubt he'd had to sit still for so long in his entire life. I'd finally taken pity on him after our noon meal and engaged him in a game of Ecarte. He'd never heard of it but had proven to be a quick study, winning two tricks in our first match and besting me with three in our second.

Initially, I had wondered at Holmes's willingness to trust Keating, but I knew from experience that he was adept at spotting a lie. The man had nothing to gain by dissembling, and his actions had shown that he was not stupid enough to think Holmes wouldn't figure out the truth eventually to his detriment. In addition, he'd had no opportunity to contact Calhoun or his friends, and I knew from my correspondence that Lady Colesworth was giving a party, just as he'd told us. The question now was her stepdaughter, Lady Helen.

I was pleased that Holmes had designated me the one who was to exert my influence to pull her to our side. She was young, and I hoped that, as Keating had asserted, she had acted as emissary only and not as accessory to murder. I tried to let her extreme youth increase my compassion for her. Many a young woman has done very silly things for love, as I knew very well; however, there is a difference between loving imprudently and turning a blind eye to murder. Calhoun must be an extraordinarily compelling man, I thought.

To ready myself for the party, I once again put on Francois's exquisite creation, but this time I also dressed my hair and put on jewellery—Mrs Hudson's, a black jade and diamond set that was old fashioned but looked very striking against the creamy lightness of the gown.

"You look nothing like I did when I wore that," she said. "I was never a beauty, though Frederick thought I looked well enough. He bought that set in Japan, to mark our first year of marriage."

For a moment, standing in Mrs Hudson's bedroom, I let myself imagine her as a young woman. If she had not been a classic beauty, she had certainly been possessed of her own charm. Even now, her face had an extraordinary sweetness and life about it. I turned and kissed her on the cheek. "If we are successful tonight, the victory will be yours as much as any of ours."

"Hush," she said. "You look very well, and you know it, and I have no doubt you will put it to very good use." With that, she shooed me out of her flat, and I prepared to meet Holmes, Watson, and Wiggins.

I opened the door with, I admit, a rather dramatic flourish, and stepped into the gentlemen's abode. All three pairs of eyes immediately locked on me, and Dr Watson's mouth fell open, which was certainly gratifying to my vanity.

"You're not an old lady at all!" Wiggins blurted out sincerely.

"Not quite, young man," I said facetiously.

"I must say—I am not surprised," said Dr Watson gently, "but it is always nice to see a lady in her most ornamented form."

"You are most kind," I said.

Holmes said nothing until both of the others had spoken. "That will certainly do," was all he finally uttered, but he smiled.

"I have hired a carriage," he said, growing serious. "We will proceed to Pall Mall in half an hour, where we will be joined by Sergeant Keating for our journey to Colesworth Hall. Upon arriving, Miss Adler will begin her task of isolating Helen and putting the case to her. That will require subtle machinations of which she is certainly capable. Meanwhile, I will study the remainder of the guests to see if any of them appear to have possible ties to the Klan."

"Your presence," he said, addressing me, "especially in your present attire, should create enough of a diversion that the guests will be less diverted by my presence than they otherwise would be. I do not wish the party to be overly focused on Sherlock Holmes, detective, lest unforeseen complications develop. Watson's task is to keep an eye on Keating, to ascertain that he does not attempt to use the party as a means of escape. We will need him if all goes well."

"How?" I asked.

"If Helen agrees to help us, we will find out from her how to contact Calhoun, and then I intend to use her and Keating as decoys."

"Have I a job?" asked Wiggins, looking a bit desperate by this time.

"Not yet," said Holmes, "but the wait will not be much longer. You must remain with Mrs Hudson one night more, but tomorrow morning, you will call the Irregulars together and bring them here, for I wish to speak to them all together." Wiggins's face had fallen at the prospect of no work for yet another night, but the idea of a meeting with his entire horde of subordinates appeared to please him considerably.

—

The ride to Colesworth Hall was a strange and silent one, for Sergeant Keating, who had been outfitted with appropriate evening attire by Mycroft Holmes, looked sullen and said nothing, while my own eagerness made my heart race and head spin. Holmes looked totally composed, as was his way, but Dr Watson seemed as tense as I was.

Thankfully, the ride was soon over, and we found ourselves at the mansion, which was white and imposing, with columns and a host of windows that placed it as dating from the eighteenth century. I almost laughed at the irony of Jane Filcher residing in such a house.

We were admitted by a crisply uniformed servant and shown into the parlour, where Miss Filcher—now Lady Colesworth—came forward to greet us. She looked older than when I had last seen her, as did I, but instead of the plain grey dress of former days, she was arrayed in a violet gown with exquisite lace at its collar. She fairly oozed money, though the smile that lit up her face displayed the same generous spirit she had always shown.

"Ir—Miss Adler!" she said, "You are exactly the same."

"That is very kind," I said, "but hardly true. I am very glad to see you and eager to meet your daughter."

"Oh, Helen is about somewhere," she said, smiling. "I'm sure she'll be pleased to see you." She turned to Holmes and Watson, who greeted her in a blandly gentlemanlike manner and to Keating, who barely nodded. We were spared from further conversation by the arrival of a middle-aged man and woman in exceedingly expensive clothing with exceedingly unpleasant expressions, to whom she was forced to turn her attention.

Scanning the parlour, my eyes immediately alighted on Sir Lloyd Allen, who was in conversation with a young man of very animated disposition. His eye caught mine at the same moment, and he smiled. For the next few moments, I was amused to watch his attempts to disengage from his conversational partner, but he finally did so successfully and made his way over to me.

"My goodness, how well you look," he said. "You were an ornament to the prison, but this is quite, well, superlative."

"You do the evening justice yourself," I answered in kind.

"No more than Holmes," he said frankly, "but ladies' eyes do not tend to be as brash as gentlemen's. I see that your beauty is escaping the notice of none of them."

"Oh, hush," I said, lowering my voice. "I am not here only to be appreciated."

"I supposed as much when I saw who accompanied you," he said, slightly crestfallen. "May I help?"

"I must speak to Lady Helen alone," I answered in a near whisper.

"She is not yet down," said the solicitor, "much, I gather, to her stepmother's consternation. I have never known her to miss a dinner, though. After the meal, the lady of the house is given to singing. You may slip out during that time."

"Thank you," I said, beginning to calculate how I might approach Helen beforehand to arrange the assignation. After that, I was like a butterfly, flitting here and there, never alighting on anything for long, but keeping my attention on the open parlour door, through which I could see the family's massive formal staircase and intercept the daughter of the house when she should appear upon it. Subtly, with glances of my eyes and barely a touch of my gloved fingers, I made my presence known to as many guests as I could, giving the impression that each had captured my fancy. Judging by the lack of a crowd around Holmes, I thought that his attendance had not created the stir he was hoping to avoid.

I wondered if my friend witnessed the skill with which I navigated the room. Had he been a woman, I thought, he could hardly have done a better job of it himself. Holmes was an exacting critic, but I did not think he could find anything to reproach in my actions. Dr Watson, too, performed his role with ease, being quietly friendly to everyone, but never getting too far away from the sullen policeman, who sat by himself and spoke to no one at all.

Finally, when I thought dinner must be imminent, I heard the creak of a banister and saw a tall, angular young woman on the staircase. Lady Helen was neither comely nor unattractive. She was what I would have called interesting, with a face that might have repelled and enthralled an equal number of admirers. I quickly made my way to the edge of the room, positioning myself near Lady

Colesworth so that I could speak to her as soon as she had greeted her stepmother.

"Roy Calhoun," I whispered as soon as she came past me. Her face paled, and I was sorry for the cruelty of the suddenness, but I knew of no other way to make my point so distinctly.

"What do you want?" she asked.

"To speak to you privately after dinner," I answered.

"Upstairs, follow me when Mother starts to sing," she said, and I nodded.

Just then, we were called into dinner by our hostess, and I went on the arm of the solicitor. Once more, I was forced to wait for an inevitable event that seemed to take ages to arrive. Dinner was relatively uneventful, but I felt Helen's eyes on me the whole evening and wanted nothing more than for it to be over.

Finally, when we had dispersed to the drawing room, Lady Jane began to sing. She had been renowned in lower circles before her marriage, and the voice that had led rousing drinking songs was equally suited to more refined compositions. With admirable quickness, Helen made her escape during the first song, and I followed suit. She led me to a blue, carpeted sitting room.

Once we were both inside with the door closed, we eyed each other, she wary, I with studied patience.

"What do you know?" she asked.

"I know that you're mixed up in something ugly and that you've possibly been an accessory to murder." I was almost certain she hadn't been, but I wanted to see what sort of reaction my words would produce. She did something then that I have seen many times in others and certainly done myself—made a valiant effort to mask instant terror with strident bravado. "Roy hasn't murdered anyone!"

"That's an interesting statement, considering that I haven't mentioned his name in connection with killing," I said mildly. "I know for a fact that he's responsible for the murders of two people and possibly another, whom he is known to have kidnapped. As for your involvement, you were seen interacting with the kidnapped man just before he went missing, and there is a man who will confirm that you were with Calhoun. When it comes to the murders, circumstances won't have trouble implicating you, and Scotland

Yard will surely find a piece of stray evidence. If I were you, I wouldn't be overly confident in my chances." I pushed again, hoping for some sign that she might be coming around.

"If all hope is gone, why are you telling me this?" she asked, sitting on the edge of her bed and clutching her skirts tightly.

"I may be able to help you if you tell me everything," I answered.

"How can you help?" she asked. I did not find her question unreasonable. For the evening, I was an elaborately dressed friend of her stepmother's, and I certainly did not appear to have any sort of legal power.

"One of the men I am with tonight is Sherlock Holmes." I hoped she would show a flicker of recognition at this in order to save me an explanation, and she did so, her eyes registering surprise.

"The detective," she supplied.

"Yes," I answered. "He's the one Calhoun has been trying to injure with all of this."

"What?" she asked, seeming genuinely shocked, which in turn surprised me.

"You don't know? Perhaps we should begin somewhere else. What was your role in the kidnapping? Remember, I already have a witness who will say he saw you with the missing man, so you have no incentive to lie. Did Calhoun coerce you in any way?"

"No," she answered, with a determined shake of her head. "He said he was in England to bring someone to justice—the man who was responsible for driving his uncle away. His uncle had been a father to him until someone accused him falsely and made it so that he could never return home."

"I know that attraction does strange things to the intellect," I said, "but I wonder if you ever delved deeper into the facts of the case." Perhaps I was harsh, but I had a hard time summoning pity for her.

"He seemed so righteous," she said, starting to really falter for the first time.

"And what excuse did this righteous man give you for kidnapping an innocent hotel porter?"

"He—he said Billy worked for a very bad man whom the police had failed to bring to justice. Roy said we were just going to talk to him, but when we got to the hotel, he convinced me that if we kidnapped the porter, he could lead us to his master."

"I think you didn't want to do that," I supplied.

"I was frightened," she admitted quietly, "but Roy said that it was the last thing, the last link in the chain that would finish the work he'd come to England to do. He said that when it was all done, he would marry me."

"I'm sorry," I said, meaning it. During this speech, my feelings towards her had softened. As much as I wished to censure her gullibility, I could not forget that I had once been younger, and a passionate man had succeeded in deceiving me as well.

"Tell me about the murders," I said, hoping to keep my bluff going for at least a while longer.

"I wasn't there!" she said, her voice high and excited. I put my finger over my lips, afraid that even the noise of singing and the increasingly loud compliments of the guests would not mask her volume.

"Roy came to call on me yesterday, and he was nearly in a frenzy. His face was cut, and he said that he had been in a fight. I pressed him, and he admitted that the other man had ended up dead. He said that he had acted only in his own self-defence, but that he was terrified he would be found out. That's when he convinced me to go to the Savoy with him. I had intended to never return home, you see, but after we took Billy, it all went wrong."

"Things went wrong long before that," I could not help saying.

"I suppose you're right," she said. "I suppose you'll tell me that Roy murdered the man instead of defending himself."

"I'm afraid it's worse than even that," I answered gently. I looked her straight in the eyes and spoke slowly. "The day before the man was killed, the body of a young woman was found. She had been stabbed. Her wound was exactly the same as the wound that killed the man Roy admitted to fighting with, and I'm afraid a button was found near the body that almost certainly belongs to Roy's coat. I don't know how he acquired the facial wound, but I expect he used it to have a way of deceiving you."

"Why?" was all she said as she sunk onto the edge of the bed, sitting very still.

"Many years ago, Sherlock Holmes succeeded in finding out that Roy's uncle, Captain James Calhoun, was part of a gang that had killed many people, but particularly one named Openshaw, who was Holmes's client. Holmes sent a letter on ahead to warn the authorities in Savannah, Georgia, that Calhoun was wanted in England, but his ship never made it back, or so we thought. According to Sergeant Keating, whom I think you know, what had actually happened was an elaborate ruse. Calhoun had friends in the Savannah police who intercepted the letter and warned him. He sailed to a different port, and, it appears now, destroyed his own ship in order to make it look as if he'd been lost at sea, most likely paying off the foreign seamen to return home other ways and say nothing. Two Americans sailed with him, but they were also implicated, so they remained with Calhoun when he fled."

"The same friends who had assisted Calhoun's flight kept in contact with him. They informed Calhoun's family, which consisted of a widowed sister and her young son, that the man was well, but that he could never return. He begged that rather than joining him, they should remain on the family's estate. They were to act as if he had died, inheriting his fortune. Calhoun attempted to reestablish himself in Mississippi, but stripped of his wealth and estate, he remained a poor man. The few people who figured out his true identity did not care. He had been a hero of the southern cause during the war, and they were willing to turn a blind eye to the possible misdeeds of a man who had been brought so low. He could not risk a return to the city where his guilt was so surely known to the law, and his nephew was left to grow up and manage the estate. I do not know exactly what happened, but Roy eventually discovered his uncle in Mississippi, and his latent disquiet turned into something more."

The girl had turned very pale during my narrative. "Are you absolutely sure his uncle was a murderer?"

"Yes," I answered, "several times over. He killed to protect his own reputation and the reputations of his friends. They were part of a group called the Ku Klux Klan. When the law in the United States of America sought to eradicate them, they endeavoured to destroy all evidence of their activities. In so doing, they took many lives. It's ironic, I suppose, that after leaving such carnage in his wake while trying to maintain his life as it was, the elder Calhoun was forced to flee from it in the end."

"If you do not trust me," I added, "I can produce proof."

The girl shook her head in the negative. "I believe you. I have always known there was something in Roy's manner that was not at peace, as if something was eating at his soul from the inside. I thought that if he could finish his task, and we could marry, that he would finally settle down and find rest. I thought I could provide that for him."

"You're not the first to have been mistaken in that way," I said.

"Will I go to prison?" she asked, as a look of resigned despair began to overtake her features. Finally, I had achieved the reaction I sought.

"That depends," I said, "on how much you are willing to help with the capture of Calhoun. You are, right now, an accessory to kidnapping. I am willing to vouch for the fact that you were goaded into it, at least partially, by your fear of Roy at the time."

"I cannot say that I have ceased to love him even now," she said, "but I will help you."

You know my methods in such cases, Watson. I put myself in the man's place and, having first gauged his intelligence, I try to imagine how I should myself have proceeded under the same circumstances.

—The Musgrave Ritual

Chapter 16: Holmes

Holmes felt like a horse that was at the starting gate, ready to spring into action. He had observed The Woman and Lady Helen leaving the drawing room, and he could not help wishing he could hear their exchange. He trusted Irene's abilities, but he was tired of the pace of a case that seemed to go at breakneck speed, only to slow down to nothing when he was getting close to his target.

It was not that Roy Calhoun had been an inordinately clever criminal. He had simply had the advantage of surprise, striking quickly and with deadly accuracy before the detective had realised he existed. His folly was in needing to be noticed, to have the object of his revenge see the hand which wielded the knife that was being twisted in his heart. That folly had led to the notes signed K.K.K. and the trusting of a young policeman who had not been nearly prudent enough to successfully shadow the detective. It was all simple, in a way, but that made it no less costly.

The Woman and the girl did not return for quite some time, and he was beginning to be concerned that their presence would be missed, because, after the conclusion of the singing, the guests began to organise themselves into tables for games. Holmes quietly entreated Watson to take up the hostess's attention to keep her from noticing, and he did so with his usual easy ability.

Fortunately, the two returned just as Sir Allen was attempting to pull the detective into a game of Loo. Irene caught his eye and nodded once, and the relief on her face communicated the same feeling to him. If they had Helen, provided they did not lose sight of her, then they would soon have Calhoun.

"Excuse me," he said to the solicitor and their other table companion, the earl's elderly, widowed sister, who seemed to be setting her cap at Sir Allen.

He moved to the edge of the room, where Irene and Helen had quietly taken their places at a table but had not engaged in a game. He sat down with them, but before he spoke, he took the stack of cards from the table and dealt three to each of them.

"This will make it look as if we're intent on our game," he said very softly, taking up his three cards and nodding at the ladies to do the same. He leaned in towards the table and spoke again. "I trust that you are with us, Lady Helen. What is your mechanism for contacting Roy Calhoun?" He watched her face carefully to ascertain her veracity.

She was pale, but she spoke with certainty. "I was to meet him tomorrow at the entrance to the Savoy. He told me that if an emergency arose and I found that I had to contact him, I could find him at the Gloucester Arms. He warned me never to go there under normal circumstances, since the risk that I might be seen would be too great."

"Very well," said the detective, "then we will give him a taste of his own medicine and pay him a surprise visit this night. Lady Helen, you must divine a way to leave the house without your absence being noted. I take it by your recent behaviour that you will not be without an idea of how to do so."

The girl blushed shamefacedly, which Holmes considered to be a mark in her favour. "Perhaps if Miss Adler were to become ill," she said, "I might volunteer to take care of seeing you out of the house, and I could simply fail to return."

"What about when your absence is noticed?"

"Chapman, my maid, is on standing orders to say that I've gone to bed with a headache if I am absent without explanation." Holmes noticed that The Woman's face showed disapproval at this, and he was momentarily struck by the extremely human hypocrisy of his formerly notorious opponent sitting in judgement on someone else's deception.

"Very well," he said. "I have no wish to be unnecessarily harsh, but if you betray us, I will not hesitate to bring you down along with Calhoun and the others. The time for blind belief in the man has passed."

"I believe you," answered Helen, her green eyes serious. "Roy deceived me about the nature of his actions. I can't act as if this completely eradicates my feelings for him, but it has begun to sour them and will probably do so more and more as I contemplate the truth."

Holmes nodded. Without his bidding, Irene suddenly slumped forward in her chair, clutching her stomach. The brilliance of the performance was in the subtlety of it. She made no sound except a low moan, and her gestures were desperate, not dramatic.

"Miss Adler, are you unwell?" Helen asked.

"I am—a bit faint," The Woman answered.

Holmes finally sprang into action, though outwardly he showed the decorous behaviour of a gentleman whose companion is in distress. He went around to the other side of the table, noting that the performance was beginning to be marked by the other guests. In a moment, Watson came and stood by.

"Perhaps we ought to get Miss Adler home," he said. "I believe it's a case of nervous indigestion." The doctor was impressively serious.

The evening's hostess had arisen now, but Helen went to her and laid a hand on her arm. "Do not leave your guests, Mama. I will help Miss Adler outside, and perhaps Keating will help us as well." Lady Colesworth nodded gratefully to the girl and reclaimed her seat, clearly relieved.

For a moment, it seemed that Keating might try to keep his place, using the delicacy of the situation to try to wrench himself from Holmes's iron grasp, but the detective caught his eye, and he rose slowly and came over to the group.

Irene got up shakily, supported by Helen on one side and Watson on the other. Holmes followed with Keating, as they slowly made their way outside the drawing room and to the door. "Evans, please call Mr Holmes's carriage. Miss Adler is ill," Helen instructed a nearby servant, who rushed away quickly.

The next few moments were awkward ones, with everyone continuing the charade in case any other guests should decide to come out and investigate. It would have been humorous if the atmosphere had been less filled with tense anticipation. Finally, Evans returned and indicated that the carriage was ready, and they clattered across the polished wooden floor to the outside. As quickly as possible, the doctor helped Irene into the conveyance, and everyone else followed.

It was a tight journey now that Helen had joined them, but the driver dutifully agreed to go to the Gloucester Arms, which was close to an hour's drive from Colesworth Hall. As soon as the party was situated, Holmes asked Watson for his revolver, which he kept casually on his knee, but focused in the general direction of Keating, who sat opposite him between Watson and Helen. The Woman was next to him, her spirits high after the apparent success of her act.

Few words were said for the first half of the journey, but Holmes finally began the speech that would herald the evening's task. "Lady Helen, you know that Sergeant Keating has acted as Calhoun's informer. This night, like yourself, he acts as turncoat. I know the Gloucester Arms well. When we arrive, you and Keating will go inside and raise Calhoun. If he has a lookout stationed on the premises, you will tell that person that all is well. Once you have spoken to Calhoun, you will bring him outside, where we will capture him.

"What about Lestrade?" asked The Woman.

"I slipped a note to Sir Allen," Holmes answered. By this time, he will have endeavoured to get word to the inspector at home, and Lestrade will be waiting for us at his office when the matter is concluded.

"I repeated," he added, looking pointedly at Helen and Keating, "that if you attempt to betray us, Calhoun's downfall will also be yours." Keating looked angry but cowed, and Helen simply nodded quiescently.

When the carriage turned onto the street that held the Gloucester Arms, the driver pulled to the side of the road as he had been instructed. The party disembarked, a strange group of elegantly-dressed revelers on a quiet street.

Holmes led them as close to the Arms as was sensible to avoid raising the alarm of any watchmen Calhoun might have placed. There were low-hanging buildings nearby, and he and the others crowded into a tiny alley that lay diagonally from the inn's entrance.

"It is time," Holmes breathed, and Helen and Keating stepped forward. "Remember, Sergeant," said the detective, "my gun is trained on you." With that, the two went towards the inn.

Holmes watched as a figure emerged from the shadows across the street, a short, muscular man, who stopped them with a low shout. As he'd expected, Calhoun had not left the place without a watchman. Keating remained silent, but Helen spoke to the man, and in a moment, he returned to his post, and the two went inside.

"What will we do about that man?" whispered The Woman.

"I will have him in a moment," said Holmes. With slow movements, the detective crept out of the alley and past one building and then another. His object was to spring unaware on the watchman, ambushing him from behind so that the man would have no time to cry out.

The process took a painstakingly long time, for he could not rush or allow himself to be revealed in the moonlight. Every moment, he was concerned that Calhoun might appear, thus complicating matters considerably, but thankfully, he did not. Holmes kept to shadows and imperceptible, creeping motions. Finally, he emerged in the alley where the lookout leaned against the sagging wall of a tiny set of miserable flats. The detective made no sound. He was much taller than the other man, so when he was ready, he sprang forward and raised his arm. He had one chance for a blow before the man could begin to raise alarm, and he took it. The watchman fell with a thud, unconscious. The detective bent down and picked up the man's gun.

Holmes stood still for a short time, forcing his breathing to return to normal rhythm, then rushed quickly back to the alley where Irene and Watson stood. "I thought I would faint with apprehension," said The Woman, grasping his hand in the darkness and squeezing it. The uncharacteristic shakiness of her tone and extremity of her statement, as well as the unusual physical contact, made him realise that he had not been the only one with rapid breath and heartbeat during the escapade.

"Well done, Holmes," Watson added, speaking low. His flatmate returned his revolver and kept the lookout's weapon.

"We have now only to hope the man remains unconscious long enough for the plan to conclude," answered the detective. Only moments before, he had hoped for more time, but he now looked towards the door of the inn and willed the American to walk through it.

In mere seconds, his wish was granted. The large wooden door began to creak on its hinges, and Holmes stepped forward, gun in hand. Irene was just behind him, and he heard her take out her own gun. Watson stood beside him, and the three waited as the door completed its rotation. Helen emerged first, then Keating, and finally—wonder of wonders—a man Holmes had never seen before, wearing a long grey coat with buttons that glinted in the moonlight.

"They're after you, Roy!" Helen suddenly yelled. Fueled by pure instinct, Holmes ran towards the young man and jumped on him. The force of the collision knocked both to the ground, and Holmes heard the American's gun fall from his hand and clatter away.

The detective was too much for Calhoun, who was slight of build and not physically strong. In a very short time, he had him lying flat, with a gun at his temple. The doctor quickly secured a gag made of his handkerchief and tied it around the man's head, then went on to tying twine around his hands. "Very solid work, Watson," said the detective with admiration.

Meanwhile, the innkeeper had come out of the Gloucester Arms because of the commotion. "Don't worry, my good man," said The Woman, handing him a fistful of coins. "There will be no more disturbances. I need only to look into the inn for one moment." The man looked dubious, but the money was generous, and he nodded.

With that, Holmes hauled the American to his feet, and he and Watson forced the man down the street to where the carriage was waiting. The doctor kept his gun trained on Keating and Helen, who reluctantly followed.

Within five minutes, Irene emerged from the inn, supporting Billy, who leaned on her shoulder. He appeared wan and weak, but otherwise unharmed.

"We must hurry," said the detective as they approached the carriage. "The watchman will come to at any moment." He did not speak to Billy, but he put a strong arm around the lad's shoulder and helped him into the carriage with extreme gentleness.

"Do you intend to let the other man go?" The Woman asked.

"He is not the primary object of tonight's raid," said Holmes. "I think our friend Calhoun may be very willing to reveal the names of his associates when his life is at stake." A series of grunts from the American revealed what he thought of this.

Trying to re-enter the carriage was a comically ridiculous business, but they finally ended up with Keating, Helen, and the doctor on one side, and the detective, Billy, and Irene on the other, with the bound American between the detective and his page. Holmes was glad he had secured a driver who was did frequent errands for Mycroft, for the strangeness of the proceedings seemed to bother him not at all. "Are you well?" the doctor asked Billy, concerned. "You are not hurt anywhere, are you?"

"No, Sir," the young man answered in his usual way, as if he had done nothing more serious than taking an evening's stroll. "They intended to kill me, but they had not yet decided on a sufficiently meaningful location at which to do so in order to show Mr Calhoun's disdain of Mr Holmes." He reported this in an immensely clinical way, of which the detective approved.

"I am glad to see you well," he said, putting out his hand, which the younger man shook solidly.

"Thank you for your pains to find me," he said simply.

The subsequent ride to Lestrade's office was a cramped and unpleasant one, though Holmes felt the glow of triumph lifting his spirits. Irene and Watson seemed similarly pleased, in spite of being crushed against their travelling companions. Lady Helen's face was impassive, and he could not tell if she regretted her last minute attempt to warn the American or not.

—

"You had better have something solid to report, after rousting me out of my home at such an hour," was Lestrade's affectionate greeting as soon as the detective emerged from the dark corridor of the Yard and into his dimly-lit office. His scowl soon turned to surprise when he saw the doctor haul Calhoun in, followed by the two women and the sergeant. Billy had remained behind in the carriage with the driver, for he was weak and tired.

"Certainly," said Holmes. "I have caught the murderer and brought along witnesses to attest to his guilt. First, I should explain the role your own Sergeant Keating has played in all of this, and you may be surprised."

With that, Holmes spun the tale of Keating's greed that had led him to become a part of Calhoun's plot. He did not dwell on Lady Helen's involvement, only mentioning her as a bearer of information that was germane to the case, not as an accessory. He did not hold a grudge against her for trying to warn her beloved. She had, after all, helped to lure Calhoun outside the inn, as she had been instructed to do, only weakening at the last moment.

Lestrade listened. After an association of many years, he had at last learned to let the detective report all of his evidence before interjecting. Finally, when it had all been laid out before him, he sat back in his chair and sighed. "I am not surprised to see that there's an American mixed up in it all. We will take Mr Calhoun's statement here and hopefully extract the names of his associates."

Watson then obligingly removed the man's bonds, since, within the Yard, he had no way of escape, and the detective finally looked at him in the light of the inspector's lamp. Roy Calhoun was a young man with blond hair that swept off his forehead in a determined wave. He had bright blue eyes and a sensitive mouth and would have been handsome if he had not been pretty. As Holmes had expected, he wore a Confederate coat with two rows of buttons. The second one down on the left side was missing.

"Good evening, Mr Calhoun, I am pleased we have finally met," said Holmes smoothly.

"You are a murderer," said the young man coldly. "I regret nothing I've done."

Dr Watson took great offence at this remark and seemed ready to cudgel him, but Holmes simply asked, "Why do you accuse me?"

"He could never go home!" said the young man, beginning to speak wildly. "You told the police he was a murderer, and we never saw him again. Do you know what my mother did? She took a pistol and sent herself out of the world. But I sought him out! I found my uncle, working in the cotton fields of Mississippi, like a common labourer. He told me about you, about the British devil who had tracked him down when all he wanted was peace and escape from his former life."

"You were not alive during the war, I think," Holmes mused. "You heard of the faded glory, but you didn't see the horror that men like your uncle carried on and even instigated themselves."

"He—he wanted to leave all that behind," said Calhoun, his arms wrapped around himself tightly.

“Perhaps,” said Holmes, “but his way of doing so was to murder, just as yours has been.”

“You have no proof of that! You slandered him!”

“On the contrary,” said Holmes evenly. “Your uncle was wise to flee. If I wished, I could build an unbreakable case against him at this moment.”

Calhoun’s nostrils flared, and he breathed rapidly, furious. “It’s not true!”

“It is,” Holmes answered, “but even if it were not, killing others would hardly have been the solution. As it is, you have taken one scandal upon your family name and compounded it exponentially.”

“I don’t care about family names,” said Lestrade, speaking up. “I care about getting the names of the others.”

“That won’t be necessary after all,” said Holmes. “I took the liberty of pickpocketing Mr Calhoun during our scuffle, and this paper from his coat pocket looks as if it will be most instructive.” The detective handed the paper to Lestrade, but the inspector stared in incomprehension at the seemingly random assortment of letters.

“A cipher,” said Holmes, “and not a particularly clever one. I’ve already begun working it out. It contains a list of names, of which his is the first.”

“Very well,” said Lestrade, “the sooner the better. Now, I will remove my prisoners.” In no time at all, the inspector had forced the sergeant and the American out of the room on the end of his gun, leaving The Woman, the detective, the doctor, and Lady Helen to their own devices.

Watson, I think our quiet rest in the country has been a distinct success, and I shall certainly return much invigorated to Baker Street to-morrow."

—The Reigate Puzzle

Chapter 17: Irene

"Do you think the young man is quite sane?" asked Watson, once we had left Lestrade and gone back to the carriage.

"That's a matter for a doctor and court to decide," said Holmes. "His actions may seem insane, even if his mind is technically sound."

"He accomplished such a great deal," I said. "I suppose insanity can be methodical."

"If he's truly insane, he never acted so to me," said Helen, who hadn't spoken since the inn.

"Lady Helen, we will shortly return you to your house," said Holmes. "You may be called upon to offer evidence, but I have endeavoured to keep you from being implicated as a part of the plot. You were foolish, and you should be thankful that you are still alive."

I didn't blame Holmes one bit for this speech. The girl deserved every word of it and more. She did not respond, but simply nodded, her expression one of cowed remorse. I knew that it would probably be some time before she let her delusion of Roy's worthiness finally go. Even after my husband had show his true colours, I had clung to my love for far longer than was reasonable, and I did not think I was unusual.

We had the driver take us to Colesworth Hall, and we watched from the street as Helen sneaked in through the servants' entrance. I wondered if she would get away with her deception, or if she would be called to testify and make it all come crashing down.

"I can't help feeling that the girl got off quite easily," said Dr Watson a bit crossly, once Helen had left us.

"Perhaps," answered his flatmate, "but I can't believe any purpose would have been served by sending her to prison. Her chief crime was being unwise in her affections, and she certainly learned her lesson there."

I agreed with both of them, but neither completely. The girl had turned a blind eye to the obvious and let herself be drawn into something disastrous; however, she would have taken full responsibility and never even considered the fear and manipulation that had led her there. In his usual way, Holmes had determined who was responsible for the crime and had dispensed justice. To him, the girl was not the instigator, and he considered her suffering ample payment for her crimes. The doctor saw things in a more legalistic light, and I understood his desire to see justice fully served. I could feel for the girl, but I still held her responsible for her actions, just as I had been for mine.

"I thought of killing my husband many times," I said, for I was thinking on the case during our journey back to the flat. "I am not proud to admit that, in my darkest moments, the main thing that kept me from it was the knowledge that I could not do it without interference and certain detection."

"I believe very few human beings have ever gone the course of a lifetime without at least a fleeting thought of helping someone else from this world," Holmes answered, "and your reasons were of greater magnitude than many who have acted on their impulse."

"Perhaps," I conceded, "but I have tried to put myself in the mind of Calhoun, and I cannot. No amount of vengeful desire could bring me to slay the innocent. I feel pity for him. I cannot fathom the amount of hatred that must have festered in his mind to bring him to such a point. There were times I thought my own hatred would overtake every other function of my mind and render me paralysed to anything but itself, yet I was nowhere near committing acts so heinous. His mind must have boiled."

"Any emotion carried to such an extreme will produce some sort of mischief. There's problem enough in letting the passions run rampant; purposefully nursing one until it grows into a giant is an invitation to disaster," said my friend.

I could not help wondering if Holmes spoke purely theoretically or if he had experienced the dangers of unbridled passion. Sometimes I longed to see what was behind his eyes, the parts of himself he shuttered off from the world.

—

When we reached Baker Street, an eager Wiggins came out to meet the carriage. Holmes helped Billy out first. He was pale, but he walked steadily over to the captain of the Irregulars and put out his hand. I enjoyed the private play that was enacted before me as

Wiggins locked eyes with him and respect was exchanged. The cocky, brash boy had finally found something to admire in the page, and I liked to think that he would be better for it. I came forward and indulged my desire to embrace Billy, which I had restrained when I had first found him in the Gloucester Arms. He blushed at my forwardness, but he smiled. Dr Watson also found his way out of the carriage and shook his hand.

While the others entered the flat, I walked a little behind with Wiggins, who was still slightly subdued. "Are you all right?" I asked.

"Yes'm," he said. "I was thinking how it could've been me in there instead of Billy, if they'd made a different decision."

"That's true," I agreed. "Both of you are very important to Holmes. They might very well have chosen you. "

"I don't think I'd have taken it so well," he continued, his brow furrowed. "I might have told them something important. I'm sure Billy didn't tell them anything important." His manner was so earnest and his distress so endearing that I wanted to embrace him as I had Billy. Instead, I allowed myself to lay a hand on his shoulder.

"You have been an excellent captain for a great many years," I said. "I daresay Billy wouldn't be able to manage the others as well as you do." At this, he smiled broadly, his usual good humour returned with interest.

"I don't mean no harm," he said, "but sometimes I can't help getting angry at Mr Holmes." He said this as if he were confessing to murder.

"I'm sure I don't blame you," I said. "I often find Holmes entirely infuriating." I did not say that I also thought their arguments perfectly normal for a father of sorts and a boy on the brink of manhood, but it certainly occurred to me.

Once we were all inside, Mrs Hudson wouldn't think of letting Billy return to his present lodgings. Instead, she installed him on the sofa with blanket and pillow and tucked him in herself with a kiss to his forehead. He was asleep before I had left the flat.

Holmes walked me out, which surprised me. "You needn't accompany me any longer," I said, a bit teasingly. "The threat is gone, and I can easily secure a cab."

"Nevertheless," he answered, "it is a fine night, and I would like some exercise." Soon, I knew that my friend would succumb to weariness and the long sleep his body craved after the deprivations of the case. For the moment, however, I enjoyed the warmth of his company. Some said that he was cold, but they did not understand him. Holmes did not speak of his feelings or declare in florid prose his devotion to Dr Watson or to Mrs Hudson or to me. I include myself on the list, for by that time I had come to the assurance that he considered me his friend. He was not a man to give gifts or write beautiful letters. What he gave us was more precious than that; he gave his friends himself. Once befriended by Holmes, one could count on him until eternity, perhaps beyond. I had never known another person so reliable. As he kept pace with me, making his long legs match strides with my short ones, I had absolute certainty that he was fully present with me, and I knew that I could afford to be fully present with him.

We say that bees have societies and queens and workers, giving human names to concepts that remind us of our own lives. It's as if we feel compelled somehow to describe the mysterious magic of the bees as they labour together in perfect harmony, the hum the music of their success. Holmes and I were a tiny hive together, two bees with jobs understood instinctively, beyond speech or definition. I had not known I could ever experience such a thing. It had come into my life unexpectedly, a halting partnership, just as when hives are shaken up and new bees are introduced. Without realising it, I had let him into my life until he'd become as much a fixture in it as the black wing chair that sat vacant in my sitting room unless he occupied it.

I had thought of my bees as stability and comfort, my ever-present reminders that all was well with the world, but as Holmes and I made the long walk to the Savoy Hotel that night, I realised that I did not need bees to give form to the chaos of my world; instead, Calhoun's malevolence had helped teach me that the shape of things was found in a chair in a flat, a pipe, and a friendship. We were not always together, but the hum of the lives Holmes and I led had gradually united themselves in a dance that was very slow, at times, but ever-present. I did not understand what it all meant, but something in me recognised it, for a moment, and I was comforted.

Perhaps, I realised, the things around us do not shape the order of our lives. Before the bees, I had had my singing and my money and then my marriage. I had thought these things formed the contours of my world apart from me. I existed in and with them, but I did not control them. When my marriage had turned sour, I had felt even more that I had no control over the world around me—order or chaos, it was out of my hands. The bees had somehow been part of this, a tiny window into a world that was perfectly ordered the way I'd always wished mine could be, but had never thought was possible. Now that they were gone, I had come to realise that I shaped my own world. My choices were the things that gave shape and colour to the plane I inhabited. I had chosen to fill my life with an Inverness cape, a Calabash pipe, and a village teeming with funny, lovely, maddening people, and I had made the right decision. The chaos Calhoun and his friends had tried to unleash had not been powerful enough to empty my world of the happiness it contained.

I did not yet understand how Calhoun had managed to poison my bees, the thing that had started it all, but I trusted that Holmes would tie up the loose ends of the mystery for me. Finally, it was over.

—

I found it strange to return to the twinkling lights of the Savoy Hotel and find them friendly instead of emblematic of a disturbing threat. "Do you plan to leave for Sussex tomorrow?" Holmes asked. "I understand that Sir Allen wishes to have dinner with you, so I assumed that you would remain here."

"Does he indeed?" I asked.

"He made his intention known to me at Colesworth Hall," said Holmes. "I expect that he will write to you tomorrow."

"Then I will certainly accept his invitation," I answered, smiling. "Good night, Holmes."

"Good night, Irene," he answered. "We have had a night of nights."

"Yes, we have."

—

The next morning, when I arrived at 221B, I heard the sound of excited voices. Mrs Hudson opened the door, and she was flanked by a small girl and boy with dirty hair and wide smiles. Upon entering, I saw what looked like a scene from a fairy tale or a factory—the flat was filled to the brim with children, who were seated on the floor in rows facing Holmes's chair, upon which he sat, like a king surveying his court. Wiggins sat in the front row with a tiny, red-haired girl on his lap. I remained standing behind.

Holmes cleared his throat. "Quiet, everyone. As you know, I have not called you together for some time. Today, I have something very serious to say to you. As you know, I refuse to employ any child who is not old enough to understand why I ask you to do things. There is a risk in being a detective and in working with the police. Some of you may have heard of the death of Anna Mason. She was killed because of her association with me. I have called you here to offer you the chance to leave my service, if you wish. I will give you a week's payment, and you will not be disturbed. If you choose to stay, I will continue to do my best to protect each of you, but each one of you knows that London is a big, wonderful place that also has frightening people in it." He spoke deliberately, and rows of wide, attentive eyes took in his every syllable.

"If you wish to leave, come up to Wiggins, and he will give you your payment." The boy stood up and posted himself next to Holmes's chair. There was a murmur of speech. After a moment, two girls got up and made their way slowly forward, amid disapproving clucking by their peers. They were given the promised compensation, and I wondered if the sight of so much money at once would persuade any of the others.

It did not. My friend waited, and after five minutes, one of the older children, a plump girl with blonde hair, stood to her feet and began to speak haltingly. "Guv'nor, we all know what you did for Anna, how you helped her instead of sacking her, even when she couldn't work no more. We don't none of us want to leave."

"Very well," said Holmes, smiling. "Rates shall remain the same, and you will report to Wiggins, as always. You may go." Over a dozen children filed happily out of the flat, but Wiggins's little friend rushed to Holmes and kissed him, which he seemed to enjoy a good deal.

"Good day, Sir," said Wiggins, the last to take his leave.

"And to you," said Holmes.

"Where are Billy and Dr Watson?" I asked, finally coming forward.

"Billy has returned to the hotel to tender his resignation, for it is time for him to return here permanently, and Watson has business at his bank. He still intends to return with you to Sussex if you find the idea convenient."

"I do," I answered. "I would be pleased if you would join us."

"I cannot," my friend replied. "I have just received a letter that requires my immediate attention. As long as nothing further arises, I will come in a month's time, when I will hope to see new hives brimming with life."

Holmes's suggestion rankled with me at first. Beekeeping had been more than a hobby; it had been my life, the thing that had given me a reason to rise every morning. The death of the bees had felt like the end of something, and I had not thought I would ever return to it after the pain of hearing the hives go silent. I now realised that I wanted very much to begin again. My life in Sussex had been wrapped up in the lives of the hives, and my feeling of rightness with the world had come to depend on my daily tasks as a beekeeper. After my husband's death, I had existed in a void for quite some time, and the bees had helped to extract me from it and set me once again on firm ground. I was no longer the broken woman who had retreated to the village. The bees would mean something different now, and the hives would be a symbol of the life I now loved.

"You're right," I admitted to Holmes. "I ought to start afresh."

"I am sorry that your loss has been at least partially on my account."

"I blame Calhoun, not you," I said.

—

That afternoon, I received an elegant note from Sir Lloyd Allen, asking me to sup with him in the Savoy Hotel's dining room that evening. I replied in the affirmative, then returned to my room and donned my pink gown, the one fine dress I had brought with me from Sussex. The grand gown Francois had made for me I had put away, to be taken home with me when I journeyed back to the cottage on the hill. I supposed I would likely never wear it again. Events that warranted such finery never came to Fulworth, and to wear it at a village party would, I knew, be seen as an insult to my poorer neighbours. I didn't mind. It was a memory, a symbol of my time in London. I had come to the city grieving for my bees, and since that time, I had learned to grieve a girl and a journalist I had never known. I had feared, and I had known what it was to wonder if even Sherlock Holmes could unravel the horror. This evening, I simply wished to let colour and scent and taste overtake me.

I met Sir Allen at the entrance to the Savoy, and he guided me gently into the dining room; I was conscious of the fact that we looked well together. Strangely, I now knew nearly every member of the staff I saw, but we had returned to our separate spheres, as if some kind of invisible curtain had been pulled between us. In desperate times, it had been pulled aside to allow fraternisation, but now that the case was over, we were separated once more.

"Beautiful," I said, as we stepped into the room. Its elaborate wooden paneling, sumptuous, deep-coloured carpets, and soft live music delighted my senses, and I felt happiness bubbling up in me for the first time in many days.

"I am glad you like it, my dear," said the solicitor, pulling out an intricately-carved wooden chair for me. I sat down and contemplated the evening's menu, which had the usual array of courses never even heard of in the country. I was particularly excited to see tenderloin of beef, for I had never been one to turn down a large slice of meat, as unladylike as the preference might be.

We began to eat, and Sir Allen regaled me with tales of his clients great and small. I laughed heartily and felt that I had not enjoyed myself so much for a long time. Finally, when we had reached a course of sumptuous apple dumplings, he took a long drink of his wine and sat forward in his chair.

"You have been a most charming listener this evening, but you must wonder why I have asked you to have dinner with me on the eve before you are to return home."

"I did wonder," I said, "but I am having a grand time."

"There is—no particularly delicate way to ask this," he answered, absently fingering his goblet. "Will you marry me, my dear?"

For once, his twinkling eyes were completely in earnest. I sighed. "You are a lovely man."

"This is a disastrous beginning!" he said. "When the lady begins with a sigh and a compliment, things don't tend to end well."

I was tempted. I could easily imagine my life as the wife of eminent solicitor Sir Lloyd Allen. He was wealthy, well-regarded, and possessed of a personality I found charming and delightful. There was nothing against it—except for the fact that I did not love him, and I knew that I never could.

"I will tell you the things that do not enter into my choice," I said. "You are neither too old, nor unattractive, nor deficient in any respect of character or personality. I do not care if it is indelicate to say; I like you very much. I should be very happy to have you as my doting uncle or my elder brother."

"Doting uncle! Elder brother!" He shook his head and widened his eyes in mock horror.

"The problem is, Sir Allen—"

"That you do not love me," he finished. "I knew it. I have always known it would be so, from our first meeting in that cursed Newgate Prison. I knew that you were destined to find me a terribly charming friend and that I was destined to fall horribly in love with you."

"Please don't say that," I answered. "It's so very bleak."

"Not at all, my dear," said the solicitor, smiling. "I've been in love before. I won't be dishonest and claim I haven't. My wife Ariadne was a goddess, and after her I have had one or two entanglements. They never came to anything either, and I'm hardly the worse for wear. I suppose I would sound more gallant if I claimed that your refusal would likely end all meaningful joys in life, but that would be shockingly disingenuous.

I took one of his warm hands in mine and squeezed it. "Thank you."

"For what? I hardly deserve praise for discomfiting you with an unwanted proposal."

"For choosing me," I said. "You know that I am a widow. My marriage, and the years before it, are parts of my life of which I rarely speak, but, Sir Allen, I thank you for introducing me to the feeling of being cared for by a worthy man. It is not one which I have known before."

"Have you not?" he asked, looking at me for a long moment. At the time, I had no idea what he meant, though his words and look would return to me much later, and I would understand them better.

—

After dinner and a remarkably friendly parting given the circumstances, I prepared to enter one of the ascending rooms to make my way to my bed, when I was surprised by a hand on my arm and found Wiggins beside me, smiling in his usual way, but with perhaps a little more gravity than before behind his gaze. "Dr Watson said you wanted to see me?" he said, his tone indicating a question.

"I do indeed," I said. "I thought you'd come to me tomorrow, but I am glad to see you now. Perhaps you'd like to walk with me for a little while." I took his arm and let him lead me back through the crowd of hotel guests and towards the street. "You'll be as tall as Mr Holmes soon," I observed. "Have you ever thought about what you might want to do when you're older?"

"I don't know, Miss," he said, staring at me with wide blue eyes as if the thought had never occurred to him. "My people are gone. They were all thieves, except me. I guess I thought I'd always work for Mr Holmes. I make money with things here and there."

"You're clever," I said. "Mr Holmes knows it, or he wouldn't have employed you all this time. Have you never wanted to do something, if you had all the money in the world?"

He thought hard for a moment. "I—I've always liked the thought of being a policeman," he finally admitted, "but not one of those that just walks about and watches. I'd want to be one who goes to the murders, like Mr Holmes does, or Inspector Lestrade, and finds the clues." This speech had obviously cost him great effort, and he stopped speaking abruptly and breathed heavily.

"I would like to help you," I said.

"You, Miss?" His face looked intensely bewildered in the light of a street lamp.

"It is not generally considered polite to talk about certain things, but I don't care," I said. "I have a great deal of money, and I want to use some of it."

"Why?" he asked.

"A long time ago, Mr Holmes did something for me, and I have never had a chance to repay his kindness. I would like to do so by helping someone who is important to him. I'm also grateful that you've looked after me so well these past few days, at great risk to yourself."

If any bystanders had looked at us then, they would have seen a gangly boy and a short woman dancing a mad jig along a London street. Wiggins didn't let go of me until he had twirled me around enough to make me breathless.

"I take it you're pleased," I said slyly, trying to catch my breath again.

He laughed. "You're the queen, just like he always says."

"What?" I asked. "Who says?"

"Mr Holmes," he answered. "He says The Woman is the queen of the bees. I never knew what that meant, but I reckon only a queen would do something like this."

I stopped dead and looked at him with mock seriousness. "Mr Holmes is, as you know, always right about such things, and you must never forget what he says." At that, we both laughed. I sent him away then, and he scampered off, grinning to himself. In truth, I had no idea if Wiggins would make something of himself, but I believed that he should have the opportunity to try.

—

I returned to the hotel, and this time I asked one of the porters to find Billy for me, for he was spending his last night carrying the luggage of the rich and wanton. I had decided to repay my debts all at once. In a few moments, he found me in the hotel vestibule. "Will you come and speak to me briefly?" I asked. "I will repay you for the time you waste."

"That's unnecessary," he said. "Mr Holmes takes care of that. In any case, I'm to return to Baker Street tomorrow."

"Excellent," I said, following him to a sofa that was situated in a quiet corner of the lobby.

"What did you wish to speak about?" he asked.

"First of all, I want to thank you," I answered. "I came to London without any idea of the horror that awaited me and everyone else connected with Holmes. You looked after me at personal risk and endured a great deal. For that I am very grateful."

"It was no trouble," he said, blushing.

"I would also like to thank you for taking care of Holmes," I said. "I know that he would never admit it, but he relies on you." At this, Billy smiled a genuine smile, and it lit up his usually-serious face. "I hope that you will stay with him," I added.

"I intend to," he answered, and that was all.

As I went up to my room, I was pleased with my night's work. I had succeeded in giving Wiggins and Billy what each desired—for the first, a chance to use his talents to become something in the world, and for the second, the assurance that he was appreciated and needed. I knew that I did not have Holmes's abilities, but I could observe people and understand their motivations. Once upon a time, it had given me the chance to get ahead in the world in ways I had no desire to do any more. Now I was glad to use what I knew to help my friends. That is what Wiggins and Billy had become. I had only known them in the past from Dr Watson's stories and Holmes's comments, but now they had become part of my world as well. I knew that I might never see them again, but I was glad I had known them for a brief time.

As soon as I reached my room, I drew a bath. I didn't bother to call the maid, glad for the solitude to collect my thoughts. I finally thought about returning home to Sussex, and my life there seemed almost as unreal as London had seemed before my journey. With a thrill of pleasure, I thought of my small house and my spare housekeeper and the tiny village where my neighbours resided. I thought, too, of my beehives, now silent, and how they would hum no more. But even that no longer depressed me. I would find joy in beginning again.

Sleep did not come quickly that night. My heart was filled with a mixture of the joyful warmth of knowing I was cared for and the cold sadness of refusal. Nevertheless, when morning came, I realised that I had slept quite well, free from the fears that had plagued me during the case.

—

Dr Watson and I left for Sussex the following morning and reached the nearest station to Fulworth in the middle of the day. Mrs Turner was standing in front of the platform when we approached. I stole a furtive look at my companion, and I saw a smile come over his face that was like pure sunshine. “She looks well,” I said quietly.

“Yes,” he answered, “very well indeed.”

If I had hoped for a passionate embrace, I would have been disappointed, but I knew them too well for that. I was very pleased with the incandescent look they exchanged and the sight of their two hands meeting.

“I take it you are too weary from your journey to enjoy a walk upon the Downs,” I heard my housekeeper say.

“Certainly not,” the doctor replied. “It’s just what I need after stuffy hours in a train.” I surprised myself by realising that I was blinking back tears.

The two returned in early evening, and the doctor took to his guest room, the better to give his lady time to speak to me. “I must leave you, Miss Adler,” she said, in the same businesslike tone with which she said everything. “I have agreed to marry Dr Watson.”

“I am very pleased for you,” I said, meaning it, “but even more pleased for him.” At that, my housekeeper blushed and smiled, and onto her thin face came, for a moment, the look of besotted girlhood.

“I will find you another to fill my place,” she said.

“You know that no one can do so,” I said, endeavouring to match her directness, “but I welcome your recommendation.”

The next morning, I penned a letter to Holmes.

Dear Holmes,

I write to inform you that your flatmate is engaged to my housekeeper. I cannot find it in me to begrudge him, since I know that she will make an excellent bride. I realise now, as the end approaches, that I have never adequately thanked you for the gift of Mrs Turner. She is a rare woman, and I have been happy with her as my companion. Dr Watson asked if I intended to employ another. Perhaps I will, but I cannot think that anyone will do as capable a job as Mrs Turner, unless Mrs Hudson should one day decide to retire to Sussex. I expect I will see you at the wedding, but if you should find yourself with time to spare before it, you know that my door is, as ever, open to you.

I remain your friend,
Irene Adler

Mrs Hudson did retire to the Downs one day, but that is another story for another time.

Epilogue: Irene

A week after my return to Fulworth, I received a letter from Holmes, informing me that Sergeant Keating had volunteered to assist with a case in Sussex at the time my bees had first contracted their disease. The malady had been introduced by no particularly mysterious means; he had purchased diseased bees from another beekeeper and introduced them to my hives in the dead of night, hoping they would transmit the bacteria. Calhoun was, of course, behind the plot. His association with Keating and, by extension, Lestrade, had given him the ability to learn a great deal about my friend's life and habits, including his association with me. He had not, Holmes wrote, had any assurance that the bees would actually become infected, but the plan had succeeded beyond his wildest dreams. Keating had paid one of Fulworth's most notorious ne'er-do-wells to report my movements to him, and Calhoun had, as a result, known of my journey to London, which had inflamed his desire to impress Holmes with his power. Such was the simple explanation at the heart of the whole matter.

The young man and two associates were sentenced to death. As he had promised, Holmes testified to Keating's cooperation with the investigation, and the policeman was sentenced to many years in prison but escaped the noose. Lestrade, my friend wrote, was beside himself with fury that he had been deceived and as a result was almost humble in his manner for some time after.

Epilogue: Holmes

One month and three days after the conclusion of the Calhoun case, Sherlock Holmes found himself on the Sussex Downs, facing two beehives that were pristine and humming with life.

The Woman was silent beside him, and after a long while, he saw that tears had sprung to her eyes. She let them come. “The sound is beautiful,” she said. The detective stood next to her, very close, still as a statue.

“You will be happy again,” he said.

“Yes,” she replied, “I believe I already am.”

The Woman reached up to pin a lock of hair that had escaped from its fastener to tickle her cheek, but the detective’s hand prevented her. He touched the chestnut strands and smiled to himself.

“It has escaped. Let it be,” he said. So she did.

About the Author

Amy Thomas met Sherlock Holmes around the age of ten, when she was scared out of her wits by an audio recording of "The Speckled Band." From there, she went on to experience heartbreak on Dr. Watson's behalf, only to be told by her older sister that Sherlock Holmes hadn't died after all. Several years later, the gift of a contemporary novel starring Sherlock Holmes rekindled her love of the detective. She re-read the original stories, and a lifelong passion was born.

Amy is a graduate of Regent University, where she majored in professional communication. When she's not podcasting with the Baker Street Babes or writing a novel, she works as an administrative support professional.

An avid knitter and crocheter, Amy has knitted a deerstalker hat and crocheted miniature versions of Sherlock Holmes, John Watson, and James Moriarty. She also enjoys reading and reviewing Holmes-related literature.

http://girlmeetssherlock.wordpress.com

The Baker Street Babes

The Baker Street Babes is an international, all-female podcast started by Sherlockian extraordinaire Kristina Manente. They cover topics as diverse as the illustrations of Sydney Paget and the preservation of Undershaw, Sir Arthur Conan Doyle's home, as well as commenting on all kinds of Holmes-related media.

The Babes' blend of irreverent, witty, and intellectual commentary has won them a devoted and ever-widening group of listeners. They were particularly delighted to be featured on NBC during the 2012 Olympic Games, and they have been featured guests of 221b Con, Elementary Con, and will be featured at Dashcon in July of 2014.

www.bakerstreetbabes.com

Kickstarter

A big thankyou to all of the backers of the Kickstarter campaign with a special mention for:

David Lars Chamberlain
Mary Ann Raley
Greg Burrell
Geoffrey Langlois
Mai Sta. Agueda-Almagro
Deb Werth
'Twister' Boote
Steven M. Smith

MX Publishing

Visit www.sherlockholmesbooks.com for dozens of other Sherlock Holmes novels, novellas, short story collections, Conan Doyle biographies, Holmes travel books, and more.

MX Publishing is the award-winning, world's largest independent Sherlock Holmes book publishers with over 100 new authors and 500 new Sherlock Holmes stories in print.

www.ingramcontent.com/pod-product-compliance
Lightning Source LLC
Chambersburg PA
CBHW030827310726
48980CB00006B/666/J
* 9 7 8 1 7 8 7 0 5 3 3 3 5 *